Waterproof

A NOVEL OF THE JOHNSTOWN FLOOD

Judith Redline Coopey

Waterproof

Published by Fox Hollow Press and the author, Judith Redline Coopey
Interior design by OPA Author Services, Scottsdale, Arizona
Cover design by Albert Chui, San Jose, California

The illustration on the front cover is adapted from the work of American illustrator Harrison Fisher (1877-1934) as part of the cover of Jane Cable, a novel by George Barr McCutcheon, first published by Dodd, Mead in 1906.

ATTENTION CORPORATIONS, UNIVERSITIES, COLLEGES, AND PROFESSIONAL ORGANIZATIONS: Quantity discounts are available on bulk purchases of this book for educational or gift purposes, or as premiums for increasing magazine subscriptions or renewals. Special books or book excerpts can also be created to fit specific needs. Contact Fox Hollow Press.

FOX HOLLOW
PRESS

Printed in the United States of America

Dedication

This book is dedicated to the memory of my father,

Kenneth Redline

who served his country well:
soldier, ball player, brick layer,
author, reader,
philosopher, student of history
and
loyal son of Pennsylvania.

Acknowledgments

Special thanks to the many people who read the manuscript,
offered suggestions and encouragement,
and made the wrinkles go out of the writing:

Mary Agliardo, lifelong friend and honest critic; Elissa Ambrose, Peggy
Campbell, Erin Coopey, Lou Coopey, Kathleen Davis, Kimberly Davis,
Amy Dominy, Kryston Eckelbarger, Sandra Geimer, Dick Gregory,
Mary Saylor Hileman, Linda Kehoe, Pamela Leipold, Dave Lettick, Jeff
Nicklaus, Pat Park, Janelle Raupp, Genie Robine and Vincent Set'tle.

Introduction

*O*n May 31, 1889, an earthen dam in the Allegheny Mountains—on South Fork Creek, fourteen miles upstream from Johnstown, Pennsylvania—failed, sending a torrent of water and debris raging downstream, devastating everything in its path. Efforts to warn Johnstown failed, and by the time the flood reached the city it had become a thirty-foot-high wall of churning, roaring devastation. More than two thousand people were killed, and uncounted lives were changed forever.

The dam held back a lake on the private lands of the South Fork Fishing and Hunting Club, owned by an exclusive group of Pittsburgh millionaires—Andrew Carnegie, Henry Clay Frick and Andrew Mellon among them. Inevitably, the South Fork Fishing and Hunting Club was blamed for the tragedy, yet no member of the club stepped forward to claim responsibility. Lawsuits on behalf of flood victims came to naught.

Waterproof, set in Johnstown two years after the flood, examines how people react to tragedy. Some recover from physical injury only to succumb to the psychological affects; some run away; some seek revenge; some rise to the challenge and become better people.

For the people of Johnstown, survivors of the flood, it became the measure of their character. Some rose to the challenge while some never got over it, just as many survive but never really recover from so many of life's calamities: war, earthquake, hurricane, tsunami or personal tragedy.

Chapter 1

1939

*I*t's already ten past two. He's late. If he weren't Laura's grandson, I'd send him packing. I'd never have agreed to a fiftieth anniversary interview if it weren't for that. Don't like looking back. I decided early on not to let the flood own me. Too many people let that happen. Let the flood be all they're about. I've moved on, long ago. I'll do this for Laura's sake, but I'd just as soon give an interview about my prize roses. I smooth my dress and give my hair a quick pat in the mirror. There's the doorbell.

"Come in, young man. Gerald, is it?" Good looking. Tall, dark. Carries himself well.

"Yes. Gerald Kirk. Sorry I'm late. I got held up at the office over a story I wrote for yesterday's paper."

I know about the story. After all, I own the newspaper. He got the names of the accused and the victim mixed up in a court story. Now they'll have to print a retraction. I may be retired, but I keep a pretty good eye on things.

He comes in and takes off his coat and hat, revealing his dark, wavy hair, cropped close. Must get unruly if he lets it grow. I hang up his coat on the rack in the vestibule and invite him into the living room. He follows and sits down, notebook on his knees, looking nervous.

"Well, Gerald Kirk, I suppose we ought to get right to it."

I'm curious as to how he'll conduct himself. Just a boy. Hasn't been around the *Clarion* for long. Out of the University of Pittsburgh. I guess that's good. Don't know how you teach a man to be a reporter from a book, though. Not the way I learned it—nor Rob, my husband. Anyway, let's get this over with.

He sits alert, watching me. Bright. Eager.

Well, young man, ask me a question. What are we here for?

He clears his throat. "I hardly know where to start," he says. No surprise there.

I rescue him this once. "Just start asking questions. Get me talking. You can organize your notes later." Experience is the only reliable teacher.

He clears his throat again. "All right. I guess I could do that." He looks around the room for something to start the conversation. I let him set his own pace.

"I heard . . . I mean, my dad told me my grandma said you lost your fiancé in the flood. Is that right?"

Well, there's a good place to start. "Yes."

Ask me a better question and you'll get a better answer.

"That must have been very hard."

"It was." Come on, boy. Open up the ends of your questions if you want a good interview. Didn't they teach you that at Pitt?

"Did you lose anybody else in the flood?"

"My brother, Geordie." I'm already impatient with his lame questions. I feel like grabbing his notebook and conducting the interview myself. I take a deep breath. Get hold of yourself, Pamela. He's young. You were young once yourself. Then.

"What's your most vivid memory of the flood?" That's better. Open ended. Get me talking.

"Oh, the noise. The noise was deafening. To this day if I hear a far off rumbling—even thunder—I get a chill. A kind of terror runs through me."

"How would you describe it? The noise, I mean." He's warming up to it now.

"Thunder, like I said. A freight train bearing down. A roar like dynamite going off, only it doesn't end. Just gets louder."

He gazes steadily at me, his young face serious. Then he writes as I speak, taking notes—busy as a shoemaker nailing a sole. I watch him, the light from the window filtering dust in the air.

I'm looking for some resemblance to his grandmother, the best friend of my youth. Handsome lad. Full of promise, even if he is untried. I don't see Laura, but I see his grandfather, Dewey Di Longo, who died in the flood. But I don't guess he knows anything about Dewey Di Longo. Probably never heard of him. Well, if he hangs around me long enough, he'll know where his swarthy good looks came from.

He looks up from his notes. "Where were you when the flood hit?"

"In our house on Bedford Street. The house I grew up in. Getting ready for my wedding. I was supposed to marry Davy Hughes on June 22nd, three weeks away."

He's writing again, head down, intent on getting things right after the talking-to he undoubtedly got this morning from James. I smile, remembering how it was to be a young reporter, trying to make your mark. Makes me want to take him in hand and show him how it's done.

"In your house when it hit?"

"Well, no, not exactly. We heard the roar and sensed what it was. We . . ."

I'm surprised at how sharp the memory still is, after fifty years. I get that stinging inside my nose. Precursor to tears. I snap my head up. What's this?

Gerald Kirk is perceptive—senses my distress.

"I'm sorry, Mrs. McRae. I didn't mean to upset you. I could come back if there's a better time." He's inept, but sincere.

I wave him off. "No, dear. There's no better time. It's just that I haven't entertained these thoughts in so long." I adjust my glasses and settle back in my Morris chair. It used to be Rob's chair—his favorite. Now it's mine, even if I don't want it to be.

"The water'd been rising all day. Terrible storms over the mountains, both rivers way above flood stage. We lived well up from the Conemaugh, so we didn't usually get flooded too badly, but the Stony Creek was closer, and it was raging."

People were used to floods. Never could figure out why you'd build a town where two wild rivers meet in a deep, narrow valley, but there it is. At first it was just a little village, but then the mills came in and the town grew. People just dealt with the floods.

"Anyway, we were at home. They'd closed the Cambria Iron Works that morning so the men could help their families clear away for the high water. Papa was moving the smaller furniture and the rugs upstairs. Mama was already mourning the loss of her beloved piano. Our house was up three steps from the street. Then the yard and three more steps up to the porch. Geordie and I were rolling the rugs for Papa and Mama to wrestle up the stairs. Geordie was eleven and I was eighteen."

I'm talking faster now, and I can see it's hard for young Mr. Kirk to keep up. I slow my pace a little, glancing over at his notes now and then to assure myself that he's getting things right. He's a very earnest young man, likable, even. I decide to be charitable.

"Papa remembered that our neighbor down the block, Mrs. Stackpole, was alone and might need some help. He told Geordie to go down and bring her up to our house. Geordie didn't want to go. He hated getting cold, and the water was already up over his shoe tops in the street and still raining. He hesitated. Whined a little. Looked to Mama to rescue him."

I take a handkerchief out of my pocket and dab my eyes, angry with myself for letting my feelings show. You'd think I could deal with this after so many years, but lately, tears well up at the least provocation. Old age, I guess.

"Papa stared him down. Told him to get on. A little water never hurt anybody. Still Geordie tried to wheedle out of it. Said Mrs. Stackpole had closer neighbors, and they'd take care of her. Said the water would be up above his knees by the time he got to her house, lower down. Said it'd be so deep and the current so swift she wouldn't be able to walk."

Young Gerald's eyes are riveted on my face.

"Papa was grunting, struggling to get a rolled-up rug around the corner of the stairway. He turned and looked hard at Geordie and said, 'Get on with you, boy, before I take my belt off.'"

My voice breaks at that. The memory still hurts.

"Geordie pulled on Papa's old yellow oil cloth slicker and went to the door. He opened it and turned to look back at us, woeful. Then he closed the door and was gone."

I feel tears making their stubborn way down my cheeks, through the wrinkles, past my nose. I use my handkerchief, but it does little to stem their flow. Drat being old and sentimental. I've got to get hold of myself.

"About five minutes later—it was just after four o'clock—we heard the roar—like nothing any of us had ever heard before. No one said a word. Papa grabbed Mama's hand and raced out the door. I followed, lifting my skirts as I stepped off the bottom step into the water. Foolish girl."

I adjust my glasses again. Tears make my nose slippery.

"There were a lot of people in the street, wading frantically, some still holding onto their possessions, their children, looking back for stragglers. Our neighbor, Mr. Zeller, waded with a baby in his arms, five-year-old Teddy clinging to the other arm and a toddler on his back. Mrs. Zeller held onto his sleeve with the little girl—Ellie was her name—clinging to her skirts Never saw any of them again."

The memory comes pounding back. I can't seem to adjust to the vividness. I didn't expect it to be this hard.

"You could see terror in people's eyes as the roaring got louder and more deafening. We turned left, struggling against the current, terrorized by the roaring, pounding noise, and made for Green Hill."

My housekeeper, Katya, appears in the doorway with a tray of tea and cookies. I nod to her to set it down. She notices my wet cheeks. "Are you sure you're all right, Miss Pamela? Sure you want to talk about this?"

"Yes, Katya, I'm all right." She's been with me for years. Knows my every thought. She could tell this story herself, if she wanted to.

Gerald lays down his pencil and gives me a moment to gather myself. I'm impressed with his sensitivity. He leans close, frowning, eager. "What about that fiancé you lost?"

"Yes. Well, he and his whole family were lost except his father. Poor man. How do you cope with that kind of tragedy?"

My young man stops writing, looks up, his face clouded. "I don't know. Hearing about it makes me wonder how anyone came away with the ability to get over it—ever." He turns back to his notebook. "I've heard some people took the flood as an opportunity to disappear and make a new life for themselves. Ever hear of anyone who did that?"

I look sharp at him. Where did that come from? I shake my head.

He lets out a low whistle. "So you made it to Green Hill, you and your parents? They made it, too?"

I nod. The memories bring unexpected grief. I thought I could do this, but now I'm not so sure. I rise and try to smile at my young cub reporter, but the smile is forced, twisted. He gets the message, folds up his papers and moves toward the vestibule.

"I'm sorry, Mrs. McRae. My father thought yours would be such a good story. I didn't mean to upset you."

"I know, Gerald. We've got a few weeks until the 50th anniversary edition comes out. Maybe later."

"I hope so. There aren't that many people around who remember. I guess some folks are eager to tell their tale every chance they get, but Dad says yours has never been told."

"He's right. I was always reticent, especially because my story doesn't stop with the flood. It goes on for years."

He buttons up his jacket, a question in his eyes. "Years?"

"Yes. There was more for me than just the flood. I got seasoned at an early age." I hope I don't sound like a braggart, just an honest person. In spite of this rocky start, I feel myself wanting to tell it all. The whole story. Or write it down. My grandchildren, if I had any, would deserve to know the truth.

I let him out the door and return to the comfort of my living room, but the memories are unleashed, and there's no way to put them away again. The noise. The deafening, never ending noise. The crashing roar of the wall of water and debris more than thirty feet high that hit Johnstown on May 31, 1889. The splintering of houses smashing against each other. The screams, the scraping, swirling, sucking water. It was dark almost immediately, and the rain wouldn't quit.

The first rush of the flood coming down the Little Conemaugh told Johnstown the calamity it had feared for years had happened. The South Fork Dam had broken. This wasn't just high water. This was a cataclysm beyond imagination.

The first wave roared down the valley through Johnstown, smashed into the mountainside above the Stony Creek, backwashed up through Kernville and most of the town. It took houses, barns, trees, railroad cars, even locomotives and slammed them against that mountain. Then it turned around and hurled it all against the railroad bridge. That held. God knows why, but it held. Acted like a dam. Collected half of Johnstown, rammed it together so tight they had to use dynamite months later to clear it away.

We made it to Green Hill, but there was no comfort there. The wind was terrible, and the rain. People were huddled together, terrified, soaked and trembling. We shivered there in the dark, calling out our peoples' names. Papa called for Geordie, but there was nothing but the steady beat of the rain and the wailing of misery—the roaring and drumming of the swirling waters. Then, as if it weren't already hell, fire broke out at the railroad bridge, and we watched the crash and rumble of its flames, listened to the screams of its victims. We watched it burn, numb, cold and out of our minds with fear for those we couldn't find— would never find again.

I sit alone in my parlor for more than an hour, remembering. I haven't thought about it in any great detail for so many years. Life goes on and takes you with it. That was always fine with me. Went with my need to throw off the tragedy and make something of myself. Guess I've done that. But now it seems as though, despite my distress, I need to bring it up again. Confront him. Confront Davy.

I go to the telephone and dial the paper. Elsie McNaughton, the switchboard operator, answers as she always does. She recognizes my voice and tries to direct my call to my son's office.

"No Elsie, no need to bother James with this. Just tell that young man, that Gerald Kirk, that he can come back tomorrow. I'll be ready to talk to him then."

Chapter 2

I spend a fitful night, somewhere between sleep and wakefulness. Sleep comes rationed to the aged. Since Rob passed, I sleep only about half as much as I did. In the morning I go downstairs to the kitchen and sit for breakfast. Katya places a boiled egg, toast and coffee before me.

"My young man is coming again today," I tell her.

"You sure you're ready to go back there?" she asks. "You were the one always said we should leave the past in the past."

I nod. "Still believe that, but fifty years bears remembering. I might need you along to check my facts, though. My memory isn't what it used to be."

"Neither is mine. No accident there. Some things I don't want to remember."

I smile at her—my best friend as well as my employee. The employee part is just a formality. She likes taking care of me, and I like letting her. Two old widows joined by a lifetime of shared joy and sorrow. If the roles were reversed, she'd come out on the short end, though. Some people are born nurturers. Some—like me—can barely nurture a flower. Just not made for the care-taking role.

"You like that young man?" she asks, hand on her hip, dish cloth at the ready.

I nod. "He's Laura Jenkins's grandson, you know."

"Now there was a pip! If there wasn't trouble afoot when she was around," Katya smiles when she says it, remembering Laura's antics.

I smile, too. Laura was a beauty of mythical stature blithely going through life without a care.

"I swear every man who ever met her fell in love with her. She relished all the attention—more than her fair share, I thought—but couldn't pick a good man to save her life. Always fell for the lowest gimcrack she could find."

I push my plate aside and reach for today's paper, folded neatly beside my plate. Katya takes care of everything. I prefer to eat in the kitchen. Dining room's too formal.

"Cut a wide swathe around this town, she did." Katya carries my dishes to the sink. "Dewey turned out all right, though."

"Yes, bless him. This boy is Dewey's son. Seems like a nice enough boy. He'll be here at two o'clock."

"Too bad Rob isn't here to tell it with you. He'd add some spice."

I smile, remembering my husband's penchant for a catchy turn of phrase. "Yes, he'd have a thing or two to say about those days. But *you* could tell it all yourself."

She smiles. "Can't. I'm busy. Got laundry to do. You're on your own." She picks up her laundry basket and makes her way down the steps to the basement.

I go into the living room with my paper and coffee and sit down by the window. Outside the morning is glorious. Bright, sunny, warm. I raise a shade to let in more sunshine. Good weather for growing flowers. Reminds me of my mother and her garden. She had a touch for flowers. Not interested in vegetables, like Katya, but every blooming thing on earth was her pet.

Here I go again. Hadn't thought of her in any real way for years. My mother, my caregiver, my joy, my keeper. I remember that feeling. Like I was her prisoner. I hated that. Hated her for going away.

My hand touches an antimacassar set she crocheted, gracing the back of the davenport. When she was here, she was such a good mother, and when she was gone, it was horrid. It still isn't easy to sort out the feelings. It wasn't the first time she went away. Ten years before the flood, in '79, she left us after my two brothers, Hugh and Jamie, died in the diphtheria outbreak. I was only eight then, feeling the guilt of the surviving child, and so afraid she wouldn't come back. She just sat there in her chair in the kitchen, staring at nothing.

Papa would try to talk to her, but she didn't hear him. I would talk, too, but she looked past me like I was wallpaper. Geordie was a baby and needed her, but she just couldn't see him. It was like she was all alone in the universe. It lasted a few months that time, and then she came back like she'd never been gone. After the flood, it happened again, only this time it was for a lot longer than a few months.

Sat in her rocking chair all day, every day, staring at nothing—like an angel, all neat and clean in her starched blue dress with a brooch pinned at the throat. I made sure of that. Shawl over her shoulders, hands folded in her lap, white hair pulled back in a neat roll. She wasn't that old, but her hair turned white after the flood.

Looking at her, you'd think she'd just come home from church and sat down to rest a few minutes before getting dinner on the table. Except that she'd been sitting there for years. Ever since we got the "Oklahoma house" they brought in as temporary housing. Before that she sat in a ward in one of Miss Barton's Red Cross buildings. She didn't speak a word after the flood.

Papa lasted a year until he couldn't take it anymore. Mama sitting in that chair. One day he just walked down the street and was gone. I think that was when he gave up hope of Geordie ever coming back. I used to wonder if Papa was still out there somewhere or if he'd gone off in the woods and killed himself. Thought I'd probably never know.

I open my newspaper. I like to keep abreast of things, even though James does a fine job of running the *Clarion* since his father died. I'm just folding it up when I hear a step on the porch. To early for Gerald Kirk. I rise and look out the window. James. Even though his father's been gone for more than two years, seeing James still gives me a start. Like a young Rob just walked through the door.

"Good morning, Mother. Thought I'd stop by for a cup of coffee."

I'm skeptical. He never stops by for a cup of coffee. Most of the time I don't see him at all unless I go down to the paper.

"Help yourself. You know where the coffee pot is." I sit down on the davenport, waiting for him to join me. James is so like his father, it almost hurts to look at him. His older brother Kenneth was more like me. Now here we are, the two of us. All that's left.

He comes into the living room and sets his coffee cup down on an end table. I hand him a coaster. He lifts his cup and puts it under. "You talking to young Kirk again today?"

So that's it. Young Gerald must have told him I was upset yesterday. "Yes. Yes. I'll be all right. No need for concern."

"I'm not concerned. Just curious. What's bothering you about the flood? It's all water under the bridge anyway." He smiles at his play on words. Just like his father.

"Brings back a lot of memories. Some I shut away on purpose. Trouble is, I kept the key."

"Just stick to the facts, Mother. Who, what, when, where. Use your old newspaper skills. No need to probe deeper." Like most men, he's full of solutions, the simpler the better. "Don't let him intrude. It's just a feature story."

"Yes, I know. Don't worry, dear. I won't come apart. Now get on with you. I know you didn't stop by to pass the time."

He rises, drinks his coffee and sets down his cup. "Sure you still want to do this, then?"

I nod as he turns toward the kitchen. "Katya! How's life?"

I hear a giggle as Katya comes into the hall to give him a hug. "James, you rascal, you. When you gonna get married?"

"Always with the marriage thing, Katya. Can't you think of anything else?"

"Thirty years old and nothing to show for it. When are you going to settle down to a meaningful life?"

I smile at their exchange. Katya has license to say things I'd never say.

"'Bout time you make your mother a grandma. She needs something to occupy her mind. If you don't do something soon, I won't be responsible for her."

James's laugh fills the tiny hallway. "You won't be responsible in any case. How's Stephen these days?"

Katya beams at the mention of her son. "Better than you. At least he's married and got two kids."

James gives her a loud smacking kiss on the cheek and turns for the door. "You'll be the first to know when I find the perfect woman."

"That was your mother, foolish boy. Give that one up. There'll never be another like her."

James bounds down the porch steps, still grinning as he settles into his new blue Packard with the tar roof and sets off for the paper. I'm embarrassed by all the fuss. Perfect woman. Really!

When two o'clock rolls around, I'm ready for the boy this time. He'd better have made a list of questions to stimulate conversation. That's what I'd really like—a good lively conversation.

He's right on time. We should sit on the porch. Such a lovely spring afternoon. We sit—I on a wicker settee—he on an old hickory rocking chair we got from my mother-in-law.

"Well, Gerald, where were we?"

"On Green Hill, as I recall."

"Yes. That's right. Well, we sat up there all night, freezing and dying inside. The morning didn't bring much relief. The rain had stopped, but it was still awful cold for the first of June. Problem was, there was no place to go, almost no houses that weren't damaged. No food supplies, medical care, nothing but the devastation."

"How long did it take for relief to get there?"

"Some local people did all they could to help right away. Loaded up wagons with food or blankets. Brought milk into town from the farms. Those whose houses weren't destroyed opened them up to all, but there were so many to be served, it was impossible to do much but put some gauze on a gaping wound."

"What about your family? What did you do?"

"My mother went catatonic by morning. Didn't speak or move. Just stared into space. I tried to lead her to a house for shelter, and she went, but her eyes were as blank as the dead. Papa recognized it, but he was almost as stricken. He stumbled about looking for Geordie, calling for him, asking everyone if they'd seen him."

"Did they ever find his body?"

I shake my head. "We'll get to that later. Now I want to talk about the day after. So many people were hurt—hungry, cold, distraught. Many without shoes, some naked. Clothes stripped right off them. The flood did incredible things to human beings. Treated them like so much chaff."

I look around at the greening spring grass and the budding trees, daffodils, lilacs, redbud. Birds singing, busily nesting as though this place were like any other. It's inconceivable that such devastation could have happened here.

"I left Mama in one of the houses on Green Hill and went down into the town. It was horrible, but irresistible—like a huge magnet drawing you in. Papa went down, too, looking for Geordie. By noon it was already starting to smell. There were dead everywhere. People, animals, plants. No water fit to drink. And the thick, stinking muck all over. What struck me was the children. Poor little waifs, hungry, cold and crying for their mothers. I met up with two or three other women and we started to round them up and keep them together so we could identify them and feed and clothe them as soon as supplies arrived."

"Was my Grandmother with you? I mean, did you see her that day?"

I scour my memory for Laura Jenkins after the flood. "No. I don't remember seeing her for some time. Seems to me she was out of town.

Gone to Ebensburg for a visit, I think." I don't tell him Laura had a knack for being gone in time of need. Then she'd come back with a smile to light up the sky when all the trouble was over and the work was done.

Still, I liked her. We'd been friends since the old Adams Street School in '76. Schoolmates. Chums. Laura was a friend to laugh with, counterweight to me. Fully expected that the world was delighted to have her in it, and would reward her presence with admiration. Maybe it was that opposite attraction that held us together all those years. Certainly wasn't commonalities. She was beautiful and irreverent. I was plain and careful. She was drawn to men of low degree like a bee to a flower. I avoided even a hint of impropriety. She behaved scandalously and relished the attention it brought. I tried my best to escape notice.

Gerald Kirk is still writing—needs a moment or two to catch up. He gives me a nod to continue.

"In the evening I went back to the house where I'd left my mother. She was sitting in a corner looking the same. I wondered if anyone had noticed her, fed her, helped her in any way. Her dress was dry, but still muddy, her hair all askew, her face and hands dirty. There was no help for it. Couldn't give her a bath or clean clothes. There were neither. Then the lady of the house, red faced and exhausted, noticed me. 'Your ma's been fed and took outside to pee,' she told me. 'Can't say much else.'"

"It was a week before there was anything close to order. They set up morgues right away and started burying bodies as fast as they could. The smell was unforgettable. Like sweet air, only nauseating. Had to bury them fast to prevent disease, so they wrote down descriptions—like what they were wearing, if anything, and anybody's guess at their age, height and weight. Identifying marks. Jewelry. What not. Some were babies, little ones, snatched from their mother's arms. Sometimes neighbors knew them. Sometimes not."

I'm surprised at how well I'm doing. No tears today. Just the facts, as James would say. The time races by, and before we know it, it's four o'clock. Gerald Kirk folds up his notebook.

"I want to write up what I've got so far, so I'll skip tomorrow," he says. After that, I'll probably have questions for you to fill in before we go on."

I nod. He seems to have good sense about him, unlike his grandmother, who had little and used less.

13

"The next thing I want to know about is your fiancé. What was his name?"

"Davy. Davy Hughes. Yes. You'll want to know about him."

Chapter 3

*A*fter young Kirk leaves, I sit alone on the porch, with Davy Hughes on my mind. Now there's someone I *have* thought about—throughout my life. It's hard to let go of what might have been. Davy was my beau, four years older, with a promising future in the iron works. Folks said they were grooming him for management. I didn't know. All I knew was, I was in love.

Our houses shared a back fence—hedge actually—and there was a path worn through it with all the comings and goings. Davy was the oldest, then came his three sisters, like stair steps, then their little brother Garreth, Geordie's age.

On the morning of that last Christmas before the flood, Davy came over around eleven o'clock with a present for me. We went into the parlor and exchanged our gifts. He gave me the diary I wrote in every night until May 30, 1889. I gave him a gold stick pin for his tie with an "H" on it that he wore to church every Sunday after that. At Mama's prompting, Geordie gave us a few moments of privacy. After all, we *were* engaged. Had been since my birthday back in September. We'd already set our wedding date for June. Mrs. David Evan Hughes. I wrote that in my diary every night, never tired of reading it.

"Come on, Davy. Beat you at checkers." Geordie liked Davy almost as much as I did, and made up every excuse he could to gain a share of his attention. Davy could beat him at checkers in about thirty seconds, but he'd put off winning to make Geordie think he was getting good.

The world was full of promise that spring. Mrs. Hanley across the street was making my dress, and the ladies of the church were busily planning our reception. So in love, I drifted through the months, barely keeping a toehold on reality.

A wedding trip to Pittsburgh, a small house we'd rented on a back lot on Franklin Street, furnished with hand-me-downs from the Hughes and Gwynedd households. I embroidered kitchen towels, pillow cases and dresser scarves. Mama crocheted doilies and antimacassar sets. The one I still have was saved from the flood because she'd sent it out to my aunt in Derry to use as a pattern. Mrs. Hughes was making us a quilt.

Davy—handsome enough to turn any girl's head—grey eyes, thick brown hair—not terribly tall, but sturdily built. A deep dimple in his right cheek that gave a lilt to his smile. And bright. Everyone knew that. Davy Hughes was the smartest boy in his class and on his way to running things in Johnstown. I never knew what attracted him to me. I was nobody great. But Davy insisted I was. Said he wanted me to be the mother of his children. My papa was proud of the match. Mama, too. Laura Jenkins said she was jealous, but then Laura could have any man she wanted, so I was grateful she left Davy to me.

Then the flood took it all away. Davy, his mother, three sisters and Garreth. Only Mr. Hughes survived, and though he stayed on in an Oklahoma house behind ours, there wasn't much left of him. Came and went with a haunted look, like a restless haint. How do you get over something like that? Losing your wife and five children? My papa only lost one child, and he couldn't take it. Sometimes at night when I looked out the back window at Mr. Hughes dark house, I wondered if he ever screamed, cried or rent his clothes.

They found all the bodies but Davy's, but that wasn't particularly odd. Davy was up in East Conemaugh by the train depot running an errand for his boss when the flood hit. There was so much destruction there from the train cars, locomotives and the roundhouse. A lot of bodies were lost, buried deep in the mud forever.

I was numb after that. Everything was gone. Nothing left to hope for. I went about life without caring. What was the use? Davy was gone. Geordie was gone. Mama was gone. Papa and I would sit down to supper and eat in silence. His face was worn and deep lines ran down from his nose to his chin. When he talked, he barely moved his lips, and his eyes seemed deeper set than before. I didn't see it coming, but when he went away, I knew why. Got up from the table one June evening, took his hat from the peg by the door and walked away. Just like that. Didn't say goodbye, or even look back. Just walked down the street and was gone.

"You planning to have supper out here?" It's Katya, coming out to check on me. "What're you doing without a sweater? Don't you know there's a chill in the air?" She brings me a sweater, picked from the hall tree on her way out.

I look up at her, glad for the interruption. Getting too sad for me. "Oh, my young man left and I was just sitting here thinking."

"Thinking? About what?" She turns a skeptical eye on me. "Or should I say who?"

"Davy." It comes out softer than I meant it to.

"I knew it. I just knew you'd end up there. You always do. Can't quite let go of him, can you?"

She hands me the sweater, and I wrap it around my shoulders. "Sit down, Katya. Let me talk about it."

She winces at the thought of dredging up old wounds, but sits down beside me on the settee. "Now don't you get the both of us crying, hear? There's a lot back there I don't want to visit."

"Remember the first sighting I had of Davy?"

"I think that was before I came to you," she says, frowning with the effort to remember.

"Yes, you're right. It was. But only a few weeks. Just before Christmas, two years after the flood."

I cover her hand with mind, give it a little squeeze. "I'd gone downtown to look in the windows. Didn't have a cent to my name. But I needed to get out of the house. Taking care of Mama was wearing me down."

Katya smiles and nods. "Guess I know a little about that."

"Remember the relief clothes I used to wear? Before you came and started sewing for me?"

Another smile. "Well, you had to take what they gave out. No money. No job and no prospects."

"Anyway, I was walking along, feeling sorry for myself, when all of a sudden I saw him. Davy!—walking about a half block ahead of me, head down, hands in his pockets, but I'd know that walk anywhere. I called to him, but he didn't turn around. I called again and started to run. Then a lady came out of a store with her arms full of packages, and I ran smack into her. Sent the packages flying. I stooped to pick them up, trying to keep my eyes on the back of his head, but by the time I'd apologized and handed them back, he was gone."

"Sightings," Katya says with a sigh. Everyone in Johnstown had the same experience. Seeing the dead. Even years after the flood."

"Remember Mrs. Yon who lived on Levergood two houses down from the Hugheses? Telling everyone her boy Roddie was back? He couldn't have been. I saw Roddie Yon's body pulled out of the river three days after the flood. I recognized him. Geordie's best friend. You can bet I looked close, too, even though it was awful. If I could have, I'd have asked him what happened to Geordie."

Katya nods and smoothes her apron. A fly buzzes past her nose, and she snatches it in mid-air. "Too early for them," she tells me, dropping the dead fly over the porch railing.

"Mrs. Yon thought she'd seen Roddie three times in a month, hanging around the shed at night. She even left food out for him, and she was convinced he was the one eating it. Now I ask you, why would a fourteen-year-old be hiding out in the hills instead of warm and well fed in his mama's house? But she wanted to believe it."

"I had sightings, too," Katya tells me. "My mama and grandma. Walking to market ahead of me, five years after the flood. And my mama came to my wedding. When I married Istvan, she was there, in the back row, smiling."

Puzzling, when you think of it. How many people could tell you the same kind of story. Is it real or wishful thinking? I don't know, but I do know it seems real when it happens.

Katya rises and turns toward the door. "You coming in? I have to see to supper."

"I'll be in a few minutes. Thanks for the sweater."

I sit looking out at the street. This journey down memory lane has gotten hold of me. For the first time in fifty years, I want to remember. It's painful, yes, but it's part and parcel of who I am. Maybe I'll write it all down. I used to think I would when I got time on my hands. Well, I've got time now, and this young man digging into the past has awakened the need.

But where do you start? Who do you start with? The flood, I guess. It always comes back to the eternal flood.

Chapter 4

It's only about five o'clock, but it feels like evening. I sit there on the porch, lost in my memories. Maybe it's because Rob is gone that life has slowed down enough for me to look back. Or maybe it's just this boy—this grandson of Laura's, with his sweet curiosity.

In a flash I'm back there on that snowy day in December, walking along looking in the store windows, wishing I had a nickel to rub against another. Puzzling over my sighting. The snow fell in large wet flakes, building up on the sidewalk just enough to make walking a little slippery.

"Pammie! Pammie!"

I turned. Laura Jenkins waved to me from across the street. I waved back. Laura was my best friend before, but the flood changed all that. She lived in her parents' comfortable house over on Willow Street, and I huddled up with my mother in a ten by twenty bare board Oklahoma house up on Bedford. Worlds away.

"Wait up!" Laura let a dray wagon pass and ran across to join me, wet snow clinging to her trim leather shoes. Her face was pink with the cold, and her breath came out in clouds. She caught up to me with a silly, flirtatious smile. That was Laura. Flirted with everyone, male or female.

"Guess what! I'm getting married!" Her voice rose with excitement and she looked around as though the news should make the world stop and take note. Laura didn't know how to temper her joy. If she was happy, the world should be happy. Still, I'd missed her, and it felt good to talk.

"Really? Anyone I know?"

"Calvin Corwyn from Ebensburg," she replied. "Works in the dry goods store over there."

I didn't know him, but I was happy for her as any friend would be. A man. The goal of every woman's strivings.

"Where did you meet him?"

"At my cousin Nora's last summer. Remember? I went up there for two weeks?" She lowered her eyes and looked up at me as though I were a man she was trying to seduce. I swear she'd have flirted with a fence post.

"When's the big day?" I asked. My happiness for Laura was tempered. This was the third—or was it the fourth?—time she'd been engaged.

"May. We want a spring wedding."

"Does he know about Dewey?" I wasn't trying to be mean, but Laura conveniently forgot to mention she had a two-year-old son when she met someone new. That's what messed up her last engagement.

"Uh-huh." She smiled, too lost in her dream to take offense.

"That's nice, Laura. I hope it works out for you." I really did hope so, even though I was jealous that Laura Jenkins, soiled as she was, could attract a man any time she wanted, and I had no prospects. I didn't understand how she did it. But then Laura's poor taste in men was notorious. Handsome and gruesome. That was Laura's type.

"Let's stop for some hot chocolate." She smiled at her reflection in a passing window. "I'm out shopping for dinnerware. Well, not really shopping. Just picking it out so I can tell Mama and Papa what to get me for Christmas."

"I'd better not, Laura. My mother's alone." Poverty chafed, but Laura saw through my reluctance and grabbed my arm.

"Come on, Pam. Let yourself have a little fun. Life isn't supposed to be grim all the time."

"Okay. I guess the water in the pitcher won't freeze if I stop for a cup of hot chocolate."

She smiled again, let go of my arm and stepped back to adjust her fur collar. "That's the spirit. Come on, let's go over to Schafner's."

She led the way down the sidewalk about four stores to Schafner's Tea Room and opened the door. The sweet smell of Christmas baking met us as we entered. The place was crowded with shoppers taking a break for a cup of Schafner's famous hot chocolate. This was one of the first businesses to reopen after the flood, a return to normal. The way we were. I used to come here often with my friends or with Mama when we were out shopping. Now it felt like it was for better folk. Still, I liked being there, back in touch with life. The room was much the same as the old one where we used to gather on a hot summer afternoon for a phosphate, or where Davy and I used to share a soda on a Friday night.

I put down my bag and slipped into a high backed wooden booth. Laura sat down across from me, a giddy smile on her face. You had to love Laura. She was as happy as if she had good sense.

Now she took a serious turn. "So how is it? Taking care of your mother, I mean." Her face was earnest. Real concern.

"Never ending. They call it catatonic. Dr. Smythe says she could come out of it any time or never. She doesn't do anything for herself. I take care of her—cook, clean, wash, iron, sew. Bathe her. Wash and comb her hair. Dress her. Feed her. Lead her by the hand up or down the stairs." In spite of my efforts at control, my eyes filled up as I related my circumstances. It was better if I didn't talk about it. "It's like prison, Laura. I don't have a life."

"Oooh, Pammie. How do you stand it?" I didn't say so, but it was a sure thing Laura never could have stood the life I'd fallen into. She leaned forward and covered my hand with hers. "You're a saint, Pam. A real saint."

Desperate to shake off the blues, I changed the subject. "So, tell me about your wedding plans."

"Oh," she swooned, "wait 'til you hear! Everything white—my dress, the bridesmaids' dresses, the attendants' suits. All white with yellow flowers. Yellow roses for me, yellow boutonnières for the men, yellow carnations for the bridesmaids. That reminds me, can I count on you to be a bridesmaid?"

Just then the waitress stepped up to the table, and Laura took it upon herself to order for both of us. "Two mugs of hot chocolate and two slices of your poppy seed cake."

I took advantage of the interruption to try to think of a reason why I couldn't be a bridesmaid—except for the obvious one, of course. Again Laura's perceptive talents came to my rescue.

"I won't hear any excuses," she admonished. "My mother is sewing the dresses and there'll be one with your name on it, so don't bother to shy away."

I forced a smile. No use arguing. We fell into a moment of silence. Then Laura reached for my hand again. "Bet all this wedding talk makes you miss Davy."

That jolted me back to my sighting, and I told her about it, my eyes growing moist with the telling. She listened, distracted, her gaze wandering around the Tea Room.

"What makes you so sure it was Davy?" she asked, clearly humoring me.

I blushed. "I'd know him anywhere. It felt so strange. Like he knew it was me, but he never turned around when I called. Kept right on walking."

She smiled over her mug. "You and Davy were a pair. Everyone thought you'd be married and having babies by now."

"Everyone including me."

She patted my hand. "Don't despair. Someone new will come along."

I supposed that might be true, but there was nothing on the horizon. We drank our chocolate and ate the cake, reminiscing about old friends and old times. Laura knew all about everyone and wasn't shy about sharing the intimacies. She made me laugh. It felt good to be normal again if even for a few minutes. I thought I really should try harder to keep in touch. Laura was good for me—pulled me out of my doldrums.

As soon as I finished my chocolate I rose to pull on my coat. It was green—from the relief. Not the style anymore. I knew Laura had noticed.

"I'd better be going. Mama's been alone too long."

Laura gathered her things and followed me to the cashier. She paid while I looked out at an accumulation of snow. It was getting deep and I had a long walk ahead of me. I said goodbye and set off up Main Street, head down against the heavily falling snow.

The little Oklahoma house sat lonely in the middle of a barren lot that used to be my mother's pride. Flowerbeds, green lawn, huge shade trees and a gingerbready two-story house. Now it was nothing—the whole neighborhood stripped of everything familiar or comfortable, though some of our neighbors had rebuilt. Still, new houses don't feel like old houses. Barren yards didn't compare with the leafy, lush lawns and flowerbeds of before. I walked the tightrope path from the street to our single front step, thoughts of Davy lingering in my mind. .

The flimsy little boxcar of a house was dark and barely warmer than outside. I'd stayed away too long, and the fire'd gone out. It'd take a few hours to warm up. I went right to the stove, lifted the lid and stuffed in some kindling.

Mama sat gazing at the stove, hands in her lap. She could freeze that way with no reaction. I warmed my hands, talking to her all the while. I told her about seeing Laura and about her wedding plans. I talked with enthusiasm and life in my voice that I didn't feel, the way I'd talked to her ever since I realized she was lost. If I could keep her up on what was happening and put it in a good light, maybe she'd want to come back some day.

Once I'd got the fire going, I pulled my chair up to the stove and opened my book. Reading was my only escape. I loved Sir Walter Scott's books. I'd read them all more than once. *Ivanhoe* about five times. I was soon engrossed in the Middle Ages, feet tucked up under my skirt, Papa's old coat around my shoulders.

After a while I got up to feed the fire and realized the wood box was almost empty, so I pulled on Papa's old boots and my mittens, picked up the canvas sling I used for carrying wood and went outside for a load. Three trips and I had enough to last the night. It was mostly quick burning pine. When Papa was here, he'd get us oak. Burns hotter, lasts longer. But I had to take what the relief sent me. As I bent to pick up one last log, I heard a call.

"Yoo hoo! Miss Gwynedd! Yoo hoo!" It was Mrs. Plummer, head of the relief for our part of town, plowing heavily through the snowy shadows, her arms full of bags.

I raised my head and smiled. She was the angel of mercy who brought our share of whatever there was to get. It was best to smile at Mrs. Plummer. She liked to know you were grateful.

"Miss Gwynedd, I bring the best news." She fairly bubbled over, so pleased with herself.

"Mrs. Plummer. Come in out of the cold." I opened the door and Mrs. Plummer filled the doorway with her ample self and the bags. She brought walnuts and two oranges, for which I was grateful, but she held out one package until last.

"Miss Gwynedd, I know you're going to be excited about this! I've found a way for you to earn some money."

What was this? Mrs. Plummer's demeanor was officious to the point of meddling, but I listened anyway. This might be interesting. I waited, my head cocked to the side. I'd been trying to find a way to make money to support Mama and me since Papa left. We went through the little money we had in a few months. Don't think I wasn't grateful for the relief. I was. But charity chafes.

"Look!" she cried, unwrapping the parts of a small loom. "You can make rugs and sell them! Won't that be nice?"

Mrs. Plummer obviously thought this was the best thing she could have come up with, and wondered why she hadn't thought of it sooner. It took every bit of pretense I could muster to express my unbounded joy and gratitude. She showed me how to assemble the loom, adding that she'd gotten twenty of them to distribute around the community. Quick arithmetic told me that the market would be flooded and no one would be able to sell a runner or a set of placemats in the whole town by spring. But Mrs. Plummer was undaunted. She bid me good day, still delighting in her enterprising style, and promised to bring some rags to get me started.

When she was gone, I stood by the door of the tiny house looking at the loom, sturdy and well designed. It would work well, and I'd probably enjoy making a rug or two, but to think of it as a means of income was foolish. I walked around studying its workings. Then I turned to Mama.

"Look at this nice little loom Mrs. Plummer brought, Mama. It's just the thing to make our lives better. I can weave rugs and sell them. Won't that be fine?"

I was suddenly overwhelmed with sadness. I hated to admit it, but I wanted to get away. Away from my mother, away from this pathetic Oklahoma house, away from Johnstown and all its memories. I was twenty-one. Eighteen plus two and a half. That's how I thought of life since the flood. I'd lived eighteen happy years before. Then that life ended in one night of horror. Since then, I was two. I wanted a life. I'd have followed Papa down the road in a minute if I could.

Chapter 5

*T*wo days later, when Gerald Kirk makes his prompt appearance at my door I'm ready for him. Ready to talk about Davy. Ready to get to the meat of this story.

I invite him into the parlor where Katya has set out a tray of tea and cookies. She likes any excuse to feed people—especially cookies. Young Gerald is dressed in his working clothes, a gray suit, white shirt, bow tie, billed cap under his arm. Not quite up with the current style, but he makes a neat, clean appearance. The Depression has been hard on Johnstown, so he can be excused for not keeping up. I'm still giving him a going over when his first question catches me off guard.

"Who was Dewey Di Longo?" His face is open, sincere. He really wants to know.

"Where did you come up with that name?" I ask, watching him for any sign of emotion.

"I've heard it around."

"Around where?"

"Around places where my dad and grandma wouldn't go."

I sit back in my chair and place my teacup carefully on the table beside me. "What makes you want to know?"

"I think it has something to do with my grandma. I think she might have had an affair with him, and I'd like to know why people still talk about it."

I smile. "Your grandma was a piece of work in her youth, my boy. My best friend, mind you, but she could cook up a scandal before you could say Dewey Di Longo. And she did—every chance she got."

"What kind of scandal?"

I can't believe I'm sitting here talking about Laura and Dewey Di Longo. This isn't where I was prepared to go. "Well, Gerald, your grandma was always attracted to men whose station in life was beneath her. Dewey Di Longo was an Italian immigrant steel worker. Laura met him on the street, and the sparks flew right away. Dewey was always in trouble with the law—couldn't stay out of bars or fights, so, of course, there was a lot of talk."

"So what happened? Did he get in a fight and kill somebody?"

"No, dear. The flood took care of that. His body washed up in the mess at the railroad bridge."

Gerald leans forward, listening with intensity. A family secret.

"Trouble was, Laura was already pregnant with your father, and she delivered the following December. The town was rocked by the flood, but, people will be people, and Laura's shenanigans brought shame."

"So Dewey Di Longo was my grandfather?" His young face is very serious. "Now I get my dad's name, Dewey."

"Yes. People got all up in arms about that, too. Like she was throwing it in their faces. But, you had to know Laura then. She relished the attention. Went out of her way to be outrageous. And couldn't keep away from the wild and exciting. She thrived on it."

Gerald is smiling now. "Sounds like my Grandma," he says.

I have to smile, too, remembering how Laura kicked up her heels and used her beauty to lure men just because she could.

"I remember one time I met her downtown—she was all excited about getting married. It was some time after the flood—a couple years, I think. Yes. It was the same day I had my first sighting of Davy Hughes."

Now my young man straightens up in his chair. "Davy Hughes? Tell me about him!"

I lay a hand on his arm. Katya comes in to take away the tea things. She notices that the cookies are all gone and goes back to the kitchen. In a moment she returns with a tall cold glass of milk and another plate of cookies. Gerald dives in without restraint.

"That comes later, I tell him. Now we're talking about Laura. Anyway, she was all excited about marrying Calvin Corwyn from Ebensburg. Well, I didn't know it then, but rumor had it that he was a drinker and a carouser, and Laura knew that, but I guess she thought her charms could bring out the best in him."

"Calvin Corwyn? I've never heard that name."

"Best you didn't."

Katya comes back into the room with a look that tells me she thinks I've gone too far. I'm chastised.

"You know, Gerald, I think we've strayed from our mission here. Maybe we should get back to the flood."

"No. I want to know about this, and no one else will tell me."

With a look at Katya, I continue. "This Calvin Corwyn beat her up one Christmas eve, and her father was so disgusted with her, he threw her out and she ended up on my doorstep, such as it was, on Christmas day. I was still living in an Oklahoma house then, even though the flood was more than two years past."

"Oklahoma house?"

"Yes, the little wooden huts, not much bigger than a boxcar—ten by twenty I think they were, two rooms down and two up—that they brought in as temporary housing after the flood."

"Oh, yeah. I've seen a few of them. Some people have them out back—use them as sheds now."

I nod. "I lived in one with my mother. It was tight in there with Laura and Dewey, but I was glad for the company. My life was pretty grim in those days. No money, no fun. Just taking care of my mother and waiting for something—anything—to happen."

Gerald gobbles cookies and drinks milk as he listens. Boys and milk and cookies. Unbeatable. I'm taken back to that long ago Christmas when a quiet knock at my door revealed a disheveled Laura holding Dewey by the hand and struggling with a heavy valise in the other.

"Laura! What a nice surprise!" I was puzzled by the unannounced visit.

Inside, she let Dewey and the valise down, removed her scarf and pushed back her hair. Her face was bruised and swollen and she had a black eye.

"What happened?" I was dumbstruck. Dewey was crying from cold hands, his coat buttoned crooked, his nose running. They looked like refugees.

"Can we stay with you, Pammie? Calvin beat me up last night—drinking a little too hearty. By the time he came to pick me up he'd already had a few."

She slipped off her coat, revealing a rich wool dress with a sprig of holly at the throat.

"Papa forbade me to go out with him, but I thought we'd just have a little fun and come home, so I went. Calvin had a bottle under the wagon seat, and the more he drank, the meaner he got."

She sat down at the table while I helped little Dewy out of his coat and rubbed his hands to warm them up.

"We went up to Woodvale to visit his cousin. He had a couple of drinks with her husband, and on the way home, he turned surly. Kept calling me a whore and slapping me. He knocked me right out of the wagon and left me bleeding in a snow bank. I had to walk home all alone in the dark."

I looked on in wonder as she smoothed her skirts. Hadn't she seen enough of drunks by now? Her bruises were more apparent as she warmed up.

"Let me get some something to put on those bruises."

"No. Just let me relax. Can we stay here? Papa threw us out."

I was amazed that Walter Jenkins would finally come to the end of his patience with this beautiful girl child he'd doted upon for years. She looked so forlorn I couldn't help but feel sorry for her.

"Threw you out? Why? Why now?"

"I don't know. I guess he's just had enough of me. That's what he said, anyway."

"Well, of course you can stay here. You and Dewey can have my bed, and I'll sleep with Mama." All of a sudden this little Oklahoma house was full to its flimsy rafters.

She thanked me profusely as she wiped Dewey's nose and smoothed his dark, curly hair. He was soon happily playing with a wooden train, the only toy his mother had thought to bring along.

At dinner I fed Mama roast beef and mashed potatoes. Like a baby, she waited for each bite, opened her mouth when it came, swallowed, waited for the next bite. Dewey stopped by her chair and looked long into her face. She looked past him at the stove as though he weren't there.

"Why don't she talk?" he asked.

I shook my head, but didn't reply. I didn't talk about Mama as if she weren't there. I thought she heard and understood most of what went on. She just didn't want to be part of it.

At bedtime I told Dewey a story from memory—one about a poor shoemaker and some elves who helped him get back on his feet. Dewey protested sleeping in a strange place, but eventually settled down. Upstairs Laura watched me get Mama ready for bed, tugging woolen booties on her feet.

"I don't know how you do it," she observed.

"We do what we have to do."

Laura shook her head. yawned and stretched. "Would you mind very much if I retired, too? I'm ready to put this day behind me."

I didn't mind. I went back downstairs and curled up in Mama's rocker with my book, enclosed by the silence in the house.

Almost a week later Laura was still there, and Dewey was wiggling his way into my heart. Why is innocence so loveable? He looked on us with such trust. How could we bear to fail him? That must have been how my mother and father felt when, twelve years ago, the diphtheria passed through and my brothers, Jamie and Hugh, died. Jamie was ten and Hugh was six. I was in between. And then the flood, and Geordie. No wonder Papa left. How can you bear the helplessness?

I found myself wishing Laura and Dewey would stay, but I knew they wouldn't. Laura flitted from one thing to another, barely lighting long enough to dry her wings.

On the day before the New Year I could see the signs she was getting restless. "I think Dewey and I will take a walk downtown today," she announced. The discoloration from her bruises was fading, so I wasn't surprised she wanted to move on.

I nodded. "Will you stop by to see your mother?"

"Maybe. At least to pick up some more clothes. I barely had time to pack after Papa and I got into it."

"He's probably over it by now. Probably just waiting for you to come back and make up." I wished that weren't the case, but my good sense told me it was. Or would be soon. Walter Jenkins's love for his only daughter was legendary in Johnstown. I was amazed that he'd let her go this long without coming for her. Surely he knew where she was.

I could tell Laura was tired of the simple life, though. The Jenkins home was very comfortable. Not luxurious, but far above an Oklahoma house which was tight enough with the two of us when Mama barely moved, but put four in it, one of them a two-year-old, and pretty soon we were tripping over each other.

"You know you're welcome here for as long as you like."

"I know that, Pam, and I thank you. You've been so nice. I'm not saying I'm leaving. I just want to stick my nose out and see if any arrows whiz by."

I laughed. Then, almost bidden by our thoughts, I heard a wagon approaching and looked out the window. Laura followed me, peering down the street. I knew what it was. Walter Jenkins come to take her home.

He stopped the horses in the street and climbed down from the wagon—a strong looking middle aged man with a thick gray mustache. He stood in the front yard, looking at the house, until Dewey saw him and ran to the door. "Grandpa! Grandpa! I missed you!"

Laura stood aside as her father entered the room, holding the little boy and stomping snow off his boots. There was an awkward moment as he set the child down and straightened up to face his daughter. "Laura."

"Papa."

"Ready to come home?"

She looked at the floor for a moment, then nodded. Walter Jenkins's smile revealed straight, even teeth. He bent down and picked up the child again. "Come on, then." Dewey grabbed him around the neck and squeezed hard.

I helped Laura gather her things and walked out into the yard with them, kissing Dewey good-bye. "You come back to see me again, Dewey, and bring Mama along."

Laura paused and turned to me. "Oh, Pam! You've been so good to us! I won't forget you. I'll be back often. I promise."

I pulled my shawl around my shoulders and smiled. "Yes, Laura. Don't be a stranger, now." I returned to the tiny house feeling empty. Back to the old life, alone with Mama.

My young guest leans forward in his chair. "Did she ever marry that Corwyn guy?" he asks.

Brought back to the present, I nod. "Yes, she did but it didn't last. Long enough for her to get pregnant again, and then another beating."

"Pregnant? You mean I have an aunt, or was it an uncle?"

"Slow down there, boy. Neither. It was a miscarriage."

"So did she divorce this Corwyn guy or what?"

"Yes, she did, but not before she'd set the town abuzz with her goings on. She was one of a kind, your grandma."

He laughs. "I always thought so, too. There was something about the way she looked at you—like she was flirting."

I laugh out loud at that one. "Couldn't help herself. But she was fun, I'll tell you that. Fun and funny. She knew all about everything that was going on, and she never missed a chance to bedevil the proper ladies of Johnstown. I was her opposite in every way, but she lightened my burden in those days."

We sit there in my parlor, smiling, remembering Laura, who died too soon in an automobile accident in 1935. I miss her.

Then Gerald gets up. "Sorry I got you off your subject, but I really did need to know all this. Can I come back tomorrow?'

"I don't know. Can you? You certainly may, but only you know if you can."

He smiles at my grammar lesson. "May I, then?"

"Yes, you may. I'll be looking forward to it.

Katya shows him to the door and returns to the parlor to pick up the cookie plate and glass. "Well, you sure educated him in a jiffy."

"I hope for the better, not the worse. I think the truth is always best, don't you?"

She nods with a raised eyebrow and carries the dishes to the kitchen. "Your boy called while you were lost in your reverie. Said to tell you he saw in the Altoona paper that a Clarence Plummer, formerly of Johnstown, passed away in his sleep last Friday. Wondered if you'd known him.

The look in my eyes when I hear about Mrs. Plummer's boy Clarence says it all. Katya's look reflects mine. It feels as though something is pulling us back into the flood days again and again. Now that it's started, will it ever end?

"He lived a long life, then," Katya observes. "Didn't deserve it."

I'm more charitable. "I hope he found some happiness there. Maybe a wife and a family. I'd have thought he'd go farther than Altoona."

Katya shivers as though to dispel Snoop Plummer's memory. "His poor mother never knew how people saw him. A mother's eyes can be blind, and you know the saying, 'Every old crow thinks her baby's the blackest.'"

Chapter 6

Katya goes back into the house. "Come on inside, it's getting cold. Too early for evening porch sitting."

I rise obediently and follow her into the kitchen. "Know where I just was?" I ask.

"Bet I could guess," she replies without a second's hesitation.

"Back to that old Oklahoma house sitting on a plain dirt lot on Bedford Street."

Katya nods. "A lot happened in that house. What ever became of it anyway? I don't remember."

I lift a shawl from a peg by the back door and wrap it around my shoulders. The kitchen smells of roast lamb, and I know Katya is up to her old Hungarian ways, cooking something delicious.

"That's because you were busy getting married and starting your farm. Rob sold the lot with the Oklahoma house on it after we were married and moved up here."

I sit down at the table Katya has set for the two of us. "Remember that first day when you ran away from home and ended up in my woodpile?"

Katya joins me at the table with a smile. "Changed my life that day." She reaches over and gives my hand a gentle pat. We eat our dinner and clean up the kitchen. Katya excuses herself to go upstairs to her room to read. I sit down in the living room, intending to listen to Fibber McGee and Mollie. But my mind won't settle in. I'm restless. I lean back in my chair and let the memories come.

Mrs. Plummer was back two days after New Year's with three bags of old clothes for me to cut up into rags. I set up the loom as near as I could to the stove. It took up a lot of space in the cramped room. It wasn't hard to string it up and get it ready to work—gave me something to do, and I was grateful for that. Not that I was ever idle. It gave me something to do *other than* take care of Mama.

Breathless with the effort, Mrs. Plummer entered the house and plopped the bags on the floor. "There! That should keep you a while.

There's lots more where that came from. When you need more, just come down to the relief center." She was still proud of her accomplishment in putting what she perceived as idle hands to work.

Her son, Snoop, was with her. I don't think she knew that everyone called him Snoop. His real name was Clarence, but I'd never had occasion to call him anything. Everything about him made me uncomfortable. He was somewhere in his twenties, not very tall, walked all stooped, like an old man, and he was wall-eyed. His eyes went off in different directions so you didn't know which eye to look at when he was talking to you. He gave me the shivers. Everyone said he was a Peeping Tom, and though it'd never been proven, I took it as true.

As his mother and I talked, Snoop stood by the door giving the house a good looking over. The need to be nice to his mother kept me polite, but it galled me to watch him chewing on his lip as he took it all in. In the old days, Papa would have run him off with a horsewhip. Sad, what you have to put up with when you're poor.

The room was warm, and Mrs. Plummer's body odor permeated the small space as she unloaded a satchel full of gossip for me. She knew all about everybody, so, if you were interested in the seamy side of things, she was the source. It wasn't that I disliked Mrs. Plummer. It was just that I didn't really care who was getting married a few months ahead of the stork, or who'd taken to the drink, or who'd gotten rich on the backs of the poor. I nodded politely, smiling and shaking my head at the appropriate times, trying not to be overwhelmed by her aroma and wishing her snoopy son were outside.

"Would you like some of these cookies, Mrs. Plummer? I felt like baking, but there're too many for Mama and me."

She smiled. "Don't mind if I do. I hear your friend Laura Jenkins is finally getting married."

"Yes, she told me about her good fortune."

"Good fortune! Ill wind, I'd call it. Now I wouldn't repeat this, but I've heard tell that her intended takes a drink now and then, and that he's known as a mean drunk. Heard he beat her up once already." She took a step back and paused to gauge my reaction.

"Oh, really? Well, Laura's a big girl. She can take care of herself."

"Pretty as she is, she can't be too fussy. Not many men would take on her bastard without a thought. Too bad his pappy got caught in the flood."

I didn't feel like getting into a prolonged discussion of Laura with Mrs. Plummer. Laura'd been the talk of the town for years, coming from a respectable family but acting like a trollop. Even so, I still felt loyal to her as a friend. I just wished she'd use a little restraint now and then.

"Yes. Too bad."

"Then she went and named him after his pappy, so everyone'd know who his pappy was, as if they didn't already. Dewey Di Longo, indeed!"

"Well, let's hope this one turns out better for her." I summed it up, hoping to cut this visit short. Truth to tell, I was rather interested in getting this loom to work.

Mrs. Plummer turned to Snoop and smiled her pride, her eyes beaming as she spoke. "Here's one's never given his mother a moment's worry," she cooed. "My good boy. Come along, dear. We've more stops to make."

Snoop left me with a sideways glance and slouched out the door after his mother. Once they were out of sight I opened the windows to freshen the air.

I cut and sorted, keeping the strips a uniform size, all the while chattering to Mama about how pretty the rug would be. I was anxious to get started on the actual weaving, but the preparation was exasperatingly slow. All right. I'd nowhere else to go. The rags were clean and colorful, and I sorted them into piles, planning patterns. By late afternoon I'd strung up the loom and started to weave. I laughed at my uneven attempts, but it was challenging, and I was always up for a challenge.

By late afternoon the cooling room told me the fire was dying, so I looked in the wood box and found not much left. I grabbed the canvas sling and headed out the door to the woodpile in back. I loaded my sling with as much as I could carry, and trekked back to the front. I really should have shoveled a path. I would have if I'd had a shovel. I pushed open the door and crossed the room to dump the wood into the box with a crash. I glanced at Mama. No reaction. I straightened up and went back for another load, since it was sunny outside and the snow was melting a little. Might as well gather wood while the sun shone.

The woodpile was dwindling. I'd have to go down to the relief and put in for another load before the week was out. Wet snow clung to each damp smelling log, and I hit the logs against each other to knock it off. I bent over to pick up a log, and saw a yellow printed scarf, lying in the mud behind the woodpile. I reached for it, and it moved. I jumped back. The scarf raised its head, attached to a girl wearing a nondescript brown coat that blended in with the color of the wood.

"Oh! Who are you?" Slowly the girl rose from behind the woodpile, young, maybe fifteen, and from the look of her, probably from Cambria City or one of the other immigrant hamlets downstream.

She stood with her back to the house, the woodpile in front of her, head down, looking up at me from lowered brows, saying nothing. Then she extended a pair of chapped, cracked hands, palms up. "Food?" she said. "Food?"

"Are you hungry?" Stupid question. She was obviously starving. "Come with me," I told her.

I picked up my sling of wood and turned toward the front of the house. She followed, looking around carefully, hunched over as though to parry a blow.

"Come on," I said. "No one will hurt you. It's warm inside."

She hesitated at the door, looking around as though to assure herself that there wasn't anyone else. She saw my mother, sitting in her rocking chair and pulled back. "It's all right. We're the only ones here."

The girl was in the house now, looking around with shy curiosity. She waited until invited to sit at the table. I set down a bowl and ladled out some soup simmering on the stove. She bent to it and ate while I cut her a piece of bread. She dipped the bread in the soup, hunched over with the bowl cupped in her arm as though afraid someone would take it away.

I watched her, wondering. Her clothes were worn, though not ragged. Her shoes, sturdy oxfords, were wet and not new. She looked hungry, but otherwise healthy. Whatever her story, she hadn't been out on her own for long. She was clean enough, and well enough clothed that I guessed she'd run away recently.

"My name is Pam," I offered.

"Katya," she replied between spoonfuls of soup. She emptied her bowl and looked toward the stove.

"Would you like more soup, Katya?"

She nodded and I refilled the bowl.

"Katya? What kind of name is that?" I asked.

"Hunkie. Papa call me Katya. Real name Katarina."

"Katya, is it? And your last name, Katya?"

"Pinter."

"Pinter?"

"Hunkie name," she replied, looking down at the chapped hands in her lap.

"Hungarian?"

A nod.

"Well, Katya Pinter, where do you live?"

She shrugged her shoulders. I was puzzled. She spoke clearly enough, but her English was limited. Maybe just by shyness. What was she doing hiding behind my woodpile? Something was obviously not right with her world. I gave her time to warm up, saving my questions for later.

I turned back to the loom while Katya watched. As I slipped the shuttle back and forth, still slow and awkward in my movements she rose and took off her coat and scarf, standing behind.

"I do that," she said.

I turned to her with a smile. "Do what?"

"Make rug," she replied.

She traded places with me and gave me a lesson. Her fingers flew as she moved through the weaving motions with practiced deftness. She sat tall at the loom, comfortable in concentration, used to the process. As I stood watching, she wove about four inches of rug. Neat. Even. Expert.

"Katya! You're good at this! Where did you learn to weave so well?"

"Mama. Nagyanya, too. Die in flood. Loom gone. Papa make me take care kids."

"Is that why you ran away? To keep from having to take care of your brothers and sisters?'

She shook her head. "No. Papa say I get married. I don't want get married."

"How old are you?'

"Fifteen."

No wonder she didn't want to get married. She'd probably seen enough of women's lives to know what was in store for her.

"How many kids?" I asked.

"Four. Two brothers. Two sisters. Oldest me."

I understood her plight. Mine was the same. For some taking care of others is second nature. For others, not. I watched the girl weaving, choosing colors, blending them into a pattern. She had a gift.

"Katya, you can stay here for a while. I don't know about your family—but you can stay here with us at least for now."

She turned and smiled—the first smile I'd seen. Straight, even teeth, a dimple in her right cheek and sparkling green eyes added up to pretty.

She stayed the night in my room, while I shared a bed with Mama, the best I could do with my limited resources. Over the next few days we talked like school girls, even the giggling kind some of the time. She understood almost everything I said, but struggled to express herself in English.

She revealed her background in bits and pieces. "Papa iron worker down river. Sang Hollow. Come from Hungary five years. Life hard before flood. Harder now. Papa work all but Sunday. Not much money. Five children and no wife. Hard life. Papa drink. Get mad. Beat us."

I listened, sympathetic, ashamed of myself for thinking *my* lot was hard.

"Who did he want you to marry?"

"Rich old man. Sandor Varga. Papa get money."

Suddenly her reason for running became clear. I hoped her father didn't find out where she was, didn't come for her. She was good company, personable, friendly, a hard worker. Her talent with the loom might even lead to some income. Not only could she weave, but I soon learned she was a wizard with a needle and thread. She knew needlework like I knew Walter Scott's books. I was thinking: when the Lord closes a door, he opens a window. Help in caring for Mama. Hope was the word.

Mrs. Plummer brought us rags about once a week. Each time she came, she looked at Katya with curiosity. One day she warned me.

"Don't get too free with that one. She'll rob you blind one of these days."

I smiled. "Don't worry Mrs. Plummer. She's honest."

"Ain't no such thing as a honest Hunkie, if you ask me. *All* those stories they told after the flood wasn't lies!"

She referred to sensational newspaper accounts that swept the country after the flood, of bands of immigrants, all of whom were called Hunkies, regardless of their nationality, roaming the countryside, robbing corpses. It wasn't true. Or, if it happened at all, it was exaggerated by irresponsible journalists trying to make their reputations on the backs of poor, misunderstood immigrants. The stories were discredited, but the damage was done.

"I'll keep an eye on her," I promised. Then . . ."Looks like the Mecklins are getting ready to rebuild. It'll be nice for them."

Always ready to spread a little gossip, Mrs. Plummer enlightened me about the Mecklins' new house and how much it cost. "I hear tell they got more than a thousand dollars insurance money. Sure is nice."

Her eyes darted from me to the rags to Katya to my mother, her hands twisting the ends of her scarf. It wasn't easy to hide her jealousy. Her dilapidated house sat up on high ground near Green Hill, out of the flood's path. The rebuilding all over town galled her.

Her eyes darted back to Katya. "How long you gonna keep that one around? Seems to me she'd be movin' on before folks get set against you for bringin' trash into the neighborhood."

"I need her to help me with Mama. I can't afford to pay her anything, but she's satisfied with a place to live."

Mrs. Plummer shook her head and moved to pick up her bags of groceries for other families. "Keep an eye on her. That's all I say."

I smiled and let Mrs. Plummer out the door. Then I turned and picked up the log sling and headed for the woodpile. Seems all I did in those days was carry wood. I got around back, picked up my wood and stood looking out at the Mr. Hughes's Oklahoma house behind ours, lonely and sorrowful where their big old house used to be. It always made me sad to look out there—to think of times gone by.

Davy's face flashed in memory. Davy, looking at me with love in his eyes. Tilting my chin to snatch a quick kiss. Teasing me about my hair (it tended to curl too much.) Playing checkers with my little brother—letting him win. I swallowed a sob. The sobs didn't come as often now, but they still came.

I turned back to look at my own house, and noticed footprints in the snow—footprints leading to my back window, and handprints on the sill.

I wake with a start. What time is it? Sleeping in my chair until almost one o'clock. I rise and turn off the static of the radio and climb the stairs to my room.

Chapter 7

*T*he next morning I rise from the breakfast table where Katya has plied me with eggs over easy, crisp bacon, buttered toast and strong coffee. It's more breakfast than I need, but Katya takes her responsibility for my well-being seriously. "Think I'll take the incline down to the city today. I feel like visiting the office."

Katya smiles. "You never could keep yourself away from that place for long."

"It's where my life began," I remind her.

I go upstairs and dress, fix my hair and gather my things. I have a book for Elsie and a picture of Laura as a young woman to show to Gerald Price. I wonder if he's ever seen it before.

As I'm going out the front door, Katya stops me. "Here. Take these to James," she says, handing me two jars of her famous strawberry preserves.

I take them with a smile and step out into another beautiful spring morning. I love spring. The promise of summer. The flowers in bloom. Then, without any real reason, I'm taken back almost fifty years to a life devoid of promise. I hate to think about it, but there it is again. Not the flood itself now, but the days, weeks and months after. As I walk through Westmont toward the incline, I'm back to the early days of 1892, pacing, restless, casting about for something—anything to pin my hopes on.

A storm blew through the first week of the New Year, snow up over the front step so I opened the door to a wall of snow about two feet high ready to fall in on the floor—a wet, heavy snow, and a mess when it melted.

I was quickly grateful for Katya. Good company, help around the house, and the offer of much-needed freedom. One day soon after the storm I set out for town in an old green coat buttoned up under my chin and a pair of tight laced up shoes, a plan in my head. I walked in sunshine through wet, slushy snow down to the office of the *Johnstown Clarion* on Main Street.

My father's friend, Harold Shaver owned the paper, and poverty had ground me down to the point where I was ready to cast my pride aside and ask for help. I hesitated before entering. Papa and Harold Shaver had grown up together in Johnstown, marched off to war together, shared their lives, even down to playing checkers every Friday night. He was always a kind uncle to me, but I'd resisted the urge to call on him for help, until now.

The office was warmed by a pot bellied stove in one corner, churning out heat with valor. My nose wrinkled at the smell of printer's ink and pulpy newsprint. The main room was plain. Wood floors, walls pinned up with old maps and a calendar, two desks, one occupied by a young man with his feet up. He looked comfortable there, like he belonged, leaning back in his chair, hands clasped behind his head.

"Excuse me." I hesitated. "Is Mr.Shaver in?"

He lowered his long legs and looked at me, obviously wondering who I was and what I wanted, but simple courtesy reined him in. "Just a minute. I'll see if he's busy." He went to the door of Mr. Shaver's tiny corner office, leaned against the doorway and spoke a few words. Impatient to get past him, I found his unhurried pace irritating.

I didn't know him. Seemed I'd seen him somewhere, but no real recognition. He was tall—lanky would be the term. Another Abe Lincoln, but this one was handsome. He seemed right at home here, and that raised the bile in me for some reason. I'd been coming here with my father since I was five. I found this newcomer's comfortable familiarity with the place off-putting.

"Pammie! Come right in. How good to see you!" Mr. Shaver stepped out of his office, cane in hand, to rescue me from his reporter turned gatekeeper. His hair was gray now and glasses rested on his nose, but he was still familiar, comfortable, Papa's best friend.

"Hello, Mr. Shaver." I stepped into his hole-in-the-wall office, books and papers piled high. He cleared away newspapers to offer me a chair. I dropped my coat off my shoulders and let it slip over the back of the chair, hoping he wouldn't notice the vintage of my clothes.

He looked at me over his glasses. "Your mother?"

"The same. Nothing's changed."

"It pains me to see her so broken, and you with the burden."

I nodded. I wanted to get right to my business. I spoke quietly so the company in the outer room couldn't hear.

"I've come about work, sir." My mouth was dry, hands trembling just a little. "There's no income with Papa gone, and we've been getting the relief for more than a year now. Most others have moved off, but with no one to care for Mother, I haven't been able to."

His brow wrinkled. "Yes. Yes. Surely there must be something you can do—work at home."

"I was hoping *you'd* have something for me."

He frowned, shaking his head. "Well, now Pammie, newspaper work is rough. Mostly men and not the most refined."

"I'm aware of that, but I'm past worrying about refinement. I need a steady income."

The frown deepened "Who'll look after your mother while you're out gathering news?"

I smoothed my skirt. "I, uh, have someone living with me. She can take care of Mama for the time being. Besides," I said with more conviction than I really felt, "Mama's going to get better. I see the signs of it every day." Lord, forgive me for lying.

Harold Shaver glanced over a paper on his desk. I was afraid he was thinking about how to let me down easy, but then he said, "I guess we could give you a trial. Happens I need someone to cover the society news, church news, news from the outlying areas. Bertha Clewell used to do it, but she's been so laid up with arthritis, she can barely hold a pencil. Anyway, young blood is needed. You could write from home, but you'll have to go get your news at first. Later on, when people get used to you, they'll probably bring their stuff in. The local correspondents drop theirs by about once a week. All you have to do is trim their verbosity and check their spelling." He swung around in his chair to face the monstrous typewriter on his desk.

"I can't afford to set you up with one of these," he said, "but if you keep at it, you can probably teach yourself to use it. Marvelous time saver, and if you'd ever seen my handwriting, you'd consider this a miracle."

"That's all right. Just give me a pad and a pencil, and I'll run my own stories down every day." My chest swelled with hope. I knew I'd have to prove myself, but at least I had a chance.

Harold Shaver leaned back in his old oak swivel chair, the arms rubbed shiny from years of wear. *Everything* wasn't taken by the flood. He looked down at his thumbs, moving back and forth behind clasped fingers. I knew he was thinking about my father—how they shared everything in life, from childhood pranks to war to the flood.

"All right, girl. Two cents an inch. That's the best I can do, but Owen Gwynedd's daughter at least deserves that."

I stood, reached around the cluttered desk and gave him an awkward hug. "Thank you, Mr. Shaver. You won't be sorry."

He gave my shoulder a pat. "No doubt."

I pulled my coat up over my shoulders and stepped into the outer office, but as I crossed the room to the door Mr. Shaver called me back.

"Pammie! Wait a minute. You'll need supplies." He opened a cabinet with a key from a ring on his belt and handed me three yellow pads and a handful of pencils. I took them with a grateful smile and a nod.

"Oh, and Pammie? This is Rob McRae, my right hand man around here since the flood. Rob? Pamela Gwynedd. Her father and I go back a long way." Then he turned back to me. "You'll report to Rob. Bring him your copy and he'll type it up and keep track of your wages. You get a free paper every day, but you'll have to come down here to get it."

Oh, great. I should have been nicer to this twit when I first came in. Young McRae stood and offered his hand, looking comfortable and confident, two things I was not.

"I'm happy to meet you, Mr. McRae."

He nodded like the well bred gentleman he was. "Miss Gwynedd."

I turned back to Harold Shaver. "Thank you, Mr. Shaver. Papa would be pleased. You won't be sorry you hired me."

Outside the world looked better already. The melting snow had all but cleared the sidewalks, and my tight shoes are starting to stretch a little. I made my way home, head full of plans about finding news. Laura's upcoming wedding would be a sure thing, but that wasn't till May. I wished I'd kept up my social contacts. Then it hit me. Mrs. Plummer!

The next morning, she stopped by with her bags of groceries, and I showed her the rugs she thought I'd made, and made a point of thanking her for the opportunity. She glowed with approval, and I invited her to sit a while for a cup of tea. That loosened her up. Katya put the kettle on and set out two teacups.

"My old feet hurt me somethin' awful in this cold," Mrs. Plummer complained. "I can't get around like I used to."

"What about your boy? Doesn't he help you with your relief work?"

"Did for a while. Not no more. He's got him a job." She unbuttoned her coat and slipped it back from her shoulders.

"Really? What kind of job?"

"Works for Ev Dailey deliverin' coal. Ev's expanding his business. Gotta keep up with the tourist trade, come summer."

Everett Dailey was one of the first businessmen back on his feet after the flood. He started by catering to the trainloads of tourists who came on the heels of disaster. Sightseers, mostly. Got in the way more than they helped, but Dailey was quick to see that they needed refreshment, so he set his wife to making iced tea to sell by the train depot.

Then it was flood souvenirs. Any piece of junk he could find, an old watch, a spittoon, a dinner plate, he cleaned up and put out on a board table to sell. People who came in on the tourist trains would buy anything connected to the flood. Business was fine that first summer, but once the weather got cold, it was clear he needed something more permanent to get him through the winter, so he started up a coal business.

Soft coal abounds in the Alleghenies. Ev got a wagon and drove over to Nanty Glo and back three times a week. Sold all he could haul, and soon had to hire more help.

So Snoop Plummer was hauling coal for Ev Dailey. In a way that was good. It'd keep Snoop busy so he couldn't go around peeking in windows, but in another way it was bad, because he could still snoop around peoples' houses when he was delivering coal.

I smiled at Mrs. Plummer and poured her a cup of tea. "How nice for you."

She looked around, keeping an eye on Katya. Then, as though she were invisible, the older woman asked, "How long are you gonna keep *that one* around?"

"I need help with Mama. Her folks are letting her stay."

Mrs. Plummer nodded and took a sip of tea. This explanation fit her view of things. Hungarian girl. The help. Even if you couldn't afford help. "I'd watch her if I were you," she warned again. "You never know."

"So what's new down at the relief office?"

That got her going. In five minutes she told me about two up-coming weddings and an engagement. Then she turned serious. "Did you hear about Davy Hughes's Pa?"

"No. What happened?"

"Apoplexy. Came over to Nonie Potter's last Sunday for dinner. Seemed like he was out of his head. Goin' on about Davy this and Davy that. She told him, "Davy's dead," but he wasn't havin' none of it. Then he just stopped talkin.' Sat down in a chair and that was that. Nonie took him home and put him to bed, then got Doc Smythe over.

"How sad. The poor man. His life ended with the flood. He's been treading water ever since."

"And him so high up in the iron works. With his money, you'da thought he'd get back on his feet in no time. Shows you money ain't everything. Some of the poorest sprung back the fastest. Course, they had less to lose."

"How do you get over losing a wife and five children?" I poured Mrs. Plummer another cup of tea. "I wonder what'll happen to him now."

"Guess they'll bring somebody in to take care of him. If he dies, more'n one has asked to get in line for his lot. Land! They're still tryin' to build new houses for all that needs it. My boy Clarence says there's a lot of tracks in the snow around the Hughes place. Better get someone in there to take care of things before the Hunkies carry everything off."

So Snoop Plummer knew there were tracks in the snow around the Hughes house. He was probably the one prowling around at night, leaving handprints on my back window sill.

Mrs. Plummer set down her cup and saucer and rose to go. "You keep workin' on them rugs," she instructed me. "You'll be makin' money 'fore you know it."

I thanked her and bid her good-bye. When she was gone, I turned to Mama and noticed her right cheek was wet. A tear? I was stunned. It was the first indication I'd had that Mama had any idea what was going on around her. Maybe her eyes were just watering, but I leaned over and gave her a hug anyway.

Anxious to get started with my work, I put my yellow pad and a pencil in a cloth bag Katya had sewn up out of scraps, and headed off toward Edith Day's house. Edith was the one Mrs. Plummer said was engaged. It was a long, cold walk back up toward Woodvale, but my sense of the importance of my errand warmed me. I knocked at the door of a double—two Oklahoma houses side by side with a passageway between. Kitchen in one, parlor in the other, bedrooms upstairs. It sat on a lot as bare as ours, but there were curtains at the windows and chimney smoke promised warmth.

"Hello, Edith. I hear you're planning a wedding. Congratulations! I'm here from the *Clarion*, looking for a story for the society page."

Edith, flattered to have her name in the paper, gave me all the particulars. I wrote them down and took my leave, careful to be business-like. "Thank you, Edith. I'll write this up and have it in tomorrow's paper." That was easy.

Next I walked over to Grace Albright's house. I knew Grace from school, so I was comfortable asking about her wedding, which took place on New Year's Eve. We spent about a half hour going over the details, and I was assured of a long article to cover it. Grace, too, was more than happy to give me a story.

Long shadows accompanied me back up our street, my cloth bag tucked under my arm. Out of curiosity, I followed the packed snow path around to the backyard and stood looking out at the Hughes place. It sat forlorn in the snowy yard, nothing to break up the expanse of white, but a light in the window let me know someone was there, looking after Mr. Hughes. Snoop Plummer was right. There were a lot of tracks around—quite a few between the house and the shed. It was starting to snow again, so the tracks would soon be filled in. I felt a little nasty, but I suspected Snoop made most of them, if not all. I shivered at the thought of him sneaking around peaking in windows at night.

The incline car thumps to a stop at the bottom of Yoder Hill. People spill out into the city. My walk is only a few blocks, and I relish the spring morning and the chance to re-visit the scene of so much of my life.

The *Clarion* office has changed a lot over the years. Rob put a new front on it the year Mr. Shaver died and left it to us. We covered the floors with linoleum and partitioned off the front into several offices, put in central heat. But for me, everything old still lingers. Mr. Shaver's cluttered cubby hole, the smell of printers' ink, the air of immediacy that hovers over any news office.

I step inside to the clack of typewriters, the hum of the presses in back, the smell of coffee.

Chapter 8

I step inside my son's office—used to be Rob's—and give him a wave. He's on the telephone, so I just put the two jars of preserves on his desk. He knows who sent them. He gives me a smile and a nod, and I move back through the newsroom to Gerald Price's desk. Poor boy almost jumps out of his skin when he sees me.

"Mrs. McRae! How nice to see you here!"

I take the picture of Laura out of my bag and place it on his desk.

"Wow! She was a looker, wasn't she?" he breathes.

"No argument there, Gerald. It's what she was known for—far and wide—all of her life."

A thought about beauty passes through my mind—how the beautiful get a free ride. How the rest of us have to earn love, but for the beautiful, it's a birthright. I used to envy Laura for that, but though her beauty brought notoriety, it didn't guarantee real love. She spent her whole life looking for it. I came out far better in the end.

"You may have that picture if you want," I tell Gerald. "When I'm gone no one will even know who it is."

"Thanks, Mrs. McRae. I'll treasure it."

I give him a nod and turn to visit with Elsie, the telephone operator, file clerk, dispatcher and general ringmaster of the place. "Morning, Elsie."

"Morning, Mrs. Can't stay away for long, now, can you?"

"You know I can't." I pull up a chair beside her and we chat over coffee and donuts, catching up on the comings and goings at the *Clarion*. Katya would frown at my eating donuts, but what she doesn't know . . .

A young woman steps in from the street, fusses with her hair and tosses a smile at Elsie. She's tall, almost statuesque, and her hair is dark—raven-like. "Who's that?" I ask.

"New one. Works social, like you used to, but a lot's changed there."

It irks me that they always think the only place for a woman in the newspaper office is clerking or writing up weddings and obituaries. "How long has she been here?"

"'Bout a month. Pitt graduate. Like young Gerald."

I smile at that. Rob was a Pitt graduate, too, as is James. Only my Kenneth went his own way and ended up at Bucknell, halfway across the state. "Maybe we can get them together," I whisper, nodding from the girl to Gerald. Newspaper offices lend themselves nicely to romance in my experience.

Elsie plugs a line into her switchboard. "*Johnstown Clarion*. May I help you?"

"He's on another line. May I have him return your call?"

I start to feel a little like a benevolent intruder—welcome, but still in the way. Elsie is busy as usual, as is James. Well, maybe I should go look around in the stores. I excuse myself and make my way out the front door to Main Street. I walk up past the Tea Room to Central Park and watch the gardeners plant pansies in a ring around the flag pole. I watch for a while, lost in thoughts of my lost youth, but it isn't long before I find my feet taking me up to Bedford Street, the old familiar route. There on the corner of Main and Bedford, sits a vacant lot. They've torn down Elder's Store. Well, it was about time. Place had sat empty for about ten years, ever since Mrs. Elder died. She was a kind woman. Everybody liked her, but the times were changing, and she spent the last ten years of her life barely eking a living out of that store. As I stand there looking at the vacant lot, the memories come flooding back.

Late one afternoon not long after I started at the *Clarion* I took three of Katya's rugs down to Elder's Store to see about trading for some seeds and garden tools. I was rushing the season; it was only late February, but I wanted to start a flower garden for Mama as soon as it was warm enough. Mr. Elder was a hard man with steely blue eyes and a lantern jaw, his wife a small, stoutish woman with a warm smile. I bypassed him and wandered to the back of the store where she was helping a woman purchase yard goods.

"Hello, Pammie." Her smile and the smell of fresh lavender—one of those people it felt good to be around. Probably why Mr. E. found her attractive to begin with. "What can I do for you today?"

I glanced at her customer, hoping she was finished. "I can wait." I bided my time perusing the ginghams and cotton prints, touching the dazzling colors with longing.

47

Mrs. Elder nodded and turned back to help the woman with her selection. As she moved toward the cash register, Mrs. E. whispered, "I'll be right back."

When she returned, I showed her the rugs and asked if she thought she could sell them. She smiled. "Beautiful work. Did you make these?"

I nodded. It was easier to take credit than to explain who Katya was and why she was with me.

"Tell you what," Mrs. Elder said, "I can sell them for you. Give you store credit. I get calls for rugs now and then, and these are especially fine. If they sell, maybe you can bring me more."

My heart leaped at the encouragement. I couldn't wait to get back and tell Katya. I suspected that Mrs. Elder was just being kind—rag rugs were common, and most people made their own. But if she could sell them, even one or two, it would help us a lot.

"Now, what can I get you for your store credit?" she asked.

"Don't I have to wait until you sell them?"

She shook her head. "Your mother and father were good customers before." People always referred to the pre-flood days as "before." No need to explain before what.

"Thank you, Mrs. Elder. I was wanting flower seeds. Mama would love to see some flowers growing. And I'll need a spade, too."

"Right over here, dear. You're early, but I understand the need to hurry up the spring." She led me to a seed display in the front window. I chose a brown paper packet of marigold seeds, hesitating. I didn't know how much the rugs would bring.

She took the seeds from my hand and put them back in the rack. "You know, I have flower seeds saved from last year. I harvest my own. Would you like me to bring some for you? You might take pot luck, because the cat dumped them over when I was drying them, and they got all mixed up, but you're welcome if you want them."

I smiled. "That would be fine."

"I'd hate to see you have to buy a spade. They're dear, and any one of your neighbors could lend you one."

She was right. "Yes. Mr. Hughes might have one in his tool shed."

"No doubt. Now, dearie, I saw you eyeing that calico print in the back. Let's go cut you a dress length for your store credit."

No use trying to hide my delight. I hadn't had a new dress since the flood. She led the way to the dry goods, and I lingered over the blue and yellow calico. A new dress. Just for me. Not something I got from the relief. Mrs. Elder measured and cut the goods and wrapped them in brown paper. She handed me the package, smiling. "If those rugs sell, I'll be wanting more."

I stepped out in the street and headed home with my calico, feeling light-hearted at the prospect of a new dress. It was warm for February—slush everywhere, and I stepped carefully to avoid getting my shoes wet.

Then I saw him.

This time I was sure it was Davy—over in the Presbyterian churchyard watching me from the shadow of a big monument.

The late afternoon light was dim. I stopped and turned my head, peering into the recesses. Davy saw me looking and ducked behind the monument. I crossed the street and entered by the iron gate. I didn't call out, but stepped carefully through the slush, keeping my eye on his hiding place; I'd see him if he moved. But I got there and—no one. I was sure I saw what I saw this time. Footprints in the slush led to the left, around the monument, to a drooping old Hemlock that had somehow survived the flood.

I lay my package carefully atop a tombstone and knelt to look under the low boughs. "Davy?"

No reply. But I wasn't to be put off this time. I crawled under the tree, unmindful of my clothes. I saw a shoe, then a leg, then—Davy!—squatting near the trunk, hunched over, cold and ragged

"Davy! Oh, Davy, where have you been? We thought you were dead."

The words tumbled out, making no sense. I fell into his arms. He held me close, rocking me against a low bough. A pent-up well of emotion broke and I cried into his shoulder. "Davy. Why haven't you come home? Where have you been?"

His presence brought back all the horror of the flood, and I cried—for him, for us, for our families, for everyone. For me. He didn't speak—just held me and let me cry. Then, as though he'd been doing it every day for two and a half years, he turned my face up to his and kissed me—a soft, gentle kiss, not our first, but surely our sweetest.

"Talk to me, Davy. Tell me about it."

"Not much to tell," he began, his voice soft in my ear. "I was swept a long way downriver, holding onto the door of a freight car. Some people down by Cramer fished me out and took me home to recuperate." He shifted his weight off his left leg, and winced. "My leg was broken, mangled I guess you'd say, so I had to stay down for quite a while. The people, the Bruners, were just poor country folk trying to help, and they even got me a doctor." He straightened the leg out in front of him. "Still pains me a little when it gets cold."

"Why didn't you come home? Why stay away so long?"

"Thought they were all dead. Never wanted to see Johnstown again." There was a fatalistic ring to his words. "I couldn't walk for about two months, and then not so well. Besides, I felt I owed the Bruners some labor to repay them for their help, so I stayed that first winter with them."

"But what about me? You didn't think I was dead, did you?"

"No. I just felt so broken—like you had enough trouble to deal with. Didn't need me."

I nestled in close, touched his face. "Oh, Davy, I've always needed you."

I pulled away for another look, not sure I believed it was really Davy, home again. The flood giving up one of its victims.

"Your father didn't die."

"I didn't find that out until last Thanksgiving. I was in Pittsburgh working for a year and a half. A friend of a friend was talking about the Cambria Works and he mentioned something about his manager, Hughes, losing his whole family."

"Have you seen him yet? Does he know?" My mind raced to a wonderful reunion, celebrations, joy, excitement, wedding plans.

"He knows, but nobody else does, and I want to keep it that way." Davy was holding me, but there was a distant look in his eyes, like he wasn't really there. Like he was somewhere far away, watching.

"Why?"

"Because." He turned away and tugged on a hemlock bough, dropping snow on both of us. I giggled, brushing the snow off my shoulders, but when I looked back at Davy, he wasn't smiling. "I don't want to burden you with my problems, but there's a lot you don't understand, so keep quiet about seeing me, okay?"

I *didn't* understand, but my joy pushed that aside. Davy was alive. That's all that mattered. Now my life could begin again.

"I've been around since early December," he continued. "Quit my job in Pittsburgh and came home. Dad couldn't believe it at first. Thought I was one of his ghosts."

"Was that you I saw downtown a week or so before Christmas? When I ran down some lady, chasing after you?"

Now he grinned. "I wanted to turn around and run to you, but I couldn't risk being recognized."

I frowned. "*Why?* Are you a criminal or something?"

"No. Don't ask too many questions. Let me come back on my own terms."

I pulled away to look at him in the waning light. It was Davy all right, but an older, thinner, harder-looking Davy. I'd do whatever he asked, whether it made sense or not. Still, this wasn't the reunion I'd imagined.

We sat on the wet ground under the hemlock tree, our backs against the trunk. I could hardly contain my joy, even though Davy was reserved, almost distant.

"My pa's not the same man he was," he went on. "Thinks he sees my mother or my brothers or sisters all the time. The stroke was no surprise after the strain he's been under. I just wanted a little time with him."

A shiver passed through me—the cold, wet ground. "Davy, come on. Let's go home where it's warm."

He shook his head. "You go. I'll see you some other time."

"Come with me. We need to talk—make up for what we've lost."

"In due time. Right now, I have some business to attend to, and it's best no one knows I'm here. I don't want you to have to answer any questions about me."

"Business? What sort of business?"

"Just business. My business." He grabbed an overhanging bough and pulled himself to his feet and offered me a hand. I rose to face him, and he took me in his arms and kissed me again. "Be patient with me, Pam. I've come for you. That's all."

I felt something nameless between us. I could see him, but when I tried to touch him, he was beyond reach. He wasn't going to share everything with me. Damn the flood.

"You can sneak into my house tonight. No one will see you."

"What about that Hunkie girl you've got with you? She'll see me." He said it without malice. The word was just a word to him.

"We can trust Katya. She never talks to anyone but me."

Davy shook his head. "I'll see you again. Don't worry. Now get on with you." He gave me a dismissive pat, and I crawled out from under the Hemlock boughs and gathered my package. I made my way home, torn between elation and confusion. Elation won out. I stepped along, full of joy, thinking, making plans, refusing to give my doubts a chance to take root. All I wanted—all I'd ever wanted—was to be Davy's wife. Now that the possibility was restored, I reached for it, savored it, wrapped myself in it.

As I made my way up Bedford Street, I saw a man standing on my doorstep—a tough, brawny looking man with shaggy hair and a too large mustache, his coat ragged, his pants muddy. He turned and saw me, anger in his eyes.

"You! You the one keep my daughter from me. You no right keep my daughter from me."

"Are you Katya's father?"

"Katya my daughter. MY daughter! You no right."

His eyes were full of anger he couldn't express. He was used to being obeyed by his family. I was a different adversary. I offered my hand.

"I'm Pamela Gwynedd, Mr. Pinter. Katya lives with me."

He ignored my hand. "Katya no live with you. Katya live with me," he thundered.

Now Katya came out of the house, pleading with her father. "Nem, Papa, nem." I understood that meant no. She spoke to him in Hungarian, a curiously musical language that would have intrigued me were I not in fear for Katya's and my own well-being.

Marton Pinter grabbed his daughter's arm and pulled her, coatless, down Bedford Street, through the slush in the gathering darkness. I followed, pleading my case. Drawn to their windows by the racket, my neighbors looked on as Katya struggled against her father's grip.

Marton Pinter saw them too. Being a member of a maligned group, deserved or not, he didn't want any trouble,. He stopped and looked at Katya. "I come for you again," he said, "You be ready." He let go of her hand and walked away into the night, slumping so that his front coat tails almost met his knees.

Katya followed me back up the street, rubbing her arm. I picked up my package where I dropped it on the doorstep and led the way into the house. Mother sat before the stove, unmoved by the ruckus.

I turned to Katya. "How did he find out where you were?"

"Coal man tell him."

Snoop Plummer. Of course. He wouldn't approve of my taking in a Hungarian girl any more than his mother would. I put my package on the table, took off my coat and warmed my hands before the stove. Katya had dinner ready—a Hungarian dish that took all day to cook and smelled delicious. I put my arms around her.

"I want you to know I'm glad you're here," I told her. "Good things are happening. Don't you worry. We'll find a way to make him let you stay."

Her face streaked with tears, she returned my hug. "You my friend, Pam. We good together."

I showed her the calico, and her face lit up. "I make dress! I make dress *you!*"

I explained about the rugs and the store credit—that we could take more rugs down if those sold—earn a little money. She beamed. "I pay rent!"

I thought about telling Katya about Davy, almost did it in fact, but no. I would follow Davy's wishes.

Later in the evening, after Katya was asleep, I lay in bed thinking back over the day. Davy was uppermost in my mind. So much depended on Davy. I longed for him, fighting the desire to run to him. I was filled with joy at having him back. I wanted to tell the world: Davy's alive! But my joy was tempered because Davy wasn't ready to tell the world. I shivered under the quilt.

Chapter 9

I move away from Elder's vacant lot, but I don't turn around. Something is pulling me back up Bedford Street. I know what it is, though I haven't thought about it in years. Bedford Street has changed. New houses, a neighborhood grocery, a small shop here and there. It isn't far to where our little Oklahoma house stood, forlorn, in the middle of nowhere. I let myself go—back to that night, the night Davy came home. My steps are drawn up Bedford. I don't know why I don't just turn around and go home, but I don't. Then I'm back in that creaky old bed, a rough blanket pulled up to my chin, thinking about Davy.

Just as I was lost in the nether-land between asleep and awake, I heard it. Tapping on the back window downstairs. I lay still and waited. There it was again. I got out of bed, felt around for my shoes, and slipped down the stairs. Davy stood outside the kitchen window, hunched over in the cold, motioning to me. In the silent house, I could hear the even rhythm of Mama and Katya's breathing. I pulled my coat on over my nightgown and stepped out the door and into his arms. We moved around back and stood in the shadows, holding each other in silence, surrounded by darkness.

I followed as he wordlessly took my hand and led me through the backyards to the tool shed behind his father's Oklahoma house, dark and lonely in the frozen snow. I didn't wonder where we were going. I didn't wonder why. I went willingly, unquestioning, eager for what was to come.

Davy slid the door aside just enough for us to squeeze in. The glow of a fire in a Round Oak heater in one corner provided enough light to define a table, a chair and a cot, all settled neatly against the wall. It looked lived in—a hideout, made as comfortable as possible without raising suspicion—surprisingly warm, almost cozy, despite its rough appearance. So this was where Davy'd been spending his time. Close enough to call out to me in the night. I wondered why he hadn't done it.

"Sorry we can't have a light." He stepped back and looked at me, his hands in his pockets. "I probably shouldn't have brought you here, but I . . ."

I touched his lips with my fingers, then leaned in to his kiss. Nothing was real but Davy, standing here, holding me. His mouth kissing me, his lips soft and warm against mine, his heart beating in rhythm with my own. I gave way to two years of longing.

We moved toward the cot, holding each other, lost in the moment. Davy slipped my coat off my shoulders. I shivered involuntarily, standing there in my nightgown. Davy looked at me for a long moment, standing back, holding both my hands, then covered my mouth with his, struggling to get out of his clothes. My heart tore loose in my chest. A whimper escaped me, then a shudder as we moved together as though this were meant to be. There was no flood, no separation, no loss. Only my Davy and me, our bodies clinging to each other, awash in desperate need.

It was over in one sweet moment of joyful abandon—the only such moment I'd ever known. We snuggled under Davy's rough wool blanket, topped by a jumble of our cast off clothing, lay there in silence, breathing softly into the pillow. He ran his fingers through my hair, and I touched his cheek, giggling at the roughness of three days' growth. "I'll have beard burn, you know."

He pulled me closer. "Next time I'll shave. Next time." He rolled over, still looking at me in the dimness. "God, Pam, I love you."

I was so full of joy I couldn't imagine happiness greater than this. To belong to Davy after all that'd happened. We lay together talking and planning until sleep started to descend, but Davy, always more practical than I, raised up on an elbow. "Gotta get you out of here. Come on."

He pulled on his clothes. I struggled into my nightgown and coat, and as he opened the sliding door the cold hit us in the face like a handful of frozen pine needles. He put an arm around me and we trekked back across the snow covered yards to my house. As we came around front we saw someone walking down the street, barely visible in the late night darkness. Slightly stooped, head cocked to the side, Snoop Plummer moved furtively along, keeping to the shadows. Davy stopped at the corner of the house, shielding me with his body. We waited until Snoop made his way on down Bedford Street, then we moved to the door and Davy kissed me softly before I opened it and slipped back inside.

I climbed the stairs, took off my coat and lay back down on my cot, trembling with the cold—or was it something else? I'd just let myself go completely, and I wondered at the momentous event. Every girl thinks about it, but this was . . . I shook my head to dispel the doubt, the rising discomfort that felt like guilt? Regret? I didn't know. I turned to the wall and pulled the quilt up over my shoulders to try to get warm. I kept telling myself, "Davy's back. That's all that matters. That's all . . ."

Johnstown is alive with activity this spring morning. I stand looking at the lot for a long time, lost in my memories. There's a new house there now. Not even new anymore. A fence along the sidewalk, a lawn, shade trees, rockers on the front porch. I open the gate and go up the walk, but I don't step on the porch. I walk around to the back, where I can see another new house directly behind. It's painted gray. trimmed in white. There's a closed-in back porch and I can see a swing through the open window. There, just a few steps from the porch stands a shed—dilapidated and sagging. Almost ready to fall down.

"May I help you?" A voice from behind startles me and I turn.

"No. I'm sorry. I used to live here. I wanted to see . . ." I'm embarrassed. I brush past the woman and out to the street. She stands watching as I make my escape. Probably doesn't know me. I hope she doesn't know me.

I'm disturbed at myself for going down that road. Some things really are best left in the past. But now I'm on that road, I feel as though there's no turning back. I want to go home and sit on the porch and drink iced tea. I want to read the paper—the *Johnstown Clarion* that Rob and I worked so hard to build. I want to talk to Katya.

It's a long walk back down to the base of the incline. I stand at the bottom looking up—almost straight up—at the cars, one moving up, the other moving down. People stand looking out the windows, waving, smiling. I wait for the passengers to get off and step in for my ride to the top. Westmont. A community that didn't exist until after the flood. The inclined plane, our answer to the threat of another one. Just move up out of the valley. Simple as that. Build a beautiful new planned community and let the rivers have the valley. More or less.

At the top I step out into unseasonably warm sunshine. This is the kind of day that makes teen-agers think of going swimming, only to find that the mountain spring-fed waters are a long way from warm. The walk home is pleasant, and I think I've shaken the discontent. But when I get there, Katya has gone marketing, and I'm alone. I didn't want to be alone. I sit down on the front porch and give way to it. Let the memories come.

Chapter 10

*W*hen I awoke the next morning, I got out of bed before Katya and washed in freezing cold water. I looked in the mirror and was surprised to see my own face looking out at me. I looked the same, in spite of last night. Strange. I thought I should look transformed somehow. I pulled on my jumper and brushed my hair, my head filled with soft remembrances. Davy holding me, kissing me, making me his own. My heart pounded anew at the memory. I looked in the mirror again. I may not look any different, but I would never be the same.

I gathered my things, pulled on my coat and took my society news to the *Clarion* office, lost in memories, feelings, hopes, plans. I opened the door to the too warm office and looked around. Always before, Mr. Shaver came out to greet me and take my stories. This morning he was nowhere about. Rob McRae was sitting at his desk pecking out a story on a typewriter, his two index fingers hopping back and forth across the keys like grasshoppers in a hayfield. He barely looked up as I waited near the door.

"In there." He indicated a wire basket on his desk. I dropped my stories in, picked up my daily paper and sat down on a bench beside the door to read my stories on the society page.

Rob stopped typing and looked up. "Did you want something?" An air of busy preoccupation.

"No. I thought I'd read the paper and wait for Mr. Shaver."

He frowned, then smiled as if he were talking to a ten-year-old. "He's out for the day, I'm afraid. Told me not to expect him back until tomorrow. Is there something I can help you with?"

His superficial kindness galled me. Spoiled rich kid. I was in no mood to deal with his condescension. "No. Thank you. I'll see him tomorrow then." I rose, folded my paper and turned to leave.

"He's pleased with your reporting. We need someone to cover the social news. Even if the ladies aren't interested in real news, they still like to see their names in the paper. Keeps them coming back. That kind of thing isn't in my realm, I'm afraid."

I felt the color rise in my face. I stepped up to his desk, ready to give him what-for as the door opened and Mr. Shaver walked in.

"Pammie! Always glad to see you here. You know, you're adding lots of interest on the feminine side, my girl."

"Yes. Mr. McRae was just telling me about that." I gave McRae a withering look and followed Mr. Shaver into his office. Again I marveled at the amount of clutter the man could cram into a tiny space. I cleared a place to sit and waited while he read something on his desk.

My errand was to beg. I hated it. Pride gnawed at my stomach as I waited. Even though Davy was back and I didn't expect to stay poor much longer, my pride chafed at my errand. Mr. Shaver looked up, and after some hesitation I began.

"I'm sorry to bring it up, but I need a little money." My mouth was dry. I twisted my handkerchief in my lap. "I wonder if you could calculate my pay and let me have a little advance. I wouldn't ask, but the relief is slowing down and I need to buy some things."

"Of course, Pammie." Sympathy in his eyes. How I hated that look.

He shouted out the door, "Rob! Come in here and bring your tabulation of Pammie's inches."

The despot of the outer office entered carrying a folder with my name on it. He dropped it on the desk and turned to go as though dismissing an annoying interruption.

"Stay here, Rob. You need to be part of this."

Quick calculations determined that I had $3.50 coming. Mr. Shaver opened his desk drawer, drew out the cash and handed it to me. I thanked him and set my feet for the door, determined to make a hasty exit.

Rob stepped around me to open the door, scrupulously polite as always, but I brushed past him and let myself out.

I stood in the outer office adjusting my coat and scarf, when I heard Mr. Shaver tell Rob, "Interesting morning. Talked to Gregg from the *Press*. Someone burned down Duncan Phillips' carriage house in Pittsburgh last week. They got the horses out, but the carriage house burned to the ground. Phillips was a South Fork Club member. Nasty business. The police are sure it was arson, and they're thinking it might be someone from around here. Revenge, maybe."

Rob replied, speaking in a low voice. "The only surprise is that it hasn't happened before. Club members have gotten away unscathed after the flood. All the lawsuits so far have come to naught. Our people are bitter, not that I blame them. We're probably in for more of this kind of thing."

A chair scraped the floor as Rob moved toward the door. Mr. Shaver spoke again. "Keep your ears open. This could amount to nothing, or it could go beyond anything we could dream up."

I stepped outside as Rob emerged from Mr. Shaver's office. Turning away I closed the door hard on his smile.

My brain was busy putting this together with that as I walked up the street, lifting my feet to avoid the deep puddles of slush. I shouldn't let Rob McRae get under my skin. I reminded myself that, after all, Davy was back. I wouldn't have to deal with Mr. High and Mighty for much longer. Then why this gnawing feeling of—what?—discontent?

I stopped in Elder's and pulled a list from my mitten. Flour, soda, washing soap, a little meat? Mrs. Elder wasn't around, and mister was engaged in a political discussion with two of his cronies congregated around the pot bellied stove in the middle of the store.

"Ask me, the whole lot of 'em should be lined up and shot," one man growled in a guttural tone. "Sons a' bitches with their private club and their wire fish screens."

"Don't stand on one foot waitin' for it," Mr. Elder replied. "Might as well roll back the flood as expect *them* to take responsibility."

"The South Fork Fishing and Hunting Club was negligent! That's the word! Negligent!" The man's face reddened as spit flew with his words.

I waited for Mr. Elder to notice me. I'd heard it all before. Everyone in Johnstown subscribed to the notion that the South Fork Dam wouldn't have burst if it had been properly maintained. But none of the club members ever stepped up to accept responsibility. How could they? Anyone who did would risk financial ruin, whether from lawsuits or from commercial and social shunning by the other club members. No single one of them could be held responsible. Why pile disaster on disaster?

One of the stove huggers aimed a stream at the spittoon. "Damn rich bastards! Don't care who they hurt. They can afford to move on, build themselves another exclusive club someplace else, while we rot in the stink of their flood."

I could hear the bitterness, feel it, almost smell it. A brassy taste welled up from my stomach.

Mr. Elder finally turned to me, raised his chin as though to question my needs. I held out my list. He left the stove and stepped behind the counter to gather my things. It totaled up to $1.36, and I handed him the money, glad to have a little left over. I noticed that one of the rugs I brought in was gone from the shelf behind the counter.

"Did someone buy one of those rag rugs?" I asked.

He looked over his shoulder. "Looks like it."

"Would you like me to bring in more?"

He took another backward glance and mumbled, "You'll have to talk to missus about that. Her department."

"Thank you. I'll ask her the next time I'm in." I left the store, full of hope.

Outside, the afternoon sun was waning. I walked along lost in thought about the bitterness that hung over Johnstown. I understood, really I did, but I wished somehow people could get over it. Move on to bigger and better things. A tall order, I knew, but life had to go on, and it was up to us to make it bitter or sweet. We had to will it. My lot was as bad as most, but I couldn't let the flood own me. Then Davy flashed into my mind, and I wrapped my mind around him to shut out the rest.

As I approached the intersection of Franklin and Main, I heard someone call my name.

"Pammie! Pammie!" It was Laura Jenkins looking like a department store ad in a soft wool coat for spring, bright eyed and full of life.

"Hello, Laura. How've you been? How's Dewey?"

"Fine. We're all fine! Guess what! Calvin and I have set the date!" Her delight was almost contagious.

I smiled—couldn't help it. "Oh, really? When?"

"Next Friday night!" She was giddy with joy.

Wasn't it supposed to be a May wedding? And why would you marry someone who'd beaten you up and left you in a snow bank? Broken up at Christmas, married little more than a month later? Could she be pregnant again? That would explain a lot. I checked her front, but her coat covered whatever evidence there might be.

Standing there in the street, I was almost overwhelmed with the urge to tell her about Davy. Not all of it, mind, but that he was alive and back and . . .

"We decided to do it up simple," she went on. "So we aren't having any bridesmaids. Sorry."

"Oh, that's all right, Laura. I wasn't expecting . . ."

"Calvin's brother and his wife are standing up with us."

"I'll be talking to you soon then, about your wedding write-up for the paper."

Laura, being Laura, didn't notice my reserve—too enthralled with her own affairs. I liked her—always had, for her good heart and the way she brought adventure into my otherwise boring life. But Laura always missed the signals people gave out. Couldn't read approval from disdain. Probably why she couldn't tell a good man from a rake.

"Oh, Pammie! You're doing so well with that. Everyone loves your stories. I can't wait to see my wedding written up in the paper!"

Her eyes wandered as she talked to me. She waved at a passerby, smiled over my shoulder at someone else she knew.

"We're getting married in the Methodist parsonage. Mama and Papa are giving us a reception at the house. You'll come, won't you?"

"Yes. Of course, Laura. I wouldn't miss it for the world."

"Oh, Pammie. You're my best friend." When she hugged me, the scent of rose water tickled my nose.

"I wanted to ask, do you know Rob McRae? Works at the *Clarion?*" Laura was always my best source for the lowdown on anybody in town.

"Why? Are you interested?" A knowing look.

"Not unless you count wanting to give him a black eye as interest. Who is he, anyway?"

"His father's a lawyer. You know, McRae and McRae. The other one is his older brother, Richard. They just built a new house up in Westmont. Rob graduated from Pitt the year of the flood, so he missed all the fun."

"Has he always been so impressed with himself, or is that a recent development?"

"I wouldn't know. He was ahead of us in school and didn't exactly travel in our circle."

"Well, he raises the bile in me just about every time I meet him. I can't explain what it is. Just annoys me for fair-thee-well."

"Endure, Pammie. Endure," she said in mock seriousness. She turned and waved at someone across the street. "I've got to run. Be sure and come to my reception."

She flitted away down the street, her mind already on who knows what? Her trousseau? New dishes? Glassware? Linens?

It was hard, but I was glad I resisted the urge to tell her about Davy. Everyone knew she couldn't keep a secret to save her mother's life.

As I came up our street, I looked out back at the Hughes place, taken with curiosity about Davy—where he was—how he spent his days. Pretty soon my curiosity became an overwhelming desire to see him. Just for a minute. Just one kiss. I knew he wanted to keep everything secret, but his reasoning escaped me. Why not just come home and pick up your life? I moved off the street and crossed our yard into theirs. It was icy now that yesterday's slush had frozen, and I almost turned an ankle in the ruts of last night's footprints. I came to the tool shed, warm with thoughts of seeing him again. I knocked quietly on the door.

"Davy," I whispered.

There was a rustling inside and the door slid open a crack. Davy stood close to the wall, peering out.

"What are you doing here?"

"I wanted to see you. I . . ."

"Get away before you get us both in trouble. *Get away!*" His voice was hoarse, angry. I stepped back. Where was the tenderness, the gentleness from last night?

"I'm sorry, Davy. I thought . . ."

"No you didn't. You didn't think at all. Now go away, and don't ever come back here in the daylight again. I knew I'd be sorry I let you know I was here."

His words flogged me, knocked the wind out of me, brought a rush of anguish and regret.

I backed away and turned toward our house, running, head down, making excuses for him. His father's illness. The grief of losing the rest of his family. Getting used to the new Johnstown. I tried to understand, but *really* . . . I wondered. Was he back after all? He wasn't ready to resume his place in Johnstown. Was he ready to resume his place in my life? It didn't feel like it.

I tore through both backyards and around to the front of our house in time to see Snoop Plummer driving his coal wagon up the street. He stopped, leering down at me, coal dust around his eyes.

"Whatcha runnin' from, Pammie? Look like you seen a ghost."

"No! I've got bread in the oven! I forgot!" I headed for the door, turning my back on him.

"What? Can't yer Hunkie girl get bread outa the oven?"

Inside I shed my coat and hung it on a peg. I wiped away tears, as I tied on my apron, keeping my back to Katya. She didn't ask, but of course she sensed something was wrong. She was sitting by the front window where the light was best, sewing my new dress, so she probably saw my encounter with Snoop.

"Don't like that coal man. Come by too often. Too slow. Look in windows."

63

"Yes, I know. He's despicable, but we have to be nice to him as long as we want his mother to keep helping us."

Katya nodded and held the unfinished dress up for my approval. I longed for a private place where I could let go and cry, but I struggled for control. She handed me the dress and I held it up in front of me. Katya was a wizard with a needle. Her stitches were tiny and even, her hemlines blind. The dress's bright colors and newness almost made me forget my predicament.

"Oh, Katya. It's beautiful. I can't wait for spring so I can wear it." Wear it for Davy.

"Wear now, around house," Katya offered.

I moved in front of Mama so she could see the lovely, new dress.

"Look, Mama! Look what Katya's making for me. Isn't it beautiful? Don't you love it?"

I twirled around beside her chair, holding the dress up. She didn't move. Not a flicker of an eye. She stared at the stove, her angel face glowing in the warm room. Then I heard it. Or thought I heard it. I wasn't sure. A sound from my mother. Quiet. Almost like clearing her throat. I waited. Nothing more.

Chapter 11

"**D**idn't stay in town very long, did you?" Katya steps up on the porch and lowers her cloth bag of groceries to the floor. "Oh, sorry. I didn't know you were asleep."

I stretch and yawn. "I must have drifted off, I guess. I've only been back for a few minutes." A kind of narcolepsy is creeping in. If I sit down and get comfortable during the day, reading or listening to the radio, I fall asleep in a twinkle. Katya doesn't sympathize. First, she never sits down, and second, she's six years younger than I am, so the failures of aging haven't reached her yet.

I pat the settee beside my chair. "Sit a minute. You don't have to be running all the time. The dust will wait."

"Just for a minute. I want to put in a roast for supper. Thought I'd go out and see my little ones this afternoon."

Katya's son Stephen lives on the farm she and her husband Istvan bought, worked on, worried over and made into a thriving business in their youth. Truck farm. They grew everything from tomatoes to corn to beans. One of those pick-it-yourself places. They had fruit, too—strawberries, apples, grapes, pears. Seemed like there was always something in season. Always an excuse to go out for a visit.

Istvan was the hardest working man I ever knew. Made me tired just to watch him, planting, cultivating, weeding, constantly bent over with the work. But he was happier than anyone knew, except maybe Katya, Rob and I. Istvan had reason to be happy, and he and Katya loved each other beyond imagination. That's why when he died suddenly of a heart attack at sixty-seven, I wondered what Katya would do with the rest of her life.

Didn't take long for events to take care of themselves. Rob followed Istvan within six months, a stroke this time, and Katya and I turned to each other in our grief. It just seemed right. Stephen needed the whole farm and the house with his three little ones, and Katya and I needed the company of a kindred soul.

"Tell Stephen and Emma not be strangers. They could drop the little ones off here every Saturday when they do the farmers' market." I wish they would. My old heart longs for the revitalization youth brings.

"Emma's afraid of taking advantage of us."

"Oh, posh! Tell her that's silly."

Katya gathers up her bag of groceries and goes into the house. I've a mind to follow her when the phone rings and I hear her answer it. "You up for another visit from young Mr. Kirk?" she calls though the screen door.

"I guess so. Just one more, though. I need to move on."

Katya conveys the message and we agree on two o'clock. I'm waiting for him on the front porch when he arrives walking up from the incline, sweat forming on his boyish upper lip.

He hands me the draft of his story and I read it while he drinks a glass of the iced tea Katya set out before she left. It's a competent story. Nothing flashy. Just the facts, as James would say. I hand it back to him and nod my approval.

"You'll make a newspaper man someday," I tell him.

He smiles his appreciation.

"You know, we never did get beyond the flood itself. What ever happened to Davy Hughes?"

I flinch at the re-opening of a subject I thought I'd succeeded in passing over. "Well, he came back a couple of years after the flood, but he didn't last long. Moved on to someplace out west. Chicago I heard."

I'm suddenly searching for a way to divert this young man's attention. I've just spent a little too much time with my memories of Davy, and I'm not ready to share them with the world.

"Anyway, that's all over and done with. You've got your story and my stamp of approval. Now off with you."

I know I'm being dismissive, impolite, even, but I'm desperate to get away from these incessant memories. Just when I think I've dealt with them—put them away—they pour in and threaten to carry me off again.

But Gerald Kirk isn't finished with me yet. "My dad said there was more to the story about you and Davy Hughes. Something about a Johnstown gang bent on revenge against the South Fork Club Members."

"Oh, that. Yes, well, that's a story for another time." Now I really want to get rid of him, but he's slow to take the hint.

"Seems to me only human for some people to feel resentment," he tries to pry the door open a little farther.

Now I'm adamant. I look at my watch. "You need to go now, Gerald. I have another appointment at three-thirty, and it's already almost three o'clock."

Disappointment shows in his young face. I'm sorry, but this has gone far enough. I rise to walk him to the steps.

"Mrs. McRae, could I maybe come back some time? So we could talk off the record?"

I smile. I know reporters well enough to know that nothing you tell them is ever really off the record, in spite of their best intentions. I'm feeling guilty for my abruptness, so I smile and say, "Yes. Maybe sometime. Give me a call."

I know in my heart that there are parts of this story that will never see the light of day in a newspaper or otherwise. My need to control has risen to the surface. Sorry, young Mr. Kirk, but you'll have to get your once-in-a-lifetime story somewhere else.

Once he's gone, I go upstairs to my room and take a book from the shelf. Historical fiction is very popular right now, and I'm engrossed in Walter D. Edmonds's *Drums Along the Mohawk*. I settle into my chair to read, but, be it age or lack of self-discipline, I find my mind wandering back there again.

All night and the day after Davy's outburst I couldn't get him out of my mind. Despite my joy at his return, fear and guilt kept creeping in. I wondered if I'd been foolish—too easy—taken too much for granted. A shiver of regret passed through me, and I fought the urge to cry. I went about my work preoccupied, concentration beyond me. I was so put off by Davy's behavior. I wanted to go back over there and take him by the ear and say, "Who do you think you are? If you don't care about me, why did you let me know you were here? Make love to me? You've taken the best I had to give. Why lead me on, if you don't intend to do right by me?"

But I told myself I didn't know how it felt to be Davy—to lose as much as he'd lost—go through what he'd been through. So I kept my peace, but my heart was breaking.

My best distraction was newsgathering. Out every morning to make my rounds, home around noon to write up my stories. Then back down to the *Clarion* to deliver them to Rob for typing.

One warmish afternoon, I was done early, so I pulled up a chair to talk to Katya, sitting by the window, working on my dress.

"Don't you get tired of sitting there sewing all day?" I asked.

"No sew all day. Cook, too. Take care of Mama. Busy life."

"Is it easier than life at home?"

"Easy. No kids. Not so much clothes to wash. You and Mama neat people."

"Do you miss your family?"

"Miss brothers and sisters. No miss Papa yell all time. Come home drunk. Beat me. Beat brothers. Not his fault. He gotta beat someone."

Her dark hair pulled back from high cheekbones framed a pretty face. In another time and place she might have been considered a beauty, not just another Hunkie girl in Johnstown.

Distracted by my own concerns, I looked out the back window toward the Hughes house, Davy never far from my mind. I felt empty. I longed to be with him, to believe things would be all right, but his odd behavior made me question everything. Day passed into evening, and I sat writing until long after Katya and Mama had gone to sleep.

The table was situated to give me a clear view of the Hughes place. How could I sit there and look at his hiding place and not run out to be with him? I was filled with fear—*for* him and *of* him. This new Davy bore almost no resemblance to the boy I loved once.

Then I saw a shadow moving through the Hughes yard into ours. Davy. I stepped to the window and slid it up a little. He reached for me. I grasped his rough, calloused hand and pulled it to my lips.

"I'm coming out," I told him.

He nodded and stood outside the window waiting as I slipped on my coat. I opened the door and stepped out into the darkness, around to the back and into his arms.

"I thought you'd never turn out that light tonight," he breathed into my hair.

"If I'd known you were watching, I have turned it out earlier."

"I'm always watching."

"Oh, Davy! I'm sorry about yesterday. I don't understand why you can't just tell the world you're here."

I didn't understand why I was apologizing, either. I wasn't the one who was harsh, angry, even cruel.

"In due time." That's all he said as we stood with our backs to my house in the moonlight, holding hands.

"Want to go back to my lair?" he asked.

"Better than shivering out here."

But instead of leading the way, he stood there, shoulders hunched, hands deep in his pockets. "I'm sorry about yesterday, too. I didn't mean to be so tough on you. It's just that I don't want complications in my life. I came back to see my dad, and now he's sick, so I guess I'll have to stay a while. But I was dead to everyone here, and I'd just as soon keep it that way."

That set me off again. "Then why did you let *me* know?" I was trying to be nice, but my tone sounded clipped, angry.

"Couldn't help myself. Knowing you're here, so near all the time. Knowing how hard it is for you, taking care of your mother. I had to reach out to you, but I'm sorry about the other night. It won't happen again."

I strained to see his face in the dim light. "What?"

"I got carried away is all. I never meant for it to happen. We'll wait now. Until we're married."

The mention of marriage brought relief. Of course we'd get married, and that would make everything all right.

I reached for his hand in the darkness. "What'll you do now?"

"Stay, I guess. Until I see how my dad fares. If he dies, I'm gone for good."

Again the stab of fear. "What about me? Us, I mean?"

He moved closer, taking me in his arms. "Oh, Pammie, don't worry. You're the other reason I came back. Had to know what happened to you. Then I heard about Geordie and your dad, and I had to see you."

He knelt beside me, held my hand. "The flood changed me, but it didn't change my love for you." He raised my hand to his lips, kissed it, held it against his cheek. "I want us to get married as soon as I know where I'm going."

It wasn't exactly the proposal a girl dreams of, hiding out in the dark behind an Oklahoma house on a cold winter night, but it's the only one I'd had, and I'd waited too long.

"Oh, Davy, I love you. I thought you were gone, and now you're here. That's all that matters."

He stood and lifted me into his arms. "Let's get you back inside before we soil your good name."

"Too late." A nervous giggle.

I followed him, compliant, submissive, eager to please, but still struggling with my doubts. He put his arm around me and guided me back around to my front door. The street was dark and silent, the frozen snow crunching under our steps. I'd be so glad when spring came.

Davy reached past me to open the door, kissed me gently, and whispered, "I'll always be here. Even if you can't see me, I'll be here. Don't worry. Good night."

Back inside, I went to the window and watched his shadow make its way through the yards. I took off my wraps and hung them on the peg, then undressed in the dark and lay down, feeling warm and full of hope. I wanted to take leave of doubt. I wanted us to be all right. More than all right. I wanted us to be jubilant. Elated. On top of the world.

The next morning, when I took my articles down to the *Clarion*, Rob McRae looked at the sheaf of papers I lay in his basket and shook his head. "Lotta typing for me," he complained.

I bristled. "That's what you get paid for."

"No. I get paid to be a reporter, covering real stories. The news. Not this junk," he said, flipping my articles onto a pile on his desk.

"It isn't junk. It matters to some people. Matters a lot. If you weren't so self-absorbed, you'd understand that."

I placed my hands on his desk and leaned across. "You think because it's about everyday life it isn't news. Well, everyday life is as significant as your police beat or county government or the latest political scandal."

He reared back, making exaggerated fun of me, but I leaned even closer, staring him in the face to make my point.

"We both write about life, Rob McRae. Real, honest-to-goodness down-to-earth life. So don't be so arrogant!"

"Wow! Where did that come from?" he asked, all injured innocence.

"It came from me, Pamela Gwynedd. Your match in all things!"

At that, Harold Shaver came out of his office, eyes atwinkle.

"Mr. Shaver! I'm sorry. I didn't know you were here." Embarrassed, I glared at Rob.

"No need to apologize, Pammie. You comport yourself very well. I might have worried that one could push you around but for what I just overheard."

Rob stood up, embarrassed, too. "I do apologize, sir. I was rude."

"Don't apologize to me. Apologize to her." He turned and went back in his office.

Rob turned to me. "I guess I *was* pretty rude." He looked down, fingering the pile of papers on his desk.

I moved to my side of the desk and looked him straight in the eye. "Apology accepted. Now, if you need help with the typing, tell me what time you go out to cover the city hall beat every day, and I'll come down and type my stories while you're gone."

He looked at his watch. "Usually around ten. I'm back by eleven thirty. Uh, it's after noon already. Have you eaten yet? Have lunch with me?"

I was pleased by his quick retreat from arrogance, but I didn't expect it to last. Might as well take advantage of the chance for a free lunch. "I guess so, if you promise not to berate me any more."

"That can work both ways," he said, reaching for his coat. "Let's see if the Tea Room is open."

We entered from the side door on Market Street and picked a small table near the rear. Mrs. Early, the owner's wife, bustled back and forth carrying trays of lunch plates, coffee mugs and teapots. Her round face was flushed with the effort, and the room alive with conversation and clinking silverware. Looking around, I felt out of place. Everyone here was well dressed, well off, comfortable. Looking down at my relief coat and shoes, I felt the sting of poverty—again.

Rob, plainly trying to make up for being a boor, turned solicitous. Could he order for me? Did I want a glass of water? Had I tried the luncheon sandwich? I enjoyed watching him squirm and decided to stretch it out as long as I could.

I was tempted to order the most expensive item on the menu, but instead I took advantage of the opportunity to tease. "So, Rob, what's a rich boy from Westmont doing working for a pittance at the *Clarion?* I'd think you'd be following your father into his law practice. Or are you the second son? Not destined to inherit the wealth?"

He gave a glance around, clearly uncomfortable. I'd hit a nerve.

"No. Nothing like that. I just love newspaper work. That's all."

"Seems like a waste of a good Pitt education if you ask me."

Now he was really ill at ease. He looked down and studied the menu with a frown. "What brought this on? I thought we were making up."

I broke into a giggle. "Sorry. I can't help needling you a little. After all, you've got it coming."

"Guess so. What's your choice for lunch? You come here often?"

"I've only been here once since the flood. Times have been hard for us."

"Oh. Sorry. I forget how tough it's been for some people. We were lucky."

"Lucky?"

"The flood barely touched us. Didn't get much more than high water on the first floor. Didn't lose anybody. My father keeps his office on the second floor of the bank. Things got wet, but that was about all."

I knew some were untouched by the flood—lots of them. But no one missed the aftermath—the body searches, the morgues. We all saw things we'd never forget.

He interrupted my musing. "Did *you* lose anyone?"

"My brother, Geordie."

"Oh. I'm sorry. How old?"

"Eleven. But that wasn't the end of it. My mother went away after. She hasn't spoken since the flood. Sits staring into space day after day. I guess you could say we lost her, too."

He lowered his head, fiddled with his teaspoon, sobered by my revelation. "I don't know how I'd deal with that sort of thing."

"You deal with it. That's all."

"Just you and your father, then, or are there others?"

"Just me. My father walked away a year after the flood. Couldn't stand the strain. Geordie, my mother, all of it. To make it worse, they never found Geordie."

I lifted a long handled teaspoon to stir my drink. "We kept hoping he'd somehow miraculously reappear. It was hardest for Papa. He'd made Geordie go down the block to help one of our neighbors in the high water. Threatened to take the belt off if Geordie didn't stop whining and go."

Rob watched my face intently. I didn't know what had loosened my tongue. I'd never told the story to anyone I didn't know before. I stopped as Mrs. Early came with our lunch.

"Go on," Rob encouraged.

"There's not much more to tell. The flood hit while Geordie was gone. We escaped by running up Green Hill with everybody else. It took our house and everything with it. We never saw Geordie again."

Rob shook his head to dispel the images. Sympathy—more than I thought him capable of. I was numb to the pain by now, living with it every day.

"I was supposed to marry Davy Hughes. You might have known him. He was about your age."

"Dave Hughes? Of course. We went through all twelve grades together. Terrible about him and his whole family. Everybody knows his dad might as well have died, too."

I looked down at my lunch, swimming before me, longing for a time when the flood wouldn't be the main topic of a getting-to-know-you conversation, a time when it would really be part of the past.

"Yes. Well, Davy's gone and that's that."

Rob caught Mrs. Early's eye and asked for the bill.

"Maybe not. I've heard some talk. Some ghosts reappear."

Chapter 12

I'm brought back to the present by Katya opening the front door, arms laden with bags of produce from her son's farm.

"What's this?" she asks. "You burning my roast?"

I recognize the smell that permeates the house—the roast has browned a bit too much. "I'm sorry. I must have drifted off for a while."

Katya's skeptical look draws more apologies. "Honestly, I wasn't gone long. I don't think it's beyond eating," I tell her. I follow her into the kitchen and watch while she pulls the roast out of the oven and inspects it.

"Not too bad," she judges. "Good thing, too. I invited James home for dinner."

"James? Really? I'm surprised he didn't have a conflicting engagement. That's what he tells me when I ask."

Katya smiles and bends over the bin to pick out some potatoes for dinner. I take them and start to peel. "Is this why you fussed so over that blueberry cobbler this morning?"

She smiles again and begins chopping green beans on the cutting board. "You just have to know how to entice him," she tells me. "There's another guest. Someone he should be interested in."

"Who?" I frown. I can't guess who would interest James enough to bring him to our table in the middle of the week.

"Miss Duncan."

"Who?"

"The new young lady at the *Clarion*. Surely you've seen her. Tall, raven haired beauty."

"Well, yes, I have," I admit. "Just yesterday for the first time. But how did you come to meet her before I did? What's her name again? "

"Ellen Duncan. Come on. You knew her mother. She was president of the Women's Club. Used to feed you stories whether you wanted them or not."

I set the pot of potatoes on the stove and turn my attention to the salad. The refrigerator yields a head of lettuce, two ripe tomatoes, a carrot and a cucumber. "Oh, yes. The Duncans. Rob and I used to play bridge with them about once a month."

"Well, I stopped by the *Clarion* to drop off some summer squash for Elsie and I saw her, and I said to myself, 'That's the girl for James.' The one he's been waiting for all these years. The one to give you some grandchildren."

"Just like that. You knew."

She smiles and waves her knife at me. "I've got a sixth sense. You know that."

"What does James think about this maneuvering on his behalf?"

"He doesn't know. But don't worry. He'll thank me some day." She goes about her business as though it were an everyday thing, this matchmaking. As though it will be accepted. Even welcomed. I shake my head.

Dinner is served at six o'clock sharp. Katya has no forbearance for tardiness. James, barely on time as usual, breezes in at about one minute to six. He's stopped cold by the sight that meets his eyes: Katya, Ellen Duncan and me, all seated around the dining room table, looking at a picture album of James and his brother Kenneth when they were boys.

Ellen greets him with a smile, then lowers her eyes to the pictures. "Why Mr. McRae, you were a little tow head! Who would have known?"

James slips into his chair at the head of the table, a nod to his young employee and a knowing glance at Katya. "Yes, ma'am. So they tell me."

"And full of the old Harry, if you know what I mean," Katya adds. "Many's the time I had to take him out to the farm and work the dickens out of him to save his mother's sanity."

I smile at that. It's true. Kenneth was the quiet one, the studious, serious, hard working one. James made up for him on the balance. Lit up my nerves, I can tell you.

Dinner goes well enough. Not swimmingly, mind you, but well enough. James is personable in spite of knowing he's being set up. Always the gentleman, like his father. Ellen is delightful. Funny, charming, very bright. Katya keeps things going with stories of James's childhood, and I add a tale or two about the *Clarion* in the old days.

"That turned out rather well, don't you think?" Katya asks as we finish up the dishes. We've given the young folks some time to get acquainted, and, judging by the laughter and talk from the parlor, they're doing a fine job of it.

I pour the coffee while Katya portions out the cobbler and we carry two trays into the room. "Anyone for cobbler?" Katya asks. "Now James, don't you pretend you're polite and well bred when it comes to cobbler. I've already cut two pieces for you."

James laughs, takes his plate and places it on the side table. He's in the middle of a story, and he's not to be distracted, not even by blueberry cobbler. "You should have seen us. Soaking wet and covered with mud. Mother was ready to hang us out to dry."

"What's this?" I ask, searching for the memory.

"The time Ken and I built the raft and took it down the Conemaugh. You know. It fell apart about 10 yards from shore and we had to swim."

"Oh, yes. Lashed it together with baling twine as I recall."

"Not very well, though. I think Ken let me tie the knots, to his regret."

"They were always into something," Katya recalls. "More inventive than my two. Stephen always did want nothing more than to be a farmer. Learned at his daddy's knee. And Andras wanted to be an accountant from the time he was ten. That's all there was for him."

Kenneth has come into the conversation, unbidden but there, nonetheless. Now, there was a fanatic. Baseball! All he did all summer long was play. Chores be damned. And spent the winter oiling his catcher's mitt, dreaming about summer and more baseball. Quit Bucknell and joined the Army because he heard they had Army teams, and he could play all year round in the warm climates. Did well, too. Scouted by some of the big leagues. Imagine his surprise when, right in the middle of it, we got in the war. Since they were already trained, his was one of the first units of the AEF to go to France. Ken didn't plan on being a soldier.

I've left the little dinner party, moved out to the trenches of France. Gone where no one but Kenneth could have taken me. I'm caught in the noise of the guns and the mud and the gas attacks. I don't want to be there, but I can't shake it. Men—boys, really—crying out in agony and rage, madness in their eyes. A frenzy of shooting, diving into the mud, rising and shooting again. Then that one loud crack and all is silence. It happens that way every time. The finality of silence.

I glance up and find Katya looking at me. I shake my head. She knows. Katya always knows. She rises and picks up the tray of empty cups. I follow with the plates. James is standing now, too, smiling. He's very cordial this evening. Makes me wonder if he might have stopped for a drink before he came. But, no. I can't help but think it's this young woman. No more than a girl, really, with her bright eyes and her quick smile.

"May I drive you home, Miss Duncan?"

"Oh, it isn't very far. Only a few blocks. I walked over."

"Oh, but now it's dark. It's not out of my way."

They bid us good-night and step out onto the porch. It's a lovely evening. Then I hear James say, "On second thought, let's walk. I could use the exercise."

They descend from the porch amid laughter and chatter. I turn to Katya with raised eyebrows. Maybe she's right about that sixth sense.

I help Katya with the rest of the dishes, smiling at her tendency to gloat over her matchmaking efforts. "They're not married yet, you know."

"Umm hmm. Give them time."

I hang the dish towel on the rack and return to the parlor. Katya follows with two cups of tea, and I accept mine gratefully, back in the Morris chair. She doesn't sit down, though. "I'm going to make mustard pickle tomorrow. Better get to bed."

I'm left alone in the parlor with my thoughts once more. Not unwelcome this time. I'm getting used to the unraveling of the story, hidden away so long behind life. This time I go voluntarily—back to the old *Clarion* office with its creaky wooden floors and the clack-clack-clack of the presses in back.

My tiff with Rob over the typing changed my daily routine. I'd go down to the *Clarion* office every morning to type my copy while he covered city hall. Usually it was just Mr. Shaver and me. He'd always offer me a mug of his very strong coffee, and I would always politely refuse. I didn't want to hurt his feelings, but . . .

Typing came easily to me, first the two-finger approach that Rob and Mr. Shaver had perfected, then I taught myself a ten-finger system that worked for me, if no one else. I got pretty fast, if I say so myself. The *Clarion* part of my life was liberating—got me out of the house and took my mind off the other parts. For the first time since the flood I felt hopeful,

Mr. Shaver's kindness and confidence buoyed me up. "Nice work, there, miss," he'd tell me, with a tap on the head from his folded up newspaper. "Try to get all the who, what, when, where in your first paragraph."

Once, when I misspelled the name of a bride in the Saturday edition, we had to reprint the correction on Monday. "Go and sin no more," he told me, with another tap on the head.

Nothing preachy—just a word here and there to sharpen my skills. Today he wandered by, whistling, looking distracted. I kept busy with my typing. The door opened, stayed open too long. Let in a draft.

I turned. "Rob! Shut the door! It's freezing out there."

He stood in the open doorway lost in thought.

"Rob!"

He looked up, nodded, closed the door and stepped into Mr. Shaver's office. I gave the typewriter a rest so I could hear their conversation. Something was up.

"I'm back from up there. Haven't seen anything like it since the fire at the railroad bridge. Nothing to do but watch it burn." Rob's voice sounded strained.

"Anybody hurt?"

"No. Place has been empty since the flood. Some of the cottages are occupied, but this one wasn't. Everyone up there says it was no accident."

I heard Mr. Shaver slip a sheet of paper into his typewriter and wind it in place. "Any idea who?"

"No. Same old talk—a connection with what's been going on in Pittsburgh." Rob cleared his throat. "Makes me wonder about some of our local boys."

"Probably not a coincidence. Trouble for members of the club. Can't say I blame the perpetrators, whoever they are."

A chair scraped. Rob was standing now. I could see his back through the open doorway. "You and practically everybody else in J-town. If they're ever identified, they'll be folk heroes. City Hall is buzzing. Everybody has a theory and a favorite suspect."

I heard Mr. Shaver's tick-tock typing begin, slow at first, but with a burst of speed here and there. "Well I don't have to tell you to keep your eyes and ears open. I just hope they have enough sense, whoever they are, not to let anyone get hurt."

"And not to get caught," Rob added. "If they're from around here, the Pittsburgh millionaires won't have much charity for them. They'd like to put Johnstown and its flood behind them."

I finished my work and moved to a vacant desk to eat my lunch. Rob came out and sat down at his typewriter, back to me, engrossed in writing his story. I ate in silence, watching him and making a list of my afternoon rounds.

Sam Wherry, the typesetter, wandered in, wearing a stained blue apron and smelling of printer's ink. Rob looked up. "Sam, hear about the cottage that burned up at the South Fork Club?"

Sam grimaced. "Ask me, they can burn 'em all down. The clubhouse with 'em. Wish *all* them damn millionaires had drowned in the flood. Them and their rich, spoiled wives and kids."

Sam's bitterness reflected the sentiments of most people in town. He'd lost a little daughter to the flood.

Mr. Shaver poked his head out of his office, nodded as Sam handed him the proof sheets. "Generalizing is dangerous business, Sam. Works both ways, you know." He glanced at the proof sheets, then went on. "We see the rich as spoiled, wasteful and uncaring—always looking for a way to exclude us. They see us as dirty, lazy, uncouth, always looking for a way to get some of their money."

He put a gentle hand on Sam's shoulder. "Neither is accurate, but it's hard to keep that kind of thinking from getting into your head. Sneaks in as a matter of course. Next thing you know, it owns you."

Sam turned away, head down, hands at his sides, probably thinking of the child he lost. Mr. Shaver stepped back in his cubby-hole office to check the galleys. I gave Sam a moment to pull himself together.

"Had lunch yet, Sam? I've some extra bread and an apple if you want."

He turned to me with a half smile. "Thanks, miss. But no. I've got my own."

Then to Mr. Shaver's open door, "I'll be waitin' for them galleys."

I returned to my list, marveling at Harold Shaver's willingness to consider all points of view. The burden of a thoughtful man. Those who don't think at all have no trouble taking sides.

I rose and gathered my pad and pencils for my afternoon rounds. As I pulled my coat over my shoulders I turned to Rob. "Any idea who started the fire?"

A frown and a shake of his head. "Could be any of a thousand people. But we'll probably know before long. Criminals always make mistakes."

I felt uneasy. I hadn't seen Davy in a while, and talk of the flood always brought him to mind. I picked up my cloth bag and stepped out into the street, wet from melting snow, and not very cold. Winter was losing its grip. I set my course for Green Hill where Mary Louise McManus lived. Word was she and Ralph Tate just got engaged.

As I turned off Main into Adams, I noticed a crowd gathered in the street, looking toward a house, newly restored from the flood. I recognized it as the home of Charlie Sipe, a former schoolmate. I stopped at the edge of the crowd to listen.

Another newcomer, a man on his way home from work, stood beside me and relieved me of the responsibility of asking the inevitable questions. I had my pad and pencil ready for the answers.

"What's happened?"

The response came from a woman standing near the front of the crowd. "Will Sipe shot himself not twenty minutes ago. Didn't you hear the shotgun blast?"

The man drew in his breath. "No. Must have been when the train was going through town."

A woman I recognized from church chimed in. "Thought I heard something. Where'd he do it? In the house? Was anyone with him?"

Another man answered. "In the shed out back. Wife was in the house. How can anybody do something like that—leave that for their family to see?"

Speculation went on in whispers. People stood mute, looking at the house as though expecting somehow more information would come—to explain, to relieve the haunting feeling that brought back the flood and the horror. Everything connected to the flood.

The working man kept murmuring muffled comments. "He'd already lived through the worst a man can endure. Why kill yourself now?"

"Some just feel they can't go on." The woman shook her head, wiped her eyes with her apron. "Police are in there with his wife. Not much to do but clean it up. Clear it was suicide. Poor missus. Now she'll have that to live with, too."

"Where's Charlie? He know yet?"

"At work."

People turned and looked down the street as though Charlie might appear at any moment. Don't send word. Let him have this last moment of blissful ignorance.

I skirted the crowd, my mind buzzing with questions asked and answered, scribbling notes as I moved on up the street. It might be a news story—Mr. Shaver would have to decide about that. Nevertheless, it was a story. One of so many played out over that lonely two and a half years since the flood.

Jack Johnson lost his wife and baby and became a hopeless drunk. The Morgans lost two children, and Mrs. Morgan moved back into her mother's house. Wouldn't even speak to her husband. Other marriages, held together by religious tradition, fear of social ostracism or poverty, carried on benumbed and beyond feeling. Drinking, fighting, all manner of misbehavior. It was how we coped. How we seemed to be coping and then cracked under some trivial, unrelated event.

As I neared Mary Louise's house, I saw her standing on the porch with her mother. Two women, arms hugging their middles, staring down the street, watching. My knees shook as I climbed the steps to the porch.

"What a shame. Makes you wonder if this will ever end." Mrs. McManus caressed her cheek with her hand. "I grew up with Will. Known him all my life. Martha didn't deserve this."

I nodded, feeling a bit like an intruder. "No one does. Is this a bad time, then, Mary Louise?" I referred to the yellow pad under my arm. "Should I come back another day?"

She placed a protective arm around her mother's shoulders and guided her back into the house. "Yes. Maybe. Maybe next week."

I had another call to make, over in Kernville, so I walked down to Haynes Street and crossed the bridge, my mind heavy with thoughts of the kind of despair that causes a person to end his own life. I tried to put the image of Mr. Sipe out of my mind. Think of Davy. *No.* Don't think of Davy.

I still didn't see much of him. He came and went in secret, sometimes letting as much as a week go by without seeing me. He always looked like he just crawled out of bed, rumpled and unshaven. Not at all like the Davy I used to know. I was puzzled by his lack of pride, but more by his refusal to come out in the open. When we were together, love and hope dimmed my doubts. When he was near, I didn't care about anything else. For a while.

Kernville was alive with rebuilding. Even though the weather was still cold, men hammered and sawed and shouted and mixed, unaware of the tragedy across the Stony Creek. Why should they be? It was just one of many. People seemed to be rebounding from the flood until something would put them right back in the gloom. Lord, deliver us from the eternal flood.

I was back home by dinner time, glad to enter the house, feel the warmth and smell of Katya's cooking. She greeted me with a smile, but was astute enough to take note of my dark mood.

"What happen today, Pammie? Trouble?"

"No. No trouble really. Just the old sadness."

Katya peered into my face. "Flood sadness?"

"Is there any other kind?" I took off my coat and hung it on a peg, then moved to the stove to warm my hands.

Katya lifted the kettle from the stove and poured boiling water into the teapot, waiting for me to share my day with her.

"I heard things today that make me think the flood will never be over. People need to blame somebody for what happened. So they point to the South Fork Club members."

"Why not? Their dam."

"Yes, but, I wonder how *anyone* would've behaved. I can't blame people who didn't know the danger."

Katya's frown reveals her disagreement. "Folks say they knew dam was problem, but didn't fix."

"Yes, but I don't share this need to blame. A tragedy happened. Somehow, collectively, the club members are a convenient target. It's easy to hate the rich, but I can't believe they don't care about what happened."

Now Katya was in full disagreement. "They act better than us. Run my papa off when he try fish there. Signs say no hunt! Keep hungry people out just because." This was personal for Katya and so many others snubbed and spit on by the spoiled rich.

"I know, Katya. Most of them had never even been to Johnstown—stayed in their protected mountain aerie, set apart and happy to be so, but I just don't think blaming and being angry for the rest of your life gets you anything."

"No get my mama back, that sure." She turned away, wiping her eye with the back of her hand.

I looked over to where she was sitting by the window when I came home, the skirt of my new dress spread over her lap. She was working on the hem, the final step. "Is it done?"

She held it up for me to admire the tiny, even stitches, proud of her work.

"You've done such a beautiful job. When I wear this, everyone in town will want one like it."

She squirmed with delight. "You like? You want me make another?"

"Not just yet, but later. I'd like a gingham check for summer."

She reached for my yellow pad and took up my pencil. In a short moment she'd sketched a dress, scoop neck, three quarter sleeves, full skirt, smocking at the front of the shoulders. I was astounded at her skill—with drawing and design.

"Yes, that's just right. In pink-and-white."

Her face glowed with pride. Then an idea struck me.

"Do you think you could make dresses for others? As a business, I mean? We could get Mrs. Elder to put one in the store window and you could take orders. Katya! It could be a way to make a real living, not just pocket money!"

She nodded hearty agreement. Full of enthusiasm, she turned the paper over and drew two more dress designs, our discussion forgotten. Each dress had some unique feature: smocking, embroidery, lace trim or insets. I smiled in admiration and recognition of real possibilities.

Suddenly a loud report—an explosion—rocked the floor and rattled the glassware. I rushed to the front window, but couldn't see anything. It must have come from farther up Bedford Street. I went to the door and looked out. Neighbors stood in their doorways, peering up the hill. Mary Hanley had come out of her house across the street and I called to her. "What was that?"

She shrugged. "Sounded like dynamite to me."

I wake with a start. Was I asleep? This was no dream. It was a memory. I stand up and turn off the reading light beside my chair. The house is quiet. Katya must have been asleep for hours. The clock on the mantel is lit by the streetlight through the window. Two A.M. I must be losing my mind.

Chapter 13

I climb the stairs, careful to avoid the treads that squeak. Waking Katya at this hour could bring on questions I don't want to answer. Why? Why am I going back over this after all these years? What is still unresolved?

I undress and pull on my nightgown. I know what waking and moving around will mean. I won't go back to sleep. I'll be left to entertain my notions. I reach for the book I was reading. Anything to put my brain on a different track. The words wiggle and dance on the page. I blink to get my eyes to focus. But the memories are not to be denied. The sound of that explosion echoes in my brain.

I pulled a shawl around my shoulders and stepped out into our front yard, looking up and down for the source of the blast. The sky was dark, but the moon's light outlined clouds floating overhead. Neighbors met in the middle of the street, looking up toward Green Hill, nodding, shaking their heads.

"What was it?" I asked, shaken by the reminder of the dynamite used to blow up the mass of wreckage at the railroad bridge in the months after the flood. The noise drove people to distraction at the thought of lost loved ones being blown to pieces.

"Sounded like it came from way up Bedford, up toward the hill." That was Theron Holloway from down the street. Usually free with his theories, he seemed bereft of any that night.

Someone else said, "Might have been clear out of town. That kind of noise can carry."

I shuddered. Mrs. Plummer's house was way up Bedford. Maybe Snoop had been up to something. Then a policeman came galloping up from downtown, looking intent. The crowd dispersed to let him through and he disappeared up the street without a word. The talk subsided. We stood around looking uphill murmuring our unanswered questions and speculating until the chill drove us back into our houses. We heard nothing else as quiet night closed in.

The next morning I hurried through my chores and left for the *Clarion* on a mission to find out about the explosion. Rob was busy typing when I came in.

"Did you hear the blast last night?" I asked.

"How could I have missed it?"

"What was it? Do you know?"

"Not yet. I'll go check with the police as soon as I'm done here. Rumor has it that somebody was unloading dynamite up on the hill and it detonated. No evidence of anyone getting hurt, though, impossible as that seems." He sat back, hands clasped behind his head, looking pleased to be a fountain of information. I was getting used to it, so I let it pass to get at the meat of the subject.

"Dynamite? What on earth would they be doing with dynamite up there? It's just houses and small farms. Didn't they know what they were doing?"

"My guess is, no. I'll be back shortly and tell you what I find out." He picked up his hat and coat and stepped out, letting a draft of cool morning air waft through the office.

I moved to his typewriter, rubbing my hands to warm them up, struggling with the thought that the explosion might have something to do with Davy. I shook my head to dispel those thoughts. I couldn't let his strange behavior color my view of everything. Surely this had nothing to do with him.

Then the door opened—more cold air—and Laura stepped in with Dewey by the hand, obviously about to burst with news. She looked around to be sure we were alone and half-whispered, "Guess what! Your friend Rob just got engaged. To Katherine Halstead."

"Who?"

"You know. The Westmont Halsteads."

I shook my head. "Katherine Halstead? Where did she go to school? With us? "

Laura waved me off. "She might as well be a Pittsburgh girl. She's our age, but she went to a finishing school there."

Dewey wandered around the office, fidgeting while we talked. He fiddled with the typewriter keys, breathed fog on the window and drew pictures in it. Little boy stuff.

I laughed. "That sounds like Mr. Snobby McRae. No common girl for him!"

"She used to come home in the summers, but she always kept to herself—never went swimming in the Stony Creek or to the church socials. Nothing as common as that."

Laura's pregnancy was obvious now, and, though most young wives stayed at home for the duration, Laura, being Laura, was out and about with enthusiasm.

"Isn't her father pretty high up in the Cambria Works? Is it *that* Halstead family?" I ask.

Laura pulled Dewey away from busily jamming the typewriter keys. She nodded, her hair dancing to the bob of her head. "Her father was one of the few Johnstown members of the South Fork Club. "

"Bet that hasn't won him many friends."

"No, but if the dam hadn't broken, my bet is the wedding would have been up there at the club, and young Mr. McRae would be on the list for membership."

"Hmm. Not the Rob *I* know. He's pretty set against the members of the club."

"Love does strange things to a person. Money, too. The Rob you know will probably disappear once he's married."

"Maybe. That's not the worst thing that could happen."

Laura looked around the plain little office, noting, the bare wood floor and the dingy furnishings. "You're all wrapped up in this newspaper work, aren't you?" She didn't say it, but I could tell she was puzzled at my devotion to such a low calling.

"It's a lot of fun. *You'd* love it. You get to find out about things first."

"That's for sure." Then she looked at me from the corner of her eye. "I've heard rumors that some people think they've seen your Davy Hughes around town. Any truth to that?"

I blanched. "Not that *I* know of. Who told you that? Really, Laura. Resurrecting the dead? Have some respect."

She laughed a typical Laura laugh and reached for Dewey's hand. "Well, if he shows up on your doorstep, let me know!"

"Sure, Laura. You're always first on my tell list."

She led Dewey out the door, and I gathered my things to go home for lunch. I was shaken and scared. Why? Why did it matter so much that anyone else might know Davy was alive? Surely they'd know soon enough anyway. Sitting at the table eating the lunch Katya had prepared for me, I studied the Hughes house for any sign of life, but it sat quiet on its barren lot, giving away none of its secrets. I pushed down the nagging doubts. Ever since that night we'd made love in Davy's shed, I struggled with the fear that I'd been a fool. I felt myself pulled down into the depths and struggled to rise back up. Where was he? Where was the Davy I needed so badly?

Back at the *Clarion* that afternoon I quizzed Rob about the explosion.

"Chief Harris says it happened outside of town in an old tumble-down stable. It's just a hole in the ground and splinters now, but nobody knows who did it. Mr. Shaver thinks it was a bomb gone off accidentally. No one hurt, apparently."

Barely satisfied with that explanation and still beset with gnawing questions, I left to go on my rounds, but instead I turned up Main Street toward the park. I sat on a bench, my yellow pad beside me, trying to enjoy the spring air and listen to the birds. In spite of my efforts to divert my thoughts, my mind raced over Rob's story. I couldn't guess why it upset me so. It shouldn't have. It had nothing to do with me, but I couldn't shake the uneasy feeling that it had something to do with Davy. After a few minutes of pursuing an elusive peace, I gathered my things and started walking toward Woodvale to track down a story.

That night, after Katya and Mama were asleep, I wandered out into the yard. There was no moon, no fear of being seen. But the neighbor's dog sniffed me out and put up a fuss. I stepped round behind the house in hope of calming him. A hand touched my shoulder.

Davy.

I turned and fell into his arms.

"Where have you been so long? I haven't seen you in weeks!"

He hugged me close, burying his face in my neck. My fears always subsided when we were together, but this time I needed more reassurance.

"Did you hear that explosion last night? People say it was dynamite," I whispered.

"Yeah, I heard it. Hard to miss. No telling who was doing what."

"I was worried it was you."

"*Me?* What would I be doing with dynamite?"

"I don't know. I just worry because I never know where you are, or what you're doing."

He tilted my chin up to kiss me. "No need to worry. I can take care of myself."

His words brought me no comfort. I snuggled my face in his shoulder, wishing I could unload my worries, but the fear that I might drive him even farther away kept me silent.

"Laura Jenkins says there's a rumor you're back in town. People are bound to ask questions." My fears tumbled out despite my misgivings. "I can't live like this. I need to see you—be seen with you. It's silly, hiding away. From what?"

"Tell Laura to keep her peace. She always did talk too much. It'll all be over soon," he promised. "We'll be married shortly."

"When, Davy? When?"

"Could be a month, maybe two. I'm going west as soon as I can, and I want you with me, as my wife."

His words sent a charge through me. Maybe my fears *were* groundless—maybe our lives would truly be joined after all. Maybe we really did have a future.

"What about Mama?"

He took a step back and searched my face in the darkness. He seemed puzzled by my question.

"What about her? Come on, Pam. She doesn't even know what day it is. You can't sacrifice your life for her. She'll probably never come out of it, and where does that leave you?"

His words were rational, but cold, empty, even cruel. How could he talk this way?

"But, Davy, I can't. I couldn't live with myself if I walked away like Papa did."

"He did what he had to do to keep himself sane, and you should, too." His words were clipped. He stood a few feet away, hands stuffed in his pockets. The smell of wood smoke filtered through the air. Still cold enough for a fire to take the chill off a spring night.

I stepped toward him, unable to see his face in the darkness, and reached for his hand. "What if it were *your* father? What would *you* do? Just walk away from him?"

Davy pulled his hand away, his voice harsh. "My father's different. He's not crazy."

"Crazy?"

I'd never thought of my mother as crazy. Crazy was violent or taking on some new identity, or babbling to people who weren't there. I'd seen some crazy after the flood. Mama had gone away. That's all. She could come back. She *would* come back. But not if I left her all alone. They'd put her on the Poor Farm and she'd die of a broken heart.

"No, Davy. No. I can't leave her."

"Says a lot about how much you love *me*." He was still standing a few feet away, but it felt like we were shouting at each other over a chasm.

A knot formed in my stomach. "I do love you, with all my heart, but I wouldn't be much of a person if I could leave my mother to the Poor Farm."

"Why not? Your father did."

That stung. I hid my face behind my hands. "Why such urgency? Why can't you get a job and stay here?"

"Because I hate this place!" he snarled. "I never wanted to come back, and I wouldn't have if it weren't for my dad. I'm getting out as soon as I'm sure he's all right. Now, you can come with me, or you can stay. But I'm going."

His words hit me with such force I turned away. The dog was barking again. Davy heaved a disgusted sigh, turned and shuffled across the yards, back toward his shed. I wanted to cry—run after him, grab him by the arm, spin him around, chastise him for his coldness. My arms rose as though to reach for him, but I was too sad to bother. I was devastated by this Davy. How did I ever fall in love with such a hateful person? Maybe I never knew him.

I stood there in the dark yard, leaning against the back of the house, searching my mind for a way out—a way to make him see how wrong he was. Nothing. Then the trembling started. I held onto myself, wrapped my arms around my waist to stop it. Shudder after shudder passed through my body. I shivered from the cold night air and from the sense of bereavement. My Davy was dead. Had been since the flood. What made me think this new Davy was the same person? After a few minutes I regained control only to realize I was crying. I pulled myself together enough to go back inside and undress in the dark.

Katya's voice in the darkness startled me. "Who you talk to?"

She must have been awakened by the barking dog and come down to see what was happening. "No one. Never mind."

"You talk to man. You kiss. Who this man is?"

I pulled out a chair and sat down at the table in my shift. Katya put the kettle on the stove and sat across from me. We talked quietly in the dark, careful not to waken Mama. Though how would we know if we did?

"His name is Davy Hughes. Before the flood we were going to get married. I thought he was dead." The story poured out of me, grateful for release. I told her all about it—all except the lovemaking—the hiding out, the clandestine visits, tonight's harsh ultimatum. Katya listened carefully, nodding now and then and barely speaking.

She reached across the table and covered my hand with hers. "He not man for you. Full of hate. Let him go, Pammie. You find better man. You leave with him, your mama never come back."

I didn't want to believe this. Didn't want it to be possible for my dear, gentle Davy to have turned cold, mean-spirited, bitter, but there it was, staring me in the face. "I don't want to lose him, Katya. I love him. I wish I could make him see how wrong he is to ask this of me."

Katya patted my hand in an awkward effort to comfort me, but the next words out of her mouth compounded my pain.

"I in love, too. With Istvan. He want marry me." Her face was alight with joy; then it darkened. "Papa not like Istvan, but I not care. Love Istvan. Get married."

My heart turned to lead.

Chapter 14

Sleep comes along late to relieve me of my meanderings, and I don't awaken until almost nine o'clock. Katya is in the kitchen putting away the good dishes from last night's dinner. She raises an eyebrow when I slip into my chair.

"About time. I was just about ready to come up there and see if you were still with us."

"No worry. I'm with you for the duration, however long that is."

"Reading late?"

"Well, yes, but there was more than that. I can't seem to get away from those old memories. Know what I remembered last night? The first time you told me about Istvan. Scared the daylights out of me."

Katya smiles. "I guess it would, having just got started with the *Clarion*. You must have thought you'd be back taking care of your mother with no place to go."

I pour myself a cup of coffee and sit back down. "It was almost terror."

"Good thing Istvan and I weren't in a hurry." She hands me my newspaper.

Then the doorbell rings and Katya goes to answer it. I'm content to sip my coffee and peruse the front page. That Hitler fellow is panting for war. I can feel it coming. Kenneth's face flashes in memory. Too soon after the last one.

Katya comes back with a vase of fresh flowers and a card. She's smiling.

"What's this?" I ask as if I didn't know. "Flowers. Wouldn't be from James would they?"

Her smile widens. "No, they wouldn't."

"Who?"

"Open the card."

They're from Ellen Duncan, thanking us for a lovely evening and hoping to see us again soon.

Katya can't contain her satisfaction with matchmaking. "Told you. You'll be seeing more of her," she sings.

I smile too, now. It wouldn't bother me a bit to see James settled down. He's a good newspaperman, smart and efficient. A good son, too, especially since his father died. But I long to see him loved and fulfilled by a wife and children. I'm willing to let Katya play with this and hope she succeeds.

"Hmm. Think I'll wander down there and visit James this morning. Get his take on last night. He'll be cagey, but I can read him."

"Go on. I'll be waiting to hear." Katya takes away my coffee cup. "Anything else this morning?"

"No, not really. I'll have an early lunch with James." I pause, back to reading the paper. "No stopping those Germans, I guess. Follow that mad man to hell, they will."

Katya's brow wrinkles. "I fear for Hungary. My aunts and cousins. They've only been independent for such a short time. I wish I could go back and visit them—and Istvan's people. Show them pictures of Stephen and Andras. The children. It's hard when you leave your home and can't ever get back."

I nod. Katya's always had a special place in her heart for Hungary. Talks incessantly about the little village she came from. Kis . . . something or other. Done her best to keep her language and culture alive for her boys. Now with this dark cloud hanging over Europe, I see worry lines around her eyes, note how she keeps the letters flowing back and forth.

I rise and go to the hall closet for a light wrap. It's still cool for early June. On the way downtown I walk along thinking about Katya and Istvan. Fine people, both of them, but what a struggle to make it in this new world. They've certainly earned their place. I smile, remembering the fear that took hold of me when she told me about Istvan. Then a shudder passes through me. Life could have been so different.

I was terrified that Katya would up and marry her Istvan and leave me with no one to care for Mama. I saw it as going back into prison. But Katya wasn't jumping into marriage. Istvan came by two or three evenings a week and they would sit out on the front step, talking. Istvan worked at the wire company, Gautier. Hard work for low pay. Still he saved every penny to buy land and return to his first love, farming. I liked that idea, selfish though my motives may have been. The longer Katya stayed, the more freedom I could savor.

One spring afternoon, unseasonably warm, as I was doing my rounds, I saw a dray wagon pulled up outside Laura's parents' house, unloading household goods. Dewey stood on the front porch waving at me.

"Hello, Dewey! Are you visiting Grandma?"

He nodded, dark curls bobbing around his ears.

"Where's Mama?"

He pointed to the open door.

I hadn't seen Laura since our talk about Rob McRae's engagement, so I stepped up on the porch to say hello. I knocked on the door frame and Mrs. Jenkins bustled into the hall, her face flushed and sweaty in the warm afternoon.

"Pammie! Do come in! Laura's upstairs. She'll be down in a minute."

She led me to the parlor, where I sat down amid boxes and trunks. It looked like Laura was moving back. In a few minutes, she entered the room, more pregnant than ever and looking pale. She sank into a chair beside me, out of breath.

"Looks like I'm bound to live here, no matter what," she said with a sigh. "Calvin beat me again."

She held up a bruised right arm, probably used to parry the blows. Bruises colored her face. "I'm ready to give up on him. He's never going to change."

"I gather this wasn't the first time since you were married. I hope you've learned your lesson." I was aghast.

"I have. No more drinkers. No more wife beaters."

I sighed and leaned back on the settee. "Why do you like these rough types, Laura? I'll never know what you see in them."

"I don't know. They're exciting, I guess. I'd hate to live with a boring man."

Her reply astounded me. "You've already had enough excitement to last a lifetime. Next time pick boring."

She tossed me a hopeless glance. "No offense, Pam, but how would you know? Your experience with men isn't all that wide."

True or not, that stung, but I let it go, knowing how distressed she was.

Now her blighted hope came to the surface. "Damnation! I never dreamed. I never *dreamed*. We'd only been married a few months. I thought he loved me. He said he loved me. And now this."

I laid a hand on her shoulder. "It'll be all right, Laura. Wait and see. A year from now you won't know why you felt so bad."

"That's what Papa says. He's furious." She wiped away a tear. "He came to get us this morning, and Calvin tried to stop him. I hope they never meet on the street. Papa's taken to carrying a gun. Do you believe that?"

Walter Jenkins appeared in the doorway, as though on cue, his shirt wet with sweat. "That's all of it," he said, and turned to pay the drayman. Laura watched him, helpless.

I tried to soothe her. "Don't worry. Next time you'll know better."

"If there is a next time," she replied, tucking her handkerchief into her belt. "A woman with two children isn't much of a catch."

"There will be. There's always a next time, Laura." I stood and gathered my things. "I have to get back to my news gathering, but I'll stop by later in the week."

She reached for my hand. "Thank you, Pam. It's good to know I still have a friend."

I nodded and moved into the front hall. And Laura followed, smoothing her dress. "Are you going to the dedication on Memorial Day?"

"Yes, I'll be covering it for the paper. Shall we sit together?"

The dedication of the new Grand View Cemetery was a few weeks away on the third anniversary of the flood. Six hundred thirty-nine new white crosses had been erected over the graves of the unknown. The cemetery boasted hundreds of flood victims and Civil War soldiers— more every year. It was a big occasion for Johnstown, the cemetery dedication. A looking back and a looking forward.

"Sure. Save me a seat. I'll find you." She took Dewey by the hand and led him back upstairs to her unpacking.

My rounds took me next to the Dailey house on the corner of Locust and Adams Streets. Ev Dailey's daughter, June, got engaged at Easter, and I wanted to write it up for the paper. The Daileys were among the first rebuilt. Ev Dailey wanted to make his house impressive, and he'd done so, in an elaborate Queen Anne Style, with a steep roof, long windows, and turrets covered with diamond-shaped shingles. I stopped to admire it before mounting the stairs to knock.

As I stood on the deep, wraparound porch, a coal wagon rattled around from the Adams Street side. Snoop Plummer was driving, and I turned away, hoping he'd pass right on by. I didn't want to be seen talking to him, but he slowed his horses and smiled. My stomach wrenched at his familiarity.

"Fancy meetin' you here," he said, as though we were old friends.

"Hello, Clarence. Yes. I'm here to interview June about her engagement."

"Better hurry up. Sounds to me like they're breakin' it up right now."

"Oh. There's trouble? Maybe I should wait for a better time."

"I would." He snapped the reins over the horses' rumps and moved slowly around the corner onto Locust Street.

I stood perplexed, not sure whether to go or stay. Then the front door opened and Rob McRae stepped out. When he saw me, his expression tightened. "Miss Gwynedd," he said with a formal nod and walked briskly past me to the sidewalk.

I hurried after him, trying to catch up with his rapid pace. "Mr. McRae! Rob! Wait. I need to talk to you."

He looked over his shoulder and slowed a bit but continued walking, not really waiting for me. I caught up in the middle of the block.

"I went up to cover June Dailey's engagement, and Snoop Plummer just told me they might be breaking up. I don't know whether to believe him or not. Should I go ahead or wait until June gets in touch?"

Rob's usual demeanor regarding social news surfaced. "I don't have time to waste on gossip. That's your department."

"I was just trying to do the right thing! Ask my "*superior*" for advice."

"You'll have to make that judgment for yourself, Miss Gwynedd. My visit with Ev Dailey had nothing to do with your social page, I can assure you."

I grabbed his arm. "A little common decency would go a long way here, Rob."

He turned to look at me and his face softened. "Sorry. I was talking to Ev Dailey about this Pinkerton thing, or haven't you heard?"

"Heard what?"

"The Pinkertons have come to Johnstown looking for whoever's wreaking vengeance on the South Fork Club members. They've got some suspects."

I blanched. "Suspects? From here? Who?"

"They're not saying. But things will probably quiet down once word gets out that they've been called in. Now what's this nonsense Snoop Plummer's been feeding you?"

I shrank from him, embarrassed. I felt foolish, silly. "He said he thought June's engagement was breaking up."

"A good reporter doesn't depend on hearsay. A good reporter goes to the source. Now, if you'll excuse me, I have a story to write." He walked away, left me alone on the sidewalk, my face burning with anger and embarrassment.

Back at the Dailey house, June answered the bell, and I was soon seated on a velvet divan in the parlor, my notebook on my lap.

"I don't think we're ready for a story in the paper yet," she began. "Paul's mother isn't well. They've taken her to Cresson to be confined." She looked away, dabbed at her eyes, struggling to keep control.

Cresson Sanitarium was for tuberculosis sufferers. Still is. It's small, secluded and expensive, tucked away in the beautiful Alleghenies not far from Johnstown. If Paul Confer's mother was going there, she must be seriously ill.

"I see. I'm sorry to hear that, June. I hope she improves."

"Yes. We do, too. But, in the meantime, our plans are suspended. Paul doesn't even want to announce our engagement, and I must honor his wishes."

I rose to go. "I understand. You can leave notice at the *Clarion* if you want me to come by again."

I put away my pad and pencils, and moved to the vestibule. "I just saw Rob McRae on the way out. He says the South Fork Club members have hired the Pinkerton Agency to deal with the trouble over the bombings and fires."

Ev Dailey clumped down the stairs into the front hall, his face drawn and hard looking. He stood with an arm around his daughter's shoulders, a forced smile on his face. "Hurry on, young lady. You don't need to be concerned about man talk. You stick to your society pages and let the men take care of the rest."

I nodded politely and stepped out onto the porch. Turning, I bade June and her father good-bye. I descended the wide steps, my face hot, my heart pumping with anger. Man talk, indeed! Stick to your society pages, indeed! I turned toward downtown, angry and embarrassed yet again.

I strode down Locust Street with purpose, lost in my hurt pride, but as I passed St. John's Catholic Church, flood memories washed over me—how the steeple caught fire that night, lighting up a sea of floating debris. We sat huddled together, Mama, Papa and I, cold and wet on Green Hill with hundreds of other people, shaken to our bones with the savage destruction all around us. We were high enough to be out of the flood's reach, but not out of its sway.

Papa held Mama's hand, trembling with the cold and his fear for Geordie. Mama had already gone away, but we didn't know it yet. We thought she'd be better when we got warm and dry. The night dragged on forever, rain pouring down, punctuated by crashes and screams of the injured and dying. Meanwhile, at the railroad bridge, the mountain of debris held back a lake of floating destruction, and the fire burned on. I shivered beside my parents on the muddy grass, people all around us talking in low tones, many injured and worse off than we.

I patted Papa's hand. "We'll find him, Papa. Wait and see. He's just gotten separated from us. When it's light we can look for him." I really believed it then. None of us had any idea of the extent of the disaster.

Morning came slowly, still raining. So many people needed help, it was impossible to know where to start. Some of the men called a meeting on Green Hill and began to organize right away.

People living on high ground opened their homes and their pantries to us, but there was nowhere near enough to go round. We stood most of the day in the rain, cold beyond measure, as people milled around, searching for lost loved ones, asking questions, trying to dry out and piece their worlds back together.

Now, as I approached the office, a shout brought me back to the present.

"Pam! Hurry up, girl! I need you to type for me."

Rob McRae stood in the doorway motioning, annoyed.

"Why do I have to type for you?" I asked, still stinging from our earlier encounter.

"Because I have to go out and get another story. I don't have time to type this one and get it all in by the deadline. Help me?"

Of course I would, earlier insults aside. I put down my things and slipped into Rob's chair as he handed me his scribbled notes. "See if you can make enough sense out of these to put the story together. I've gotta run."

He was gone before I could ask another question. I read through the notes, established some semblance of order and started to type.

Pinkerton Agents from Pittsburgh arrived in Johnstown today to investigate several incidents of vandalism and destruction of property believed aimed at the former members of the South Fork Fishing and Hunting Club. Authorities suspect those responsible may be from Johnstown. Residents are warned that withholding information or refusing to cooperate with the investigators could result in charges of complicity. Johnstown authorities are working with the agents in an effort to uncover information leading to the arrest of anyone involved. A reward is offered for the apprehension and conviction of the perpetrators.

As my fingers tripped over the keys, my heart felt like lead in my chest. No one in Johnstown would cooperate, no matter how big the reward. Resentment against the SFFHC members was always there, simmering below the surface.

The vandals could be anyone.

Davy.

Even Davy.

Especially Davy.

Chapter 15

*T*he *Clarion* office is abuzz with activity when I arrive, stopping to chat with Elsie and to look over the editorial room for Miss Ellen Duncan. She's busy at her desk, but I walk over to thank her for the flowers and lovely note.

"Oh, Mrs. McRae. How nice to see you again." Her tone is gracious, serving notice of good upbringing. I can't help but be impressed. We chat for a few moments before I excuse myself and depart for James's office.

"Good morning, Mother. What brings you downtown today?" He gives me a look that says he knows what brought me down town, but he wants me to admit that I'm meddling.

"Just thought I'd stop by and see how you enjoyed your evening last night."

"I enjoyed it very much," he says, turning back to his typewriter.

Not to be so easily dismissed, I continue. "Think you'll be seeing more of her?"

He lowers his hands from the keys and turns to face me. "Is this a mother-son talk?" he asks.

"Why yes, as a matter of fact, it is."

"Is it the one about it's being time for me to settle down and have a family?"

I smile. "More or less."

"Well, hold your horses, Mother. This may not be the ripe plum you were hoping to pick."

"Really? Why not?"

"Because Miss Ellen Duncan is engaged to be married to a young man she met at Pitt."

I'm stopped dead in my tracks. "She told you that?"

He nods, a little too complacently to suit me. "Last night."

"Well, I never."

James is into it now. He leans forward, elbows on the desk. "See, Mother? You and Katya can try all you want, but you can't control much beyond 306 Tuscarora Street." He's laughing at me.

"Why are you so resistant? Doesn't every man want—need—to be married? Do you want to end up old and alone?"

He leans back in his chair and looks beyond me, out the window. "To tell the truth, I don't give it much thought. That was supposed to be Kenneth's job. Making you a grandmother."

"Who made that rule?"

"I guess I made it myself. Figured Ken would get married when he got home from the war, take over the paper and give you grandchildren."

I watch his face, taken aback by his view of things. I didn't know James felt second to Ken in so many ways. "It wouldn't have relieved you of all responsibility, you know. I'd still have expected you to marry and settle down."

"It changed everything. I figured on going off to Pittsburgh or Philadelphia and getting on with a big paper. Thought I'd make a name for myself. Be the boy wonder. But I was only nine when he died. Not set in my ways—not by a long shot. I grew to see it as my responsibility to take up where Ken left off. Keep the family—what was left of it—together."

He's very serious now, and this revelation shakes me to my soul. I never wanted to be a demanding mother. This marriage talk is just frivolous as far as I'm concerned. And yet, I can feel my life ebbing away, and I can't let go of the idea that it might stop with James. My family. All of it.

I look at my hands for a long time, afraid if I look at him, I'll cry. "I'm sorry, James. I wish you'd felt free to follow your dream. I don't want anything for you but what you want for yourself."

He reaches across for my hand. "Thank you, but I've adjusted nicely and I no longer think of myself as missing anything. I've learned to love this simple little newspaper the way Dad did. I wouldn't go now if you sent me."

"I'm glad to hear that, but it still doesn't absolve you from the responsibility of getting married." I'm trying to tease us both out of this sad little corner we've painted ourselves into.

"Well, it won't be to that one. Mr. David Hughes will see to that."

I stop and look at him. "*David Hughes?* Is that what you said? Where from?"

"Pittsburgh now, but he grew up in Michigan. His dad's an executive with one of the auto manufacturers in Detroit. Ellen said his family was from around here, though."

I rise and excuse myself rather abruptly. It can't be. Can't be the same family. This has to be someone else. I make my way through the editorial room to the street, feeling short of breath. I see Miss Duncan out of the corner of my eye, but I go on as though I'm in a hurry. I am. I wish Laura were here. She'd know, or she'd find out for me in a flash.

When I get to the street I'm still breathless. I walk up to the park and sit down on a bench beneath towering elm trees just leafing out. Davy. Surely not Davy after all these years. In and out of my life like a ghost. I remember him the day they dedicated Grand View Cemetery.

That was difficult for Johnstown. We'd so looked forward to it, anxious to see the new memorial to the flood victims. But as I sat on a slatted folding chair beside Laura, listening to the band play and dignitaries speak, I wondered how long it would be before we ever got over the flood.

The whole week before the dedication the newspapers were full of articles and talk of it. Three years wasn't long enough to fade the memories. People talked on street corners, in church and in the stores, re-living that painful night, crying anew.

My own thoughts were mostly of my mother. Papa and Geordie were lost. Why go back over that? What I wanted was for Mother to take up her bed and walk.

Laura sat beside me, keeping track of Dewey and scattering her come-hither smiles around the gathering, more pregnant than ever. I still marveled at her blithe view of the world. She knew people talked about her endlessly, but it made not a whit of difference in her behavior. I would have given my daily bread to be so free of concern.

"Do you think she ever will?" Laura asked.

"Ever will what?"

"Take up her bed and walk."

I wasn't conscious of having given voice to my thoughts. "I don't know. I hope so. Fervently."

She patted my hand. "Well, at least Katya gives you a chance to be out in the world. I was worried for you for a while. Thought the flood would take you, too."

Her meaning was clear. My deepest fear.

An old neighbor, Mrs. Green, passed by in the aisle between our chairs and stopped. "Pamela! How fine to see you! How is your dear mother?"

I rose to speak with her, used to inquiries about my mother. People did care, even if they didn't know how to express it. As we talked, I looked over her shoulder and saw Davy standing back near the tree line, away from everybody. I hadn't seen him in such a long time. I'd no idea where he'd been. Ever since I refused to leave Mama, he'd been elusive. I struggled against the urge to run to him.

When he saw me looking at him, he moved his hand in a furtive wave. I nodded and went on talking to Mrs. Green while Laura chased Dewey around among the tombstones. There were flowers on almost every grave. Flags flew in the breeze from the graves of the Civil War dead. My papa should have been there with a flag on his grave rather than out somewhere, unknown to us.

Mrs. Green moved on, and I picked out one of the crosses for Geordie. Third one from the left in the third row. In my mind that would be my brother's grave, no matter whose bones lay beneath. I walked among the graves, listening to the quiet talk, watching for Davy out of the corner of my eye. To my relief he'd moved back into the woods.

Now and then a sob ripped the air, countered by laughter from someplace else. I still couldn't get over the way people experienced the whole range of emotions at a time like this. I moved past the crosses for the unknown flood victims and wandered through the family plots. There was hardly a surname I didn't know.

Suddenly, I was confronted with the most familiar: Hughes. Mother 1842–1889, and five smaller stones with brother or sister atop and a name carved beneath. Emma, Annie, Agnes, Garreth. David. A stone for Davy! Of course! His father thought he'd drowned, too, so why not? I wanted to cry. I didn't know why, exactly, but I couldn't find comfort in knowing that he was alive, watching me that very minute. Life might be simpler if he were really dead.

Dewey ran around taking flags off graves, and Laura chased after him, putting them back. I stood alone at the Hughes plot, lost in thought.

"Remembering an old beau?" Rob McRae appeared near my right shoulder, notebook in hand.

Surprised, I turned and nodded. "Davy."

"Hard to look at, isn't it?" His arm swept the cemetery.

"Yes. But I think we should, anyway. So they're not forgotten."

"Few people will be remembered for so long. The way they died writes their names in stone."

"Maybe, but my guess is they'd rather have had life. So many were children."

I moved on to the next plot, watching my step on the uneven ground. Rob stayed by my side.

I turned to him. "Why aren't you out among the people, interviewing?"

"Got my fill. I could write about this stuff for a week and not get it all said."

I nodded, walking on. "Sometimes I think I'll write a book about it. Collect flood stories. I know a lot's been written, but there're still so many stories to tell."

"Looks like the story's still unfolding, if recent events are a sign. The Pinkertons report says there's a whole gang working from here, sabotaging the South Fork men's homes, businesses—generally disrupting their lives."

I shuddered, then looked to see if Rob had noticed. "I suppose if you scratched anyone in Johnstown, you'd find some bitterness. Heartbreak. We all know it. But somehow—some way—we have to get over it and get on with life. If we don't, our lives ended on May 31, 1889, just like theirs." I nodded toward the rows of white crosses beneath the monument.

"Some people's did." He nodded back over his shoulder. "Think *he* ought to get on with his life?"

I followed his gaze to Mr. Hughes, looking old and beaten, kneeling at his wife's grave. Several friends stood at a respectful distance, giving him room to grieve. Tears welled up in my eyes, and I turned away, lest Rob see me. Then I felt his hand reach out to steady me.

"What life?" I asked.

"See what I mean?"

"Well, I can't walk in anyone else's shoes, but *I* want to move on." If I could just find a way.

Suddenly, Laura came hurrying across the cemetery, holding Dewey's hand, as he danced behind her. She looked upset, but when she saw Rob, she slowed to a walk and bent down to brush the grass off Dewey's knees. Rob hailed someone he knew and strode down to the gravel lane that encircled the memorial plot.

Laura was breathless. "You'll never guess what just happened," she whispered.

"What?"

"I saw Davy Hughes!"

"No! No, Laura. It can't be. Where?"

She motioned toward the edge of the woods, the exact place I'd seen him minutes before.

"Dewey was running away with the flags, and I was chasing him, when all at once I looked up and saw this man watching me. He was right there, right near the woods. It was Davy, Pam. I swear! Dirty and ragged, but I'm sure it was him. When I saw him, he slipped away among the trees. But I'd bet my last nickel it was Davy Hughes."

I kept walking, looking at the ground, shaking my head. "No, Laura. It couldn't have been. I was just standing by his grave. It couldn't have been."

"I know. But it was. I swear it was!"

I turned toward the road leading down the hill. "Let's start down now. I've got to get back to Mama. Katya and Istvan want to spend the holiday together."

"Let's take the path through the woods. We might run into Davy again."

"Don't talk nonsense, Laura. It wasn't Davy. Just someone who looked like him." My heart beat a quick tattoo in my chest. "Let's go by the road. It's quicker."

That night, back in our house, I read by lamplight, trying to keep my fears at bay while Katya and Mama slept upstairs. I'd been agitated all day, ever since Laura's sighting. My eyes rose from the page and scanned the backyard, deep into the space between our house and the Hughes place.

I knew he'd show up. I put out the light and waited in the dark, watching. Before long I saw movement. I sat still, waiting to be sure. Then a pebble hit the kitchen window. I rose, picked a shawl off the peg, and let myself out the door. Down two steps and off to the right around the house.

As I rounded the corner into the back yard, he grabbed me and pulled me into the shadows next to the house. His mouth covered mine. To keep me quiet? Settle down, Pamela. A kiss is a kiss.

"Davy," I whispered. "Where have you been? Why did you come to the cemetery? Laura recognized you. Did you know that?"

He held me tight, didn't answer. He buried his face in my hair, silently breathing into it. "I know. That was dumb. I wanted to be there. That's all."

"Why all this secrecy? Why don't you just let people know you're alive and get it over with? Are you involved in this trouble? This burning and bombing that's been going on?"

"No. Don't be silly, Pam." His fingers caressed the back of my neck as he reached for me again, pulled me to him. "I know it's hard, but you have to trust me. I know what I'm doing."

""What *are* you doing? Tell me! Where have you been?" I asked again. "It's like you don't really exist. Sometimes I think you're a ghost I've conjured up."

"This ghost wants to marry you." He stepped back. "When you're ready."

"This is tearing me apart. I can't *know* when I'll be ready. Mama could come out of her shadows tomorrow or never. My life isn't my own."

I couldn't see his face in the darkness, but I felt the frown.

"Well, maybe you'll just have to choose, Pam. Maybe you'll have to decide who's more important to you." His tone had turned angry again.

We'd been over this enough. I stepped away from him, turned away, then turned back.

"You know Laura will trumpet the news all over town. She wouldn't take my word that she was mistaken, and if Laura knows, everyone knows."

I stood with my back against the house. Davy moved up to face me, his hands flattened on the wall above my shoulders. He leaned down and kissed me again, then stepped up and pinned me against the wall.

"Don't worry about Laura. I know how to keep her quiet. Now, what does your boyfriend at the newspaper say about the trouble?"

I frowned. "I haven't heard much. Rob—and he's *not* my boyfriend—says they've hired the Pinkertons to look into it. There's a reward. That's all I've heard. Oh, and they think there's a gang working out of Johnstown, but I don't think anyone here will cooperate with them."

Davy snorted. "Guess not. They'd be dead if they did. Reward or no reward."

"Davy! What do you mean?"

"Nothing. I just know that anyone who even talks to any Pinkerton man will be dealt with, that's all. So tell your boyfriend to be careful."

"Stop calling him my boyfriend. I don't even like him. Besides, he's engaged. I'm *your* girl, remember?"

He smiled and touched my cheek. "I remember. I'm waiting for you to realize that your mother's already dead and come make a life with me."

Stung again by his cruel words, I looked around the dark yard, struggling against the hurt. How cold could he be? Was he trying to push me away? "She's not dead. She'll come back, Davy. Please, let me be patient."

"I don't have forever, Pam. I'm leaving as soon as I can get out of here. I want you with me."

I reached up and traced the line of his nose. "Oh, Davy, wait for me. Please wait for me. I've waited for you."

One more kiss and he was gone, a shadow moving through the yards, past where the hedge used to be. I sighed, alone in the dark, struggling with the feeling that I'd been a fool. As I turned to go inside I was stopped by the sound of a wagon rattling up the street. I peered around the corner at Snoop Plummer driving his coal wagon along in the empty darkness. I watched him move slowly up Bedford and turn on Adams toward Ev Dailey's house. Then I moved around to the front and in the door.

As I mounted the stairs, Katya stirred in her sleep. "You talk to Davy?" she asked.

"Yes, it was Davy."

"He still mean about Mama?"

I sighed. "Yes, Katya, he's still mean about Mama."

"I tell you that one no good. You find better man."

"He used to be good. One of the best. I know what's happened to him, but I can't find it in myself to understand. I want the old Davy back."

"Old Davy gone. You find better man."

I undressed in the dark and lay down in my bed near the end of my patience. Davy'd better come up with some kind of explanation for his behavior, or I'd . . . what? What would I do? What choices were open to me? Davy could be in big trouble, or he could just disappear into the night. Or I could go with him, or . . .

Then I heard it as plain as day. My mother's voice. She said, "Geordie?"

Chapter 16

Sitting there in the park, I know I'm not ready to go home. I need to know about this David Hughes who's claimed Ellen Duncan as his own. Is he Davy's son? Is Davy still alive? How can I find out? Oh, where is Laura when I need her?

Then it dawns on me. Of course. Katya reminded me the other day. Rob and I used to play bridge with the Duncans. I could call. Make a date for lunch. The topic would come up as a matter of course. Once decided, I get up and walk back to the incline with a purpose, anxious to get home to make the call.

When I arrive, Katya's upstairs airing out the bedding, an old European custom she can't let go of. She leans over the banister while I tell her about Ellen Duncan's engagement, but she's not even ruffled by the news.

"Engagements can be broken," she tells me. "As I recall, Rob McRae was engaged to someone before you. That didn't work out, and neither will this. This is meant to be. It's in the stars."

I chuckle as I take up the phone book to look up the Duncans' number. The call is made "tout de suite" and I'm on for lunch at the Duncan's home tomorrow at eleven thirty.

"Did you hear the name of her fiancé?" I ask Katya when she comes downstairs.

"Yes, Elsie called and told me, and now I suppose you'll be beside yourself until you find out if it's your Davy's son. Lord, Lord. I can read you like a book."

I smile and go into the parlor, but Katya is right behind me with her dust cloth. "What you need, Pamela, is a job. You're at loose ends around here—wandering around dredging up old memories. I'm surprised at you. You were always the one to leave the past in the past."

"I know. Makes you wonder, doesn't it? Maybe I do need something to keep me busy. Grandchildren would fit the bill."

"Be patient. I'm still convinced this will work out to everyone's satisfaction."

I go upstairs to get my book and find a place to sit on the sun porch. The book's engaging enough to keep me reading until Katya calls me for lunch, but once she's cleared the table and done the dishes, she returns, wearing a light jacket.

"Thought I'd go over and see poor Mrs. Hanley. She's bedridden and alone. Sad how her children all live in Pittsburgh and only come to see her once in a coon's age. I hope Stephen and Andras don't treat me that way when I'm old."

"Don't worry. They won't. I never saw two boys who loved their mother more. Tell Mary I said hello."

She's gone in an instant, and I find myself relieved to be alone again with my thoughts. There are so many of them, racing around my brain, giving me no recourse but to sort them out.

The fact that my mother spoke even one word made me think she would, indeed, someday come back. I tried not to let my hope run away, but inevitable thoughts crept in. The interlude was only an instant, though. She said no more and retreated back into her preferred world. Still, I waited and hoped.

Summer was upon us, and with it, the notorious Pennsylvania humidity. Local boys swam in the Stony Creek, hooting and hollering as they swung out on a rope and dropped into the cold, sparkling water. I could hear their shouts where I sat at the table, organizing my appointments and planning my afternoon. Katya sat by the window, sewing a dress for Mrs. Ev Dailey. I'd moved Mama's chair out into the yard where she could sit in the shade of the old elm tree that survived the flood and look at the flowers. Pansies, marigolds, zinnias—a colorful profusion from the generosity of Mrs. Elder. They seemed to bring Mama joy, but as Katya said, more like it brought me joy to see her out there—to think that it brought her joy.

Katya rose to stir some Hungarian concoction she had simmering on the stove. The smell of paprika, onions and cabbage filtered through the neighborhood. I hated to have a fire on so hot a day, but Katya knew only one way to cook: long and slow, the Hungarian way.

"Honestly, Katya. Don't the Hungarians know how to make anything that doesn't take all day?"

She smiled, returning to her sewing. "Outside kitchen be nice. In Hungary, summer cooking outside."

Katya sat by the window, content, her needle moving with speed and deftness I could only envy.

"Is Istvan coming by tonight?"

She smiled and nodded. "Tonight we count money." She beamed.

Once a month, on the first, the two of them would sit down at our table and take their money out of a metal box Katya kept under her cot. They counted every penny and made a note of the date and the amount. The clink of each coin counted and dropped into the box sounded like prosperity. After the counting, they would sit out on the front step and dream together about how long it would take them to save enough for a down payment on a farm, and what they'd grow, and how many children they'd have.

I liked Istvan. He was dark and brown eyed—not what you'd call handsome, but neat and clean looking. Kind of like an Ohio farm hand. How would I know that? Anyway, he was quiet and polite, and he treated Katya with gentle respect. I found myself hoping that their dreams would come true—as soon as mine did and not before.

"When you finish that dress, you'll have some coins to add to the box," I told her.

"More dress orders come. I work till week from Sunday." She was proud of how her reputation as a seamstress had grown, and with good reason. She could turn out a dress in about three days and make a neat profit. The orders kept coming.

Suddenly Katya motioned over her shoulder out the window. I rose to look, and saw Mrs. Plummer laboring up the street, her face red from the effort.

I hailed her. "Mrs. Plummer! Come in. Sit down."

She lifted her ponderous self through the doorway and lowered her body into the only empty chair.

"Oh, Miss Gwynedd, I'm about to melt." She was panting, and sweat beaded on her forehead and upper lip.

I went to the cupboard for a glass and poured her some water from a pitcher in the dry sink. Most people had running water by then, but most people had rebuilt by then, as well. I carried mine from the pump down at the corner—or Katya did. Backbreaking work. Mrs. Plummer took the water—tinged by the sweetness of Pennsylvania iron—and drained the glass. Then she wiped her brow with a piece of cloth she kept tucked in her belt. Her bags surrounded her on the floor.

"Mrs. Plummer, it's too hot for you to be laboring so. You should make people come down to the commissary on their own."

"Oh, I do, most of them. But there's a few that can't. Get downtown, I mean. You know. The infirm." She'd recovered from her near heat stroke, and was back to her businesslike self.

Much as I disliked Mrs. Plummer's officiousness, I had to give her credit for taking care of the elderly and sick since the flood. That's why she was so attentive to me—because of Mama.

"You need a boy to help you, then."

"My Clarence used to help, but, you know, Mr. Dailey can't get along without him these days. He's a rare one, that 'un."

She sat looking around the house, taking in everything. "Your Hunkie girl sewing again?" Her own eyes could tell her that.

"Yes. She's making a dress for Mrs. Dailey right now."

Mrs. Plummer sniffed. "Guess I better take that loom back, then. Mrs. Elder tells me the Hunkie girl does the weaving. Them looms is for the local folk, you know."

"Katya is local folk. She weaves beautifully, too. Mrs. Elder has sold several of her rugs, even though almost everybody weaves their own. Hers are so different."

She puffed herself up. "Hunkie designs, if you ask me. I wouldn't give 'em house room. You mark my words. If you don't get her out of here, before long she'll be movin' *you* out *and* your poor mother with you." She talked about Katya as though she were a table leg, unable to hear or comprehend.

I struggled to control my Welsh temper, which has been described as an Irish temper without the moderation. Mrs. Plummer was goading me into a fight. No. I wouldn't rise to the bait.

"You can take the loom with you now, if you wish. I can dismantle it and pack it up for you."

She looked at her bags on the floor and decided against taking on another burden. "I'll send my Clarence by to pick it up when he has time." She rose and reorganized her pack, all business again. "Thanks fer the water."

"You're more than welcome, Mrs. Plummer." I tried to sound gracious, all the while fighting the urge to shove her over backwards out the door.

Katya kept working, intent on her sewing, barely looking up.

I turned back to Mrs. Plummer. "I really do appreciate all you've done for us since the flood. I don't know where I'd be without your help."

Flattery got me a reprieve, and she was all smiles as she let herself down the steps to the dirt. "You're more than welcome, Miss Gwynedd. I hope your poor mother doesn't get the flux from all that spicy Hungarian cooking. I'd keep my eye on that one, if I were you."

I nodded and smiled as though her advice were welcome, glad I didn't have to depend on her kindness so much anymore. I'd be careful what I said, though. Very little escaped Mrs. Plummer and her snoopy son.

I was soon out the door and on my way to an afternoon interview with Mrs. Aaron Sullivan, president of the Johnstown Women's Club. Her Vine Street home was new, built up several feet from the street, brick and much cooler inside than an Oklahoma house. She took me into her parlor, where large framed pictures hung on long wires from the molding near the ceiling. The room was dark, quiet, and crowded with furniture and bric-a-brac—a perfect refuge from the heat of the outside world.

"Come in, Miss Gwynedd. I'm anxious for you to write about our Fourth of July Ice Cream Social."

She offered me a seat on a brocade covered platform rocker. I sat and listened, dutifully taking notes.

Mrs. Sullivan was only a few years older than I. She was ahead of me in school, but we were only passing acquaintances. Though their home was lost, the Sullivans didn't suffer much in the flood. She and her baby left town, went to Derry to stay with relatives while her husband rebuilt his business and the house with insurance money. Now she had two little ones, a beautiful home, and social position. I struggled with the inevitable comparison of our lives.

We'd finished up our discussion of the social news when she asked, "Have you heard about Davy Hughes? Weren't you betrothed to him? The town is buzzing with rumors that he's back."

I nodded and smiled, trying not to seem nonplussed. "No. I think it's just talk. Laura Jenkins thought she saw him at the cemetery dedication. I'm sure she was mistaken, but there's no convincing her. But, yes. Davy and I were engaged."

She was watching my face, trying to read me, and I wondered how I could put this to rest. I waited for her to continue.

"Well, it isn't unheard of for people to surface after a long time. Who knows how many walked away that night."

"I agree it's possible. But I haven't seen him." I felt the heat rise in my face. I've never been any good at lying. "I wish it were true." I picked up my notebook and turned to leave.

"If it is true, I hope he isn't mixed up with the ones that are terrorizing the South Fork Club members. He could be sorry for that.

The Pinkertons are asking a lot of questions. It would be hard to escape their notice."

A white light of fear flashed in front of my face. I wanted to be outside, anywhere but here. "Well, Mrs. Sullivan, thank you for your time and information. I hope you're pleased with my efforts."

Hearing my fears put into words was unnerving. I rose and turned to the vestibule—waiting for her to let me out, breathing deep to conceal my anxiety. With great effort I regained control as I descended to the street, not sure where to go, what to do.

I turned toward town. I should have gone home to write up my stories, but I needed to walk this off. I headed blindly down Vine Street to Market and turned toward Main. I wasn't conscious of having a destination, but the *Clarion* office appeared before me, almost deserted when I arrived. Nobody around but the printers in back. I sat down at Rob's desk, my head on my arms. I heard the clickety-clack of the presses turning out job printing. I wondered where everybody was, but I was too upset to worry about it. I needed a good cry.

"This is no place for that."

The words came out of nowhere. Clipped. Masculine. The last person I wanted to talk to—Rob.

I raised my head. "For what?" I asked, feigning innocence.

"For a good cry. That's what you were about, isn't it?"

I could have protested, but he'd never believe me, so why bother? I looked up at him as a tear wended its way down my cheek. His expression changed in an instant from teasing to caring.

"Hey. I was kidding. What's the matter?"

I couldn't tell him about Davy, but maybe I could find out whether the talk about him was serious, or just hen talk.

"Nothing. Nothing you'd care to hear about, anyway."

"Try me. I can be very sensitive."

I laughed out loud at that.

"You? Sensitive? About as sensitive as a copperhead." I wiped my eyes. "I just heard something that made me sad, that's all. Somebody's flood experience. You know how it is. The cemetery dedication brought out all the old stories. So sad."

I watched him taking in my explanation. When he seemed to be buying it, I turned to the typewriter in relief. "Can I do some work for you?"

My offer was met with silence, and I looked over my shoulder to see what he was up to—looking through his notes, distracted. "No. Thanks. I have to do some more digging before I'm ready to write this story."

"Digging?"

"Yeah. The South Fork Gang. I think I might be onto something."

Again the flash of white.

"Onto something? Like what?"

"Like nothing that would concern you, my pretty." He stuffed the notebook into his shirt pocket and reached for my hand. "How about a sarsaparilla for a hot day?"

Anger at his usual arrogance rose in my cheeks. I hated to be talked down to. I sat there, angry, thinking of all the retorts I could use against him.

"Come on, you need some refreshment," he teased.

I *was* thirsty and flattered to be asked, so I put aside the insult and rose from my chair. We left the office and walked through the muggy afternoon to the drug store, with its modern soda fountain. Four fans slowly moved the air beneath the high, hammered-tin ceiling as Rob steered me toward a table in back. Wire chairs and small round tables sat on a floor of tiny, octagonal white tiles. Everything gleamed with newness.

Rob ordered our drinks while I concentrated on collecting myself. Insulted though I was, I felt drawn to him today for some reason. Drawn, not attracted. Maybe it was because he had access to information I could only guess at—and guessing didn't make me feel safe.

"Now, are you ready to tell me what's bothering you?" he asked, setting down a round tray with two sweating, cold glasses.

"I thought I already did."

"No. I'm not that easy. You've got something on your mind. What is it?"

His persistence was unnerving, so I formed my question carefully. "What have you learned about the Pinkerton investigation?"

His eyebrows rose. "Not as much as I'd like to know. Why?"

"People are talking all over town. I wonder if they've found out anything yet."

He turned in his chair, stretching his long legs out in front of him. "They left town this morning. Said they were going back to Pittsburgh. As far as I know, they haven't had any co-operation. But then, I don't guess they'd want it in the paper if they had."

I listened, Davy heavy on my mind. Was he a suspect? How could I find out what Rob knew? I still couldn't imagine my Davy deliberately hurting anyone. I knew there was bitterness in him, but there was bitterness all over Johnstown.

"Well, then, what's *your* take on it? Do *you* have any suspects?" I kept my eyes down, played with my napkin, trying to look casual.

But Rob was on it like a duck on a June Bug. "Why? You worried about your beau?"

"Beau? What beau? I don't have any beau."

"Used to. Your old beau, then. Davy Hughes."

"Davy's dead. You know that. We were looking at his grave the other day." I sat tall and looked straight at him, showing confidence I didn't feel.

"Not his grave. His tombstone. There's talk he's been seen around town. I'd think you'd know that by now."

"Laura was prattling about seeing him at the dedication, but I took that as her imagination working beyond the limit. What have you heard?"

"Question is, 'what have *you* heard?'" His blue eyes stared at me, level, intent. I felt like a schoolgirl called to the teacher's desk.

"Only what Laura said, and I told her she was imagining things."

"I can't believe he'd be in town and not seek you out." Again the penetrating eyes.

I looked down. "Even if he were in town, does that necessarily link him up with the crimes against the South Fork Club?"

"Makes me wonder. Guess if I were a Pinkerton man and somebody told me Davy Hughes was back from the dead after two years, and sneaking around town, I'd wonder."

I couldn't look at him. My hands were shaking under the table. Rob took a drink, still looking steadily at me. I reached for mine, searching for a way to shake him off, make him think he was mistaken.

Suddenly the front door opened, ringing a little bell above it. The fountain boy stepped up. "Hi, Mr. Shaver! What can I get for ya?"

Harold Shaver let his eyes get used to the darkened store, peering toward the back. He ordered a soda and turned toward us.

"Thought I'd find you here." He brought up another chair to our table. "Big doin's in Pittsburgh. Somebody threw a bomb under Thomas Clark's hansom. A little too anxious. It went off in front and killed the horse, barely injured Clark, but he was the obvious target."

Rob looked up. "Another South Fork Club member?"

Harold Shaver nodded. "That's the word. You'd better take the evening train in and find out what you can. You can telegraph your story back for tomorrow's paper."

Rob was out of his chair, notebook in hand with barely a glance at me. "You'll excuse me, Miss Gwynedd. Looks like I'm off to Pittsburgh." He strode through the store and out into the afternoon glare, clearly on a mission.

Mr. Shaver settled back with a smile at me. "Nice to see you and Rob getting along better. But I'd be careful lest anyone get the wrong idea. He's engaged, you know."

"I know, Mr. Shaver. We were just talking about the South Fork Club crimes. I was curious about what the Pinkertons found out."

He nodded with a detached expression, then changed the subject. "How's your mother?"

"She spoke the other day. Night, I mean. She said Geordie, plain as day." I was relieved the conversation was taking a different turn.

Mr. Shaver nodded again, still not entirely attentive. "Yes, that's a good sign."

I was disappointed that he didn't seem to share my perception of Mama's progress. He was clearly distracted—probably following Rob in his mind. Neither of us really felt like making small talk, so we finished our drinks and left the drug store, he to walk down Main to the *Clarion*, I to walk up toward home.

A strange sight greeted me as I turn up Bedford Street—Snoop Plummer's coal wagon drawn up outside our house and Katya standing in the yard by Mama's chair, her hand on Mama's shoulder. Snoop was nowhere to be seen.

"Katya! What's going on?" I asked.

"Man come for loom. I give."

"Where is he?"

She nodded in the direction of the house where Snoop was coming out the door with the dismantled loom under his arm. He nodded to me, his eyes white in his coal blackened face.

"My ma told me to come and get it," he explained, plopping the loom parts into the coal wagon with no care for the soot-infested floor. Then he pulled himself up to the wagon seat, clucked to his horse, and rumbled slowly up the street, his eyes never leaving mine.

"That one no good," Katya half-whispered.

"I know. If I had any silverware, I'd be counting it right now."

Chapter 17

My curiosity about Ellen Duncan's fiancé can't be satisfied by any subtle means. I have to know. It's been such a long time since I've heard anything from or about Davy, I doubt that this young man could be his son, but still, I have to know. I'm impatient all morning, waiting for Katya to get done with the ironing and go shopping. Once she's out the door, I rush upstairs and change into my soft blue walking dress—one that Katya made for me—and check myself in the mirror before going out. I'm reminded how pleased I was with that first dress— the blue and yellow calico. She was so proud, and I thought it the height of style. How times have changed. No more full skirts and tight waists. This dress almost seems to hang from the shoulders, as though to defy any fitted appearance. Well, it's been fifty years now, hasn't it?

The walk to the Duncans' house isn't very long, and I rehearse my reasons for wanting to get back in touch. Widowhood, you know. Elizabeth Duncan has always been more of a social being than I. She surely doesn't need more friends, but maybe she's tired of the old ones and looking to revive some from the past. She meets me at the door— barely a knock—and leads me through the house to the backyard. There's a small gazebo down at the end, where we sit down in blessed shade, surrounded by the sweet scent of honeysuckle.

"What a lovely garden," I compliment her.

She smiles. "How nice to see you again, Pamela. I don't know how we ever drifted apart, but I'm so glad you called." She looks up to motion her maid to bring the tea tray. The table is set with a beautiful embroidered cloth that I recognize as one of Katya's. She used to do them for sale at the farm. She only had four or five designs, so it's easy to tell which ones are hers.

We sit talking and sipping our tea while bees visit the honeysuckle and butterflies light on the flowers in her immaculate garden. I'd forgotten that she was a flower grower like my mother.

"We're delighted to have Ellen working at the *Clarion*," I tell her. "Such a bright young lady. You must be very proud of her."

Elizabeth nods, smiling. "Yes. She's always given us much to be proud of. She's getting married, you know. Next spring."

"No, I hadn't heard," I lied. "Who's the lucky young man?"

"No one you'd know. She met him at Pitt. He was raised in Michigan. His father's an auto executive."

"Oh. What's his name?"

"Hughes. David Evan Hughes Junior. His father grew up around here, but left after the flood. His whole family died."

Elizabeth Duncan isn't from Johnstown, so she wouldn't have known about Davy. She goes on about her daughter's wedding plans and where they'll live. Tells me Ellen won't continue to work after she's married.

"I'm sorry to hear that. I couldn't get that newspaper out of my blood, so I raised my boys in a corner of the office."

"Yes, well, you were good at both reporting and mothering as I recall. We'll see about Ellen."

We spend a pleasant afternoon catching up with each others' lives, and once it is over, promise not to let so much time pass between visits. The warm walk home takes me past Rob's old house. James lives there now, took it up when his grandmother McRae died seven years ago. We expected a wedding to follow, but he's kept to himself and concentrated on the paper. The house is big and old now—going on fifty—as is the neighborhood of Westmont. There's a big back yard and lots of shade trees. The school is just across the street. A perfect place for grandchildren. I let myself muse as I make my way home.

Katya isn't there when I arrive, but there's a note. She's out visiting her grandchildren again. I change into a cotton dress and pour myself an iced tea. As the afternoon wanes, a sultriness descends. I should be writing a thank you note to Elizabeth Duncan, but I let myself sit on the front porch my curiosity about Davy running free. There's no doubt this young man who wants to marry Ellen is his son. I wonder that I haven't heard anything about him over the years. The next thing on my agenda is to get to meet this child of his. See if he looks like Davy. Can't wait to tell Katya.

That's the way it's been almost since we met—Katya's and my friendship. Cemented in those days when Davy was such a puzzle. Life has bonded us well, she and I. Then, as though on cue, I'm taken back to the summer of 1892, when she'd been with me for about six months. What a summer that was!

We hadn't heard from Katya's father in some time. I counted that as a good thing, but one summer evening, without notice, he showed up at our door, his hair slicked back, his mustache trimmed, his suit coat brushed, his shoes free of dust. He handed her a small bouquet of wildflowers as he stepped into our tiny front room.

"Daughter. Good to see." He smiled a crooked, yellow-toothed smile.

I offered him a chair, my nose tickled by the smell of garlic. "Mr. Pinter. What brings you here this evening?" His obvious purpose made me wary.

He looked away from me to Katya, uncomfortable. He'd come to talk to his daughter, not me. "You come out. Talk in yard," he told her.

I wasn't sure I should let this happen, but my faith in Katya's ability to take care of herself won out. They rose and went outside. But Katya was no fool. She wandered around to the back of the house, where I could hear their conversation through the window.

Not much good. They spoke Hungarian, but I could tell from the tone that things were tense. Their voices rose as their speech accelerated. Then he reached for her arm, and Katya pulled back. I took that as my cue to intervene. I was out the door and around the house in time to see Katya yank her arm free. She stood facing her father, her posture telling him and all comers that she was nobody to push around. I stood aside and smiled to myself. Good for you, Katya!

Mr. Pinter marched past me to the street, then turned and shouted something in Hungarian, unintelligible except for the word 'Istvan.'

I turned to Katya. "What's he saying about Istvan?"

"Say Istvan is Gypsy. No good. Say I be sorry for marry him, but too late. Papa no want me after I bed with Gypsy."

"Is he really a Gypsy?" I didn't know a thing about Gypsies, except that in stories I'd read they kidnapped babies and stole for a living.

"No. In Hungary to say Gypsy is insult."

"Why would your father hate Istvan? He's planning a good life for you."

She sighed. "Same old Papa. Want me marry Sandor. Old man with money. I pick Istvan."

I hoped we'd heard the last of Mr. Pinter, but the next evening he was back, this time with an older man, better dressed, but with a yellowed gray mustache and small mean eyes. I was thoroughly dismayed by Mr. Pinter's refusal to accept things as they were.

This time Katya didn't want to go outside. "That Sandor Varga, man Papa want me marry."

She was clearly afraid, so I went to the door. "Mr. Pinter, Katya doesn't want to talk to you."

"My daughter. My daughter talk to me," he insisted.

I moved to close the door, but he beat on it with his fist.

Mama was sitting in her chair, where I'd been combing her hair. Her back stiffened at the noise. I bolted the door and leaned against it while Mr. Pinter kept on pounding.

Then I saw Katya raise a hand to her mouth, her eyes on the front window. I turned to see what she was looking at, and there was Istvan coming up the street. Too late. Her father saw him too, and rushed out through the yard to confront him. We watched through the window as the three men stood in the middle of Bedford Street, shouting in Hungarian.

Suddenly Mr. Pinter hauled back his fist and smashed Istvan in the face. Istvan retaliated with a fist to Mr. Pinter's stomach, doubling him over. Then Sandor raised his walking stick and brought it down on Istvan's head with a mighty crack. Katya screamed as the younger man turned, dazed, and gave Sandor a mighty shove that knocked him off his feet and sent him reeling. Sandor's head snapped back as he fell with a thud, like a sack of butter beans in the dirt.

I was dumbfounded at this turn of events, frightened and sickened at the sight of the old man lying still in the dusty street. Fear and anger rose in me, and I swallowed hard at the taste of vomit. Katya opened the door and we rushed out. She held her hands to her face, crying.

Mr. Pinter rose slowly, brushing off his jacket, and he and Istvan stood looking down at Sandor, their faces blank. A strange silence descended on the neighborhood.

Down the street someone yelled, "Police! Call the police!"

Two of our neighbors, attracted by the noise, ran out of their houses and grabbed Istvan and Mr. Pinter. Old Sandor lay motionless, dust settling on his yellow mustache and his scuffed, brown shoes.

Then Katya and I were joined by neighbors from every direction. Old Sandor's neck was twisted at an odd angle, his eyes closed. It took some time for the police to arrive, but no one touched the old man. He looked dead. The two neighbors, strong men seasoned by years of hard work in the mills, held Mr. Pinter and Istvan, their arms twisted behind their backs. Katya clung to Istvan alternately crying and screaming at her father in Hungarian. Somewhere on the other side of town a train rumbled by, whistling at the crossing, the sound of normalcy.

Then Mrs. Plummer came, bustling her way through the crowd, shaking her finger in my face. "I told you no good would come of having that Hunkie girl in your house. Now look at this. A Murder! Right here in our street. What kind of low folk do you associate with, Miss Gwynedd?"

I put a protective arm around Katya. "She's done no wrong! Her father was trying to force her into a marriage she doesn't want. Don't blame her for this."

Mrs. Plummer flounced away to discuss the matter with the neighbors who were standing around, talking among themselves, murmuring in disbelief. Finally, a policeman rode up and got off his horse. He knelt by the man lying motionless in the street. Sandor was indeed dead. The policeman made his way through the crowd, asking questions. I stepped forward and offered my version of things, and Katya affirmed it. The policeman listened very nicely, took a few notes, and then arrested both Istvan and Mr. Pinter. Katya stood helpless beside me, tears streaming down her face as Istvan was led away.

The next thing I saw was Snoop Plummer driving up with his coal wagon. He and a neighbor hefted Sandor's limp body up into the bed, covered it with a dirty tarp, and shut the tailgate Then Snoop climbed back up and nodded to me as he lumbered off down the street. His mother stood aside, beaming with pride at her son's importance, as the crowd slowly dispersed.

Katya and I walked slowly, arm in arm, back into the house. I was going to need help with this. There was so much prejudice in Johnstown, it would be easy to jail both men and forget about them. Katya, heartbroken and hopeless, moved about the kitchen as though in a dream. I turned to finish getting Mama ready for bed.

I went back to combing her hair, soft as silk in my hands, comforting to feel in the face of all this tumult. But my mother was restless, anxious. Her hands flew to her mouth at every sound, as though she sensed something else was about to happen. I led her up the stairs to her bed, and she lay down, staring at the ceiling, but didn't sleep. I sat beside her bed and spoke soothingly, but to no avail. Turmoil always made her tense, and though she couldn't express it, her fear was obvious. Her eyes darted from here to there, her fingers kneading the air. Desperate to calm us both, I began to sing to her—Sweet Hour of Prayer—one of the beautiful old hymns she used to play on the piano at church. Finally, after about an hour, she drifted into shallow sleep.

I went back downstairs and put out the lamp. Katya and I sat talking in the dark.

"What happen now, Pammie? They hang Istvan?" Her voice shook with emotion.

"No. I guess they'll have a trial. If they find him innocent, they'll let him go. If they find him guilty . . ."

I was in unfamiliar territory. I didn't know anything about the workings of the law, but I did know that immigrants were lesser citizens. Little would be done on Istvan's behalf. I couldn't be honest with Katya about his chances. I needed to talk to someone who knew more than I did. This night I couldn't offer her hope or comfort, knowing as little as I did. I put my arms around her and held her as she cried.

The next morning, after a hurried breakfast, I set off for the *Clarion* with a purpose. Mr. Shaver was already there, tapping at his typewriter. I stepped into his office and poured out my troubles amid the clutter, grateful for a sympathetic ear.

He listened, frowned, leaned back in his chair. "They'll probably blame it on Istvan. Charge him. He'll need representation, that's for sure. Mr. Pinter will testify against him, is my guess. You'll probably be called, too, my dear, and your housemaid."

"It was self-defense," I assured him. "I saw all of it. Mr. Pinter hit Istvan first, and Sandor joined in. Surely they won't find him guilty!"

Mr. Shaver shook his head. "It's hard when they don't speak much English. Hard to give them their say. Hard to defend them. I'll ask around and see if I can find someone who'll take the case for little recompense."

"Recompense for what?" It was Rob, carrying a coffee mug that he set down beside his typewriter. I repeated the story for him.

He frowned. "Lot of anti-Hungarian feeling around this town. Bottom rung of the ladder and all that."

"I feel so sorry for Katya. She and Istvan don't deserve this." I told them how the couple saved their money and dreamed of buying land.

"She's a master seamstress. I've never seen anyone do such wonders with a needle and thread."

"She'll probably need every penny she can scrape together for his defense," Rob added.

I sighed and turned my attention to my stories. Nothing I could say about Katya and Istvan would make any difference. Their fate was in the hands of the law, and, though I knew I was supposed to trust the working of the legal system, I was still uneasy.

Rob puttered with a lot of loose papers on his desk, trying to find something in his notes. I remembered I hadn't seen him since he returned from Pittsburgh. "What did you find out about that carriage bombing?"

"Not much. Whoever threw it got away clean. Lobbed it over a board fence and got out before anyone saw them. The horse was killed, but the driver and Mr. Clark just had a few scratches. No leads, but a lot of speculation about a Johnstown connection."

"Now they're hurting people. It was bad enough when it was only property damage, but they're either getting bolder or just plain careless," Mr. Shaver muttered, disgruntled.

I sat there worrying about Davy, unable to give voice to my fears.

Rob looked my way. "Type up my story for me? I have to make my city hall rounds."

I nodded and picked up a sheet of paper to feed the typewriter. He tore out his notes, handed them to me and left. I read them over, trying to make sense of his private shorthand. I was almost finished when I saw the name Davy Hughes circled with a question mark beside it. What did that mean? I started typing and forming the notes into a story, but I couldn't see how Davy's name fit with the rest of it.

Once I was finished with Rob's story, I took out my longhand articles and typed them up. By the time that was done, Rob was back from city hall. I knew I should be on my way home for lunch, but I lingered to ask about Davy's name in Rob's notes.

His response was evasive. "Don't know. Can't remember what I was thinking when I wrote it. Maybe somebody said something and I just jotted it down. Anyway, thanks for writing it up for me." His smile was dismissive.

Frustrated, I ruminated about it all the way home. Can't remember, huh? Just jotted it down, huh? Sure, Mr. McRae. I believe that. Then as

I was turning into Bedford Street, I heard a commotion—singing, loud laughter. A wagon full of people rattled down Main—a wedding party. But it was a Thursday, not a Saturday, the day for most weddings. I searched my mind for an engaged couple who might be getting married early. They sang and hollered as they rode along, toasting the bride and groom, the wagon driven by a fellow I'd seen around Elder's store. It was one of Ev Dailey's wagons, cleaned up and festooned with bunting and flowers.

Inside, seated high on a crude bench fashioned for the occasion, the bride and groom sat surrounded by bridesmaids and groomsmen. The bride turned and waved to me. June Dailey. So her intended had decided to go through with their plans after all. Then the groom turned to face me, and I drew in my breath. Snoop Plummer, looking furtive and sneaky as ever, in a Homburg hat and a new suit. He looked me right in the eye as though daring me to question his right to be feted for his good fortune.

Chapter 18

I'm sitting at the kitchen table drinking an iced tea when Katya arrives with her arms full of groceries. The first word out of her mouth is, "Well?"

"Well what?"

"Well, is Miss Duncan's fiancé the man we think he is? Or should I say the son of the man we think he is?"

"Um hmm. Looks that way. Now what, Mrs. Matchmaker?"

She puts down her bags on the table and turns to open the refrigerator. It's the newest thing—an ice box that doesn't need ice. Keeps food cold all by itself. I think of the days when the ice man drove the streets with his wagon loaded with ice, followed by a gaggle of ragtag children begging for a chunk. His deft expertise with an ice pick was a pleasure to watch. He knew just how big a block Mrs. Johnson needed, or Mrs. Swatiak, and chopped it off with expert speed, picked it up with his ice tongs, balanced it on a leather patch on his shoulder and delivered it to her ice box with nary a drip. People should appreciate skill no matter where it shows itself.

Katya puts the food in the refrigerator and turns to me. "I feel sorry for him, is all. Thinks he's found the girl of his dreams, but he's wrong. He's destined to keep on dreaming."

"Oh Katya, how cryptic!" I laugh. "What does James think about this engagement?"

"He's disappointed, but not disinterested. I know that boy. He's ready to make his move and he finds out she's taken. Not one to be put off, our James. He'll bide his time. Something will come up. You wait and see."

I take an apple out of one of the shopping bags and pick a paring knife from the drawer. I go out on the back porch and sit down on the swing with a paper bag in my lap to peel it. Katya is busy in the kitchen, so I let myself go back to my musings. Where was I? Oh, yes. June Dailey's wedding.

Full of curiosity about Snoop and June, on Saturday morning I made my rounds for the paper and then headed over to Laura's house. Her advancing pregnancy was slowing down her social life these days, but she kept up her contacts around town, and if anyone knew how Snoop Plummer managed to get married to June Dailey, it would be Laura.

She met me at the door and hustled me into her mother's comfortable parlor, bursting with fervor to talk. We sat on the settee, and Laura leaned over and patted my hand, obviously glad for some company. She threw back her head and laughed when I asked about Snoop and June. "I guess she's in the same condition I am. Gaining weight and getting lonely." She smiled like a fellow-conspirator.

"June is pregnant? To Snoop? What was she thinking?"

"Oh, honey, it's not Snoop's. Paul Confer dumped her when he heard about the baby, and she's been getting more desperate by the day. That explains Snoop. Word is her father offered him part of the business to marry her."

Now my visit to June Dailey for her engagement write-up made perfect sense. Even Snoop's warning fit.

"This happened pretty fast. No announcement or anything. They just up and got married," I commented.

"Would you want it in the paper if you were marrying Snoop Plummer?"

I shuddered. "Guess not. Too bad. June's a nice girl. I always liked her."

Laura nodded. "She's in for it now. If you think Calvin Corwyn was bad, even *I* wouldn't have anything to do with Snoop Plummer."

I giggled at that. "Yes, Laura. It's good to know you have your standards!"

Dewey was out in the kitchen in a tug of war with his grandmother, and from the sound of it, wearing her down. Mrs. Jenkins appeared in the doorway with a tray of tea. Dewey followed, carrying a plate of cookies, two of which he snagged for himself.

"Dewey, those are for Mama," his grandmother admonished. "You put them back now."

Dewey gave her a mischievous glance and popped both cookies into his mouth. He grinned at her with sparkling brown eyes, mouth brimming with cookies, crumbs falling on the carpet.

"Away with you, you scamp. Back to the kitchen before I wear you out." She swatted at the seat of his retreating pants, with a hopeless look at me and followed him back to the kitchen.

Laura frowned. "She spoils him."

I smiled and turned back to her. "Do you have any plans? For when the baby comes, I mean."

Laura shifted her weight in the brocade settee and poured each of us a cup of tea. "I've been seeing someone."

What? I marveled again at how Laura always managed to attract a man, no matter her circumstances. Even her advanced pregnancy didn't slow her down. "Who is it this time?"

"Danny Kirk." She looked at me from under lowered brows. Expectant.

"Danny Kirk! Well, at last a respectable one!"

A year ahead of us in high school, Danny Kirk was the son of one of Johnstown's rising professional men—in the same league as Katherine Halstead, Rob's fiancée. But Danny was shy, quiet—bland looks, no backbone, as far from Laura's type as he could be, except for the money. I was taken aback by this news. Danny Kirk. Of all people. I wasn't surprised that Danny would be attracted to Laura. He always did like her. But Laura? Had she finally given up her lust for excitement? And Danny? Could he really overlook Laura's past indiscretions, to say nothing of two children? That's a forgiving man!

"Of course, we're keeping it quiet until after the baby comes. But we're thinking about a winter wedding." She smiled.

So Laura was getting married *again!* And here I sat wondering if there was any future for Davy and me, and if not, if there was any future *at all* for me. I couldn't help but be glad for Laura. A little envious, but glad, nonetheless. Maybe she'd learned her lesson about low-lifes.

"Did you hear about Katya's Istvan?" Of course she'd heard. It was all over town.

"Yes!" Laura's face lit up, delighted by the excitement. "Tell me all the details!"

I launched into the story, sharing my fears for my friends. "They're such good people, Laura. Really. They work hard, save, live clean, and don't bother anybody. If anyone doesn't deserve to spend time in prison, it's Istvan."

"He won't get off without at least five years or so. You know how it is for Hungarians around here." Laura wasn't unsympathetic, just realistic.

"He'll be lucky if they don't hang him," I sighed. "I wish I had some money. I'd hire a good lawyer."

An idea-hatching look came over Laura's face. "What about Rob McRae's father? He's a lawyer! If he won't do it, maybe he knows someone who will."

"Rob knows about it. I half expected him to make some kind of offer, but he hasn't. Probably afraid of getting his hands dirty."

"Rob's a puzzle."

I nodded. "I know. I like him and I don't like him."

Laura smiled. "He's at home in circumstances we can only dream about, and yet he seems to be perfectly happy in that drab little newspaper office." She cast an apologetic glance in my direction. "No offense, Pam, but you know what I mean."

I let that go by. "I wish he'd step up and offer, but I guess that's not going to happen."

We sipped our tea and meandered through the latest gossip. Laura's grasp of everybody's business was deep and wide.

After a brief silence, Laura opened the subject she was waiting for. "What does Rob say about the South Fork Gang—or whatever they are?"

"Nothing. He says he doesn't know anything, but I think he just doesn't want it talked about before he gets to write the whole story." I took a bite of a sugar cookie.

Laura tilted her head back and looked down her nose at me. "I think he knows a lot—about a lot of people. I wonder what he told those Pinkerton men when they were here snooping around. Probably told them plenty."

"Then why did they leave? If they knew so much, why weren't there any arrests?" A pause to think about that. "I don't think Rob would tell them anything. He knows the feelings around here. That'd be professional suicide."

Laura was the skeptic now. "Depends how much the reward is. Nobody's ever said. Probably enough for Rob to take off and get comfortable somewhere else."

"Rob doesn't care about money." I felt I was in a position to know about this. "If he cared about money, he wouldn't be working for a poor little newspaper like the *Clarion*."

"That's going to cost him, too, so I hear."

"What do you hear?"

"Just that his sweetie has given him an ultimatum. Marriage or the *Clarion*. Not both."

I was caught up short. "Rob doesn't talk to me about things like that, but it doesn't surprise me. He never mentions Katherine at all. It's almost like she lives on one planet and he lives on another. Marriage of convenience or something."

"No wonder she's jealous of his attachment to the paper. Anyone would be. He's there all the time." Laura rose and picked up the tea service. "It really does look like a step down for Miss Halstead to be marrying a common reporter, even if he does come from money."

"Yes, I guess so." I caught myself frowning. "Do you think they'll break it off, then?"

"Why Pammie? Thinking of moving in?" Again the conspiratorial tone.

"Of course not. I can barely abide the man. Such an insufferable snob."

Even though I said it, I didn't really feel it as much as I used to. Rob had been nice lately. Still when his superior attitude surfaced, as it inevitably did, the sting came back.

Laura moved to the kitchen with the tea service, and Dewey ran to my arms, all giggly little boy. He really was a beautiful child, I'd say that for Laura. The one she was carrying now would probably be blond and blue eyed. Quite a contrast with Dewey. Danny Kirk would have his hands full.

I was moving toward the front door when Laura's next remark stopped me in my tracks. "I'm not the only one who's seen Davy Hughes."

I turned, a little too abruptly. "Who else?"

"My cousin Alice Pheasant. Lives in Pittsburgh. Knew Davy from her summer visits here. Says she's seen him coming and going from a rooming house in Pittsburgh lots of times. She thought everyone here knew he was alive."

I sat down on a wicker rocker on the porch, my eyes fixed on Laura's face. I couldn't talk to her about Davy. "When? When did she see him?"

"She says he's been around Pittsburgh since about a year after the flood. She hasn't seen much of him lately. I take that to be because he's here."

Laura was matter of fact about her news, but the shock sent me reeling. Maybe that's where Davy went when I didn't see him for days or weeks: Pittsburgh. Just the place for access to the South Fork Club members. The news made me shiver.

I tried to head her off. "You're both mistaken. Really Laura, you shouldn't be spreading this kind of thing around. You could cause Mr. Hughes some real grief."

She looked at me, an eyebrow cocked as though wondering if I were stupid or just too stubborn to accept the truth. "What are *you* so upset about? I'd think you'd be glad Davy's alive. Are you angry because he hasn't been to see you? Is that it?"

I rose, shaking my head in annoyance. "Laura, please. Don't speculate about Davy and me. He's dead. Gone. Whoever you or your cousin saw, it wasn't Davy."

I moved toward the porch steps. "Anyway, I've got to go." She reached out to hug me, and I gave her a half-hearted hug in return. "Take care, Laura."

Walking down Franklin Street toward Main, my head was spinning with the disturbing news. Instead of turning down Main, I headed up toward Bedford Street. I wanted to go home. I walked quickly, keeping my eyes on the sidewalk so I wouldn't have to meet anybody.

Then I heard a wagon behind me, laboring slowly up Bedford. I hastened my steps to keep ahead of it. I kept my eyes on the sidewalk, afraid it'd be someone I'd have to greet. I could see the horse out of the corner of my eye—the big, plodding beast that pulled the coal wagon. I heard a growl, and the horse came to a stop, right beside me. I had to look. Snoop Plummer, back in his dirty old work clothes, delivering coal. He motioned me over to the wagon. What could he want with me?

When I was right beside the driver's seat, he spoke to me in a low tone out of the corner of his mouth. "Tell Davy to lay low." Then he snapped the reins over the horse's rump and moved on up the street, hunched over, one foot up on the front board, the reins dangling over his knee.

I was within sight of my own house, rooted where I stood, dumbfounded. Snoop Plummer? Davy? How could I tell Davy anything? I hadn't seen him in weeks. The thought of Davy having anything at all to do with Snoop Plummer made me cringe.

I found my legs and hurried up the street. Mama was sitting out under the Elm tree, watching the flowers weave and bob in the breeze. She started when I came up from behind and laid a hand on her shoulder. "Aren't they beautiful, Mama? Especially the pansies. I remember they're your favorite." I kept my hand on her shoulder to calm us both.

Then I went into the house where Katya was waiting for me, all dressed up in her Hungarian best, full skirted with an embroidered bodice and laced weskit. Her head was covered by a colorful babushka, and she looked at me with pleading eyes. "I go see Istvan," she said.

"I'm not sure they'll let you in, but go."

She carried a basket of food, good Hungarian sausages, cabbage rolls and pastries. I watched her make her way down the street, my heart aching for her. What would she do if she lost Istvan?

I turned to see lunch already laid out on the table for Mama and me. I went out into the yard to get her. As I led her into the house, her grip on my arm was so steady I wondered who was leading who. I sat her down at the table and tied an old apron around her neck for a bib. She sat complacently as I fed her, chewing slowly, swallowing. I wondered how many times in the past three years I'd fed my mother. How many more times I'd have to. When she was satisfied, I took off the apron, wiped her chin, and moved my chair across from her.

She sat tall and straight, and just as I was about to take my first bite, she smiled at me. A beautiful, warm, loving smile. I straightened up and smiled back, but before I could get any words out of my mouth, the smile faded and was gone. I was left with the hollow shell I'd come to know so well.

Chapter 19

*I*t's about four o'clock and shadows are getting long when Katya comes out and sits with me on the front porch. "What's next?" she asks, shading her eyes against the afternoon sun.

"I don't know. You're the matchmaker. You tell me."

"Maybe just wait and see. James can make his own move."

I smile at that. My second son always was a charmer, able to negotiate his way around whatever obstacle stood in his path. Even as a little boy, aware that his older brother could best him in many ways, he still managed to arrange the world to his liking. "Do you really think James is that smitten?"

Katya gives me a wise look. "I know he is. If he wants Miss Ellen Duncan for his own, and I think he does, nothing as paltry as an engagement will stop him."

The afternoon sun slips behind the big elm in front of our house and gives our eyes a rest. Katya has brought out some potatoes and a colander with her, and she sits peeling potatoes for our dinner.

"I guess we've done what we can do—getting them together for dinner. Wouldn't want to be too obvious. There should be something else, though."

"You always were impatient, Pam. I wonder where James gets that. Let's just sit back and watch for a few weeks. Let nature take its course."

A sigh escapes me. "You'll never guess what I was thinking about before you came out."

"What, pray tell?"

"Your first visit to Istvan in jail. Remember?"

Her face clouds at the memory, still painful after all these years. "You really are living back there these days, aren't you? Why?"

"I don't know. That young man, Gerald Kirk—Laura's grandson— has stirred it all up for me. I can't seem to leave it alone."

"Well, I'm still not interested in spending any time back there. But this thing with Davy Hughes resurfacing has me all discombobulated."

I know what she means. Ever since the flood, Davy Hughes has been a source of discomfort for me, first one way, then another. But I still have a need to go back and examine it one more time. Maybe this time it'll make sense.

Katya picks up her colander and goes back in the house. Still sipping my iced tea, I get up and go around back to look at the rose garden. Rob was the keeper of the roses, out there trimming and puttering every day after work. I miss him. There's the old swing Rob hung from a branch of our cherry tree. I wander out and sit down, remembering many a warm afternoon, reading there and sipping tea while Rob puttered. Slowly, I relax and let the swing move me with the soft, gentle breeze. If I didn't know better, I'd think I dozed off, but no. I'm just time traveling.

Katya was back in about two hours, her face flushed with the heat, her eyes sad. "No see Istvan. Say visitors only Saturday morning. They take food, but I think *they* eat. Not Istvan."

She sat down on the front step and poured out her story. "Jail men not nice. Tell me wait, and I do, but nothing happen. Wait and wait. Jail men not nice."

Folding my skirt under me, I sat down beside her. Flies buzzed around our faces in the sultry afternoon.

"Man ask what's in basket. Say not allowed take food to prisoners. Say they inspect." She turned her hands palms up and sighed.

"I open basket and they take. One man with knife open every cabbage roll, every sausage." There was anger in her voice—and frustration. The system was working against her, and Katya was no fool. She knew it. "They laugh at my dress. Call me Hunkie girl."

"What did they do with the food after that?"

"They take. I no see again, but not see Istvan either. They say wait. Maybe when police chief come, so I wait more. But when he come, he say no. Come back next Saturday."

I put my arm around her shoulders to comfort her, but there wasn't much I could say, even less I could do. I doubted they'd let her see Istvan on Saturday either, but I didn't tell her that.

On Monday morning Katya was still in a gloom. I wished there was something – anything – I could do to fix things. I made up my mind to work on it, grovel if I had to.

"I have to get going on my rounds, Katya. Chin up, you'll see Istvan soon." Rising from the breakfast table, I gathered my notes and trekked across the grassless yard, heading down to the *Clarion*.

The office was already stifling in the dead, humid air. I slipped into Rob's empty chair to type my stories. Mr. Shaver was in his tiny office, clacking away at his typewriter, against the noise of the presses in back. They were always printing something. If not the paper, then job printing. Every time someone opened the door to the print shop, the clackety-clack of the presses overpowered conversation. The odor of printer's ink on the men who worked there announced their presence well before they appeared.

I finished typing my stories and looked around for something to keep me there until Rob got back from city hall. Mr. Shaver came whistling out of his cubby hole and gave me a smile as he passed. "You keeping busy these days?" he asked.

"Busy enough."

"How's your mother?"

"You know, Mr. Shaver, I really do think I see some improvement."

"That's good news. I'm sure it's because of the care you give her." He was rooting around in a file cabinet, looking for something.

"Katya's more responsible for that than I am."

At the mention of Katya's name, he turned to face me. "I've been meaning to talk to you about that business the other night. What do you make of it?"

"I have to find Istvan a lawyer. I saw it. All of it. There's no question he was attacked first—by both of them."

"Jolly time you'll have getting a jury to believe that."

"I know. That's why we need a good defense."

He frowned. "Who'd pay for it? No lawyer of any account is going to take an unpopular case for free."

This was the kind of talk I heard at every turn. Frustrated, I vented my anger to the only ears that would listen. "That's the problem. Nobody cares a whit for a poor immigrant unjustly accused. All I know is he shouldn't be convicted. He's a decent human being, and he's innocent. Couldn't you write an editorial or something? To influence?"

Mr. Shaver shook his head, frowning again. "I sympathize, but I don't see much chance of meaningful help. I could write one, but you know how people are when it comes to immigrants. Might get the citizens all up in arms and do him more harm than good."

"We're all immigrants. Why should that work against him?" I hated the negative talk—wanted someone to agree with me. Good people ought to be able to hope for a better life—get an even chance with the law. I turned back to my work, weary of feeling hopeless. Just then the door opened and Rob came in, looking hot and tired.

I seized the opportunity to shore up my alliances. "There's a jar of cold lemonade in the icebox. Katya made it. Help yourself."

Rob opened the ice box with enthusiasm and drank long gulps of the cool lemonade right from the jar. Well, then, it was Rob's lemonade now.

I waited for him to quench his thirst and sit down before I launched into my request. "Rob, would your father know anyone who could defend Istvan?"

He took off his jacket and rolled up his sleeves before answering. "I guess I could ask him."

Rob's lack of enthusiasm was puzzling. Was he just going through the motions to placate me? If that was the case, why bother?

Nevertheless, I grasped at hope. "Would you, Rob? They have some money saved. Maybe enough to pay some, if not all of the fee."

"I'll see what my dad says. but I wouldn't be optimistic. Few lawyers are willing to take on a case like that, even if they can pay something. Any lawyer's trial record is important to him. Why take on a hopeless case if you don't have to?"

I knew the outlook wasn't good, but I winced at the word hopeless. "Well, talk to him and let me know what he says."

That job done, I gathered my things and stepped out into Main Street. The other disturbing thing on my mind was Snoop Plummer's warning for Davy. I didn't need to tell him to lie low. He did that by nature. But I wanted to know what Snoop had to do with Davy, or if he was just probing to find out what *I* knew. The place to start figuring that out was with old reliable Laura.

I turned down Franklin Street toward the Stony Creek and followed it to the Jenkins house on Willow. The local boys were beating the heat with a raucous swim in the Stony Creek. Their shouts and laughter made the day seem almost refreshing. I was tempted to shed my dress and shoes and join them. If I'd been Laura Jenkins, I would have. Afternoon shadows were lengthening, which suited me fine. The sooner night came, the sooner it would cool off. I wished I lived up on one of the high hills that surrounded the town. The valley would hold the heat much longer. I stepped up on the Jenkins's porch and knocked on the frame of the screen door. All was quiet inside. I wondered where they could be. Then Mrs. Jenkins came down from upstairs and opened the door. She put a finger to her lips.

"What's wrong? Is Laura sick?"

"Miscarry. The baby's gone."

"When?"

"This morning."

I sighed. My concern for Laura competed with the awareness that this might simplify her life. "Where's Dewey?"

"My man's taken him to Geistown to stay with my sister for a few days. Let Laura recover."

The house was quiet, cool, dark. Mrs. Jenkins, ever the kind hostess, offered me refreshment. "Sit a while, Pammie. I'll get you something."

I protested, but she was gone before I could get the words out. I studied the parlor while she was gone. Not rich, but certainly comfortable. It underscored my awareness that everybody else had rebuilt—lived in a nice house—enjoyed the comforts of a modern home. I couldn't help but sigh.

Mrs. Jenkins was back in a few minutes with a tray and two glasses of iced tea. I accepted mine gratefully and sat back on the settee while she sat in a cushioned rocking chair beside me. Her face was care worn. It must have been hard being Laura's mother, knowing how people loved to talk.

"We, Walter and I, appreciate your friendship with Laura. She needs a friend so, now. There's so much talk about her. You know how people love to gossip."

I smiled. "Oh, Mrs. Jenkins. We've been together since the day you and my mother took us off to first grade at the Adams Street School. That kind of friendship lasts forever." I smiled at the memory of Laura and me sitting side by side in the front row in first grade. Even then she was the adventurer and I the careful one. "Laura says she's seeing Danny Kirk. I hope it works out."

Mrs. Jenkins's face clouded. "I hope so, too. She can be so willful. And poor little Dewey needs a father. I just hope we don't have to do what the Daileys did and bribe some no account to marry her."

"No worries there. They'll always be lined up to marry Laura."

I took my leave in a discreet twenty minutes and walked home, pondering twists of fate. Laura was free again, in a way. I hoped for her sake she'd make this thing with Danny work out. Even Laura had to be tired of the ups and downs of being Laura. I'd have to wait to talk to her about Snoop, and that bothered me. It gnawed at my gut—thinking about Snoop in the same sentence with Davy.

When I arrived home, the late afternoon was still sticky. Katya was sewing, as usual, seated on the front step. Mama sat in the yard in a straight-backed chair, watching the flowers. I stooped to pick off the dead blooms and feel if the soil needed water. Then I went into the stuffy little house and changed my dress and shoes. I went around back to weed the bed, but my attention was drawn to the Hughes house.

It sat quiet, shades drawn. It could be uninhabited for all I knew. There hadn't been any movement around there in weeks. Sometimes I wondered if Davy had taken his father and gone away. But just as I was about to get back to the weeding, I saw Mr. Hughes step around the side of the house and walk, bent over like an old man—to the shed. I recalled his vitality before the flood—gone now. Nothing left but a shell. I couldn't see from where I knelt in the flower bed, but the shed door must have been open. He stood about a foot in front of it and talked— had a conversation with someone inside. I couldn't take my eyes away.

Then, as routinely as you please, Mr. Hughes turned and went back into his house. Davy must still be living in the shed. He was probably vexed with his father for coming out and talking to him in the broad daylight. He felt so far away, and I was torn between wanting to see him and hoping I'd never see him again. I was sorry I ever let myself go— gave myself to him. His relentless anger backed me off, filled me with regret. I wanted to love him, but I wasn't sure how I felt anymore. Kneeling here, looking out at his house, I wanted to cry.

After a little while I shook off the blues, got up and went around front to talk to Katya on the step. "I'm hoping we can find a lawyer for Istvan."

She stood, holding her sewing against her, excitement in her voice. "We pay. Istvan and me. We have money." Hope brightened her face. How do you describe hope? I didn't know, but I could see it, feel it. Katya radiated it.

I didn't tell her it wasn't likely she had enough saved, or that all the money in the world probably wouldn't help Istvan. "My friend Rob McRae's father's a lawyer. He might know someone."

"My papa out of jail." She said it softly, with resignation.

"He is?" I couldn't keep the surprise out of my voice. This didn't bode well for Istvan.

"Come here today. Tell me I be sorry for go against him. Say Istvan kill Sandor—hang for it." She turned away and wiped her eyes with her apron string. "I scared, Pammie. Scared my papa right. Scared they hang Istvan."

So, that's how it was going to be. They'd blame it all on Istvan. Mr. Pinter would get off when it was his doing that caused the fight in the first place.

"They probably let your father go in exchange for his promise to testify against Istvan." I swatted at a fly crawling over Katya's work. "I hope he stays away from here. If he comes back when I'm here, I'll run him off." The bravado in my voice sounded hollow.

We gathered our things and took Mama inside while Katya finished preparing supper—chicken paprikash. I was so grateful for Katya's help with Mama that I could overlook some of her Hungarian foibles, like firing up the stove on a hot summer day. I fed Mama, then ate in silence while Katya cleaned up the dishes. It was so warm I wondered if I'd be able to sleep. I sat outside reading until the light waned. Then I put my book down and wandered into the back yard, wishing Davy would appear—afraid Davy would appear.

By ten o'clock, Mama and Katya were long asleep, and I was still outside wishing, when a pebble hit my skirt. I peered into the darkness. I waited for him to step out of the shadows, and we moved to precious little privacy behind the house.

"Where've you been?" I asked, holding off his attempts to kiss me. "So much has happened. Where've you been?"

He stood with his shoulders hunched, hands in his pockets. "Not far. I know about Istvan, if that's what you mean."

"What about Snoop Plummer? He told me to warn you to lie low. How does he know about you?"

As he stepped away I felt the distance between us grow.

"I guess I'll have to tell you something. I wish I didn't. The less you know, the less you'll have to lie about."

"What is it, Davy? Tell me!" I couldn't see his face in the darkness, but I could smell that Davy scent that used to be so familiar, so dear.

"I know a little about the South Fork Gang. Some of them, anyway. Snoop is one. He's not as bad as you think."

"Snoop Plummer? Is he the one who's been burning down cottages and throwing bombs?"

"Not that part of it." Davy sank to a squat beside the house and pulled me down beside him. "But he knows who's doing it."

"You, Davy? Is it you? Is that why he's warning you?"

He shook his head. "There are a lot of us. I don't know exactly who's done what. I just know things are getting a little too hot around here, and I have to go away for a while. When I come back, I'll be ready to leave for good and take you with me."

As I was about to reply, my words were interrupted by a scream from inside the house. Katya! And by the sound of it, she was in trouble. I rose and peeked in the window. Katya struggled in the shadowy doorway against a man trying to drag her outside.

Davy and I rushed around to the front as Mr. Pinter hustled a screaming Katya toward the street. Davy ran up behind him and elbowed him hard in the back of the head. Mr. Pinter stumbled to the ground as Katya wrested herself free. Her father was down on all fours, groggy, shaking his head. I grabbed Katya's hand and we ran back in the house. Davy'd already disappeared around back. Mr. Pinter picked himself out of the dirt and brushed himself off. He turned toward the house, shaking his fist.

I went to the window and shouted at him. "Go away, Mr. Pinter, and don't come back. If I ever see you on my property again I'll call the police!"

He turned and stumbled down the street, still groggy from the blow. Lights shone in most of the houses by then. Katya and I went upstairs and sat on her bed in our dark room. I put my arm around her as she cried. "It's all right, Katya. I don't think he'll be back. What's he want with you, anyway? Old Sandor's dead."

"Want me home. Help with kids. Make me marry some other rich old man so he can get money."

My anger at men who view women as property rushed to the surface. "Maybe he'll live long enough to learn a little respect. Maybe not, but at least he'll think twice before he comes around *here* again."

"Who hit him?" she asked.

"I did. I hit him with all my might." I prayed no one saw Davy—that he got away without being recognized and bringing more suspicion down on us.

"*You*, Pammie? How *you* get so strong?"

I made a fist and bent my arm to show her my muscle. We laughed. "I'm as strong as I have to be," I told her.

She smiled and looked beyond me, out the back window. "I think Davy come. Davy the strong one."

Upstairs Mama lay still in her bed, curled up on her side, knees to her chin, paralyzed by the commotion. I went in and sat down beside her and rubbed her back—her muscles tight beneath my touch. It took almost an hour of back rubbing and soothing talk before I felt her relax and drift away to sleep.

I returned to the room I now shared with Katya and undressed in the dark. Both of the windows were open, one in our room and one in Mama's. Both doors were open, too, to let the air flow, but there was little movement. I lay down, pondering Davy's need for revenge. Just as I was about to fall asleep there came a knock at the door.

Chapter 20

I got up and made my way downstairs, carrying a lantern to the door. No one was there, but on the step lay a loosely tied burlap bag with a note attached. I picked it up, straining to read in the lantern light. It said: *Get that Hunkie out of here!* in big crude letters. Something in the bag shifted. Sensing that it was alive, I untied the bag carefully, keeping my hands close to the top. Then I dropped it and watched a big, black snake crawl out and slither across the yard. On the back of the paper was scrawled: *Next time it'll be a copperhead!*

I went back into the house, shaken to my soles. Mama slept on in blissful ignorance, but Katya, aroused from sleep, came downstairs and quickly took stock of the situation, fear in her eyes. "What we do, Pammie? They hurt you because of me?"

I tried to comfort her, but my words sounded hollow in the darkness. I thought of Davy again, keenly aware that he wouldn't be there to protect me every time someone got ugly. He was gone. Maybe for good. His father would probably recover and go back to work at the iron works, and Davy would leave for the west without me. I went back to bed, anxious and full of despair, yearning for sleep that wasn't going to come.

In the morning, my rounds took me into Laura's neighborhood, so I stopped by to see how she was getting on. She came to the door herself, looking pale, but her face was animated and her voice alive with the latest gossip. Same old Laura.

"Don't Snoop and June Plummer look every bit the happy couple?" She sat on the divan in her mother's parlor, looking beautiful—and just a bit conspiratorial. "Snoop isn't driving the coal and ice wagons anymore. He works in the Dailey Company office and has taken to wearing white shirts with stiff collars and sleeve garters."

"Really? I don't have much occasion to see him now that he's off the street. When our paths do cross, he gives me that knowing look, like we're fellow conspirators. Makes my flesh crawl." Davy could trust him if he wanted, but it was too far a stretch for me.

Laura leaned forward with a wink. "Outside of June and Snoop, Danny and I are the talk of the town."

That brought a chuckle from me. Some girls would cringe at the negative attention, but Laura thrived on it. She patted the divan beside her, inviting me to move in closer for her juicy tale. "I was downtown the other day," she said, "and I overheard Mrs. Whithers ask, 'Why would a young man with such a bright future want to go around with one so soiled as that? A common trollop, if you ask me.'" Laura threw back her head and laughed. "She was talking about me. Danny and me. She didn't know I was standing right behind her." Such an experience would have reduced me to tears, but Laura was frankly delighted by it.

I knew why a young man with a bright future wanted Laura. I couldn't name it, but she had an allure men couldn't resist. None of them. Yes, she was pretty, but that wasn't enough to make every man she met fall in love with her. It was the way she made them feel. Like maybe—just maybe—they could have a chance. I swear, Laura never met a man she didn't like, and the more dangerous, the better. Made me wonder whether Danny Kirk had any idea what he was getting into.

We shared a cup of tea and continued our confidences. I couldn't wait to tell her about the snake incident.

"Who do you think it was?" she asked, making a cringing face.

"I don't know, really. I'd suspect Snoop or Mrs. Plummer, but it seems pretty outlandish, even for them. I can't understand why anyone would object to Katya. She works hard, minds her own business and doesn't bother a soul."

"Of course it's that trouble with Istvan. People make up their minds about things like that—no matter what the evidence."

"Well, anybody with eyes could see Istvan was attacked first."

"People believe what they want to believe. Always. No matter what."

Laura was right. I knew it, but I still struggled to believe Istvan still had a chance, somehow.

The next day, at the *Clarion*, I got the official word about the breaking of Rob's engagement. He told me himself—seemed a little brought down by it.

"Guess you've probably heard my betrothed sent me packing."

"Well, yes, I did hear something like that." I wanted to be careful here—this was personal territory.

He checked my reaction before sitting down to type. "Guess everyone in town knows—and the reason why."

"I'm not sure I do, but if it's what I've heard, you're better off following your calling." My face reddened. I'd said too much.

He gave me a questioning look. "What have you heard?"

"Just that she doesn't want to marry a newspaper man."

He sat down at his typewriter and wound a sheet of paper in place. "That's about it. Can you believe it?"

I laughed. "Yes, I can believe it. You'll spend your life pounding a typewriter and running around the county hounding people for news. Sounds like a low profession to me."

"Pounding and hounding, huh? I'd never thought of it that way, but it's a pretty good description. Low profession? You're doing it, aren't you? You and your silly little society column." He was sneering again.

I cast him a warning glance. "Watch what you say, McRae, or you'll be typing your own city hall beat."

He backed off right away. "Sorry."

"Now that's what *I'd* dump you for. Scoffing at women."

"Scoffing?" He turned to me with that innocent, confused look. "What's that supposed to mean?"

"You know very well. Belittling our interests and treating us as though our heads were full of rags. Women read the front page as well as the society news. One of these days, you'll be writing about us getting the vote."

He bent over in his chair, grabbing his head. "Oh, no! Not a suffragette, too! Mr. Shaver! Come out here! You've created a monster."

Mr. Shaver wasn't in his office. I glared at Rob and turned my back, concentrating on my notes. I heard him snickering behind me.

We sat back to back, working our stories. The presses were up to their incessant clacking, and the office was stifling. I wished he'd ask me to go for a sarsaparilla, but he was deep into his work. At about four o'clock I rose and gathered my papers to leave. As I passed his desk I looked over Rob's shoulder at his story. My heart stood still.

"Rob! They've set a date for Istvan's trial? Why didn't you tell me?"

He nodded. "Three weeks. My father found him a lawyer, a young guy from Latrobe. He's been working on the case."

"Does Katya know?"

"About the lawyer? No, I guess not. I don't think he's going to charge much, though. Barely passed the bar exam a couple of weeks ago."

"What do you think of Istvan's chances?"

He shook his head. "Not good, I'm afraid."

I moved toward the door. "Can I go with you to the trial? Sit with you, I mean? Katya and I?"

"Sure. I guess so." He turned back to his story, not anxious to pursue it any more.

Walking home, I worried over Istvan's chances, but as I approached the house I pulled myself together to face Katya.

"Istvan has lawyer? Oh, good! Soon this be over and Istvan and I marry." She beamed at the prospect.

I hadn't the heart to tell her how slim his chances were.

On the day of the trial, Katya wore her best dress and I mine—the one she made for me out of the blue and yellow calico—for the morning ride to Ebensburg in a trap Mr. Shaver had rented, Rob driving. He dropped us off outside the courthouse just before one o'clock and headed to the livery to get the horses taken care of. Katya and I waited on the lawn under some huge old oak trees, grateful for the shade, until Rob returned. He escorted us into the courthouse, an impressive building of brick and stone. Katya gazed up, awed by the structure. Rob led the way to the upstairs courtroom and showed us into the gallery, where some local court watchers had taken up the front row. I glanced around and saw two or three familiar Johnstown faces—Mrs. Plummer—I expected *she'd* be interested—Mr. Elder from the dry goods store, and Ev Dailey, probably here to see how it came out for an immigrant. He hired immigrants from time to time. Ev nodded to Rob but ignored me. Mrs. Plummer looked the other way.

We sat on straight oak chars, behind a railing that separated us from the attorneys and the defendant. The jury, chosen that morning as we drove up from Johnstown, sat in a little, raised gallery to our left. The judge sat on a high bench above the court, looking out over the room with clear authority. Overall, the place was intimidating. Above our heads, four fans on long poles descended from the ceiling in a vain effort to move the air and defy the heat. Rob saw some acquaintances and left to talk to them. When he returned, the trial was about to begin.

A mean looking guard escorted Istvan into the courtroom in shackles. He looked helpless. He'd lost weight and his jail clothes hung on him like old rags. Dull, brown eyes looked out from an unshaven face. To me, he looked as though he was quite aware of how it was for him. His eyes searched the room for Katya, but when he saw her, he looked away. Katya giggled with joy at the sight of him, but his pitiful appearance sunk in, and she drew in her breath. For the rest of the trial she sat beside me in brooding silence.

The proceedings were short. The prosecution stated its case perfunctorily, relying on the testimony of Katya's father—playing the role of the concerned and loving parent—and on a surprise "eye witness:" Mrs. Plummer. I watched as she waddled up to the witness stand and was sworn. She was wearing the same brown dress she always wore—one she probably got from the relief. It might have been stylish once, but now it hung loose about her flabby frame, faded and forlorn. She averted her eyes throughout her testimony, as though she were studying something peculiar on the ceiling. She was afraid to make eye contact with me. I knew she was lying.

"Mrs. Plummer, will you tell the court where you were on the evening of June sixteenth of this year?"

"I was comin' up Bedford Street at about six-thirty in the evening. Home from the Flood Relief Office." She drew herself up to emphasize the importance of her position.

"Did you see or hear anything out of the ordinary on Bedford Street that night?"

"Yes. I did. I saw that Hunkie there fighting with another Hunkie over that Hunkie girl."

Istvan's attorney didn't object to her demeaning language or to speculation by the witness. He sat at the table, fumbling feebly through papers as though absorbed in looking for something. He was young— too young to have someone else's fate in his hands—and untried. If a pale countenance and trembling hands could attest to it, I concluded he was nervous–shaken to his roots by the responsibility. He let the prosecution state its case without so much as raising a finger.

Mrs. Plummer went on as though asked for her take on the Hungarian question. "Don't know how to act around civilized people. Shouldn't even be in our neighborhood. Shame on Pamela Gwynedd for taking her in. No wonder it led to murder. That one . . ." she pointed to Istvan "up and kilt the other one over that Hunkie whore. I seen it. Seen it all."

I couldn't believe what I was hearing. Hunkie whore? What was she saying? And why was this boy-lawyer letting her go on without raising an objection? I looked at Rob, vexed beyond belief. He gave me a warning glance, then went back to taking notes.

The young lawyer, sweating and wiping his brow, accepted Mrs. Plummer's testimony without even cross examining or trying to discredit her. Her satchel full of lies was allowed to stand.

The judge seemed bored with the whole proceeding. He leaned back in his chair, steepled his fingers, closed his eyes. I kept thinking he'd wake up and nudge the defense attorney into action, but he seemed content to let the trial go on at its own pace.

I glanced over at Katya, sure she was getting all of this. She reached frightened fingers and touched my hand.

The boy-lawyer looked to be about nineteen, smooth-faced and uncertain. His effort at defense was hardly worthy of the name. He rose and called Istvan to take the stand. Holding up his hand to take the oath, Istvan sat down in a slump on the witness stand, looking at the floor. I cringed at disaster in the making. Istvan's broken English shored up the prosecution's case. He mumbled through his side of the story, barely audible. He looked like a ruffian, spoke hardly an intelligible word, his grayed and wrinkled shirt soaked with sweat. Why didn't this lawyer prompt him to sit up and look lively? Why wasn't he given a chance to bathe and get a haircut?

Then, as if to add to the mounting evidence of his incompetence, the attorney rested his case without calling a single other witnesses to support it—didn't even call Katya or me to the stand—eye witnesses!

The trial was a sham, and my anger rose with every weak and whining act of incompetence. I scribbled a note to Rob: "Where did your father find this fool?" He shrugged.

The jury was out barely ten minutes. The verdict was read to a hushed courtroom. Guilty of murder in the second degree. Both lawyers approached the bench. We could hear murmuring about "extenuating circumstances." The judge listened very nicely and then sentenced Istvan to ten years in prison.

In front of us, the court regulars murmured their approval. The judge rose and pounded the gavel three times. "Court adjourned." He was out the back door into his chambers before we could move to the aisle.

I caught Mrs. Plummer's eye, but she looked away before I could convey my anger. She turned and hurried out the door, down the wide wooden stairs to the street.

Katya sat quiet ever since Mrs. Plummer took the stand. I didn't know if she really understood all that had been said. But she fully understood Guilty. And ten years. She covered her face with her hands and pushed her way out of the courtroom as though gasping for air. I stood helpless, looking at Rob, shaking my head.

We rode back to Johnstown with hardly a word. Katya sat with her head in her hands, crying, wiping her tears with a once white embroidered handkerchief. I tried to comfort her, but when I put a soothing hand on her back, she stiffened and turned away. What do you say to someone whose life has just been shattered? Things will be all right? This will work out? Hardly.

Rob drove up Bedford Street to drop Katya off at our house and I went back to the *Clarion* office with him to give her time to grieve alone. Rob and I sat down at our desks, our backs to each other again. He hammered out his story, two-finger typing, punching the keys hard. I stared into space, unable or unwilling to believe such a miscarriage of justice. I turned to Rob.

"I suppose that sniveling little rat will expect to be paid for his services."

He shook his head. "I'm sorry, Pam. I don't think my dad expected a performance like that. This must have been his first case. I think his uncle is a friend of Dad's or something. Dad can't know him very well."

I sat with my chin in my hands, wondering what Katya would do now, wondering how Mrs. Plummer could be so hateful and vicious. What had any of us ever done to her?

After five o'clock I walked up Main Street, still full of anger and resignation. When I got home, I expected to find Katya crying on her bed, but she wasn't there. I called, but there was no response. I looked outside. No one was in the yard, front or back. Mama was sitting in her rocker by the stove. There was a fire going and the kettle was steaming away. Dinner was on the back of the stove, smelling like stew. There was bread and butter on the table. I went upstairs—no one—then I looked for the money box under Katya's bed. It was gone, along with her clothes and few meager belongings.

I sat down on my bed and looked around the room. There was no evidence that Katya was ever here. Even her sewing box was gone. The room was bare, the walls plain, the curtains drawn. It was so quiet. I doubted she would go back to her father's house in Cambria City, but I couldn't think of where else she might have gone. My own situation closed in on me. Here I sat with Mama, back to the way it was.

When Katya calls me to the table, my heart is beating as though the trial just happened. I can't tell her that. It'll just upset her to think about it. We eat in relative silence, forks clinking on plates, water glasses ringing against the silverware. Just as we're finishing up, the doorbell rings. Katya goes.

"Well, look who's here," she says in a joyful tone. Only one person brings out that much happiness by just appearing at the door. James.

Chapter 21

*W*hen Katya calls me to the table, my heart is beating as though the trial just happened. I can't tell her that. It'll just upset her to think about it. We eat in relative silence, forks clinking on plates, water glasses ringing against the silverware. Just as we're finishing up, the doorbell rings. Katya goes.

"Well, look who's here," she says in a joyful tone. Only one person brings out that much happiness by just appearing at the door. James.

I wait at the table while Katya and James banter their way into the kitchen.

"I thought I'd see you around my kitchen if I baked a blueberry pie," she tells him.

"Right, as usual, Katya. I smelled it all the way over at my house."

He leans over and kisses me hello, then sits down in his father's place, opposite me.

"To what good fortune do we owe this visit?" I ask.

"Just stopped by to pick up some of Dad's tools. I'm helping out with hobby club this year, and we're collecting tools for the kids to use. Hammers, saws, folding rules, squares. You know. The basics."

"Where does this sudden interest in hobby club come from?"

"Gerald Kirk talked me into it. He did it last year. Said it was kind of fun. Anyway, Dad did it, so I thought I'd continue the family tradition."

Katya chimes in. "I hear they've opened it for girls this year. Teaching them sewing, knitting, embroidery. They asked me to teach a sewing class. Twelve-year-old girls. Told them I would. I'm glad it's not just for the boys anymore."

I give her a look. "This is the first I've heard about it."

Katya places a generous serving of blueberry pie before James, and he attacks it with enthusiasm. "You could take over the world with this pie, Katya."

She smiles and kisses him on top of the head. "And you could take over the world with your flattery."

I watch my son devour the pie, trying not to dwell on the thought that he's all I have left. My parents, three brothers, a husband and a son, all gone. Getting old is hard. I don't want to be a burden to him. I want him to have a good life—his own life—but he *is* all I've got. I think about that big back yard, the house right across the street from the school and picture it full of grandchildren. All of this I keep to myself, waiting, hoping.

"I wonder who else will be teaching the girls classes this year," Katya asks, with a knowing glance at me.

"I guess Kirk has talked Ellen Duncan into teaching knitting," James replies.

Katya smiles.

When James is finished with his pie, he excuses himself to go down to the cellar and gather up some tools. He returns carrying an old wooden toolbox of his father's, hammer and screw drivers sticking out at odd angles. "Guess this will do it. Thanks for the pie."

"Why the hurry, James? Hobby Club doesn't start until after Labor Day." Katya's curiosity prompts her to dig deeper.

"We're having an organizational meeting of all the instructors tomorrow night. Get things set up, plan the projects and get to know each other. See you there, Katya?" He seems interested in the prospect of community service, maybe even just a little excited by it.

Another sly smile from Katya. I suppress a giggle. Maybe she's right. Maybe she does have a sixth sense.

When James is gone, I turn to her. "Well, it looks as though young Mr. Kirk has far reaching influence."

"He certainly has *you* thinking about the past. Maybe if he works at it, he'll be able to turn you around to face the future."

I rise to help her clean up the kitchen. We talk of friends and neighbors and her grandchildren until darkness descends.

"I think I'll go upstairs and read for a while," I tell her.

"Yes. Well, I'll listen to 'Amos 'n Andy' before I set up the kitchen for breakfast."

As soon as I'm in my bedroom, I close the door and settle down in my chair, fully intending to read. But it isn't that easy these days. The past keeps intruding—wants to tell its story, almost as if I were watching a movie.

They transferred Istvan to a prison in Pittsburgh within a week of the trial. I had no idea where Katya had gone, but I feared for her safety. If she went to Pittsburgh, maybe she could find work as a seamstress, but her poor English would certainly limit her options.

She'd more than likely end up in a factory doing piecework for a pittance. I didn't blame her for wanting to get out of Johnstown. For her it had been a hateful place, but losing her changed my life—and not for the better.

I struggled to balance my newspaper work with taking care of Mama. I asked Mary Hanley from across the street to sit with her while I did my rounds. She and Mama were once best friends. It'd been hard for her to watch Mama given over to despair, and she was willing to help when I needed her. Still, I tried not to take advantage. I only asked when I really had to go out.

One fall morning I looked out the front window and saw Rob McRae walking hurriedly up our street. I'd never seen him in this neighborhood before, so I wondered what brought him to my door.

"Rob! What a surprise!"

"Good morning." His tone was abrupt. He wasn't bothering about the niceties. "Mr. Shaver asked me to come get you. If you can find someone to watch out for your mother, we need you at the office."

"Why? What's happened?"

"There's word out of Pittsburgh that one of the South Fork club member's children was hurt. Someone threw a burning torch through a basement window. Landed in a pile of clothes. They handled it, but not before a seven-year-old boy badly burned his hands trying to put it out. Mr. Shaver wants me to go look into it. He needs you to help him get the paper ready for print."

"Are you leaving right away?"

"On the ten o'clock train."

I glanced around the room. Mama was up and dressed and had eaten breakfast, so I could take her across to sit with Mary for a while. "Tell Mr. Shaver I'll be down as soon as I can."

Warming up, he nodded and smiled. "Thanks, Pam. This means a lot." He turned and strode back out to the street, heading toward the depot, strength and resolution in his step. Rob was all business when it came to the *Clarion*. I liked that about him, but I guess it didn't meet with the approval of Miss Halstead.

Five minutes later, I was ready to leave. Mama followed willingly when I told her she was going to see Mary. I took her arm and led her across the street. Mary was waiting at her door, welcoming Mama into her kitchen where the smell of baking bread made the world seem right.

On the way to the *Clarion* office in the crisp October morning, I reflected on how far I'd come in less than a year. I had a real job. I was accepted, even needed, at the *Clarion*. Still, I worried that all of this would slip away unless I could get someone to stay with Mama all the time. Opportunities were opening up for me, and I wanted so much to be able to take advantage of them.

I hadn't seen nor heard from Davy since summer. Funny how he used to occupy almost all my thoughts and now I only thought of him once in a while. He seemed lost to me. I wondered where he was and what he was doing. Thoughts of the burning basement and an injured child sent a chill through me.

Mr. Shaver greeted me warmly and set me to typing copy for the day's edition. I worked my way through pages of local news rather quickly, but as fast as I typed, Mr. Shaver finished another story and added it to the pile. By one o'clock I'd managed to get caught up. Mr. Shaver came out of his office, wiped his brow with his handkerchief, and smiled. "How about some lunch, young lady?"

We walked through a lovely afternoon to the tea room, the acrid smell of autumn leaves in the air. In Johnstown, if you only look up, autumn treats you to a kaleidoscope of color. The hills all around are a mixture of yellow, red, orange, brown, accented here and there by evergreen. I stopped in the street to take it all in, and Mr. Shaver joined me in appreciation of our beautiful part of the world. Johnstown itself may have been gritty, scarred and industrialized, but the world right outside was still a gift.

At the Tea Room we'd missed the noon crowd, and we slipped into a booth in anticipation of a quiet lunch. Mr. Shaver ordered a bowl of their famous corn chowder for each of us. Everyone in Johnstown loved the Tea Room's chowder.

"Have you heard anything from your Hungarian girl?"

I shook my head. "I may never hear from her again."

"Shame for that to happen. They seemed a nice young couple."

"Life is hard enough when you're a native. I can't imagine being as bright as Katya and Istvan and being on the bottom of the ladder. No respect, no money, and not much hope."

Mr. Shaver screwed up his face into a scowl. "You'd be surprised at how far they might come in one generation. I remember when the Germans were the low ones. Or the Irish. First thing you know, they're running things."

I raised a skeptical eyebrow. "If they don't throw you in jail for defending yourself, maybe. I wish now I'd done more to make sure Istvan had a good lawyer."

He leaned toward me across the table, his bushy gray eyebrows drawn close. "It wouldn't have mattered, Pam. Rob tells me that jury's minds were poisoned from the start. Goes clear back to the flood and beyond." He looked around the quiet lunch room, filled with the smell of corn chowder and fresh baked bread. "People were more than happy to believe Mrs. Plummer's testimony. They heard what they wanted to hear. Don't berate yourself."

The waitress brought two steaming bowls of chowder, soda crackers and a small loaf of bread. Mr. Shaver dived into his lunch, but I sat back and gave mine time to cool. I watched Mrs. Early wipe tables and rearrange wire backed chairs.

"Don't you ever get tired of the flood, Mr. Shaver? Don't you wish we could put it behind us forever?"

He sat up from his soup and wiped his mouth on his napkin. "I do. But it's been my experience that these calamities have an almost supernatural hold over peoples' minds." He tore off a piece of bread and slathered it with butter. "I'm not sure you can just decide to get over them. They imprint you. Like the war. Those of us who experienced it were never the same."

I thought of Papa and Harold Shaver, young Johnstown boys marching off to war. Boys. Nothing more. "Is that why men who've been in war don't talk about it?"

Mr. Shaver's brow furrowed. "I guess so. The ones who spout off about their war experiences probably never had any. The ones who really saw the fighting bury it. Too painful."

"I think it's the same with the flood. The people who lost the most don't stand around on street corners telling their stories to all comers." My chowder had cooled, and I took up my spoon, but I leaned in to continue our talk.

Mr. Shaver was with me now. He held his bread at mid-chest, looking thoughtful. "It's best to get it out in the open, no matter what happened, but so many can't do that. There's more than the deaths and injuries. Lot of guilt, too. Guilt about surviving—about things said and unsaid. Some people just can't deal with it." He took a bite of his bread and chewed. "Your mama, for example. When things got too painful, she built herself a cocoon and hid in there, where the world couldn't hurt her anymore."

My eyes filled up, and Mr. Shaver pulled his handkerchief from a pocket and lay it on the table in front of me. "Papa, too. He felt guilty about Geordie. That's why he went away. Just couldn't handle the guilt." I looked out the window of the Tea Room at the autumn afternoon. "I'm not sure it works. Hiding away, I mean. Or running away. I think you have to know what's going on inside your head and make a conscious decision not to let it own you, be it war, flood, or any other disaster."

He shook his head. "Not everyone can do that. It may depend on how old you are when your tragedy comes. If you're young enough—still a child—you can get past it. But if you're coming of age—that coming of age time is crucial. It turns you in a direction and gives you a shove. If you're old . . . well, it has a different effect. You get that helpless feeling, like you're past making a difference." He pushed away from the table. "We'd best be going back."

After he paid the bill, we stepped out into the October sun. It seemed I'd opened a door to his soul. He continued as we walked back to the *Clarion* office. "For my generation, and your pa's, it was the war. I'll wager none of us has really gotten over it. It's always going to be with us. For yours, it'll be the flood."

"I understand, but I don't want it to be that way with me."

"I'm not sure you have a choice."

I thought of Davy, measured his losses against my own. He'd lost more in numbers, to be sure. But I'd lost as much, too, in a way. Davy still had his freedom, and a future if he wanted it. I'd nothing left of either.

"I think I do," I said. "If I decide not to let the flood own me, I can make it happen. But you have to *decide* that. If you don't, it'll take you along with the tide, caught in it forever."

Davy, never far from my conscious thoughts, intruded again. Right now the flood owned both of us, but I couldn't let that be the end of it. I had to struggle against it—make myself waterproof. And Davy, too, if only he'd let me.

I picked up my satchel at the *Clarion* office and started on my rounds for tomorrow's news. As I walked out the door, Mr. Shaver stopped me, "I think you'd do well to start staying at the office and get folks to bring their news to you. People from the outlying towns bring theirs in once a week. You could get the churches to appoint someone to do the same. Get up a form for weddings and engagements. It's getting too big for you to cover it all this way."

I smiled. "If I could get Katya back, I'd be able to do that."

"If you get someone to look after your mother and do this job full time, I'll pay you a living wage. You bring a woman's perspective. This place needs a little tempering sometimes, don't you think?"

I could hardly contain my joy as I made my rounds through the autumn afternoon, pondering the possibilities. Delighted that Mr. Shaver saw me as a credit to the *Clarion,* I saw myself, years hence, editing the paper—even owning it, maybe. A respected editor and community leader, renowned for her clear perspective on the issues of the day. I chuckled aloud at that. Still, there was a new spring in my step as I went about my interviews.

The streets were littered with leaves and horse chestnuts, both having lost their final grasp, blown down by the gusts channeling down the river valleys. The smell of burning leaves filtered through the air as here and there I passed a smoldering pile, carefully tended by some older man with nothing better to do than give nature a hand.

When I got home I put down my satchel, put the kettle on to boil, and went over to Mary Hanley's for Mama. Mary's sweet smile welcomed me. "Thank you so much, Mary. They really did need me down there today."

"You're always welcome, Pam. The poor soul doesn't even know me, but I'm glad to help."

"Sometimes I think she does. Know us, I mean. She's just not ready to come back. I still believe she will, someday."

Mary's smile waned as she let out a sigh. "I think maybe not," she said gently. "I think she's happier there."

I took Mama's hand and led her back across, leaves fluttering by in a race down the street. Those autumn days turned cold as soon as the sun went down. It was a short walk, set to Mama's slow pace. By the time we were across, I was starting to shiver.

As I approached the house I remembered having left the door ajar when I went out. Now, crossing back over, I could see it was shut tight. Maybe the wind . . . I stepped up and turned the knob, but someone had slid the wooden bar in place. With no window in the door, I couldn't see inside. Fear gripped me.

I turned to Mama, speaking carefully in a calm voice. "Here, Mama. Why don't we sit you down out here for a while so you can look at the fall colors?" I turned her so she could see the leaves, and brought her old wooden chair up behind.

All the while, my mind was racing. Who's in the house? Katya? Davy? I went around back, as though gathering firewood, and looked in the window. There stood Davy in the middle of the kitchen, hands clenched, angry, almost menacing. I went around front and tapped for him to open the door.

"What are you doing here?" I almost shouted when he let me in. "Why did you lock me out of my own house?" I stepped up to face him, my eyes ablaze. "Honestly, Davy, I'm getting tired of this!"

"I didn't lock you out. I locked myself in. So no one could come in while you were gone." His tone was flat, nonchalant. "They're looking for me."

I was annoyed by his matter-of-fact manner. "Who's looking for you? What for?"

"The law. They think I threw a torch into a house in Pittsburgh last night."

"Did you?" I fully expected the reply to be yes.

He lowered his eyes. "I might know something about it."

"Davy! Why? What were you thinking?" My pent up frustration finally exploded. "I've had enough."

"I didn't say I did it. I said I might know something about it." Now he was being short with me, annoyed by my show of anger.

"Well, do you? I want the truth. No more evading me. Just tell me what you've got to do with this insanity."

He sat down on my mother's rocking chair. He was unusually dirty and unshaven. It was hard to connect this ragged man with the Davy Hughes I once wanted to marry. He pointed to another chair for me to sit down.

I looked out the window. Mama sat patiently in the yard. It was getting colder. "I can't. I have to bring Mama in."

He looked away in disgust. "Looks like you'll always have to bring Mama in." He shoved his chair back from the table with a sneer.

I awaken with a start, still sitting in my chair, and look out at the street light across the way. Why do I always feel such anguish when I think of Davy? Why haven't I been able to shake that feeling after all these years? Do I still harbor love for him? Or is it just curiosity about what happened to him, where his life led? Now I might have a chance to find out, it's disconcerting—almost upsetting.

I crawl into bed, missing Rob. Wishing he were here to help me through the uncharted paths of aging. His steady hand was exactly what I needed and still do. I wipe away a tear on the corner of my blanket and let myself drift into sleep.

Chapter 22

W e're into summer before we know it, and Katya is already making preparations to spend days and weeks on the farm with her son's family. A truck farm is busy in the summer with customers coming to pick their own vegetables as they come into season. Katya runs the produce shed, helps with the canning and preserving of food, sells her jams and jellies. It's her livelihood, beyond working for me, and it affords her some independence and discretionary funds.

June is seasonally warm, but we know better than to expect a whole summer of moderation. July and August will bring the oppressive heat and humidity that make Johnstown sizzle in the summer. With no one to distract me from my thoughts, I decide to start writing my memories down. It takes the greater part of June to record what I've recalled so far, and by the time July rolls around, with its higher temperatures and humidity that makes you stick to yourself, I've caught up.

Looking back has a strange effect on the mind, especially if you strive to be honest about it all. You wonder if you've misread or unfairly judged. You wonder how things could have been different. Old angers and old hurts well up and take over your thoughts. In remembering how it was, you're faced with the inevitable what might have been. I want to get through this—to come out on the other side with satisfaction that it all turned out for the best. I'm back to that October night in 1892, the last time Davy and I would ever be alone together.

Davy sat on the straight kitchen chair, staring at the floor, while I fetched Mama and got supper ready. He didn't speak, just sat there, looking sullen. I kept busy because I didn't know what to say to him anymore. Well, I did know what to say, but I didn't think he'd be listening. I boiled potatoes and opened a jar of canned green beans Katya put up last year. I cut off some bacon and fried it, filling the house with the smell, then browned the potatoes in the grease.

I no longer felt comfortable with Davy. His demeanor set me on edge, made me anxious. I wanted to find the magic words that would make everything right again, but there didn't seem to be any. I concentrated on making supper to keep from thinking too hard about how I felt, and worse yet, acting on those feelings. How I felt was angry, hurt, disappointed. And even if it wasn't Davy's fault, he was somehow responsible.

I chopped up some of the fried bacon into the beans and put the rest on a plate. Mary Hanley had sent a loaf of her fresh bread home with us, and I sliced off some to eat with butter I'd brought up from town. When the table was set, I led Mama over and nodded to Davy to join us.

He took his time coming to the table—sullen, ill tempered. He watched me feed Mama before I addressed my own meal, then shoved his plate aside. "I guess this is the way it's going to be, then, huh?"

"Yes, Davy. This is the way it is, and will be, unless something changes." I was tired of going over this with him.

He looked away in disgust.

Again the frustration. "Wouldn't you do the same for your own mother? Or your father?"

He looked down at his plate and said, "I've a feeling you'd not be so quick to care for *your* father."

"Yes, I would. If he showed up on my doorstep tomorrow, I'd take him in and care for him, too."

He was eating now, and I wiped Mama's mouth and took up my own fork. She sat quiet, hands in her lap, looking at nothing, but I could tell she was upset by the way her eyes darted here and there, and she gnawed on her lower lip, an old habit.

I looked back at Davy, wanting him to go. He was too wrapped up in his anger. The bond that once joined us was shredded, beaten down. Gone.

I rose and cleared the table, carried the dishes to the basin in the dry sink, and poured hot water over them. I added some Octagon soap powder and picked up a dish cloth, scouring each plate harder than I needed to. Davy sat with his elbows on the table, his head resting on one hand, watching. "Mind if I put out this light? They might be lookin' for me. I'll be goin' time it gets good and dark."

"Where to?"

"I don't know. Back to Pittsburgh, I guess. By the railroad. I'd like to see my pa, but they'll be watchin' his house." He raised his head and studied the ceiling. "Don't know when I'll be back. This might be it for us."

The finality of his words sent a shiver through me. I dried my hands on a towel and went to his side. He rose and reached for me. I went to his arms, still looking for the old feeling, but it was gone. We stood in a loose, silent embrace, unable to bridge the gaping chasm.

"I'm sorry, Davy, but I don't know what to say—what to do to fix us."

He nodded, pulling me closer. "I know. It's the damn flood. Ruined everything." His voice was hoarse. He buried his face in my hair, and I felt a sob shudder through him.

"Davy, don't. We don't have to let the flood own us. We could beat it if we really tried."

His arms dropped and his eyes searched my face in the darkened room. "It's too late, Pam. I'm so full of hate I can't think about anything else."

He sighed and looked again at the ceiling, as though the answer were somehow up there. "Those bastards up on the mountain, with their private club and their private lake, their private hunting grounds, their fish screens. They can do as they please, and when what they please unleashes hell on those down the valley, they can walk away and go on with their lives as if they had nothing to do with it."

He stuffed his hands into his pockets and hunched his shoulders. "I want to make them pay. Make them remember Johnstown every day of their rotten, rich lives."

His bitterness filled the room. I reached for him again in the dark. "Davy! I'm not saying you're wrong. But your hatred will kill you in the end. Nothing you do to them will change anything."

"I told you, Pam. It's too late."

"Have you actually done any of these things they're talking about?"

"Some." His voice sounded flat. Lifeless. "That's why I have to get out of here before they catch me."

I took his hand and raised it to my face, held it against my cheek. He stepped closer and lifted my chin to kiss me—a sweet, warm, gentle kiss, like one we shared three years ago. For those few seconds I wanted to believe we could still beat the flood. But he stepped back with a sense of finality. "Good-bye, Pammie Gwynned. I'll never forget you."

He turned toward the door, looked out both front windows, checking that the street was empty. I heard the door open, saw the pale moonlight on the floor, and he was gone.

I stood there in the dark little hovel, alone again. Forlorn. Forsaken. Was this what it felt like when love died? Like there really *was* no tomorrow? I would mourn. I would grieve. This was not my first bitter life lesson, but it was the most painful because if love can die, so can hope.

The next morning, before I went over to talk with Mary Hanley, I busied myself with the house for the first hour or so, waiting for the town to awaken.

"Mary, I don't want to take advantage of you, but I need your help again today."

"My stars and garters, girl, bring her over anytime," Mary assured me.

"Thank you, Mary. You'll never know how much I appreciate you. I promise to find a caretaker as soon as possible."

When Mama was settled in, content to sit and watch Mary go about her household chores, I started downtown. I walked briskly, wrapping my scarf close against the morning chill. The frost on the roofs glistened like crystals. A wagon rattled along toward me—the police chief and several of his officers, accompanied by two well-dressed strangers. They'd gathered a few curious followers. I stopped, even though I was anxious to get in out of the cold. Rob McRae appeared from the fringes of the crowd and moved to my side.

"You'd better get along to the office, Pam. This looks like it isn't going to be pretty."

"What is it?"

"They've got a warrant to search Mr. Hughes' house." His face was grave.

"Mr. Hughes? Why? He's an old man. What could he do?"

Rob continued. "The two men in suits are Pinkertons. They think Hughes knows something about that torch-throwing incident on Monday."

I stared in disbelief. A shudder of fear for Davy passed through me. He was right. They really were looking for him.

"They arrested Snoop Plummer in Pittsburgh yesterday, and I guess he's been cooperating with them. Says there's a whole gang of Johnstown men involved. Your 'dead' Davy Hughes is one of them *and* his father." He gave me a pat on the shoulder, intended to direct me away from the action, and moved on up the street. "You get down to the *Clarion* office and wait for me. This is big!"

I stood there, dumbfounded, fighting the urge to follow him, terrified for Davy. Surely, he'd left town last night without going to see his father. Still, the need to know was overwhelming. Despite Rob's admonishment I turned and followed the rattling wagon back up Main to Bedford Street, then off to the right on Levergood.

Mr. Hughes' Oklahoma house stood desolate in the middle of a bare yard that was once his beautiful shaded lawn, looking small and vulnerable in the cold morning light. The police chief strode up and pounded on the door hard enough to rattle the window panes. Two of his men swaggered around back to close that escape route. The crowd, grown larger by the excitement, waited in silence, the air clouded by their breath.

The door opened and Mr. Hughes stood in his undershirt, with his suspenders down around his knees, white hair blowing in the morning breeze. He looked calm, almost serene, and he didn't resist as the men handcuffed him and led him out into the yard. I heard them rummaging through everything inside, pushing their way through the tiny house, the sounds of their search grating in my ears.

Someone yanked open the shed door and yelled to the chief to come look. Davy's hiding place was exposed to public view, but to my relief, it was empty. Still, they turned up the mattress on his bed, threw the pillow and blankets on the floor, and shoved everything off the table and shelves.

I watched, shivering, filled with pity for Mr. Hughes. How much could one man take?

The crowd grew even larger as word got around that Mr. Hughes was part of the gang taking revenge against the South Fork Club Members. That stirred them up, Johnstown folk all, and they moved threateningly toward the police chief and the Pinkertons.

"Let him go!" they shouted. "He's an old man. Let him go!" Some of the onlookers picked up rocks. Another grabbed a shovel leaning against the shed.

"Who says he done it? Who says?"

"Yeah! Even if he did, they had it coming!"

The mood was menacing, and the police chief moved to protect his prisoner. He ordered his deputies to draw their guns and, with the Pinkertons, they formed a small circle around Mr. Hughes, who stood in their midst, head bowed.

A shout echoed from inside the house. The crowd moved as one, turning its attention to the doorway where one of the deputies stepped into view. A cry escaped my throat as I saw him dragging someone else out of the house. My heart cried for Davy, but I saw soon enough that it wasn't Davy. *It was my father.*

The crowd stood in hushed confusion. Most of them didn't recognize Papa; his hair was gray, his face unshaven. He looked like a railroad tramp, but I knew him. I looked around and saw Rob standing nearby, taking notes as fast as he could scribble. I ran to him. "Rob! That's my father!"

He stopped writing and looked at me like he didn't understand what I was talking about. "What? What did you say? Whose father?"

"*My* father, Rob! Owen Gwynned. They're arresting him, too!"

I must have looked like desperation in a dress, standing there on the street, watching them shackle my father to Mr. Hughes. My eyes darted from one to the other—two old men, bent and shrunken—not from age, but from shared tragedy. My heart pounded like a trip hammer. I felt a weakness in my stomach that extended down to my knees. I looked around for a place to sit down, but there was no place except the ground.

The police and the Pinkertons pushed their way through the crowd, leading the two prisoners to the waiting wagon. The crowd parted reluctantly, standing a little too close, murmuring epithets and threats. The chief turned to them. "Step back! Step back, now. I warn you, I'll do my duty here. If one of you lays a hand on one of my men or one of these prisoners, I'll shoot." The gravity in his voice left no room for speculation.

A rock hurtled through the air and hit one of the Pinkertons on the side of the head. He reached up and felt the wound, looked at his bloody hand, and raised his gun. Another rock sliced by, barely missing the chief. He fired into the air. "One more rock and somebody's gonna get shot!"

Rob was at my side, his arm around my shoulders, moving me against my will into a space between two houses. He stood in front of me, blocking my view. "You don't need to see this."

I pushed out from behind him, standing on my tiptoes, desperately trying not to miss anything. "Yes I do! He's my father!" Rob extended an arm to block my only escape route, then lowered it enough for me to see.

Slowly, deliberately, they urged the two shackled men into the wagon. The chief and the Pinkertons climbed up and seated themselves around the prisoners. The wagon started and made a slow, laborious turn toward Main Street. The deputies followed, with the crowd moving along behind, anger spreading like a low-lying fog. A chant went up from the crowd, swelling with every heartbeat: "Let them go! Let them go!"

As they passed my vantage point, I pushed my way around Rob to get a full view of my father, sitting on my side of the wagon. He recognized me and raised his unshackled hand in a slight wave. I rushed into the street, running beside the wagon.

"Papa! Papa! Where have you been? Why did you leave us?"

He stared down, his face grave. "Go home, Pammie. Go home to your mother." He turned away, looking down Main Street toward the jail. The wagon kept rolling, and even though I could keep up with it, I stopped, tears streaming down my face.

I felt Rob's hand on my arm, holding me steady. He fished a handkerchief out of his pocket and dabbed my tears. I let myself lean on him as we watched the crowd make its way slowly down the street.

I forgot where I was, who I was with. I gave myself over to misery. Rob held me while I sobbed in anguish. Warring emotions clashed within me. Anger mixed with joy. Relief that my father was alive. Bitterness toward him for leaving. Shame that he was nothing more than a common criminal, destined to spend time in jail.

Rob stood patient in the middle of Levergood Street, his arms around me, stroking my hair. I leaned into him, crying, struggling to regain my self control. People were standing around watching, wondering, but I was past caring what they would think. I just needed to let it all go.

When I'd recovered enough to walk, we made our way down Main Street, past the *Clarion* office, where the door was open but no one was visible. Mr. Shaver must have joined the crowd in the street. I didn't know whether to stay or go. Then I saw Laura walking along with little Dewey on the other side. I released my arm from Rob's and ran across to meet her.

"Laura! Laura! It's my pa. They've taken my pa!"

She looked at me as though I were mad. "What did you say?"

"Davy's pa and my pa! They've arrested them for those crimes against the South Fork Club Members!"

"*Your* Pa? Where'd they find *him*?"

"At Mr. Hughes' house!"

Laura stopped and looked at my tear-streaked face. "Are you all right? Do you want to go inside and sit for a while?" She indicated a small eatery.

"No. I'm all right. Rob has had the worst of it, though."

Laura looked across the street at Rob, watching us from in front of the *Clarion*. She gave him an 'I'll take it from here' wave and tucked my hand over her arm. People moved in the general direction of the jail and we followed. The crowd had swelled to an almost unmanageable size. The police chief stood in the wagon bed, warning them off.

"These men will be jailed until their trial. Back off. Let me do my job."

The deputies helped the two men down from the wagon and into the jail, their shackles clanking as they walked. The door closed behind them with a dreadful finality.

Dewey turned to Laura. "Mama, why they got guns?"

Chapter 23

*I*n summer, when Katya is gone, James stops by more often to check on me. I smile at his attentiveness but attribute it to his need to run things. I don't resist. It's nice to have him around. One July morning he stops on his way to work.

"Where were you yesterday?" I ask, noting his absence from church on Sunday.

"Went to Altoona on the train. Remember? I told you Friday I was thinking about it."

"Oh, yes. How was it? Your visit with Catherine, I mean." Catherine Powers is the closest thing James has to a girl friend. They met in college, and she is now the Director of Nursing at the Altoona Hospital. "What did you do?"

"Went to Lakemont Park for a picnic with some of her friends. The weather was fine, nice day for boating on the lake."

I expect an announcement. Has he finally decided to propose? I shouldn't ask, so I wait. "How is Catherine?"

"She's well. Sends you her best. I won't be seeing her again, though, I'm afraid."

"Really? Why not?"

"I went there to tell her our little romance, if you can call it that, is over." He looks around the kitchen table, coffee cup in hand. "Got any scones, Mother?"

"Yes, in the breadbox. What's this? I thought you were going with a commitment in mind."

He smiles as he butters a scone and takes another drink of his coffee. "I'm sure you did. But—no."

I'm nonplussed. "James! You're turning into an old bachelor. What *are* you thinking?"

"I'm thinking my interests lie in another direction."

I rise and take my coffee cup to the sink to rinse it. "Care to share what direction that will be?" I ask.

"Not just yet, Mother. I have work to do in that direction." He stands and takes a last swig of coffee. "Gotta run. See you later." He kisses my cheek and is out the door before I can ask the next question. I shake my head and go to the mud room to put on my smock. I'm going outside to trim the roses.

It'll be too hot to work in the garden by ten o'clock, so I work quickly, making sure they have enough water and picking off the dead blooms. My mind wrestles with James's announcement. I think I know what other direction his interests lie in, but I wonder how he expects to carry it off. The girl is engaged, after all.

After lunch I go upstairs and spread my yellow, lined tablet and pencils on the library table in what came to be Rob's office. It's comfortable working in there, on the shady side of the house. I can still feel his presence, comforting and saddening at the same time. I only hope James gives himself a chance to feel the joy and the intimacy that a long marriage can give.

I start to write, haltingly at first, but before long I'm back to the old days, remembering. The days after my father reappeared were difficult. I wanted to be happy to have him back, and I was, but his situation overwhelmed me. I wanted nothing more than to make it go away.

Once Papa and Mr. Hughes were safely locked up and no longer a threat to civilized society, the excitement died down. The crowd dwindled as people wandered away to spread the news. New faces came and went, but the furor that accompanied the arrests was over. Back at the *Clarion* I tried to work on my typing, but my mind wouldn't engage; I was dying to go down to the jail and see my father. My chance came after lunch, when Mr. Shaver stopped by my desk, his face drawn.

"I guess you'd like to talk to him, eh, Pammie?"

"Yes, sir. I would."

"Well, come with me. We'll go around the back of the jail. Chief Harris promised he'd let us in."

A block before the jail we turned left into an alley that ran behind the building. Halfway down, in the middle of the block, an armed guard leaned back against the building on a wooden chair, a rifle across his knees. As we approached he lowered his chair and rose to greet us.

Mr. Shaver nodded to him. "Afternoon, Fred. Harris said we could get this girl in to see her pa."

Fred moved quickly to comply. He looked both ways down the alley, then rapped twice against the door with the butt of his rifle. A window in the steel door opened, and Fred mumbled something about Gwynedd's girl. I heard a steel bar slide away, and the door swung open. It was dark inside. The floor, the walls, the ceiling were all constructed of cold, hard, unyielding steel. Our footsteps scraped and echoed in the narrow, empty hall. The cells on either side each had a single, narrow, barred window, high up, but little light penetrated the dirty glass. A slop jar sat in one corner, and the "bed" was a slab of iron suspended from the wall on thick chains.

We moved through the semi-darkness past empty cells, to the two closest to the front door, across from each other. Harold Shaver asked the guard for a chair, and he produced one from around a dark corner. Mr. Shaver pulled it up to the bars of Papa's cell, his back to Mr. Hughes. Papa sat on the bed, hands clasped, elbows on his knees. He looked up, but didn't rise.

"Pammie! I . . . I'm sorry. So sorry for you to know this." His voice faltered.

Tears ran down my face as I reached through the bars for him. He stood and shuffled over, head down, like an old man. Two years since I'd seen him, and he'd aged ten years at least.

"Papa. Why did you go away and leave us like that? Where have you been? I thought you were dead."

He clutched the cold bars, looking at me with a sadness I could barely describe. I'd seen it before—when Jamie and Hugh died, and for days after the flood as he searched for Geordie.

When he spoke, his tone was flat, like someone reciting lines from rote memorization. "Dead to you. I couldn't take it anymore, Pammie. Your mother. I had to do something."

"Do something? What did you do? Bring more ruin on us?" I sank into the chair. Harold Shaver stepped around me, standing close to the cell, peering in at his boyhood friend, old army pal, Friday night checkers partner. "Yes, Owen. What *did* you do?"

Papa looked up at him and sighed. "I don't expect you to understand. The flood hurt your pocketbook, not your heart. I thought the war was as bad as life could get, but even in the war, it wasn't *my* child, *my* wife, *my* own. I looked for him for months, Harold. I couldn't let myself forget I sent him out with a threat to thrash him. Sent him to his death."

"Papa, you don't know that Geordie would have lived anyway. He could have been swept away from us on the way to Green Hill or hurt by debris. You can't blame yourself."

My father raised himself up as tall as he could stand, his knuckles white on the bars, and shouted. "He would have lived! I killed him! Once that sunk in, I didn't care about anything else." His hands clung to the bars, but his body sagged until he was sitting on the floor, leaning against the cage, sobbing. "Why do you think your mother can't face it? She was there. She knows I killed him!"

I reached down and touched his shoulder. He was wearing a thin chambray shirt, and I could feel his aging bones against my hand. No one spoke for a long time. I heard Mr. Hughes's labored breathing behind me. I couldn't look at him. I could barely look at Papa.

What could I say? I was there, too. I heard him order Geordie out into the floodwaters to help old Mrs. Stackpole up to our house. Heard Geordie beg not to have to go. Heard Papa threaten to take his belt off. Papa was halfway up the stairs—he and I—struggling to get Mama's chifforobe to the second floor, out of the rising water. Her piano was destined for ruin, but Mama had salvaged her music from the cabinet, and she stood at the foot of the stairs, holding it against her chest with the glass-footed piano stool in the other hand. Water already seeped in under the front door.

Geordie would have had to wait for his thrashing. Papa was in no position to mete out punishment and would probably have forgotten it. But Geordie went. Head down, wearing Papa's old oilskin, out to the porch and down the flooded steps until he was in water halfway to his knees. He turned and looked back at the house once, then waded slowly down toward Mrs. Stackpole's, halfway down the block. The water deepened as he went, sloshing his way out of our line of vision and out of our lives.

The roar came not five minutes later—like a freight train bearing down on the town. By that time we had the chifforobe upstairs, and Papa came flying down, grabbed Mama by the hand, dragged her outside and up Bedford Street as fast has they could wade through the high water. I was right behind, all of us looking back for Geordie and Mrs. Stackpole, but the street was a river of brown, swirling water, full of debris, empty of anything recognizable except a swarm of people like us, slogging against the current, crippled by fear.

The roaring got louder until it was unbearable, houses crashing into houses, tree trunks cracking, people screaming, and that huge, brown wall of destruction bearing down. We struggled toward Green Hill. All around us people moved—maddeningly slow, achingly distraught. It was unreal—the noise, the faces, the anguish. Even when we reached the hill we stared in disbelief as the whole town floated and crashed, bobbed and receded, floated and crashed again.

It was about four o'clock in the afternoon, but darkness came with the flood. That night on Green Hill was the coldest, most agonizing of my life. The rain came down, unremitting. There was no shelter, no place to go, no relief from the wet cold.

All around us, people tried to help the injured. Mrs. Swanson, the stationmaster's wife, lay a few feet away, her left arm badly mangled. Her husband worked to relieve her pain, but his efforts only resulted in more screams. Farther down the hill, a man I didn't know was laid out, the clothes torn from his body, his scalp ripped from his head, babbling about money he left in a jar. People huddled together for whatever warmth they could make. The hill was alive with voices crying, groaning, murmuring. So many children were separated from their families, filling the night with cries of "Mama! Mama," wandering lost among the mass of injured and dying. Every hour on the hour the clock in the tower of the Lutheran Church tolled, like a death knell.

We could sense rather than see the pile-up at the railroad bridge—buildings, animals, people, indescribable wreckage. Then the fire. The inevitable fire from a hundred kitchen stoves, setting the wreckage aflame, fed by kerosene and spilled oil. It lit up the sky, and we could but sit, huddled on the hillside, watching, numb. Not close enough to hear the cries of the burning, but not far enough away to mistake the blended noises of flood and flame for anything but hell.

I came back to my father, slumped against the bars of a jail cell. "Don't berate yourself, Papa. You couldn't know. You loved Geordie. We all did." I heard myself talking softly to him, still holding onto his shoulder, reaching across the chasm.

Harold Shaver rested his hand on the back of my chair. "See what I was talking about the other day, Pammie? It never lets go."

Papa sat on the floor looking up at me like a child caught in some severe transgression. I couldn't bear to look at his tired, tormented face.

Where was the man I looked up to, the man I thought could right all the wrongs, the man I thought stronger than strong?

He shook his head; his eyes welled up with tears. "I left because I had to. I couldn't stand watching your mother sit there day after day. I tried to talk to her, begged her to come back, but she was too far gone. I doubt we'll ever know her more."

That brought the anger up in me again. "What did you think *I* was going to do with her? Did you ever think of me? Or were you too busy feeling sorry for yourself?" I didn't mean to be hurtful, but the years of poverty, sadness and worry would have their say.

He cringed as though he'd been hit. "Yes, girl. I thought of you. I've thought about little else *but* you since I left. I've tried every way I know to head Davy off his course and turn him back to you. But there was your mother all the time. Your mother."

"How could you ever expect me to leave her? Couldn't you explain that to Davy?"

"Lord knows I tried. A hard head, that one. As mad as *I* was, and then some. Bent on destruction—of himself or the whole South Fork Club."

Harold Shaver stepped up to the bars again, the newspaper man in him coming to the fore. "What'd you have, a whole gang?"

Papa nodded. "Uh huh. They've got the Plummer boy and us, and they know about Davy, but there's more. And when the word gets out, there'll be more again. They'll never stop us."

"Why, Papa? Is it ever going to make any difference? Even if you could kill them all, would it bring Geordie back?"

My father stared at the floor. "Won't bring back what's gone. Might catch some of them up short, though. Make 'em think twice about havin' their pleasure at others' expense." He winced. "Oh, God, I know we can never hurt them like they've hurt us, but I want them to feel *something*."

Harold Shaver stepped back from the bars and crossed his arms. "You're fools, the lot of you. And you're lucky no one was killed in your reprisals. It's bad enough your spite has the whole town talking. You'll probably groom a whole new crop of fools just like yourselves. Shame on you, Owen. You were a better man when you were a boy!"

I rose and turned toward the back door, still unable to look at Mr. Hughes. "I'll probably be back, but I don't know when. I need time to think. You might have wronged Geordie, but you've wronged Mama and me even more. Poor Geordie is dead, but we're still here, and we're still suffering and will more, thanks to you."

I stepped around the chair and made my way toward the door, followed by Mr. Shaver. "Guard! Let us out, please!"

I walked back up the alley, shaking. At the corner, I glanced down the street at the crowd of supporters clustered in front of the jail and shuddered at the way people love to wallow in the muck of hatred, anger and revenge. Children in the crowd. That's right. Teach them to hate, too. Raise up another generation of revenge seekers.

As we walked back to the *Clarion* office, another wagon rattled slowly down the street, armed deputies riding watch at the four corners. Ev Dailey sat bent over on a wide wooden seat, his hands shackled behind him. So that was the connection between him and Snoop Plummer!

We didn't go a half block before we ran into Mrs. Plummer herself, marching up both sides of the sidewalk, her face red, her jaw set. "You, Harold Shaver! You have the power to set them all free. You write the editorials. You command peoples' thoughts. You can say the right words and give me back my son. This is all a lie." Her eyes blazed with denial. "My boy would never do anything to hurt nobody. My Clarence is a good boy! And him with a baby coming! How does that look?"

I wanted to remind her that the baby wasn't Clarence's, but I restrained myself, given the current circumstances. She stood right in front of Mr. Shaver, blocking his way.

He showed no compassion, though. "Your Clarence should have thought of all that before he got himself into this mess, Mrs. Plummer." He raised his cane, brushed past her and continued down the street.

She turned back to me, hurling insults. "And you, Miss High and Mighty. I guess you knew all along what your pa was doing. And your little boyfriend. While *you* were collecting relief. A trollop if I ever saw one!" She moved in front of me, hands on hips, head forward like a banty rooster. I stepped around her and moved on to catch up with Mr. Shaver. She maintained her pose, shouting abuse at my retreating back.

At the office, I slumped into a chair, my face in my hands. I wanted to cry, but no tears would come. Which was stronger, the need to cry in anguish or scream in anger? I couldn't tell. Rob looked up from his typing when we arrived, hands suspended, waiting for the report.

I shook my head, sighed, and pulled out my pad. Meaningless gesture. I'd nothing to write. Even holding a pencil was a task, my hands were shaking so.

Rob stood up, reached over my shoulder and took the pencil from my hand. "Come on. You need to go home." He waited while I gathered my things, then took my hand and led me out the door. He walked along beside me, his hand under my elbow, moving with a resolution I'd come to associate with him. It was a long, silent walk home. Rob asked no questions. I was grateful for that. When we arrived at our doorstep, I turned to thank him.

"Where's your mother?" he asked.

I nodded in the direction of Mrs. Hanley's house across the street.

"Good," he said. "Leave her there for a while. You need some time alone. I'll tell your neighbor to bring her back after supper."

I let him direct me, tell me what to do. My mind was so numb I didn't want to think about anything. I turned away and opened the door. When I turned back, he was already halfway across the yard, heading for Mrs. Hanley's.

"Thanks, Rob," I called.

He turned with a wave of dismissal.

Inside I was greeted by the familiar smell of cabbage soup.

I sank into a chair, shaking with sobs. Katya came over and sat beside me, wrapping her arms around me.

"Sooo, Pammie. Can't be so bad, now. Katya back. Take care of you."

I smile at the remembrance of the joy I felt when Katya came back. Just when I needed her. It felt so right to have a friend to share my anguish —one who knew a little something about anguish herself.

Chapter 24

*T*he afternoon passes quickly as it always does when I'm engaged in reminiscing. By four o'clock, I'm thinking about dinner. With Katya staying out at the farm, I'm on my own, and, to be honest, cooking has never been my favorite endeavor. I don't even think about eating until I'm hungry, and by then it's too late to do much but fry an egg. That's why Katya's and my relationship has worked so well. She loves to cook and fuss over me, and I love to let her.

Sometimes I wonder what I would have done if she hadn't come back to my mother and me that summer. If things had turned out differently. So many things could have. Life is perilous and we don't even know it, going from one day to the next, unaware of the possibilities. At any rate, I was glad to have her back. Words couldn't have expressed my relief and joy.

We sat down to supper, and while I fed Mama, Katya related her adventures. She seemed well and healthy, but the sadness in her eyes spoke of more.

"I go Pittsburgh. Stay with aunt. Try get work, but only piecework. Istvan in jail in Pittsburgh, so I go see." Katya spooned some stew onto her plate and began to eat.

"How is he? It must be awful, being in jail." My thoughts turned to Papa, right that minute sitting in an iron cell. I had a lot to tell Katya.

"Istvan say, go back Johnstown. Come visit on train. Not good do piecework. Say I better than that."

"You are! You could make a tidy living sewing clothes for rich people. Maybe you could even save up enough to buy a sewing machine."

"I live with you now? I stay and make dress?" Her eyes were sad, but she brightened at the mention of a sewing machine.

"Of course, Katya. When you're here I don't have to worry about Mama. I'm so glad to have you back."

Her eyes lit up and she nodded, excited. "Istvan say keep save money. Lawyer no ask for pay yet."

"He's probably embarrassed at the poor defense he made. You might not ever hear from him again."

She smiled, crossing her fingers. "I hope. I sixteen. Istvan twenty-one. We not so old when jail over. We save. Buy land then."

I didn't tell her I doubted they'd make it through ten years in jail. That would have to take care of itself. I was just grateful to have her back, help in sharing my burdens. Now I took a turn and told her about Papa, Mr. Hughes, Davy—all of it.

"Mr. Shaver wants me to start working at the *Clarion* full time. No more tramping the city to get news. People will have to bring it in or send it to us."

I was giddy with joy telling her this. I should have been sad at Papa's predicament, and I was, but here was Katya to help me with Mama, and that meant I could be a real newspaper woman. Rob could laugh at that, but it made me proud.

The next day, at the *Clarion* office, Mr. Shaver directed me to the desk back to back with Rob's and swept a litter of books and papers off the top with a wave of his arm.

"Here you go, young lady! Rob, get my typewriter and bring it out here." He smiled like he was watching a child open Christmas gifts. "You'll need this, now that you're official!"

Rob brought the heavy machine, set it down on the desk and stepped back.

"But, what will *you* use?" I asked Mr. Shaver.

He shook a finger back and forth. "Not to worry, my dear. Gives me an excuse to buy a new one. I love these machines. Best invention known to man, and *you* can manipulate it better than the rest of us, so I defer to you."

I sat down, opened and closed the desk drawers, adjusted the tilt on the oak chair, and slid out the desk extensions.

"Let's put it here," I suggested, pulling out the extension on the left side, and Rob jumped to comply. I put my yellow pads in a side drawer, my pencils in the middle one. Mr. Shaver returned from his office with a calendar—the one the *Clarion* put out every year for its subscribers—and hung it on the wall beside my desk. I planned to bring a vase for flowers and maybe my own mug for coffee.

Rob looked around the changed office. "Hope there's room in here for both of us."

"As long as you don't stomp on my rights," I warned him.

"Me? Stomp? Why, my lady, you must have me confused with some insensitive lout!"

"Experience gives me pause," I told him, with a hint of a smile.

I turned away and began work on my column. Mr. Shaver made one more trip back into his office and returned with two stacked wire baskets that he positioned on the outer corner of my desk. "Copy in—copy out," he said with a wink. He was having as much fun as I was.

The door opened, and Paul McGirk, one of the rural mail carriers, entered amid a gust of chilly October air. He nodded to me and Rob, then turned to Mr. Shaver. "They found some remains downriver, by Nineveh," he announced. "Naught but a skeleton, but they'll try the usual ways to identify it."

Mr. Shaver shook his head with a glance at me. "What was that, Pam? You wanted to be shut of the flood? Won't happen working here, I'm afraid." He turned to Paul. "Bringing it to Johnstown, are they?"

Paul nodded. "The morgue. Guess they'll see what else there is, but I doubt there's anything left, this long. Just thought you'd like to know."

When he left, Rob said, "I'll wander down there tomorrow and have a look. Everybody who's still got someone missing will be trying to lay a claim. Wish there'd be something definite, though. This kind of thing always opens old wounds."

The next afternoon I sat at my typewriter, keeping myself busy waiting for Rob to return from the morgue, apprehensive about this find. I wanted it to be clearly identifiable, so that someone got some peace and the rest of us could go back to our lives. Unidentified bodies still cropped up here and there, would for years. Sometimes I thought they should just bury them and not make them public. But if it was your loved one, you'd want to know, to grieve, to mourn, to say good-bye.

Rob was back just before three o'clock. "Appears to be a young boy." He hung his hat and coat on the clothes tree, rubbing his hands together. "Getting cold out there."

My heart jumped. "How young? A *little* boy?"

"Twelve or so, I'd say, from the size of the shoes."

"Shoes? There are shoes?" Hope, excitement, fear mingled in me.

"What's left of them. And fragments of some kind of old oil cloth. Yellow once."

"Could I . . . Do you think they'd let me . . . you know . . . look at it? The shoes, anyway? And the oil cloth?"

My mind raced. I could see Papa bent over a cobbler's last, fixing Geordie's shoes. High top, leather, farm-boy shoes, with thick, new soles and nail-adorned heels so Geordie wouldn't wear them out so fast. I'd recognize them. And the yellow oil cloth? Papa's old slicker?

Rob frowned. "Maybe the shoes and the oil cloth, but I don't want you to see the skeleton."

"Why not?"

"It'd be too hard. You think you're up for it, but just seeing it could set you back a ways."

"Will you go with me?" I asked.

Without a word he reached for his coat and hat and handed me mine. As we walked across town through autumn leaves, I chattered about Geordie as though I had to tell his story for it be him. Geordie laughing that laugh that crinkled up his face until his eyes were almost shut, freckles dancing across his nose. The little scamp. I tried often to conjure up his face in my mind, but for a long time it eluded me. Would almost come into focus, then fade again. How can you forget what your brother looked like? Sometimes I felt like I was almost there—like if I just had a few more seconds, his face would appear before me, grinning and full of the dickens, but it danced just out of reach.

Rob held my elbow steering me toward the morgue on Railroad Street.

Going there brought back memories of the horrible morgues set up right after the flood. The business of identifying the dead and getting them buried quickly to ward off an epidemic was ghastly.

"Remember the morgues, Rob?" I asked.

"Yeah. Pretty awful."

"I wondered then and I wonder now how anybody could stand that work."

"Some people rise to the call," he replied.

"I marvel at their strength."

He nodded. "Were you downtown right after?"

"Oh, yes. Working for the relief. When I wasn't working in the commissary, I went to every morgue looking for Geordie. Papa did, too. So many were beyond recognition, and some who weren't didn't have any survivors to claim them."

I stepped around a puddle as Rob took my arm again. "I remember one little girl in particular—about five years old. Dressed in a yellow pinafore. It was filthy with mud, but you could tell it was clean and starched before. Lying there on a table in the morgue like she was taking a nap. Nobody knew who she was."

"I was busy keeping records for the Relief Commission, so I missed a lot of the first-hand encounters. When I wasn't there, I was over at the Lime Kiln, rubbing elbows with all those out-of-town reporters."

"I hope you chastised them for some of their made-up stories. Heroism and depravity. Who knew what to believe?"

"I'll say this: I learned to report the facts—no matter who was helped or hurt. Beyond that, don't call it news."

Rob left me standing in the vestibule of the morgue while he went to talk to the coroner. I waited, nervously biting my lip, afraid it'd be Geordie. Afraid it wouldn't. There was a big open room with a couple of offices on the outside walls. Through the glass windows I could see three bare tables. The front-most one had something on it, but I couldn't make out any detail.

Rob was talking to a man in a white coat. They gestured toward me and then Rob came back with a small tagged bundle under his arm. The tag read "personal effects #3323." The oil cloth was tattered and muddy beyond recognition. It might have been yellow once. Could have been Papa's slicker or someone's old table cloth. I looked at the shoes. One sole was ripped away. The leather, stiff and discolored, barely resembled a shoe. I looked closely at the heels. Two neat rows of nails outlined the curve. Papa did that to make them last longer, but lots of papas did that.

Rob placed a steadying hand on my shoulder while I studied the fragments.

"It's too old and rotten. Could be anybody's shoe."

"Right," Rob replied. He waited for me to decide what to do next.

"I want to see the skeleton." My voice was firm.

Rob picked up the bundle and wrapped it again with the tag on the outside. "I don't know, Pam. I'm not sure it's a good idea."

"I need to, Rob. If it's Geordie, I need to know."

"How can you be sure, anyway, looking at bones?"

"Geordie had a chip out of the corner of one of his front teeth, cracked it on a walnut shell. If there's that, along with these other things, it'll be enough."

"Okay, but . . ." He looked into my eyes, straightened his shoulders and took my hand. "Come on."

Inside the morgue, the bones were laid out on the table. I walked toward it, my knees weak, a tingling in my ears. I was afraid to look and unable not to. Rob stayed close. I felt his hand on my arm, but my eyes were only on that table. There it was—a complete skeleton—relief that maybe he died intact—not torn limb from limb as many were. I looked down at the skull. The teeth were all in place, shining white. One of the front teeth had a chip out of the lower corner. I turned to Rob and nodded, holding myself around the waist. The hardest thing I'd ever done—look at Geordie's bones.

Rob put his arm around me, led me into one of the offices and sat me down on a chair in front of a huge oak desk. He knelt beside the chair and took my hands in his. "Go ahead and cry." Gentleness again from one I thought so callous.

I leaned into his shoulder and let my tears flow. Geordie. My little brother. Mama's baby. Gone from us. What must it have been like? The roaring, twisting, grating fury of the flood. I hoped it was quick. Rob handed me his handkerchief and put an arm around my shoulders. I felt his closeness and didn't resist. After a good cry, I pulled myself together, and Rob called the morgue attendant. There was paperwork.

I attended to the details, even down to choosing the undertaker, with Rob standing by. When all was in order, the attendant handed me the bundle of personal effects, and I tucked it under my arm. We went back out into the cold afternoon, and I shivered against the wind and the pain in my heart. Most of the way I was quiet, thinking about Geordie. Thinking about the way we were before and what we had become. Rob stayed close, but let me grieve on my own.

"I wonder if they'll let Papa out to go to the funeral. Do you think?"

"Mr. Shaver could probably swing it if he takes responsibility for him."

When we were back at the *Clarion* office, I turned to Rob at the door. "I don't think I want to go in. I want to go see Papa and then tell Mama."

"Sure. Want me to go with you? You shouldn't be alone."

I turned toward the jail without responding, and Rob followed. I talked about Geordie—remembering him. "We had three pictures, one when he was a baby, one when he was six years old, starting school, and one when he was ten, but they're gone," I mused.

"Funny how pictures turned up in the strangest places after the flood. A picture of a baby floated ten miles down river and came to rest on top of a trunk, like a loving mother placed it there." The memories were painful, but talking was a kind of relief.

"I found a wedding picture face down in the muck, scratched so bad you couldn't read the faces. People collected pictures and pinned them up in public places so the owners could find them."

"Yeah, I remember that," Rob replied. "Sad when you saw pictures of families you knew were gone. No one to claim even the pictures."

It was quiet outside the jail today, but the rumblings of support for the jailed conspirators continued. Here and there a crudely lettered sign was tied to a pole or nailed to a storefront: *Let them go.*

We entered by the front door. The guard at the desk rose and picked up his keys. He unlocked the door to the cells, and Rob and I moved into the dark, cold steel structure that was my father's abode.

He stood at the bars, holding his cup. He'd heard the noise and must have thought it was suppertime. Then he saw me and a questioning look passed over his face.

"Pammie! Oh, thank you, girl, for coming again. I didn't want to leave it at yesterday."

"I'll be by, Papa. I won't walk away and leave you."

"Like I did you, eh, girl?"

I studied his face for a few moments, screwing up my courage. "Papa, they've found a body. Remains, I mean. It's Geordie."

I opened the bundle and showed him the oil cloth and the shoes. There was also a belt buckle I'd overlooked. His face twisted in agony. He nodded. He reached through the bars, took a decayed shoe in his hands and examined the heel.

"Yes. Yes. And the buckle. One of my old belts I cut down for him."

He stepped back to his steel bunk and sat down, head in hands. "Oh, my boy. My poor little boy, sent to his death by his own father."

"Papa, listen. This wasn't your fault. You were trying to help someone. Geordie didn't want to get wet and cold, but he was glad enough to be helping. He wanted nothing if not your approval. He wanted to be a man, just like you."

My father rocked back and forth on the bunk, arms around himself, keening. "My boy. My little boy. My only boy left."

"Isn't it better to know, Papa? Isn't it better to have an answer?"

When he didn't reply, I turned to Rob. "He needs time. I'll come back tomorrow and talk about the arrangements." I gathered the sad little bundle and turned toward the door.

Outside, dusk had settled over the valley. Rob walked me up Main Street to Bedford, shepherding me along toward home, my mind filled with thoughts of Geordie and Papa.

Katya had a lamp lit, so Rob took his leave at the step. He reached down and tilted my face toward his. "Are you sure you're all right, now? Is there anything else I can do?"

I shook my head, thanked him and opened the door, only vaguely aware of his gentle concern.

Mama sat in her usual place by the stove, her hands clasped in her lap. I went over and took one of her hands in both of mine and held it up to my cheek. "Mama, they've found Geordie. Down by Nineveh. He's all gone but the bones, but we can have a funeral now, and a proper burial. It's Geordie, Mama. I'm sure."

She didn't move. No change in expression. No acknowledgment. Then a tear —a real tear this time. Unmistakable. She sat staring at the wood stove. Except for the tear, there was no evidence she'd even heard. I enfolded her in my arms and cried with her.

Chapter 25

Sitting at home, alone in the summer afternoon, I am suddenly taken with the need to go to the cemetery. Go visit him—visit Geordie, and Mama and Papa. They're all there at Grand View. It's barely a mile from our house, and though I pass it often in my comings and goings, I haven't really stopped and thought about them, except for Decoration Day, in years. I get up from my chair and put on my hat, pick up my purse and set out. It's warm for June, and I walk at a fairly steady pace, intent upon my mission.

The Gwynedd family plot is in the oldest part of the cemetery. All of it established just after the flood. I marvel at how fast 50 years can go by—how weathered and old the earliest tombstones have become. There they are, all in a row. Father, Owen, 1840—1910, Mother, Nell 1842–1899, Son, Geordan, 1877–1889. Jamie and Hugh, buried in the old church cemetery down in the town, are gone, their bones washed away by the flood. I can barely remember them. I stand looking at the grassy space under which my family lies, thinking about Geordie—wishing he'd lived to grow up. Memories flood over me, piercing my soul with grief anew. They say time heals all wounds. Yes. Until the next time you let yourself really think about them. The sadness here is for Geordie. How different life might have been if he'd survived. To have a brother to share—not just childhood but all of your life. If I could go over to his house, sit with him on the back porch swing, talk about his garden and his grandchildren, maybe I wouldn't feel so alone. He'd have been there to share all of it—Kenneth, Rob, everything. I feel cheated.

It's getting near to dinner time, so I take myself away, slowly, still thinking about them, remembering Geordie's funeral. My route home takes me past James's house. Not of necessity, but by choice. I like looking at it, imagining it full of grandchildren. Wrong to put so much on your only surviving son, I know. I try to keep it to myself.

As I'm about to cross the street in front of his house, James drives up in his Packard. "What brings you over here?" he asks as he gets out of the car.

"Cemeterying." I tell him. "And you? It isn't even five o'clock yet. Are you playing hookie?"

He smiles. "Can't get anything past you, can I? Came home to get my bathing trunks. Some of us are driving up the Stony Creek to Kirk's cottage for a swim."

"Some of us?'

His smile widens. "Gerald, Ellen, Cynthia and me."

"Cynthia?"

"Gerald's cousin. From Derry. She's visiting his family this week. Friend of Ellen's, too."

I nod as he turns toward his back door, pleased at the company he's keeping, but left to wonder what Miss Ellen Duncan considers proper behavior for an engaged young woman. Oh, well, it's not my place to question. I'm glad enough that she spends any time at all with James. Keeps the glimmer alive.

"You young folks have fun, then," I say as I go on my way.

My thoughts aren't long in turning back to the subject at hand—Geordie's funeral. Finding the skeleton and identifying it were just the beginning.

The next morning I took Mama by the hand and we walked down the street to the Methodist Church through dry, crunching autumn leaves, subdued reminders of their former glory. Katya followed, giving me space to deal with Mama. It was the longest walk Mama'd taken since the flood, and she let me lead her, head down, as though she were blind. But she wasn't blind. That was apparent by the way she knew when to step up on a curb, or aside to avoid a puddle. I noticed, but didn't remark on it. When we got to the church, the sanctuary was cold and the small chapel reserved for private gatherings empty. A simple, pine coffin sat on a bier in front of the altar. Katya sat down in the second row, while I took Mama up to the coffin, our breath fogging in front of us. I wished I had a flower for the coffin. A pot of bronze chrysanthemums sat by the choir loft, left over from Sunday's service. Reading my mind, Katya rose, went over and picked off the biggest, nicest bloom and laid it on the coffin.

I held Mama's hand, rubbing it to warm her. "Geordie's in there, Mama. We'll bury him up at Grand View today. It'll be nice to have him here, so we can go visit him and take flowers on Decoration Day. He's fine now, Mama. He's with God."

She stood there, head down, not responding, and I worried that this news might have sent her farther back into her own world.

We sat down in the creaking front pew on the right. Reverend Snyder entered quietly, Bible in hand, smiling. He'd been through a lot of these services. He patted my hand, nodded to Katya, and touched Mama's shoulder. Then he straightened up and looked toward the back of the chapel. I turned and followed his gaze. There, in the back row sat Mrs. Plummer, eyes down. I wondered what brought her here. We weren't friends before the flood. I doubt that she even knew Geordie. She looked at Katya, gave her head a slight shake, and rearranged her coat. Mr. Shaver and Papa entered and took seats across the aisle from her. Mr. Shaver nodded to her, but Papa didn't seem to take any notice.

I wasn't sure how to handle Mama. I was afraid just seeing Papa would upset her, to say nothing of his arrest. Afraid she'd withdraw even more, I took pains to keep them apart.

"I have to talk to the organist, Mama. You stay with Katya." I left her sitting in the front pew, gazing at nothing.

Papa looked like a tramp. They hadn't given him a chance to take a bath, and his clothes looked like he'd been living in them for months. They'd let him shave, though, and he'd tried to pat down his hair with water.

I nodded to Mrs. Plummer, but she seemed to deliberately avoid looking at me.

"You should stay back here," I told Mr. Shaver and Papa. "This is hard enough for Mama. I don't want to send her farther away." They nodded, and I returned to Mama's side.

Rev. Snyder opened his Bible and stood in front of us, ready to begin. "I hope you don't mind, Pammie, but I've asked my daughter to play a hymn before we start."

I nodded, and the strains of "Beyond the Sunset" filled the chapel— a touching hymn, and a favorite of Mama's. I glanced sideways and saw her fingers move to the rhythm almost as though she were playing the piano.

When the music was done, Rev. Snyder proceeded with a brief service for Geordan Gwynedd, beloved son of Owen and Nell, beloved brother of Pamela. It was unutterably sad, and yet it brought relief. I was soon lost in my memories of Geordie. A toddler carrying a soft blanket with him everywhere he went, a six-year-old off to his first day of school, so proud of his new satchel, a ten-year-old robbing the neighbor's pear tree, filling his shirt so full of ripe pears he couldn't squeeze under the fence. Pear sauce. And always the wide grin, the ready laugh, the mischief.

When the brief service was over, I shepherded Mama past the coffin to the minister's office to give Papa time alone with what was left of Geordie. When I looked back into the church, Mrs. Plummer was gone.

Mr. Shaver, leaning on his cane, supported Papa's arm, leading him along much as I led Mama. Through the partially open door I watched Papa stand by the coffin, head bowed. As he touched it, tears streamed down his face. My heart ached for him, still ridden by guilt. I hoped some day he could know Geordie's death wasn't his fault. As Mr. Shaver led Papa out the back door, two volunteers from Rev. Snyder's congregation lifted the pathetic, light burden and carried it to the waiting horse-drawn hearse. One of them handed me the chrysanthemum, and Katya, Mama and I followed the coffin out of the church. Papa and Mr. Shaver were gone around the side of the building by the time we got outside, and Mrs. Plummer was nowhere in sight. I wondered why she even came.

Mama walked along beside me, head down, watching her feet, as I held onto her arm. How much of this did she understand? What, if anything, was she thinking? Her face offered no clue.

I'd hired a hansom to take us to the cemetery, and the pall bearers loaded the pine coffin onto the sleek, black hearse, fancy beyond description. I was struck by the irony of Geordie's last ride. He would have loved it.

At the cemetery, high on a windy hill above the city, we descended from the cab and stood beside the open grave in the cold October sunshine. In the distance, near the Flood Memorial, Papa and Mr. Shaver shivered against the cold wind. I sensed someone to my left, and as I turned, Rob McRae stepped up beside me. He took my arm and bowed his head as Rev. Snyder said a brief prayer and dropped a handful of dirt on top of the sad little wooden box.

I let go of my flower and watched it drift down onto the coffin, biting my lip to keep back the tears. I didn't want to upset Mama. Katya stood a little behind us, to the left, ready to help when needed. The cemetery men waited politely for us to be gone so they could finish and get back to the tool house for some hot coffee. I turned to Rob, reached for his hand—someone to lean on. "Thank you for coming."

He nodded and gave me a few seconds to gather my senses. Geordie. Gone. No doubt now. My only brother. In spite of my efforts, the tears made their way slowly down my cheeks. Rob, patient, took Mama's hand and led her away from the grave. She looked up as though she knew him and followed like an obedient child, Katya just behind. I stood by myself for one last moment with Geordie before turning away. As I did so, I saw Mrs. Plummer standing alone a few rows away. She didn't wave or acknowledge me—just stood there, watching as Rob shepherded us back to our cab.

"Ride with us?" I asked Rob as he tucked a lap robe around mama's knees.

"Sure." He pulled himself up into the seat and signaled the driver to go. The ride down the hill was slow because it was so steep. The driver kept a steady hand on the wooden brake. I sat beside Mama, across from Rob and Katya, lost in memories.

At home, I settled Mama into her chair, took off my best dress and changed into my workaday clothes. Katya was busily sewing and cooking; the house was alive with the smell of paprika, onions and garlic. Life goes on.

Mr. Shaver was already back in his office when I got to the *Clarion*. "Your father needs you, too, you know. You should go down to the jail and talk to him. He's devastated by all this. I went through the whole war with him, and I've never seen him so distraught."

"I know, Mr. Shaver. Thank you for bringing him to the funeral. I wanted to talk to him this morning, but I was afraid it was too much for Mama."

"You're right, of course. But do make time to visit him. The man's lost in despair. He'd kill himself if he had the wherewithal today."

I shuddered. Just what I needed. *Two* helpless parents and no place to turn. Then, ashamed, I replied, "I'll go after work." I couldn't call up any more enthusiasm than that.

The afternoon passed quietly. I had a lot of typing to do, and Rob was gone somewhere on a story. It gave me a chance to make up for the morning's absence.

Just before five o'clock, Rob burst in, rubbing his hands together from the cold. I shot him a critical look. "If you wore gloves you wouldn't have that problem."

"Can't hold a pencil with gloves on." Shivering, he sat down in front of his typewriter.

"Thank you for coming this morning."

He nodded, almost absently. "You're welcome. Nothing less to be expected." Then he turned and looked squarely at me. "I have some news you aren't going to like."

"What?" I waited, tense.

"They arrested Davy Hughes in Pittsburgh last night. He'll wait there to be tried with his father and yours. Along with Ev Dailey and Snoop Plummer, of course."

He wasn't exactly gloating, but I thought I could hear a tone of satisfaction that made me bristle. "I suppose that makes you happy. Knowing you were right about Davy."

He turned to his typewriter. "No. It doesn't make me happy or sad. It just *is*. I thought you'd like to know, in case you wanted to write to him or something."

I turned back to my work, waiting for some feeling to arise. None did. It was almost as though my Davy was dead and this other Davy an imposter. Oh, I'd write to him, I supposed. But I was past caring beyond the hope that somehow he'd get his life back together. No more dreams of shared happiness. No more hope that somehow my old Davy would come back. And yet it hurt. Ached. Wouldn't let me go without one last twinge of bittersweet memory.

"Yes. Thanks. I guess I should."

Behind me Rob pounded hard on his typewriter, beating up the keys with barely disguised hostility.

I was glad when the workday ended and everyone went home. I thought I was the last to leave, and instead of turning up Main Street toward Bedford, I turned left and walked down to the jail, the cold wind cutting my face. No snow yet, but threatening every day. Papa, Ev

Dailey and Mr. Hughes were the only prisoners. Snoop and Davy probably had better accommodations in Pittsburgh, though not much.

It was hard to talk to Papa with Ev and Mr. Hughes so close by. They engaged themselves in a card game to ease my discomfort, but I still couldn't bring myself to discuss intimacies—Mama, Geordie, me.

I did my best to comfort him—held his hand through the bars. "Mama's making progress, Papa. I see little signs of it every day. I hope after all this is over, you can come home and then maybe she'll be able to get better."

"I will, if they let me. I guess there'll be jail time. The others have hired a Pittsburgh lawyer to speak for all of us."

I hoped he'd get a better defense than Istvan did. "If you get jail, it might not be very long. Public opinion's on your side. They'd break you out of this place if they could."

A rueful smile crossed his face. "I had to do it, you know. I couldn't live with myself, knowing how little responsibility they took."

"How can you hold club members accountable, Papa? They didn't know the dam was faulty."

"Some did. Talk was of the dam failing for years. Any one of them could have insisted on inspection and repair."

I sat on a straight-back wooden chair in the corridor between the cells. I'd heard it all before. What if, who should have, why . . .? I changed the subject to talk about Geordie's service. Relief at knowing where he was.

Papa nodded and wiped away a tear. Ev Dailey and Mr. Hughes continued playing cards through the bars, talking quietly to fill up the silence. Suddenly, my whole situation bore down on me and I wanted to scream, cry, pour out my anguish, collapse in a heap—all the things a girl was supposed to do when life got to be too much. Maybe some day, but not that day. I forced myself back to the problems at hand.

"Would you like me to bring you something to read, Papa?"

"Yes. Yes, that would be nice."

I felt a strong desire to be gone, to put some space between my papa and me. "I'll come by to see you after work tomorrow," I assured him. "I'll bring you the newspaper." I rose and moved toward the door, glancing back at my father, sitting on his steel plank bed, head down. How much longer could I bear the burden of two shattered parents? Damn the flood.

It was a long walk home through the cold October evening. The house looked warm and almost cheerful as I approached. I could smell Katya's cooking out in the street, and it made my mouth water. As I crossed the yard someone stepped out of the shadows into my path.

"Been to the jail, have you?" It was Mrs. Plummer, her gray hair standing out in wisps, her face sagging, almost like she'd had a stroke.

"Mrs. Plummer. Thank you for coming to the funeral. That was kind of you."

She continued without acknowledging my thanks. "Least you can *see* your pa. They're keeping my boy, Clarence, in Pittsburgh. Him and your Davy Hughes." She stood squarely in front of me, blocking my path. Her face was drawn, almost menacing.

"I'm sorry I didn't get to talk to you this morning. It really was nice of you to come."

Again no response.

"Guess you're proud of Davy Hughes, then. And yer Pa. All of 'em. Heroes, every one. Brave enough to do what everyone else thinks should be done."

She stood too close, her breath coming out in clouds. I looked down at her feet, clad in a pair of old castoff rubber boots, and my sympathy was aroused. Snoop was all she had, and now she had to share him with a wife and wait for him to get out of jail. Respectability was slipping out of reach.

"It's that Ev Dailey's fault." She shivered in the cold. "I wish Clarence'd never started to work for him. None of this would have happened but for him. None of it." She brushed away a tear, which I thought might freeze on her face. "Gettin' him to marry that June of his, like she was some kind of catch and not used goods."

Her words were random, disjointed, like she wasn't altogether there. I still didn't know what made her come to the funeral—or even how she found out about it.

"Mrs. Plummer, come inside with me. We can sit down to a nice, hot supper and talk. It smells like Katya's made cabbage rolls." I reached for her arm, but she pulled away, almost making me fall.

"No! I ain't eating none of that Hunkie girl's cooking! You know what folks are saying about you? They're saying you're bringing down the neighborhood, letting any Hunkie stay with you just so's you can go off and be a career woman. Any self-respecting woman would stay home, take care of her own mother and wait for a decent man to come along."

I drew back. The poor woman was so distraught, she didn't know what she was saying. But I was distraught, too. All I wanted was to get warm, eat supper and go to sleep. I wanted this day behind me. Stepping around her, I stumbled up the hard path to the door.

"Bet Davy Hughes could tell a tale or two about you, too, dearie. Laying around with him and pretending you didn't know he was alive. My Clarence saw you, more'n once. We'll see what the town thinks of you once that gets around. You ain't no better'n your friend Laura Jenkins! Trollops! Both of you!"

I hurried inside, closed the door firmly and took off my wraps. Mama and Katya had already eaten, so I sat down to a plate of stuffed cabbage, still upset by the Mrs. Plummer's harangue. No use to talk to Katya about her. Katya had every reason to despise her.

I made a conscious effort to eat slowly, giving my emotions a chance to subside. There was nothing to do but clean up the dishes, set the pot of cabbage rolls outside on the step for the night and go to bed. Katya took care of the domestic chores while I got Mama settled.

When I lay down I listened for Mama's regular breathing, and Katya's. Both were deep in sleep long before I could let go of this day. Goodbye, Geordie. Goodbye, Davy. Goodbye, dreams.

Chapter 26

By the time I get home from my walk to the cemetery, daylight is fading. I open the refrigerator and look for something quick and easy. I cut up a salad and take it out on the back porch. I miss Katya. Think I'll go out to the farm for a visit tomorrow. Tell her about the latest developments in James's love life. I chuckle at the thought of James even having a love life, but then I guess most mothers have a hard time imagining their sons as lovers. I wash my dishes and climb the stairs to my bedroom. *Smokefires in Schoharie* occupies me for an hour or more, but I drift off to sleep before nine o'clock.

The next morning dawns a little dreary, but we need rain, so I accept the clouds. I wanted a sunny day to go visit Katya, but she'll have less to do if it rains. More time to talk. I'm pouring myself a second cup of coffee when the front door opens and James steps in. "Good morning, Mother. Seems we're seeing a lot of each other these days."

I smile, always glad to share a few minutes of his time. "Yes. That's nice." I pour his coffee. "How did the swimming go?"

"Cold. Too early for the Stony Creek. July and August are better."

"I meant the company, not the water."

He casts me a knowing glance. "Oh, that. That went well. Warmer than the water."

"Really? Did you and Miss Cynthia get on?"

He smiles widely. "No, Mother. I'm not interested in Cynthia. You know that. Just come out and ask what you want to know."

"What I want to know is, what are you and Ellen Duncan up to? Doesn't the fact that she's engaged deter you?"

"It does, but only up to the point where she realizes that she's making a mistake. How's that going to happen if she never gets to know me?"

I get up to clear the table. "You sound like Katya. So sure of yourself. I'd wait for the breakup if you're so sure it's coming. No need to get ahead of yourself." Dishes clatter into the sink. I'm not comfortable with the way this younger generation does things.

James rises, takes a last sip of coffee, and puts his mug down on the table. "Gotta run, Mom. Don't worry. She's going to Pittsburgh this weekend to see her intended. If I get lucky, she'll find him dull compared to me."

I laugh at that. "You can hope!"

Before I know it he's gone—off to the *Clarion* and the little world he's carved out for himself down there. I can relate to that. I gather my purse and a cloth bag for the produce Katya will send home with me. The walk to the incline is pleasant, though a bit dreary. It isn't really raining yet. Just thinking about it. I board the bus for the ride down. The bus rides the incline like a tram car, all the way to the bottom where it drives off and up to the park. That's where I transfer to a bus that goes out to Geistown where I can walk the half mile from the end of the bus line to Katya's farm. Walking along in the morning gloom, I take myself right back to the old days, give myself over to memories again. Mrs. Plummer was a puzzle back then. A mother's love for her son was something I could understand now, but then . . .

The next day was Saturday, and I awakened early and lay abed pondering Mrs. Plummer's bitterness. As dawn cast its first light on the room I rose and splashed cold water on my face from the pitcher on the washstand. It wasn't frozen yet, but in a week or two it would be that cold. I shivered at the thought of spending another winter in this tiny, drafty house.

I could have slept in—no reason to get up—but I was restless. Might as well get up and move around. I dressed quickly, trying to keep my thoughts of Mrs. Plummer at bay. I loved my work, and it hurt to think that some people might see me as selfish. Katya stirred in her sleep, and I slipped quietly down the stairs and out the door into the cold October morning. I didn't really have a destination. It was too early to shop or visit, so I found myself walking the old familiar route to the *Clarion*.

Down Main Street, toward Franklin, I sensed someone walking on the other side of the street, a little behind me. I looked around to see Rob, on his way to the office. His parents lived on Jackson Street near Locust then. He worked on Saturdays, even though he didn't have to. He'd probably have worked Sundays if Mr. Shaver had let him. No wonder Katherine Halstead sent him packing. I stopped and waited for him to cross and catch up with me.

"You going to work on a Saturday?" he asked.

"Uh huh," I lied, "I have a story to work on."

He raised his eyebrows, but continued. "Did you see your father after work yesterday?"

"Yes, but we didn't have much to say to each other. He's lost." After a few steps I decided to confide in him. "Mrs. Plummer is acting strange."

He laughed. "How can you tell?"

"I don't know why she came to the funeral. Then she accosted me in my yard as I was going home last night."

"Probably just upset about Snoop. Who knows what motivates old women?"

We walked along for almost a block before Rob broke the silence. "Guess I'll be going to Pittsburgh for the trial. Soon as they set a date."

"I'd go, too, but I don't know how I'd arrange it. Mama and Katya might be all right without me, but with you gone, I don't know how Mr. Shaver would get the paper out."

More walking in silence. The town was waking up. The milk wagon rattled through its rounds, here and there women swept porches in the gray morning. Lights showed in some of the stores. We passed Mr. Marchetti's produce wagon, and Rob picked up two apples and flipped a coin into the vendor's palm. He handed one to me and pocketed the other. "Mid-morning snack."

"Snack? It'll be breakfast for me."

He grinned. "I have something else in mind for that." He guided me into the café on the corner of Main and Walnut Streets. We sat down at a table for two and were soon facing heaping plates of eggs, bacon and toasted homemade bread. The smells took me back to our house before the flood. Mama cooking breakfast. Me getting ready for school, wrapped up in thoughts of Davy Hughes, Papa shaving at a tiny mirror above the kitchen sink. Geordie sitting at the table, head down, barely awake, staring sullenly at his plate. Geordie wasn't a morning person. In that moment, his face came back to me—as clear as if he was there. I smiled.

Rob and I soaked up the warmth, along with his coffee and my tea. I look around and realized that apart from Mrs. Muller, whose husband operated the café, I was the only woman present. Again, the fear that people would judge me as too ambitious. Rob rose to pay the bill, and I reached for my purse.

He shook his head. "I can't let a lady pay for breakfast."

I smiled and thanked him. He could be almost gallant at times. Other times, he was as irritating as a splinter. I'd settle for gallant.

We arrived at the *Clarion* and I sat down at my typewriter and pretended interest in a story while Rob stoked up a fire in the pot-bellied stove that huffed and puffed in a valiant effort to ward off the cold. I typed a few words, but my fingers were stiff, almost brittle, in the cold room. I could see my breath.

We'd been working for about twenty minutes when Mr. Shaver came in, took off his coat, and warmed his hands at the stove. He gave me a questioning look and entered his office, where we heard him rattling away at the typewriter. In a few minutes he returned, motioned to Rob and shut the door. Strange. He rarely closed his door. I tended to my typing, dying of curiosity.

In a few minutes, Rob came back and sat down at his typewriter, rifling through hastily scribbled notes. "You'll never believe this one. Snoop Plummer's getting out of jail today."

"Why? I thought he was one of the gang."

"Me, too, but Mr. Shaver has it over the wire that he was working for the Pinkertons and helped them crack the case. Named everybody, including his father-in-law."

I stared in disbelief. "Well, who would have thought? Are you sure, Rob? I hope he doesn't intend to come back to Johnstown. He'd be lynched in five minutes!"

I thought about Mrs. Plummer, even more defensive now that her boy Clarence had shown his true colors. And June. If I were her, I'd see about getting a divorce. I'd be darned if I'd stay married to a man who was responsible for putting my father in jail, right or wrong.

Rob spun around in his chair to face me. "You never did like old Snoop, did you?"

I shook my head. "He made me uncomfortable, all hunched over and looking sideways. I wasn't the only one. Wait until Laura hears about this."

I glanced at the clock. Nine-thirty. I hoped it wasn't too early for a visit. I rose and put on my coat. "I'm done here. Think I'll go see her."

The Jenkins house. modest and middle class, sat on the corner of Willow and Franklin Streets, smoke rising from the chimney. I rang the bell, hoping for Laura and not her mother. I got my wish.

"Pam Gwynedd! Where have you been?" She was dressed in a soft flannel wrapper, her hair still askew from sleep.

"I could ask you the same thing." She led the way into the kitchen where we sat at the table. The house was quiet.

"Where's Dewey?"

"My parents got up early and took him to my uncle's farm to pick out a pumpkin for Halloween."

"I just had to come tell you the latest news." I broke into the Snoop Plummer story as Laura poured tea, listening intently.

Her response was quick. "I hope they paid him well. He won't be able to hide in Cambria *or* Allegheny County once this breaks."

"Why do you think he'd do something like that? What did he think it would get him?"

"Respect, my dear. A sense of his own importance. Snoop doesn't get that anywhere else. That and money."

Then I remembered my encounter with his mother. "Poor Mrs. Plummer. She's always had lace curtains in front of her eyes where her Clarence was concerned. I hope he's prepared to take care of her now that he has money. That poor woman won't be able to show her face in this town anymore."

"People have been ostracized for a lot less," Laura said with a laugh, clearly thinking about her own status in the community. "Anyway, how do *you* feel about this? He's turned in *your* father, too."

I hesitated, sorting out my thoughts. "I don't like his reasons for it, but I thought my father was dead, so in a sense, he's given him back to me. Some good might come of it if they don't give Papa a sentence to die in jail."

"No doubt they'll be found guilty. Depends on how hard the upper crust wants to push. People around here will be so mad, it could lead to worse than what's already happened, so maybe the court'll ease up a little."

Laura got up to pour more tea. "Say, how'd you like to take a ride with me up to Westmont? I want to show you our new house. Danny's and mine."

"You have a house?" My napkin slipped off my lap and I bent over to pick it up, my face burning. How did Laura always manage to come out of her adventures in the pink?

"Yes. Brand new. You know how they're building up there. Well, Danny bought a lot and had a house built for us. We're moving in right after our wedding. Did I tell you we've set the date? January 25th."

A lot of information at once. Laura and I hadn't talked in a while, but this was more than I expected. "January 25th. My mother's birthday? How nice for you."

I said it, but I didn't really feel it. I'd always struggled with jealousy for Laura. New husband, new house. Everything the way she wanted it, and here I was still living in an Oklahoma house with a mother lost in her own world and a father sitting in jail, to say nothing of a former fiancé who might as well be dead. I tried to be gracious, but Laura's good fortune tasted like bile. All right, Pamela, enough self pity.

Laura was already putting on her coat, handing mine to me. "We can ride up on the incline. It's just a short walk from there—on Bucknell Avenue."

Westmont was a new development then—up on Yoder Hill, across the Stoney Creek. High above the old town, away from fear of flood, it was part upper class, part working class. The dinner side of town and the supper side of town, divided by the trolley line.

Swept along by Laura's enthusiasm we walked down to the incline and paid our fare. The ride up the mountainside was breathtaking. You could see the whole valley below, Johnstown after the flood, rebuilt and rebuilding. I couldn't help but marvel at the beauty of the Y-shaped valley, surrounded by forests and hills on top of hills. At the top, we walked a couple of blocks to Bucknell Avenue where a neat cottage sat in the middle of a large lot. Trees had already been planted, and a brick sidewalk led to the door.

"I have to choose curtains for the bedrooms," Laura told me as she turned the key in the door. She led me through the bare rooms, excitedly pointing out where this or that piece of furniture would be. Now I really struggled with envy. Why should she be so privileged? Weren't there any wages of sin? Why didn't I just go out and make myself the talk of the town and see what it got me?

My silence wasn't lost on Laura. She stopped her chatter. "Oh my, Pam, I'm sorry. I just remembered I have to meet Mrs. Stapley at the dry goods store to pick out my fabric. She's making the curtains for me."

We rode back down the incline, quiet. At the bottom I gave her a half-hearted hug and started up along the Stony Creek without looking back. No need to explain. She knew me well enough to get it, even if she didn't completely understand. I needed to be alone. It didn't matter where.

When the late afternoon paper went out, the talk in the streets was all about Snoop Plummer. I'd have been surprised if someone didn't go to his mother's house and harass her. I'd walked off my low feelings, and by four o'clock I headed down Main Street to the jail. People looked at me as though I was a celebrity and stepped aside as I passed, talking behind their hands.

The jail was quiet. The guard on duty let me into the back without comment. The inmates hadn't heard the news yet, but it didn't come as any surprise.

"I shoulda knowed better than to take up with that sniveling little weasel," Ev Dailey said. "Lost my sense when that young swell got my June in a family way and then took off. She into cryin' and moanin' about the baby not havin' a name. Well, its name won't be Plummer now, that's for sure."

Mr. Hughes and Papa were older than Ev Dailey by a decade or more, and neither had much property, so they had less to be in a temper about.

I turned to Papa. "It'll probably go hard with you, with Snoop's testimony."

He nodded. "I don't doubt."

"If you ever do get out, where'll you go?"

"Like to come home to you and your mother. Don't know how much good I can do, but I owe it to her—and you—to try."

I was pleased by the sentiment, but skepticism stalked my brain. From here it looked like he'd be in jail a good long time. Too long to be much help.

"I can't believe you gave Snoop Plummer the time of day, Papa. You used to say he was a snake. You were right. What made you want to trust him?"

"I didn't come into it until things were under way. Davy Hughes was the main one. Him and Ev did most of it. I wandered back from Altoona looking for a warm place to sleep and Hughes took me in."

He sat on the edge of his bunk, elbows on his knees. "I just helped plan and hid Davy once in a while. There's a cave upriver a ways. He'd hide out there, and I'd carry him provisions at night. I meant to come home, but. . . . couldn't bring myself to face your mother."

He studied the backs of his hands, which hung drooping between his knees. "Ev thought Snoop'd be loyal because of June, so he urged us to let him in. Davy didn't like him, either. Kept him out of the inner workings. That's why it took him a long time to get enough to turn on us."

I listened to my father, unable to believe he'd let himself get involved in such crimes and that he'd let others' opinions go against his better judgment. But I didn't know him anymore. Maybe I never had.

"Your mother, Pammie. How is she, really? Do you think she'd know me?"

"Sometimes I think she knows everything that goes on. Just doesn't want to be part of it. I see signs of her coming out of it. Get my hopes up, but then she'll go for months with no change. She's docile—goes wherever I lead her, but doesn't try to do anything for herself."

He listened, nodding. "Same as before I left."

"No. Better. But not enough to build much hope on. Still, now and then she'll do something that gives me pause. One night she said Geordie's name."

He looked down at the floor. "I was getting real close to coming home when this came up. Now I don't know. Depends on how much jail time there is."

I didn't tell him I thought it would be a very long time before he could come home. I didn't need to. He knew.

"I hope this lawyer they've hired is a good one." I launched into the whole long story about Katya and Istvan and how poorly he was defended. Papa listened with interest, apparently glad to have something else to think about.

The guard came in with three tin trays, my signal to be on my way. "Good-bye, Papa." There was a catch in my voice as I turned to leave. I nodded to Ev Dailey and Mr. Hughes.

"I'll probably be seeing Davy when they take us to Pittsburgh. Anything you want me to tell him?" Mr. Hughes asked, hope in his voice.

"No. Tell him . . . Tell him I'll write to him." It came out flat, without feeling.

Mr. Hughes nodded and sat down at a checkerboard he and Ev had on the floor, split under the bars. I turned to my father. "Too bad you aren't close enough to join in the game."

Outside, I started up Main Street. Childish of me to have been so petty with Laura. As I passed the *Clarion,* Rob stepped out of the doorway and placed a guiding hand on my back. "Thought you might be passing this way."

The leaves scrunched under our feet, releasing the dry, tangy smell of autumn. We moved along briskly through the cold. I pulled up my coat collar with a shiver. Rob talked all the way along about the whys and wherefores of Snoop's treachery. Suddenly, a local prankster rolled a huge pumpkin down over a lawn. It fell from a low wall and smashed at our feet. Boys! Always up for a bit of Halloween mischief. I thought of Geordie—sneaking out of the house this time of year, meeting up with his friends, knocking over outhouses, hatching trouble. A weak laugh escaped me.

"What's funny?" Rob stepped around the smashed pumpkin.

"Boys," I responded. "All of them."

"Even me?"

"Especially you."

He reached over and tucked my hand over his arm. Whether he was just being gentlemanly or something else, it felt right to walk along beside him in the October twilight.

Chapter 27

Katya's all smiles when she sees me, drops what she's doing and comes for a hug, taking off her dirty work gloves as she walks. "Lord, you're a welcome sight," she tells me. "How's everything at home?"

"Boring and quiet without you. How long are you going to keep this up?" I ask.

"Oh, another week or two. There's so much to be done out here— strawberries are about over, and peas, but peaches will be coming on, and grapes. There's always plenty to do here in the summertime." Her seven-year-old granddaughter sidles up to her, risking a shy grin at me.

"Hello, Carol. Looks like you're keeping Grandma busy."

The child nods, then runs off to chase a kitten hiding behind a watering can. She catches it and brings it around for me to admire. I pet it and make a fuss over it as though it were the first kitten I ever saw. Little Carol wanders off with the kitten held in front of her with both hands, pleased with herself.

Katya leads the way to a bench under a grape arbor, and we sit down for a chat. "What's new with our boy James?" she asks. Leave it to Katya to get to the heart of the matter with dispatch.

"I'm worried that he's taking the wrong tack. Seems bent on ignoring the fact that she's engaged. Doesn't that mean anything anymore? Getting engaged to Rob was the greatest moment of my life up until then."

"Engaged is a promise, but it's there to give some time before the final commitment." Katya's giving me a lesson in the conduct of life.

"I know all that," I respond, annoyed. "But a broken engagement is a scar. Not to be taken lightly."

"Not as bad as a marriage mistake. If she finds herself attracted to someone else, now's the time to find it out."

"Yes, but I keep thinking James is a home wrecker. I don't like that."

Reaching up, Katya pulls down a fat bunch of deep red grapes and hands them to me. "Try these. New variety. Take a long time to mature, but they're worth it."

I'm sucking away on the grapes while Katya takes off her broad-brimmed hat and wipes her brow. She studies me for a moment, then adds, "You have to butt out, Pam. Remember when you were young, how sure you were of Davy until . . . ?"

"Well, yes, Davy and I were engaged, but that was different."

"How different? You found out you weren't in love any more, and you moved on. How different?"

Her logic silences me, and I sit in the shaded arbor eating the juicy, succulent grapes, thinking back to the waning days of my relationship with Davy. "Well, I hope she knows it sooner than I did. I clung to old hopes, I'm afraid."

"You knew when it was over. You just didn't know where else to go."

"Remember those days? You and I were both lost souls. Neither of us had any idea what the future held."

Katya gives me a pat on the arm. "The best thing about us then and now is the friendship. We knew then and we know now neither of us will ever be alone as long as the other lives."

"Yes. I knew when you came back from Pittsburgh you'd stay. It made all the difference for me then, but now I have James to worry about. What am I going to do with him?"

"Let James make his own way. Those grandchildren you want so badly will come in their own time. You may have to wait, but you'll get them."

"I hope before I'm too old to enjoy them."

The sky opens and a deluge of rain falls all around the little arbor, but we stay dry under the grape leaves. I need Katya's steadying hand, her sensible take on the world. Rob used to do that for me. Now it's Katya.

"Know where I've been lately?" I ask her.

"I shrink from the possibilities," she laughs.

"Back at the trial. When Papa and the rest were in Pittsburgh and people were so down on Mrs. Plummer.

"Hmm," Katya muses. "When will you get done with this trip to the past?"

"I don't know. Maybe when I get another chance to meet Davy Hughes and settle a few things"

"What? Where are you going with this? Surely you don't think you'll meet him again, do you?"

"I might if his son marries Ellen Duncan. He'll come to the wedding, to be sure."

Katya stares at me, dumbfounded. "I don't know what would ever make you want to see Davy Hughes again."

"Curiosity, mostly. I'd like to know what his life has been like—if he ever got over his bitterness."

"And what if *your* son pushes his son aside and marries Ellen Duncan? What then?"

"Then maybe I'll have other things to keep my mind occupied. In the meantime, Miss Duncan and the young Mr. Hughes are still engaged."

We sit under the arbor and watch it rain. No use trying to get inside, and getting home in this downpour is beyond thinkable. So we sit and talk, laugh and catch up. After about a half hour, the rain abates and Katya's son, Stephen, comes looking for us. He gives me a warm smile and a hug. "Auntie Pam, good to see you! Mother misses you. She complains all the time about having no one to talk to around here." He pulls down another bunch of grapes and pops three into his mouth. "Great grapes, eh? Come on in the house. Time for lunch."

Lunch with Stephen's family isn't exactly relaxing. The children compete for attention, Stephen talks endlessly about his produce, his wife worries over the menu, and Katya sits there with a benevolent smile on her face, taking it all in. I feel like a fly on the wall, a detached observer. As soon as the rain stops, I gather my things, the bag I brought bulging with fresh fruits and vegetables.

"How do you expect me to eat all of this without you to help?" I ask Katya.

"Make some preserves. Do a canner full. What? Have you forgotten your old skills?" She stuffs another bag of grapes on top with a smile.

"All right. You've shamed me enough. I'm leaving." I step outside and look up at the sky. "Looks like a break in the clouds. I'd better hustle to the bus stop."

I walk along, carrying my bag of produce, reflecting on Katya's family. She enjoys her grandchildren, but isn't smitten with them like some women are. Of course not. They came along in good time, as summer follows spring. Her other son, Andras, lives in Pittsburgh with his wife and three daughters. The girls come out every summer for a week. Then our house gets a good shaking up! Katya is blessed.

The half-mile walk to the bus line is long this time—the bag of produce is heavy. I stop and rest under a tree, keep an eye on the sky. Pretty soon my mind is past thinking about Katya's grandchildren and wandering around back *there* again. Back at my father's—or should I say *Davy's*—trial and all that went with it.

In the weeks leading up to the trial, set for December first, I tried to keep busy writing articles on just about anything to keep my mind occupied. Mr. Shaver ran some of them, but not all. He could see that I was filling the time the only way I knew how. I came and went from the *Clarion* every day, anxious for the verdict but afraid of what it would mean for me. They'd all be tried together in the Allegheny County Court in Pittsburgh, and while there was sympathy for the four of them on every corner of Johnstown, I couldn't take comfort from that. Maybe it was the time of year—gray skies, bare trees, cold wind, the threat or promise of snow. Papa wouldn't be coming home for a long time, and Davy probably not at all. My life stretched out before me with no promise of change.

I wrote to both of them, but my heart wasn't in my letters. By the second letter to Davy I had to will myself to keep it up, and my will was weak.

I kept telling myself their crimes weren't *that* serious. Only one minor injury—mostly property damage—but property damage to the most powerful was the equivalent of vile murder in the lower classes. I clung to the hope that public sentiment in Johnstown would hold sway and that leftover sympathy for Johnstown's suffering would bring—maybe not the verdict, but the sentences—up short.

Rob seemed distant—preoccupied and businesslike—and went about his work without much conversation. I was too involved with my own problems to pay him much notice, but Mr. Shaver sensed a rift and asked me about it.

"You and Rob not on speaking terms these days?"

I was embarrassed. "No. We're fine. Just busy."

He gave me a skeptical look and went back to his typewriter, leaving me to wonder how he sensed so much. Rob *had* been quiet lately. Maybe he was afraid I'd taken his attentions wrong. No danger of that. I could tell sympathy from attraction, any day.

Laura came by the *Clarion* the Saturday after Thanksgiving, dressed in a new wool coat, the height of fashion, glowing with wedding plans—again. She went on about her evening candlelight ceremony, gushing over each detail until I felt like stuffing a sock in her mouth. But, being Laura, it didn't take her long to get down to the real purpose of her visit. She knew the Pittsburgh gossip almost as well as she knew Johnstown's.

"They've got a good lawyer. Word is, someone from Johnstown is paying him. No one is saying, but there are only about five people in town who could afford to."

I was puzzled. Who would actually put up money for their defense?

Laura put a hand aside of her mouth as though to keep anyone from reading her lips. "There are rumors—just rumors, mind you—that it isn't anyone from Johnstown at all. There's talk that some of the South Fork Club members are doing it to ease their consciences." She leaned back to study my reaction.

I frowned, pondering the idea. "Well, maybe, but it's a sure thing *some* of them want our men's heads on a plate."

Laura smiled. "It'll be interesting to see what comes of it. My money is on a guilty verdict and long sentences. Sorry, Pam, but that's how I see it."

Her words cut through me. "Gracious, Laura. You're stomping on my hopes."

"Whatever will be will be. It doesn't matter what we think, anyway." She rose and smoothed her skirt down over blooming hips. "Let's go over for tea and a scone. This is my last one, though. If I don't cut short on the scones, I'll look as matronly as my mother before I'm thirty."

At the Tea Room we slipped into a booth and were soon sipping tea and laughing over reminiscences. Laura prattled on, telling outrageous stories about half of Johnstown.

"How do you know all this?"

"Keen observation. You know I never miss a thing!"

Then she was up from her seat, mimicking a pregnant Mrs. Pritchert, hand at her back, groaning as she hung her laundry with one hand, yelling at her kids and cursing her husband, exaggerating every movement. Never happier than when she was the center of attention, Laura soon had everyone in the Tea Room watching in amusement. I laughed with them. It'd been a long time since I'd laughed, and it felt good.

Her performance done, Laura sat down and turned her attention back to me. "What's going on between you and Davy? You're not saying much about him these days. Are you going to wait for him?"

Such a direct question deserved a direct answer. "There's nothing left for Davy and me."

"Why not? You were so head-over-heels in love with him. He hasn't done anything *that* bad, has he?"

"More to luck than to reason if he hasn't. He's eaten up with hatred. He'd probably kill a few South Fork members if he had the chance."

Laura's eyebrows went up. "Don't you think he's learned his lesson by now? Won't he be glad to put all of it behind him and get on with his life?"

"No. He can't let go of his anger—not that it should be easy—so, no. He's consumed by it."

She gave me a long look, head cocked to one side. "Would you give him another chance if he promised to change?"

I held my teacup poised before me, searching for any feeling at all. "It's gone, Laura. Dead. There's no resurrecting it."

"Well, then, it's time you moved on. Rob Mc Rae's available. What about him?"

"Laura! Don't go around making matches for me. I can take care of myself." The mention of Rob's name set me off, but I couldn't lay my finger on the why of it.

"Some job you're doing." She rose and picked up the check. "Careful you don't end up as Miss Gwynedd, that old spinster who's worked at the *Clarion* forever and still takes care of her mother."

"Yes, Laura. I'll watch out for that."

She whisked up to the counter, paid the bill and gave me a good-bye hug. "Don't forget, Pam. All work and no play."

Back at the *Clarion*, gathering my things, I found myself struggling with the blues again. Thoughts tumbled around in my head like feathers shaken from a tick. I tried to sort them out and look on the bright side, but it was elusive—the bright side. I looked around the little office, now a place of belonging, and sighed. Maybe I *would* spend the rest of my days here. But somehow there was comfort in that. I smiled, turned out the light and closed the door.

As I came up to the corner of Bedford and Main, I noticed a crowd gathered near Mrs. Plummer's house. Someone had built a huge, menacing bonfire out front, and people stood around yelling insults. I was drawn to the scene, unable or unwilling to mind my own business. The newspaper woman in me.

Someone had stuffed old clothes with corn husks, and a man I didn't recognize raised the effigy on a long stick above the fire. It danced crazily, just out of reach of the flames, while people chanted "Clar-rence, Clar-rence" in a menacing monotone.

"Tell yer boy this is what'll happen to him if he ever sets foot in Johnstown again!" someone yelled.

"Good fer nuthin' snitch!"

"You shoulda drowned him when he were a baby! Save us a lotta trouble."

I elbowed my way to the fire's edge and looked toward the house. The curtains were drawn, but a slight movement revealed a presence behind them. Poor Mrs. Plummer! These were the same people she labored to help after the flood. She was guilty of nothing worse than a mother's love. I couldn't help but feel sorry for her, in spite of the pain she'd caused Katya and me.

Then a rock sliced through the air, followed by the sound of shattering glass. The window in the front door was smashed, broken glass lay over the front step and the curtain waved in the breeze. Still no one was visible inside, and I hoped Mrs. Plummer had the good sense to keep her head down.

I looked around at the crowd, all plain working folk, neighbors, most of them familiar to me. I understood their anger, but I couldn't bring myself to join them.

Someone in the crowd yelled, "You, Pammie Gwynedd! Tell her yourself what her sniveling son took from you."

I shook my head. No. No more. Enough pain. I turned away. No use trying to reason with them. They'd only think I was a hateful daughter, unwilling to defend my own father. I faded into the back of the crowd and made my way back home, barely watching where I was going.

I spent the next day, the Sunday before the trial, with Mama and Katya, reading my old friend *Ivanhoe,* trying to keep my mind off what was coming. Katya showed me her latest creation, a wedding dress for one of the city councilman's daughters. She'd designed and made it herself, and she was justifiably proud. It was beautiful.

"Your work is fine enough for the wife of the president!" I told her.

She shook her head. "Happy here. Order sewing machine. Mr. Elder say two weeks."

"Two weeks! There'll be no stopping you once that gets here."

She smiled, a little ruefully. I knew she was thinking of Istvan. And I was thinking of . . . the best laid plans.

Suddenly I was overwhelmed by the need to write. I picked up my pencil and pad and began scribbling down words, sentences, as they came without regard for anything but getting the words on paper. I wrote into the evening by lamplight, stoking the stove to keep out the cold. Katya and Mama were long asleep when I finally turned out the lamp and slipped into my nightgown.

The next morning, my editorial efforts tucked into my cloth bag I hurried down Main Street to the *Clarion*. Mr. Shaver greeted me with a warm office and a cup of his extra-strong coffee, which I was too polite to refuse.

"Today's the day, eh, Pammie?" His words were light and cheerful, behind a tone of resignation.

"Is Rob gone already?"

He nodded. "Sent him off on the eight o'clock train. He'll send his dispatches every afternoon on the eastbound. If you want to stay around until six every evening, you can find out the latest along with me."

"Yes. I'd like that. I'll tell Katya not to expect me home early."

"In the meantime, I'll keep you busy. You know what they say about an idle mind."

"You needn't worry about that," I reassured him. "The devil has much more promising playgrounds!"

"Old Mother Worry likes an idle mind, too."

I took out my pad and began to decipher my scribblings of the night before. They still made sense, so I transcribed them on the typewriter and slipped them into a pile of copy for Mr. Shaver to edit. Then I returned to the typing task before me, wondering what Rob was doing, wishing I were in Pittsburgh with him.

Mr. Shaver read through the copy pile one after another without comment. I waited for him to come to mine, struggling with the idea that I was foolish to try to write an editorial. He called me into his office. "This yours?"

"Yes, sir. I came upon that shameful demonstration outside Mrs. Plummer's house on Saturday and I couldn't get it out of my mind."

He held the pages in one hand, looking over his glasses at me. "You know this won't make you any friends in Johnstown."

"I guess. But right is right. Someone needs to tell people it's time they moved on. Mrs. Plummer is just a plain old woman, like any of them. She loves her son, that's all. If *I'm* not blaming her, I don't see why other people should."

Mr. Shaver leaned back in his chair, hands clasped behind his head. "I'll print it as an anonymous letter to the editor, but you might want to lay low for a while at any rate."

"No, sir. I want my name on it, and I'd be honored if you'd print it as a staff editorial. If we don't have courage here, where's it going to come from?"

He stood up, looking at me over his glasses. "I'd be proud to print it as a staff editorial for the writing, but I can't let you put yourself out there where they can hurt you, Pam. I won't have it."

"Mr. Shaver, I want to be a newspaper woman. I want to write the truth as I see it. I've worked hard, and I think I've earned the right to have a voice. This is *my* voice, and I want to be heard."

He closed his eyes and held the bridge of his nose between his fingers. Then he sat back down, silent for so long I worried that I'd offended him—maybe even lost my job.

When he spoke his voice was tired—like he'd seen too much of this world. "All right. But don't say I didn't warn you. They'll be burning you in effigy next."

My editorial came out in Tuesday's paper . . .

Johnstown knows tragedy well. Maybe better than any other town in the world.

We share a history with places like Pompeii and Krakatoa. Such adversity can strengthen us, or it can turn us into angry, bitter, vengeful people.

Last Saturday evening outside the home of Mrs. Grace Plummer on Bedford Street I witnessed a gathering of the latter. It was distressing and disappointing to see people I've known all my life bent on exacting payment for perceived wrongs from a woman whose only crime is being a loving mother.

Clarence Plummer has wronged us, to be sure, but his mother has worked tirelessly to provide relief to those of us for whom the flood continues to bring pain. She carries food and clothing to people who can't go downtown to pick up their share. She makes sure her distribution is fair and that specific needs are met. We owe her gratitude and the respect due any human being, not fires, effigies and broken windows.

This editorial is about moving on. Standing tall. Maintaining order and dignity. How do we want to be remembered? As a people who bore up under the worst that life has to offer, or as mean little miscreants bent on making someone else pay for the wrongs we feel have been done to us— wrongs some of us want to nurture beyond all reason?

This brings up the events that caused the demonstration outside Mrs. Plummer's house: the criminal vandalism against members of the South Fork Fishing and Hunting Club . . .

Walking home that night, I half expected to be accosted, upbraided, spat upon or something, but I passed several people on the street and no one took notice of me. I laughed at my overinflated sense of self-importance. Then Wednesday morning rolled around.

The first person in the *Clarion* office was one of the policemen who'd guarded my father. He stepped in, nodded to me, and said, "Careful who you side with, miss."

He was followed by the mayor, who cautioned me with a pointing finger. Then the Presbyterian minister came by and warned me that some of his parishioners were quite offended that I would chastise someone for standing against the likes of Snoop Plummer.

"You got courage, girl, I'll say that for you. Lots of courage, but not much sense." That was the verdict of Mr. Elder who'd been pulled away from the pot-bellied stove in the middle of his store long enough to give me his two cents.

A letter to the editor berating me for disloyalty to my father, my town, my sex, and any other connection I might have was slipped anonymously under the door. One woman I hardly knew hustled into the office and tore up her copy of the *Clarion* and threw the pieces on my desk. At least three customers cancelled their subscriptions, and one advertiser pulled his half-page ad from the next edition.

The majority of opinion, spoken and written, was against me. I knew it would be. It's hard for people who've suffered as they had to find charity in their hearts. Still, someone had to stand up for right, even unpopular right. I was beginning to learn what the newspaper business was all about, and to my surprise, I was up to the challenge. The opposition didn't matter. They could agree with me or disagree. At least I had them thinking.

Just after noon on Wednesday Mrs. Plummer stepped into the *Clarion* office, wrapped up against the cold. She stood inside the door, her face twisted as she struggled for control. I fully expected another of her tirades, even though I'd spoken in her defense, but her voice came out shaky, almost gentle.

"Miss Gwynedd. Can you forgive me? I've been so wrong to you." She collapsed in Rob's empty chair, her fingers laced over her ample middle.

Confused by her pleading, I turned and took her cold hands in mine. "It's all right, Mrs. Plummer. You didn't know what your son was doing."

"No. It's not about my Clarence. I know why folks are set agin' him. No, I've wronged *you*. You and your Hungarian girl. I lied when I said I saw that one Hunkie kill the other. I didn't see no such thing." Her shoulders shook, and she pulled her hands away from mine, given over to sobs.

I was stunned. "I know that, Mrs. Plummer. I was there. Remember? But why? Why would you want to hurt someone who'd never done a thing to you?"

Mr. Shaver came out of his office as the poor woman straightened up, pounding the air with her fists. "What's this? Mrs. Plummer, a man's in prison because of you."

"I know," she sniffed. "I know, and I'm sorry. I want to make it right. I'm sorry about Clarence, too. Poor boy. He didn't mean anything by it. He just wanted people to like him." She reached up to Mr. Shaver, took his hand. "Help me make it right, Harold."

A chill went through me. Snoop Plummer wanting people to like him. This poor, sobbing woman would have to leave the only home she'd ever known or suffer every day for her son's pathetic lack of common sense.

Mr. Shaver dropped Mrs. Plummer's hand. "Madam, you and I have to go to Ebensburg. The county attorney needs to hear about this. You'll have to rescind your testimony."

I thought of Istvan and what this could mean for him. I wouldn't tell Katya, for fear it wouldn't change anything, but I hoped with all my heart that Mrs. Plummer's efforts really would make a difference. When she left, still tearful and full of regret, Mr. Shaver went into his office and composed a letter to the judge. When he was finished, he put on his coat and stepped out the door. "Got to post this before she changes her mind," he said.

Rob's first dispatch came in on the eastbound at six o'clock. I hurried to read it, but little had happened. Jury selection would probably take up the first two days. Then the prosecution would present their case. It'd take several days for testimony and cross examination. The waiting weighed heavy on me—like waiting for Christmas, without the promise of presents.

I stayed late every day to wait for Rob's dispatches, empty and afraid. So much depended on the verdict and the sentences. I was alternately full of hope and despair. Then one day, tacked on the end of one of Rob's dispatches, was a note for me. I read it with more excitement than I wanted to show.

> Dear Pam,
> Great editorial. I agree wholeheartedly. Guess I'd better start looking over my shoulder at the competition.
> Rob

I smiled, cut the note off the bottom of the page, and tucked it away in my desk drawer. He had nothing to worry about, but it wouldn't hurt if he thought he did.

Chapter 28

I'm barely through the front door when James's car rolls to a stop in front of my house. Stopping by on his way home from work? That's odd. I get a quick a kiss on the cheek as he settles into his father's chair and smiles like the proverbial cat.

"My, you certainly are attentive these days. What's the matter? Afraid I'll get so lost in the past I won't come back?"

He laughs. "You never did get very far out of the past, so, no. I'm not worried about you at all, but I thought you might be interested in this."

He hands me the Pittsburgh paper, pointing to a front page headline. "Former Johnstown Resident Honored by Michigan Group."

I read the story quickly. David Evan Hughes, born and raised in Johnstown was honored by the Wayne County Chamber of Commerce for his contributions to the local hospital. Seems Davy had donated a hundred thousand dollars to the hospital for a new wing. The story goes into detail about Davy's Johnstown connection and notes that his son is now engaged to marry a prominent young Johnstown woman, Miss Ellen Duncan, daughter of Mr. and Mrs. Bert Duncan, but it skips right over his terrorist activities, arrest and trial. Funny how financial success glosses over a lot of inconvenient details. I'm more interested in reading about Davy than I want to show, but I fold the paper and turn to James.

"Looks like Miss Duncan is marrying money. I'm not surprised Davy Hughes was successful, but I am surprised at *how* successful. A hundred thousand dollars is vast wealth to people like us—like Davy was when he was young."

"Didn't you know him back then? Weren't you neighbors or something?"

"Neighbors, yes. Back fence neighbors. That's all." James has never been privy to my life before his father, and I'm satisfied with that. No need to rake up old rotted leaves.

Rising, I ask if he's eaten yet. "I brought half of Stephen's farm along. How about some fresh peas and carrots? I've got a nice slice of ham to go along."

"Sure. So you think Ellen's head is being turned by money?"

"Can't hurt." I say over my shoulder. He follows me to the kitchen. It feels like old times, getting dinner with James hanging around, talking about his day. When he was a teen-ager he used to come in from school after basketball practice, drop his books, and start eating. He'd eat while I made dinner, then he'd eat dinner, then he'd eat after dinner. I never saw a boy eat like he did.

He picks a raw carrot out of the bag, washes it and starts to chomp. "I'll make you a bet she comes home from her weekend visit a free woman."

"Oh? What makes you think?"

"I don't want to make too much of it, but I think she's cooled off on him."

"What makes you think?"

"Nothing. Just a gut feeling. I think she loves the paper, and she'd hate to have to leave it to go off to Pittsburgh or maybe even Detroit and be a lawyer's wife."

"Convenient that you own the paper and will be there until the four horsemen ride."

"My sentiments exactly," he says, setting the table while I prepare the meal.

"So this sounds serious, James. Are you sure you want to bring about this breakup? Sure you want to pursue it?"

"Yeah, Mom. I'm sure."

My heart flutters just a bit. "You're not just doing this to please me, are you?"

He turns and gives me a look that would turn a raging bull into a mewing kitten. "No, Mom. No danger of that. I love you, but I wouldn't do this just to please you. This is for me."

As we sit down to eat, I feel a welling up of joy—all I've ever wanted from this boy. Too bad his brother died and left all the responsibility to him, but I try not to lean on him too heavily. I leave him to his own life—for the most part, but I can't help smiling over my ham, peas and carrots. Katya will love this.

James helps me with the dishes, then makes his excuses and leaves. Ellen Duncan is still in town, until Friday. I get the feeling her evenings will be taken up with whatever social events James can contrive without arousing suspicion as to his intentions. Probably thinks he has her fooled, but I'm a woman. I know better.

The evening lies before me, empty but comfortable. I turn on the radio and listen to Jack Benny, laugh a little, work on my knitting. It isn't long before my needles are still and I'm off thinking about Papa's trial and the aftermath.

Every evening for three weeks I hurried down cold dark sidewalks to meet the six o'clock express. Back at the *Clarion* Mr. Shaver and I would read Rob's dispatches and weigh the evidence, especially Snoop Plummer's testimony, which was heavy against the defendants. I wished I could be there to support my father, but it was just as well I couldn't see Davy. His last letter was as angry and defiant as ever. He wasn't going to change, no matter the outcome.

In our off moments Mr. Shaver and I exchanged opinions about the trial. "I guess it's a foregone conclusion they'll be found guilty," he said.

"Yes. I'd be surprised if it were otherwise."

I couldn't disagree. Even though people stopped in the newspaper office every day with overblown expectations, telling me they'd be found innocent and set free. Telling me the law wouldn't dare give them harsh sentences after all Johnstown had been through. My own opinion was that they'd have to pay for their crimes, but I hoped, mostly for my father's and Mr. Hughes's sakes, that the penalty wouldn't be too harsh.

Mr. Shaver glanced at me over his glasses. I turned away lest he see my eyes fill up.

"You should get out more, Pam. You don't do anything but work and go home. Get out of here for a while. Call on your friend—what's her name?"

"Laura. Laura Jenkins."

"Yes, yes. That one. Go see her. Have tea. Join in some of the young folks' activities."

I smiled at his concern. "Thank you, Mr. Shaver, but I'm not *totally* bereft of social contacts. Laura and I get together once in a while, and I do have other friends." I knew it wasn't true, just a desperate attempt to divert his concern from my empty social life.

He gave me a skeptical look. "Any beaux? What about Davy Hughes?"   "What about him?" He was getting too close. Mr. Shaver was like a father to me, but I wasn't ready to open my innermost confidences to him. As though to my rescue, the office door opened and in walked Laura.

"Yes, what about Davy Hughes?" She stepped right into the conversation, full of opinions and not about to shield them from the light. "I can't really believe you've given up on him. Doesn't he still want to marry you?"

Everyone had an opinion about my private life. "It always includes the condition that I leave town with him, and you know where that leaves Mama."

"Mama, Mama, Mama." She tilted her head from side to side to emphasize her frustration. "I admire you for taking care of her, but at what price, Pam? Is it worth your only chance at happiness?"

Mr. Shaver slipped into his office, uncomfortable with this turn of the conversation.

"My only chance?" I felt prickles on the back of my neck. "Is that really how you see me? So lacking in charm and attraction that I can't hope for anything better than what Davy offers? You're never satisfied yourself, but you think *I* should settle for the first thing that comes along, as if it's the *only* thing that'll come along."

Laura's shook her head. "Don't take it that way! I didn't mean to be insulting. I just want you to re-think this absurd devotion to a woman who's likely never to change, and never to thank you for giving up your life for her."

"I'm not expecting thanks. I do my duty because it's my duty."

She sniffed. "Honestly, I'd think you'd want to get out of this town before you succumb to the aftermath."

Typical Laura. Do as you please and let the rest of the world take care of itself. "I might want to get out of this town or not, but it has to be by choice. I'm not going as a runaway. If I go it will be as a woman with a future. I don't see a future in shirking responsibility. It would always be back there, clouding my life. Besides, Laura, I've told you before, Davy can't get over the flood. I need someone who can."

"Well, I just hope you don't end up wasting your life is all."

"Thanks, Laura. You're a real friend." I made no effort to hide the sarcasm in my tone.

She rose to go. "I'm sorry, Pam. I didn't intend to be mean. It's the farthest thing from my mind." She placed a tin box on my desk and hugged me close. "Christmas cookies—from my mother. I'm sorry. Really I am. I should mind my own business."

I couldn't disagree with that, but after she'd gone I sat alone in the office, staring at my typewriter. Mr. Shaver stepped out, leaned his cane against the door frame, and put a sympathetic hand on my shoulder. Grateful, I reached up and placed my hand over his.

"Maybe I shouldn't be so quick to give advice, either," he told me. Then he laid some copy on my desk and pointed to it. "Two o'clock deadline." The tension was gone. We were back to normal.

I started to type, but Mr. Shaver hovered near, hands behind his back, perplexed. "I can't get that Plummer woman out of my mind. I've asked three lawyers in town their opinion of her lying on the witness stand, but there's no consensus. One says there should be a new trial. Another says it doesn't make any difference—that Istvan was guilty anyway, and the third says his conviction should be overturned by the judge."

"Do you still plan to take her to Ebensburg to speak to Judge Patterson?"

"Yes, but finding time to do it is hard with Rob gone, and she's so overwrought about her son's testimony in this trial she's barely coherent. I think we'd better wait until we find out how this is going to turn out before we try to reopen Istvan's case. People are still harassing her, day and night, I hear."

I shuddered. In spite of everything, I couldn't help but feel sorry for Mrs. Plummer, alone in her house with no one to care about her, poor soul.

"Do you think I should stop by and see her some evening?"

"It'd be a good idea. You never know what she might do in the face of so much stress. I don't want her to get so distraught that she goes back on her confession."

Okay. Another sad case to tend to. I wondered how many of these I could shoulder. But Mrs. Plummer had taken good care of Mama and me after Papa left, even if she did want to be thanked for it. I owed her at least some payment in kind.

That evening after we read Rob's dispatches, I took myself home through the cold December evening, past my own door, where the light shone from the windows and the smells of dinner spilled out into the street, on up Bedford to Mrs. Plummer's house on the hill. The house was dark, with a couple of boards nailed haphazardly across the broken window. It looked uninhabited, but I went around back, where there was a light in the kitchen. I knocked and waited, stamping my feet in the cold, as Mrs. Plummer moved the curtain aside to see who it was. She opened the door.

"Oh, Miss Gwynedd. How nice to see you. I have to be careful, opening my door these nights. There's been a lot of fuss about my Clarence." Her voice quavered when she said his name.

She stepped aside and motioned for me to come in. She'd lost weight, and her face sagged. The rest of her sagged, too, beaten down.

In the room, dimly lit by a single oil lamp, I saw she'd just finished her supper. The room was cluttered, piles of old clothes on chairs, old newspapers and magazines on the floor, with barely room to pass from the stove to the pump to the door. She offered me a chair at the round table, and I sat studying the worn oil cloth.

"Can I get you some coffee, Miss Gwynedd? I'm sorry I don't have any sweets to offer. I don't have much need to bake without Clarence here to help me eat." Though she tried to sound cheerful, her tone was empty.

"Coffee would be fine. I'd like that."

The room wasn't warm, and I opened my coat but left it on. I watched Mrs. Plummer move slowly from stove to table and back again, her once bulky figure drooping, her dress fairly hanging from her shoulders.

"How've you been, Mrs. Plummer?"

"How've I been? How could I be? Chastened and chastised for nothing *I've* done. Sad for my boy. Everyone's so agin him. S'pose they think it's all right, what your father and the Hugheses done. They broke the law, is what I say. Broke it and should pay. But, no. Everyone's down on my Clarence for respecting the law and helping bring them in."

This abrupt change in her perception of the accused was to be expected, but it still grated on me. I fought the urge to remind her that she once thought them heroes. No use. She set a cup and saucer in front of me and poured the steaming coffee. The spout of the coffee pot nicked the top of the cup and spilled most of it into the saucer. She drew back, confused.

"It's all right, Mrs. Plummer. This is fine."

I lifted the half full cup to my lips and blew on it. At this temperature, it'd be cold before very long. "I know it looks bleak right now, but this will pass. You have to believe it will."

"Then where'll I be? That Dailey girl has already filed for divorce, which is right enough with me. But we'll have to leave Johnstown. Clarence'll never get another job here." She wiped a tear from the corner of her eye. "I've got a sister in Greensburg. Maybe we'll move over there."

I couldn't tell for sure how old she was, but probably not much more than fifty. She'd seen a lot of pain—the flood and its aftermath, her husband's death from the typhoid that followed, countless friends and neighbors who succumbed either to the flood or to the depression and shock. She rose to the challenges of distributing aid to all in the weeks after the disaster. One of those women who never knew her own strength until called upon in a crisis.

"Someday you and your son'll have a new life in a new place. You'll get over this."

She turned a tearful face to me. "I was born here. I never knowed any other place. I'm too old for anything new. My Clarence, too. He's never knowed other than Johnstown."

"I'd leave myself, if I could." The words were out of my mouth before my better judgment could stop them.

"What? *You'd* leave? What about your poor mother? Where'd she be without you?" In an instant she'd turned hostile.

"I said I'd leave if I could," I spoke evenly, aware that almost anything I said might be misinterpreted. "I know I can't leave Mama."

"Leave your poor mother! I can't believe you'd do that. I thought you was a *nice* girl, even if you did take up with Hunkies. My God! What's happening to this world?"

It was clear she was confused. Try as I might, I couldn't get through to her. I sipped my coffee quietly, waiting for her to calm down so I could take my leave. What did I come here for? To try to be nice? To let her know *everyone* wasn't against her? Now I couldn't convince her I wasn't going to walk away and leave my mother, but at the same time I had to wonder if *her* son would ever come back. *She* might be the one whose child left her to struggle alone.

I rose and buttoned my coat. "I'd best be off, then, Mrs. Plummer. You know, if you need anything, anything at all, you can call on me." I touched her hand and turned to go. I left her standing alone in her kitchen, muttering to herself.

The trial dragged on until almost Christmas, taking over my mind—squeezing out everything else. I did crossword puzzles and read the geography quiz every day to divert my attention, but nothing kept me occupied for long. Time and again I found myself back there, thinking about Papa, wondering if he'd ever get to come home. I'd push my worries aside and five minutes later, there I was again, right in the middle of it. Then, one cold afternoon four days before Christmas, I was writing an article about the Presbyterian Christmas pageant when the door opened and in walked Rob McRae, leather briefcase in hand, his face serious.

"Rob! What are you doing back here?" I asked.

"Trial's over."

My stomach tightened. I was short of breath. "Over? What, then?"

"All four found guilty. Sentenced to six months hard labor, including time served. Davy's lucky he didn't get more. Couldn't resist being defiant. Got up and yelled at the whole courtroom—called the South Fork Club members parasites. The judge added a month to his sentence for contempt. The rest of them should be home before summer." He lowered himself into his chair, tired, his eyes on my face.

I let out a sigh. "I'm glad it's over. I guess the moneyed men of Pittsburgh would just as soon not hear any more from or about Johnstown and its flood."

"Looks that way. Guess you'll be going to see your father and Davy then." He spoke without emotion, matter of fact, like he was interviewing someone for a story.

I hesitated. "Oh, yes. Of course. I guess so. I'd like to see my father because now he can . . ."

Rob watched me with disquieting intensity. "Come home?"

I nodded.

"Come home so you and Davy can get married and get out of Johnstown?"

"That's not going to happen."

"Why not?"

"It's over between Davy and me. The feeling's gone."

Rob snorted. "It'll be back once he's out of jail. I'd be careful, though. Life might be hard married to a convict."

My head jerked back as though he'd struck me. I turned away—sat tall—went back to my typing. He attended to the stack of papers on his desk. For the next two hours, not a word passed between us. I heard him typing up his story—wanted to ask him more about the trial, more details. Never mind. I'd read about it in the paper. He sat with his back to me, making a great pretense of being busy, and I did the same, though keenly aware of his presence. When the clock struck five I rose, put on my coat and hat and stepped out the door without a word.

Walking home, I swallowed a lump in my throat, fought tears. I didn't know what I was so sad about. It was finally over. Papa would be home in the spring, and I could expect him to keep his word about coming back to us. I'd be free for the first time since the flood—free to plan my life, to pursue my own goals. I should be happy. To hell with Rob McRae. He could stay in Johnstown and drown in the next flood for all I cared.

At home I told Katya the news, and after we'd eaten I led Mama upstairs and sat down on her bed, taking her hands in mine.

"Mama, I've good news. Papa's coming home in the spring. Won't that be fine, Mama? We can be a family again."

She turned and focused her gaze on me, frowned and said, "Owen?"

I hugged her tight, but when I let her go, she was gone again. Back to her refuge, beyond the light.

Chapter 29

The next morning, I dial up Katya on the phone and read the newspaper article to her.

"A hundred thousand dollars? How'd Davy Hughes get that kind of money?"

"In the car business, I guess. Davy always was smart. He must have seen the possibilities in automobiles early. Linking up with the right people probably didn't hurt."

Silence on the other end of the line. "What's James got to say about Ellen marrying his son? That kind of money would turn any girl's head."

"That's what I told him, but he's confident the romance is dying on the vine."

"I'll call Elsie and see what she thinks the forecast is."

I'm taken aback at the widespread knowledge about this love triangle. I would have expected James to be more discreet. "Does everyone know? About James's interest in her, I mean."

"Not everyone, just anyone with any people sense. You, me, Elsie, Ellen herself and . . ."

"That's enough! Good Lord, what will happen if word gets to Davy's son in Pittsburgh? He'll come here and challenge James to a duel!"

Katya laughs. "Not likely, but it would break the monotony. James can take care of himself."

"Maybe so, but I think he's being a little reckless. He could lose this one, you know."

Again the silence on the line. "My money is on James. If Miss Ellen Duncan has any sense."

I sniff. "Well, she's going to Pittsburgh for the weekend. We'll know soon enough."

We turn the conversation to other things—like when Katya is coming home—and make a plan for one more week. I'll be glad to get her back. She's always been like a rock for me. Full of common sense and good advice—about Davy, Mama, even Rob.

I put down the phone and turn my attention to household duties. Dusting. I've always hated that chore, but with Katya gone, the fates are against me. I start in the living room and move on to the dining room, proud of myself for sticking to it. Then I open a buffet drawer to look for a set of candlesticks I think would look nice on the table, and there it is – a picture of Rob on our wedding day. Now how did that get in there? I must have put it away absent mindedly. It was always my favorite picture of him – so handsome and sure of himself. The resemblance to James stands out. I sit down in a chair by the window to study it. That's all it takes to carry me right back there again. Dusting be damned.

My life was so busy in those days—filled with concern for my father, my work at the paper, hope for a life of my own, undefined as that may have been. I didn't think much about my mother, except to make sure she was comfortable and well fed. I'd about given up any real hope of improvement, though I didn't admit it to myself. She was always there on the fringes of my consciousness, but I didn't allow myself to hope out loud. I guess what I expected was that Papa would eventually come home, take over her care, and free me of the burden. Sad to think of your mother as a burden, but I did.

Her brief episodes of clarity were just that: brief and fleeting. I still believed she could come back, but only if she wanted to, and I didn't see why she would want to. Katya was becoming better than I was with her. Patient. Gentle. She didn't have as much at stake as I did. She had a future, even if it was ten years away. Once the trial was over, we settled into a routine of work, winter and waiting.

"'Spose you and Davy Hughes'll be making wedding plans, now, eh?" It was Dan McIntyre, the haberdasher, stopping by the *Clarion* to pass the time of day with Mr. Shaver.

I gave him a weak smile and went on with my work. It amazed me how people commented on my private life as though I'd asked for advice—as though their speculations were welcome. My ears wearied with the repetition. Protest just brought more questions, but a smile seemed to put them off. I entertained the notion of going to see my father in the Pittsburgh jail, but I couldn't bring myself to make any plans because it meant I should also see Davy, and I wasn't ready.

Mr. Shaver expressed relief that the trial was over. "I hope your father comes home and puts your family back together. No more of this revenge nonsense."

"Tell *him* that. He needs to hear it from someone besides me."

I sat at my typewriter, transcribing Rob's notes from the trial. He needed a record for future reference, so I'd been assigned his typing. After his "convict" remark about Davy, I resented being his handmaiden, but I kept my feelings to myself. Mr. Shaver had been so nice, I didn't want him to think I wasn't grateful.

"I'll tell him that when I see him, but I don't know when that will be. Things are buzzing around here, and I can't even get free to take Mrs. Plummer to Ebensburg. *If* she'd still go with me and *if* she'd stand by her story."

I looked at him in alarm. "Do you think she'd go back on it?"

"I don't know. The woman seems unable to keep her mind working. She's befuddled by all the meanness surrounding her son."

"Anyone would be, but this is a chance to make things right. Surely, she won't let it pass."

"Perhaps. If I keep after her. And I'm not sure, even then. I'm going to try to clear next Wednesday to take her to see the judge."

"Things should be quiet in the middle of the week after Christmas," I said. Then I wondered, "Is Snoop home yet?"

Mr. Shaver gave me a sharp look. "Haven't you heard?"

"Heard what?"

"Snoop Plummer got a four-hundred dollar reward for his help in tracking them down and another two hundred dollars for his testimony. My guess is he won't be home soon."

I drew a sharp breath. "From whom?"

Mr. Shaver shrugged. "South Fork Club members would be my guess."

Six hundred dollars was more than most people in Johnstown would see in a lifetime. "I'd go west and start over if I were him." I couldn't resist a certain meanness in my tone.

"People are saying he'd better not show his face in Johnstown. I don't know where he is, but if I were him, I'd lay awfully low."

"What about his mother? Don't you think he'll take her with him?"

Mr. Shaver looked thoughtful. "I'd be surprised if he did. Remember his character, Pam. He's not exactly what you'd call upstanding."

"How is his poor mother going to get along without him? If you think she's confused now, wait 'til this sinks in."

"I know. That's why I want to get her to Ebensburg before she changes her mind, or shuts down the memory, or whatever it is people do when they feel hopeless."

"Mr. Shaver, take her today."

He stared at me. "Today? How can I get the paper out and be gone to Ebensburg? Besides, it's two days before Christmas, and I haven't heard back from the judge yet."

I saw myself as Istvan's only advocate. No one liked a miscarriage of justice, but when it was a poor immigrant who could barely speak the language, people found it easier to be busy elsewhere.

"Come on, Mr. Shaver. Time is short. Rob and I can get the paper out. Just go."

I spoke for Rob as though I knew he wouldn't mind my volunteering for him. We hadn't exchanged more than a dozen words in the past two days, but I was ready to take whatever scorn he dished out to get help for Katya and Istvan.

Mr. Shaver stood in the middle of the room, lost in thought, then he turned and walked back into his office, taking his coat and hat from the peg.

"You're right, of course. We may not have any time to waste."

He grabbed his cane and walked out the door, turning left toward the livery. Fifteen minutes later I saw him driving a little, light trap up Main Street toward Mrs. Plummer's house. The day was cold, overcast. He should have had a lap robe to keep her warm. I closed my eyes and prayed she'd go with him and speak the truth.

Five minutes later, Rob returned from his city hall beat. He looked in Mr. Shaver's office, then turned to me with raised eyebrows.

"He's gone to take Mrs. Plummer to see the judge in Ebensburg. I told him you and I would get the paper out."

He frowned, swinging a long leg over his chair. "Okay. We can do that, but it'll probably take us half the night."

"With your professionalism and my dogged typing, we can accomplish anything, Rob."

He laughed. "That we can, Miss Gwynedd. That we can." It was a relief to hear him laugh.

We worked through the day at a steady pace. I typed and Rob worked on layout with the printer. We stretched stories to fill in holes, added features, composed headlines, changed the order of things, cut minor articles that could wait for the next edition. I was exhilarated by the process, glad to be part of it. Rob seemed to enjoy it, too, even though he maintained a business like air. It did, indeed, take us until almost eleven o'clock to get it all done.

We were closing up when it dawned on me that we hadn't heard from our boss. "I wonder where Mr. Shaver is. He should have been back in town by no later than eight o'clock. Surely, he would have seen the light in the office and stopped in."

Rob shrugged and guided me to the door with a hand under my elbow. "Maybe he took Mrs. Plummer home and just went on home himself. Got tired. I'll walk you home. This is no time of night for a woman to be out alone."

We walked briskly along in the cold, hardly talking at all. The rift between us hadn't hampered our ability to work together, but work done, we returned to our private worlds. Halfway up Main Street, we saw the light of a trap coming slowly in our direction. Rob's grip on my elbow tightened. It was Mr. Shaver, and he was alone.

Rob waved him down. "What's wrong? Where's Mrs. Plummer? Why so late?"

Mr. Shaver stopped the rig beside us and stepped down. "Gone, poor woman. Collapsed on the courthouse steps. Couldn't take the stress of all the goings on."

I was aghast. "Mrs. Plummer? Dead?"

He nodded. "Four-thirty this afternoon. Coming out of the judge's chambers. They carried her back inside and called a doctor, but by the time he got there, she was gone. Her heart." He shook his head in despair. "Wish I'd never insisted that she go. I feel terrible about this."

"Did . . . did she talk to the judge?"

He looked at me, his eyes sad. "Yes, she did. Told him she'd lied on the stand and begged him to do something to help Istvan. Poor sad soul. At least she died having done the right thing."

I knew I should show proper concern for Mrs. Plummer's plight, but I was more interested in the outcome of her exchange with the judge. "What did he say?"

"Said he'd study it and make a decision after the New Year."

"Does it look promising?"

"Can't say. He listened carefully and had one of his young protégés take notes. Said he'd have to research it—look for a precedent. I've no idea which way it'll go." He climbed back into the rig. "Is there anyone besides Clarence Plummer who should be notified?"

I shook my head. "I don't know of anyone. Oh, wait a minute. She mentioned a sister in Greensburg, but who knows what her name is? Or where Snoop is?"

Snow began to fall, the first snow of the winter. We'd been waiting for it. Rob took my arm again. "We put the paper to bed a few minutes ago. I'll take Miss Gwynedd home, now. See you in the morning."

We walked up the dark street through a gentle snowfall that quieted the world, wrapping it in soft whiteness. I lay my hand on Rob's arm, comfortable for his support.

"I guess you'll be going to Pittsburgh to see them soon?" he asked.

"I suppose I should. I want to see Papa, but . . ."

"What's really up with you and Davy? You don't seem in a hurry to see him. It's almost as though you're trying to avoid it." His question jerked me awake.

"I guess I am. Davy isn't the boy I used to know. The flood changed him. Got him in its clutches and won't let go."

We walked along in silence for a while, as the street got slick with snow. I started to slip and tightened my grip on Rob's arm. He clasped his hand over mine to keep me from falling, then said, "I hate to admit it, but I'm sorry for what I said about you marrying a convict."

"Why do you hate to admit it?"

He smiled. "Because I hate to be wrong. Don't say you hadn't noticed."

"I *did* notice. That makes it even sweeter. Apology accepted."

"But he's still a convict." He stopped under a streetlamp and turned to face me, his eyes searching mine. "You can do better, Pam. I hate to see you clinging to the memory of something that went down with the flood. Some of these survivors are more wounded than the dead. Davy's one of them."

His eyes held mine for a long moment. He was saying what I'd been thinking for months, but I felt strangely insecure, standing here with him under the streetlamp. I started to walk again—a little faster, and slipped again. Rob caught me in mid-fall. For a few seconds my eyes were level with his, and I felt myself pulled toward him, unable to decide whether to run or stay. In that tiny second a spark lit between us. Maybe it had been there all along, I didn't know. I regained my balance and we continued up the street. Rob didn't take my arm again. We turned off Main onto Bedford, and I could see a light in the window of our Oklahoma house. Katya must be asleep by now. Surely she hadn't waited up for me. At the door I turned and offered Rob my hand.

"Thank you for helping with the paper. I shouldn't have volunteered for you, but I was determined to get Mr. Shaver to take her to Ebensburg."

"Not at all. I enjoyed it. I hope I haven't offended you with my talk about you and Davy. It's none of my business. I should keep my opinions to myself."

"So should we all. Good night, Rob. Thank you for walking me home."

He bowed low on the snowy sidewalk, and I stepped up into the house, feeling as though I should have said something more. Like what? *"Thank you for walking me home, and I'm not sure, but I think I might be falling in love with you?"*

Katya was indeed awake, sitting by the window watching the snow fall. "Evening, Miss Pammie. You out late."

"Yes. I had to help Rob McRae get the paper out. Mr. Shaver had business in Ebensburg." I didn't tell her about Mrs. Plummer's recant— didn't want to get her hopes up.

"Mrs. Plummer died today."

Katya frowned, then her features twisted into a sneer. "Too bad she not die long time ago."

After all of Mrs. Plummer's anti-Hungarian harangues, and her testimony against Istvan, Katya had a right to her feelings. Still, one day she might be able to see Mrs. Plummer in a different light.

"Pammie?"

"Yes?" I turned out the lamp and headed for the stairs, so tired I couldn't think.

"I just think of home. Hungary. Because Christmas come. Think of Mikulas day when children put boots by window for Mikulas to fill with treat and small gift. I love Christmas. You think we have tree this year, Pammie?"

"Yes, Katya. We'll have a tree. Papa used to go out to the mountains and cut one for us. I'll see what I can do. Tomorrow. I'll go tomorrow."

"Good. I decorate with cookies and ribbon bows." She was quiet for a while. Then . . ."Pammie? You think I go Pittsburgh, see Istvan after Christmas?"

"Yes, if you want to. I'll go with you. I can see Papa then, too."

"And Davy?'

I hesitated. "I don't know. Maybe." My voice sounded flat.

She was quiet for a long time. "Why you stay out late with Rob McRae? You like Rob McRae?"

"No, Katya. I don't like him. I work with him, that's all. He can be very tiresome."

Katya smiled. "I know. Istvan tiresome, too. But I love."

I got into bed, exhausted but now wide awake with Katya's prattling. I lay there for maybe an hour before sleep finally descended, thinking about poor Mrs. Plummer, her sniveling son, and Istvan rotting in jail, and—despite my best intentions—Rob McRae.

Chapter 30

I hate to admit it, but I view the weekend with trepidation. What if Miss Duncan comes home radiant, full of wedding plans, a date set? What then? Well, I tell myself, James will just have to look elsewhere. But I've never seen this look in his eye before—this spring in his step. I do believe my son is in love, and, like any mother, I'm prepared to shower scorn upon any woman who spurns him.

I spend the weekend writing letters, listening to the radio, reading, knitting—like a caged lion. I go out for a couple of long walks—even as far as the woods outside town. That brings up another whole series of memories. Christmas, Katya's baking, getting a tree.

The day before Christmas I awakened to the smells of cinnamon and sugar. Katya'd been up since five o'clock, creating marvelous, intricate Christmas cookies. Her early morning smile was full of exhilaration and Christmas spirit. The house felt warm in spite of the snow piled up at the door—maybe four inches fell overnight. Mama was dressed and fed, seated as always in her rocking chair, close to the stove. She seemed to sense the holiday air and rocked just a little from time to time.

"You go get tree?" Katya asked, her face alight with anticipation.

"Yes, Katya. I get tree," I assured her. "I'm not quite sure how I'll accomplish it, but I'll get us a tree today."

After breakfast I put on my coat, hat, mittens and boots and went out into the beautiful morning. Crisp, quiet, undisturbed snow all around. Crystalline whiteness that covered all the scars and revived hope. I stopped to breathe in the wintry air, actually feeling the Christmas spirit for the first time in three years. I went around to the back yard and looked toward Mr. Hughes's shed, where Davy used to stay. I remembered seeing an ax hanging on the wall in there, and if it was still there, that would solve one problem.

The shed stood lonely and forlorn, its door closed but not locked. I slid it open and looked inside. The place was a shambles, left that way by the police after the raid. It was only a few months ago, but it seemed like a different century. A light trace of snow lay on the floor inside the door. Davy's cot stood against the wall under the window, the mattress turned up, the pillow on the floor. It felt colder in here than outside. A shiver ran through me as the memory of our one night of love-making resurfaced. I looked away, shaken by the memory. Once I found the ax, I lifted it from its peg, holding it carefully by the handle. I looked back at the rumpled bed—a stark reminder of times past—mistakes made— and was flooded by a need to get outside again, into the sunshine.

As I slid the door shut, I noticed tracks in the snow through Mr. Hughes's yard. I dismissed them as probably made by neighborhood children taking shortcuts. But it was pretty early for children to be out, even on the Saturday before Christmas. I stood looking at the Oklahoma house, more sorrowful than the shed. Tracks led up to a back window, and curiosity spurred me to wonder who'd been looking in— nudged me across the snowy yard to the house. I stopped again and wondered at the contrast with the lovely large home that stood here once. Full of children, full of life. Poor Mr. Hughes. No wonder he turned hateful in despair.

Pulled like a pin to a magnet, I moved toward the back window and peered in. It was much the same as the shed, a mess left over from the police search. I put both hands on the sash, surprised when it raised with little resistance. Why not? I boosted myself up and crawled through, leaving the ax outside, resting against the house. I don't know what I expected to find, but as soon as I put my feet on the floor, I turned around and found myself face to face with Snoop Plummer. I started and let out a scream. Snoop's hand was over my mouth before I could make another sound.

"Hush. Don't give me away. They'd kill me if they caught me." His voice quavered with fear.

He released me and stood hunched over, looking worn out, his clothes dirty and torn. He needed a shave; his hands shook—with the cold?

I brushed myself off, straightened and looked him in the eye. "What in the world are you doing here?"

"Don't talk so loud. I came back to see my mother—help her get to my aunt's house in Greensburg, but she must have gone already. There was nobody home when I got there last night. I came over here because it was snowing and I figured they'd be watching my mother's house."

"Your mother. Oh, Clarence. I'm so sorry. She's dead. Your mother died yesterday." I watched his face, wishing I could soften the news. "I'm sorry."

He stared dumbly at me, unable to comprehend. "Dead? She's dead? How did she die?" His face twisted in disbelief. I was afraid he was going to cry. I didn't know what I'd do if he cried.

"Her heart."

"Where is she? Where'd they take her?" The urgency in his voice made me want to take back all the bad things I'd said about him leaving her to her fate in Johnstown.

"To Fullerton's Mortuary. That's all I know. There'll be a funeral notice in Monday's paper."

He stepped back, letting the news sink in, shrinking visibly. He looked more lost and alone than I'd ever dreamed of being.

"Snoop . . ."

"Don't call me Snoop!"

"Clarence, you'd better get out of here before someone discovers you. Talk in town is pretty nasty, and now they don't have to care about offending your poor mother."

Snoop Plummer's posture, never full of confidence, drooped even more as he sank onto a backless kitchen chair. He lowered his head to his hands, elbows on his knees. His hands were dirty, grime under his nails. I looked around in the dim morning light at the cold, barren little room. The windows were smudged, the floor needed sweeping. There were dirty dishes on the table. The room smelled damp and musty, even in the cold. Why was I thinking these things when the man before me reeled in anguish? I waited for him to speak. Say anything. Just don't turn mean on me.

I was way beyond comfortable, not exactly afraid—but wary. My back was to the open window, and I edged in that direction, measuring the chances while Snoop sat quietly, head in his hands, engulfed in grief.

"I was gonna take care of her. She always took care of me." He looked up, eyes full of tears, as though I might have an answer for him—a truth that'd make it all better.

I nodded. "That's true. Her love for you was as solid as the railroad bridge."

Now he was talking to the floor, his feet wide apart. The leather of his shoes was split, one of the soles pulled away. "I only did it to be somebody. When I took up with Ev Dailey, I seen right away he was in on somethin.' I just joined up to find out what they was up to. When them Pinkertons come to town, I seen my chance to make somethin' of myself. Maybe even get June to care for me 'stead of pinin' away for Paul Confer like she did."

"June? Where is June, now? Are you still married to her?"

He barely shook his head. "Naw. I got a letter from a priest, sent to the court in Pittsburgh, an' they give it to me. Said the marriage was annulled. Said it wasn't consummated. I had to ask what that meant. Meant we never even done it. She wouldn't let me touch her. I slept on the daybed in her room, over there at the Dailey house. For appearances, she said."

In spite of all that'd happened, I felt sorry for this sniveling little slip of a man. He couldn't help what he was. The sad truth was, he thought he was going to gain respect. Well, not here. Not in Johnstown.

"You still gonna marry Davy?" he asked, looking up from his hands.

"No. Davy and I are all over." I didn't want to discuss Davy with this poor wretch. "You'd best lay low here until dark and then get out of town as fast and as far as you can."

"My mother's funeral. Guess I can't go to that."

"The whole town'll be watching for you. Your mother would want to know you're safe. Maybe sometime, after this has blown over, you can visit her grave."

I'd only seen a more destitute picture in the aftermath of the flood. Snoop Plummer sat head down, body shrunken, hands shaking. There was nothing more I could say. I took two steps back toward the window. He didn't move. I sat on the ledge, swung my legs over and dropped to the ground, my coat cushioning my landing. I lowered the window and grabbed the ax.

I walked along, thinking about the sad excuse for a man I'd just left and thanking my guardian angel he wasn't Davy. I trudged through the new snow, turned toward the Stoney Creek, and passed through Kernville on my way to the woods, lost in thought about Snoop and his mother. I felt a little foolish, going out after a Christmas tree by myself.

Maybe I should just buy one from one of the hucksters downtown. But the need to restore the family tradition spurred me on, and within a mile, I was in the woods. I followed an old lumber road up into the hills, watching for suitable pine trees. There was one. Nicely shaped. Not too big. I waded through the ankle deep snow toward it.

"Not that one. It's a hemlock."

I started at the sound of a man's voice, far enough away that I couldn't place it right away. Not Snoop. Surely he wouldn't have followed me. I stood still, waiting for whoever it was to reveal himself.

"This one's better. White pine."

Rob McRae stood by a nice little tree, a hundred feet or so from the one I'd chosen. "Hemlocks don't make good Christmas trees," he said, shaking the snow from the pine.

"What are you doing here?"

"Getting a Christmas tree, what else?"

"You weren't following me?"

"Following you? Why would I do that? To see you climbing in and out of your neighbor's window? Stealing an ax? Trespassing? Or to keep you from cutting off your foot with that ax?"

He stepped toward me. I was relieved it was Rob and not Snoop Plummer, and that he was here to help me cut down a tree, which I might or might not be able to do by myself. I navigated a few drifts and made my way to his side, holding out the ax.

"If you came to cut a tree, why didn't you bring your own ax?"

He grinned that annoying, smug, superior grin of his. I would have turned my back and walked away, except that I wanted his help with this tree. He took off his jacket and knelt in the snow. Trimming away some of the lower branches, he cleared himself a space, stood back, and took a good, solid swing at the tree trunk. After only about six swings the little tree folded over in the snow.

He handed me the ax, put his coat back on, and grabbed hold of the tree trunk. Dragging it behind him, he led the way back to the road, which was getting a little muddy now that the sun was up and melting the snow. I followed with the ax, wondering how much he saw of my morning adventure and why he was there to see it.

Once on the road, we kept to the snow-covered edge and swung into an easy gait, heading back for town.

"Thought you were here for your own tree. Change your mind?"

He walked along in silence, ignoring my question.

"Why were you watching me this morning?" I was irritated. Glad for the help, but miffed at the way he just stepped in and took over. Thought he was smart. Sometimes I found him insufferable. So here I was tripping along at his side, ready to invite him in for some of Katya's Christmas baking when we got home. No pride whatsoever.

He countered with a question of his own. "What was so interesting in Mr. Hughes's house this morning?"

"Nothing. I just looked around. That's all."

"Talking to yourself, were you? People will think you're daft if you do that."

"Talking? Where were you? Close enough to hear?"

"Close enough to hear a man's voice."

I stopped and looked up at him. "If I tell you, will you promise to keep it to yourself?"

"What? I'm a newspaper man. I don't make promises I can't keep. But I can guess who it was. In fact, I know who it was."

"Well, then I've no need to tell you."

We walked along in silence while Rob digested that comment. "Well, I don't *really* know who it was. I merely suspect it was Snoop Plummer and that you told him his mother died. Am I right?"

My silence buoyed his confidence, and he grinned down at me. "I'm right, huh? I figured as much."

"Rob, don't tell a soul. He's pathetic, that's all. He has no one. No place to go. He'll have to start life again somewhere."

"Six hundred dollars should take the sting out of that."

"Maybe so, but even if he's a sniveling little twit, he doesn't deserve what he'd get at the hands of a Johnstown mob."

We made our way up Haynes Street and down Bedford to my house. Rob set the tree on the step and gave it a shake to clear off the snow. "Here, hold this while I take back the ax you stole. Might be some wood in that shed I can use for a tree stand."

I did as bidden and found myself standing there in the cold for almost five minutes before I asked myself, *"Why am I standing here in the cold? Just because Rob told me to? What's wrong with me?"* I leaned the tree against the house and went inside to tell Katya to put out some refreshments. She was more than glad for the company.

We heard Rob struggling with the tree, and I gave Katya a wink. "He's determined to be the man, so let him."

He opened the door and wrestled the little tree into the tiny room. Katya giggled with glee and started to decorate it right away with cookies and popcorn she'd strung this morning.

"You miss excitement, Pammie. Some men come and find Snoop Plummer in Mr. Hughes house. Take him downtown in wagon. They kill him, I think."

Chapter 31

*R*ob didn't even have time to set the tree in place before I grabbed his arm and tore out the door and down the steps. "Come on. They've got Snoop. Katya says they took him downtown."

We rushed across the snowy yard and turned down Bedford Street to Main. Far down Main Street a crowd had gathered. "Rob! They're going to kill him. We have to stop them."

We ran, pell mell, down Main Street, jumping over puddles, swerving to avoid icy spots. The street was crowded with wagons on the day before Christmas, and the melting snow made running treacherous. We ran all the way to Union Street and stopped, breathless, where the crowd milled around in front of the jail. Snoop Plummer stood in an old, broken-down wagon, arms tied behind him, head almost resting on his chest. People shouted insults and shook threatening fists. The look of terror in his eyes was beyond human. He saw me, and a look passed between us that told me he thought I'd betrayed him. I shook my head.

In front of the crowd, Johnstown's police force stood ready to take Snoop into protective custody. Apparently the mob was on their way to the Point, where the Conemaugh and Stoney Creek Rivers meet, in order to have a very public punishment, betting the police wouldn't intervene. They were wrong. Chief Harris stepped up and confronted the leaders of the vigilantes.

"He hasn't committed any crime," the chief said evenly. "You have no right to abuse him. If you do, I'll have to arrest you, and I'd hate to do that."

One of the ringleaders, a burly steel worker named Mike, brushed him aside. "You wouldn't do that and stay in this town. You know he deserves what he gets."

"Deserving has nothing to do with it. You have no right to decide who's done what and how to punish them for it. I can't . . . won't . . . let that happen."

The crowd was restless, anxious to get on with their business. They looked on down toward the Point, and someone slapped the horse on the rump. The start threw Snoop off balance, sending him crashing to the wagon floor. Rob stepped forward and grabbed the horse's head to calm him. The crowd pushed in around him so that I could barely see the top of his head. He pushed back, stepped away, and swung himself up onto the horse's back. The crowd pushed in again, and Rob raised his hand to speak.

"Get back. Get out of the way." He looked over heads at the chief of police. "I'm taking this man out of town. I need a police escort. Are you with me?"

Chief Harris nodded and motioned for three of his men to get in the wagon. They climbed up, guns drawn, positioning themselves to watch in three directions. A fourth man pulled himself up into the driver's seat and took the reins, but it was Rob who dug his heels into the horse's belly and turned down Union Street toward Washington. The wagon turned slowly, sagging and wobbling in its rickety state. Snoop sat on a box in the middle, blood trickling down the side of his face from a cut above his temple.

The steel man, Mike, turned to rally the crowd. "Come on! Let's follow 'em. They don't have no dominion outside of town. Let's git 'em then!"

Terrified for both Snoop and Rob, I hitched up my skirts and ran after the wagon. Its progress was slowed by all the Christmas traffic, but people fell back when they saw the police officers with guns drawn. I had no trouble catching up.

I reached for the tailgate and pulled myself up. The officer in the back of the wagon offered no help, but he didn't try to stop me either. Once I was in, he pushed me unceremoniously to the floor. "Stay there and don't make no trouble," he growled.

I watched Rob's back as he guided the horse through the crowds, up Washington Street to Clinton where he turned right and followed it into Bedford Street. We drove past our house, bare and bedraggled in the melting snow. The crowd followed about a half block behind, dwindling now. One of the policemen yelled at Rob. "Don't know what yer gonna do once we get outa town. They'll probably rush you then."

Rob turned and saw me for the first time. He grinned. "Let me worry about that."

As we neared the edge of town, Rob turned and shouted to the four policemen, "Jump out when you can. I'm not going to slow down. See how long you can stall them."

The police took orders from him as though used to it. They seemed to admire his courage, and even if they wouldn't mind seeing the crowd do its work, they were conscious of their responsibility. As we passed out of town they jumped off the wagon, one by one, and formed a four-man barrier across the road.

As soon as they were out, Rob larruped up the horse and we went careening along the rutted, muddy road, splashing snow and water waist high on pedestrians. They set up a howl, but Rob heard none of it. He turned and shouted to me to untie Snoop. I did that, with some difficulty—the knots had obviously been made by a man. Snoop's face was white with fear.

"I didn't turn you in," I shouted over the noise of the wagon.

Rob was yelling again. "Snoop! Get ready to jump!"

We'd gained some distance on the angry crowd, and Rob looked for a place for Snoop to jump out and get into hiding—around a bend where they couldn't see. The horse was getting tired—probably not used to such carrying on—so we didn't have much time. We came to a sharp curve to the left, and Rob slowed enough for Snoop to jump out and scramble into the woods beside the road. He was gone in an instant, his old, brown coat blending in with the bare trees. We continued on around the curve at a pace that had me holding on tight.

We kept up speed as long as the horse could run, and then, having put some distance between ourselves and the crowd, we let him have his wind and slowed to a walk. After about five minutes, Rob pulled up and got down from the horse's back. He walked back to the wagon, his face red from the effort of riding without saddle or bridle. I offered him a hand as he climbed up beside me on the wagon seat.

"There. That's about all we can do. They'd have caught up with us eventually. Some of them anyway." He took the reins, urged the horse into a wide turn and let it set its own pace back to town. Along the way we ran into remnants of the crowd.

"Think yer pretty smart, don'tcha, McRae?" someone shouted.

"Smart enough to save you from yourselves. What's the matter with you? Do you want to wind up in jail with Gwynedd, Dailey and the Hugheses? Think, man. Snoop Plummer! Is that little worm worth going to jail for?"

They grumbled and grouched, but the fight had gone out of them. They were still in a bad mood, but no one was for tracking Snoop through the woods.

"Besides," I told them, "you've already frightened the daylights out of him. He won't be back. And he won't have a happy life, either."

"Six hunnert dollars'd make me pretty happy," the steel worker named Mike called out.

"Not if you had no home, no family and no place to go," Rob reminded him.

We left them grumbling among themselves, already talking of other things. Christmas. The work schedule. Stopping at Callahan's for a beer.

I rode along beside Rob in the wagon, hoping Snoop would get away—far away and never come back. He didn't deserve to die, but he didn't deserve much pity, either. At least he had something to start him on a new life. What was left was up to him.

Rob interrupted my thoughts. "Think Katya'll still have some cookies left?"

"I think so. She baked enough for the whole county. Those Hungarian women are hard to stop when you get them in a kitchen." Then, thinking of Katya, I wondered what was in store for her. Whether next Christmas would find her with Istvan or alone again.

"Know whose wagon this is?" Rob asked.

I shook my head.

"We'll drop it at the livery. They'll know where it goes."

I'm sitting in the kitchen sorting recipes on Monday evening when James comes in the back door. "Hello. I didn't hear you drive up."

"I walked." He helps himself to a cruller from the breadbox and sits down. "Got any coffee?"

I nod to the pot sitting on the stove. He rises and picks a mug out of the cupboard and pours. "Want any?"

I wait for him to start the conversation we both know is sitting around the fringe of the kitchen. He rubs his forehead with his fingers, eyes down. When he looks up, I see he's struggling with unfamiliar feelings.

"She didn't break it off. I thought she would. Thought she was ready. Now I don't know." He sounds dispirited.

"What did she say—beforehand, I mean. To make you think she would?"

"Nothing, really. But we were getting along so well. I could see it in her eyes. She was thinking about it."

My heart goes out to him. My James. Always so confident, like his father. But here he is, a helpless specimen, in love with nothing to do about it. "What did she say about her weekend?"

"Not much. Just that they had a nice time. She stayed with her aunt, and he brought his dad to meet her."

My heart stops. "His dad? I thought he lived in Detroit."

"He does. In Pittsburgh on business or something. Anyway, you know he's rich. Maybe that does turn a girl's head."

Davy Hughes in Pittsburgh again. That must be some visit. It passes through my mind to wonder if he'd stopped by the jail where he'd spent some of his youth, or if he'd visited the homes of some of his late enemies, the South Fork Club members.

"Wouldn't have turned mine. You can bet, if she's any kind of worthwhile girl, it won't turn hers."

I feel the bile rising in me. Davy Hughes could just go back to Detroit and take his son with him. Hadn't he done enough to mess up my life? Why did he have to come back into it now?

"I don't know, Ma. Don't know if I should pursue this or not. Don't know what she's thinking."

"Have you kissed her yet?"

"No."

"Well, try that. She's either waiting for you—dying for you to do it, or she'll let you know on no uncertain terms where her heart lies."

He stares at me, dumbfounded. "Really? That easy?"

"Really. That easy. You'll know where to go from there. No doubt about it." I hear myself giving advice on love and smile. Then I remember Davy Hughes. Well, maybe I do know a little something about love.

James pushes back his chair and turns toward the kitchen door. "Think I'll drive over to Highland Avenue and see if she wants to go for a ride."

"Good idea."

He's barely out the door before I call Katya. "Davy Hughes is in Pittsburgh. Ellen Duncan met him for the first time this weekend. What do you think of that?"

"What do *you* think of it?" she asks.

"I think . . . I think he's probably the same old Davy, but I'd like to know."

Katya listens as I probe my feelings. My life has been good since Davy's been out of it. Better than I ever hoped back in those dark days after the flood. But I can't help but wonder if he's ever really gotten over his wrath. Is he happy? I know he's accomplished a lot—gotten rich—but is he whole and healthy and fulfilled?

"Why do you care?" Katya has a way of getting to the core of things.

"I don't know. I don't know, Katya. I loved Rob with all my heart, never a regret there, but . . ."

There's a sigh on the other end of the phone. "You want to tell him to back off and let your James have the girl? Is that it?"

"Not very realistic, now, is it? I mean, it's really up to the children to decide. But I don't like the idea of Davy Hughes lurking in the background."

"He probably doesn't even know Ellen Duncan knows James. How could he have anything to do with this romance?"

"He knows she works for the *Clarion*. That much I'm sure of. Who knows, maybe he's rich enough and nosy enough and controlling enough to have her followed or investigated or something."

Another sigh. "You take a pill and go to sleep, Pam. You need rest. This'll all look different in the morning."

I doubt that. I put down the phone and settle into my reading chair. The book holds my attention for about five minutes before my mind goes wandering again—back to the day we saved Snoop Plummer. Rob and I riding that rickety wagon along the muddy road, talking about Snoop and his chances for a new life.

Back in town, we headed slowly down Main Street toward the scene of this morning's drama. I saw Laura walking along with her arms full of parcels and Dewey at her side.

"There's Laura. Stop, Rob. You can let me out here."

"Hey, what about my cookies?"

"I'll bring you some on Monday."

He stuck out his lower lip like a petulant child. "Not 'til Monday? How about later today? Christmas Eve day. Should call for some kind of celebration. After all, I did help get the tree."

"All right. Come over at suppertime. I'll tell Katya to set another plate."

I climbed down to talk to Laura.

"Look at you!" she cried. "Mud all over your coat. Your boots scuffed. Your hair's a mess. I'm afraid to ask what you and Rob McRae have been doing!"

"You won't believe it," I responded and fell to telling her about my adventures. She listened quietly with a knowing look.

"No, Laura. It's not what you think. Don't go jumping to conclusions about Rob and me. We're just friends. That's all."

"Maybe you think so, but I saw the way he looked at you when you got out of that wagon. He's got other ideas."

Her words gave me a turn. I was still uncomfortable—almost panicked—with the idea of Rob as a prospective beau. I turned my attention to Dewey as he fidgeted and played in the sloppy snow. "Going sledding today, Dewey?"

"Yes. Poppy is taking me soon as we get home," he replied with an impatient glance at his mother.

"Are you all done Christmas shopping?" Laura asked.

I stopped, puzzled. I hadn't made anything for Mama this year, but what could I get her? She barely noticed whether it was day or night. I couldn't give Papa much besides food or reading material in jail. There wasn't anybody else but Katya. The light dawned. I saw a beautiful gold plated thimble in Elder's window one day last week. I could get that for Katya.

"Almost. I just have one more thing to buy."

As Laura and I parted company, I hurried on up Main to Elder's. Mrs. Elder looked harried, waiting on customers one after another. I had time to browse as I waited in line. Then I saw it. A beautiful soft watercolor of a river, flowing gently between banks of trees and flowers. The kind of thing I'd wished for, for Mama. I asked the price, surprised to find it was painted by one of our local women, and that she was asking only a few dollars for it. A few dollars was still a lot of money then, but I wanted it so much for Mama. Something beautiful to look at instead of the rough, unfinished boards of an Oklahoma house.

I hurried home with my purchases. Katya had the tree all trimmed, and the smells of pine and cinnamon raised my spirits. There was a package under the tree, marked "For Pammie" in very careful print.

"What happen to Snoop? They kill him?" Katya asked.

"No. Rob saved him."

"What he do that for? Snoop no good."

"I agree he's not much good, but he didn't deserve to die. Really, Katya. He's just a sad, sorry excuse for a man."

Katya sniffed. "You want cider?" She offered me a mug of hot mulled cider, just the thing after my hard day. I sat down in the other rocking chair beside Mama and took off my wet boots. I sat in my stocking feet watching the stove, sipping my cider, listening to the crackling of the fire.

Suddenly there was a knock at the door. Rob! I forgot! Katya opened it and ushered him in. The room was too small—barely big enough for two. There was no place for him to sit but on one of the two chairs at the table. He smiled and pulled one of the straight chairs up beside mine.

"Some day, wasn't it?"

"Umm. I wouldn't want too many more like that stacked together."

There we sat, Mama, Rob and me in a little semi-circle in front of the fire. Katya brought Rob a mug of cider. I sipped my cider, feeling self-conscious, embarrassed by the inadequacy of my position—poor as a church mouse, as they say. Rob Mc Rae in my house. Must be an adventure for him. There it was. Nothing to be done but make the best of it.

"Would you like your cookies before or after the repast?" I asked.

He grinned that boyish grin. "Both," he replied.

Katya, delighted to have company, turned out a dinner to be proud of. We ate, pulling two straight chairs and two rocking chairs up to the table. Rob watched as I cut up my mother's food and fed her like a baby. His face softened. "You need better living conditions."

"Tell me about it," I sighed.

Katya added her opinion. "We get along. Pammie and me. We do. But need more room. Maybe another Oklahoma house hitch on."

We laughed at the prospect of a train of Oklahoma houses trailing across our lawn. "Yes, we could have a very large house if we wanted. Even use one of them for a bathroom!"

"Have you looked into the possibility of getting some help from the Relief Commission? People poorer than you have gotten housing vouchers."

"There aren't any people poorer than I, Rob. Believe me."

We talked for an hour after dinner, a little self-consciously, considering Mama and Katya were close at hand. He sipped his cider, munched cookies, and looked at the stove, showing its flame through an isinglass window. When he rose to go, I felt a flutter of regret at the evening coming to an end. It was surely the nicest Christmas Eve since the flood. I went to the door with him, and he motioned for me to step outside. The sky was dark and full of stars. We walked across the yard arm in arm, looking up at the dazzling display, the frozen snow crunching under our feet. Rob touched my shoulder, and I turned to him, knowing what was to come. Wanting it. Fearing it. He pulled me close and tipped my chin up with his hand. My lips rose to meet his—the stirrings of old feelings awakening in me.

Chapter 32

Morning doesn't bring relief from my worries about Davy Hughes. I wander around the house, restless. I want to do something, but I don't know what. What are my alternatives? Nothing. Just wait and see what happens. I'm not good at that. I want to make something happen.

I decide to do some gardening to distract myself, but just as I'm pulling on my gardening gloves, the doorbell rings—almost sets my hair on fire. I enter the vestibule and look out the window. There in front sets a very large, very black car with a spare tire molded into the front fender and a chrome winged goddess on the hood. It's the biggest car I've ever seen—a Cadillac—I can tell that much. On the porch in front of my door stands a smallish man with a broad white mustache and white hair, hat in hand. Davy Hughes.

I open the door and smile. "Davy! Davy Hughes! I'd know you anywhere." I'm lying, of course. He's shorter and broader than I remember. Lines about his still gray eyes. His clothes certainly didn't come off the rack. Fine wool tailoring. Impeccable fit. The stories are true. Davy's done well for himself.

He stands on the porch, rich bowler hat in hand, sizing me up as I did him. I must look a fright in my gardening smock, gardening shoes and gloves. I raise a hand to my hair, but it's too late. He's already taken in the gray and, most probably, the unruliness. The wrinkles, too, I'm sure.

"Come in, Davy." I open the door wide.

He steps inside and hands me his hat, which I hang on the hall tree in the corner before ushering him into the living room. "Can I get you something? A cup of tea? I've got some delicious coffee cake I made myself."

He shakes his head and takes a seat on the davenport without saying anything. Awkward silence. I wonder if he's lost his voice.

"What brings you back to Johnstown after all these years?" I ask. Even now I get the feeling I need to brighten things up with Davy— never one to take life lightly.

He doesn't answer right away. Busy taking in the room. His eyes measure every square inch—curtains, furnishings, carpets, without the slightest effort to hide his stock-taking. I watch him, not sure how to take this odd silence. .

When he finally speaks, it's abrupt—disconnected with my question. "Evan. I go by Evan now. Easier to keep track of."

"Evan. Yes, that would be a more mature name than Davy." My mind goes to the need to change one's name if one wants to forget one's past. "I'm surprised to see you here. Do you have business?"

"Some. You might say. I'm here on behalf of my son, David Jr. He's living in Pittsburgh, but has somehow managed to get himself engaged to a Johnstown girl. Ellen Duncan is her name. Do you know her?"

"Ellen Duncan? Why yes, of course. She's Bert and Elizabeth Duncan's daughter. You wouldn't know them. They came here some time after you left."

Davy's very direct. Used to being heeded and obeyed. He certainly must have found his niche in the automobile business. There is no passion or gentleness in his eyes—no emotion at all. Just business. I get the message quite clearly. This isn't a social call.

"Yes. Well, as you would understand, there's some history here that I'd like to keep in its proper place. The past. I've managed to make a name for myself in Detroit, and I'd like to keep it separate from my past life. I'm sure you understand. I'm frankly worried that David's marrying a Johnstown girl will bring up old stories that are better left in the trash bin of history."

"Yes. I know. You've done well, and now you're in the same position as those you once hated. How does that feel?"

"I didn't come here to delve back into all that. It's over and done with. I've paid my debt, and you can't blame me if I want to keep the past in the past. I have connections. Business connections, that would be damaged by any sort of revelation about my youthful indiscretions."

"I see. And that brings you to my door?"

"Yes, Pamela. You and your husband . . ."

"Rob. You knew him. His name was Rob."

"You and Rob owned the *Clarion*. Newspapers can suppress stories that are, shall we say, inconvenient?"

I nod.

"I understand your son owns the paper now, and, much to my distaste, the young lady, Miss Duncan, works there."

I nod again. "Yes, she does. She hasn't been there long. I hardly know her. Why is that to your distaste?"

245

"Newspapers always did give me pause. Tend to take up causes they don't understand. Defend the downtrodden. Poke around in places beyond their realm. That sort of thing. But more to the point, I don't want anyone using this betrothal as an excuse to stick their nose into my business, delve into my past. This is damned inconvenient, I want you to know."

"I'm sure. So you want me to use my influence to get my son to suppress any story that might come to light about your past?"

"That's right, Pam. That's what I'm asking. Tell your son I can make it worth his while to keep on my good side. I make philanthropic donations all the time. Does Johnstown need a new hospital? New library? New community center?"

"Well, Davy, I understand your point of view, but what kind of newspaper man would James be if he allowed himself to be bought? If you can do it, anyone can do it. I can't answer for my son, but my take on it is, he wouldn't dream of suppressing news for any reason."

"News? News? This wouldn't be news. It'd be salacious gossip. Not newsworthy at all."

"I guess we'd have to let the editor of the *Clarion* decide that, if and when such a story would arise."

"Are you telling me you won't cooperate? Not even for old times' sake?"

"I'm telling you I won't intervene on your behalf with my son. He'd send me packing even if I did. And if *I* were still in charge down there, you couldn't turn *my* head with your money either."

He stands, his eyes sparked with anger. "You always were a simple soul, Pamela, with your insistence in doing the right thing. I see that hasn't changed. Well, I hope you're happy here in this poor, God-forsaken place. As for me, there's a whole world out there you know nothing about. I'll fix this. You wait and see."

He steps around the davenport and into the vestibule. I rise and follow, but not too close. My mind races with memories. How lucky I was not to have married Davy. How lucky I was that Rob McRae came along when he did.

"I'm sorry, Davy. When I saw you at my door, I hoped for a joyful reunion. I'm sorry it didn't turn out that way. Are you going back to Pittsburgh?"

He turns in the doorway and pulls his hat down from the tree. "After I visit the cemetery. Want to lay flowers on the graves of my family."

"I visit their graves often, Davy. Theirs—and my family's, too. And Rob's, of course. I don't want any of them to be forgotten."

He stops on his way out the door and turns to me, his eyes downcast. "Damn the flood, Pam. Damn it to hell. It ruined our lives, yours and mine. Ruined them. And nobody paid."

"In the whole scheme of things, I don't see it that way. It didn't ruin my life. It brought it to fruition. Made me whole. Brought Rob and me together. We had a nice life. Fulfilling. Meaningful. We didn't get rich, but we've always been comfortable. The flood gave me a sense of what's really important."

"There you go, putting a nice polish on a clinker. Well, best you and I parted ways way back then. We'd have clashed mightily, I'm afraid."

"Yes, I guess. We did then, and we still do. I do still wish you well, though. You're not the man I thought you were, but you have a right not to be. A right to be who you are, I mean."

He reaches out with his left hand and grasps mine. "Life takes us on unexpected paths. Let's leave it at that."

He turns and crosses the front porch as his driver steps out and opens the back door of the limousine. I watch as he ducks into the back seat and settles into comfort and luxury. Then I close the door and go back out to my gardening. Thank you, God, for Rob McRae.

Digging in the roses calms me. It always has. Guess I inherited that from my mother. Despite my agitation pretty soon I'm back there again—back to that Christmas, the fourth one after the flood. Katya's gift to me was a beautiful new dress, a pink gingham check with intricate smocking at the shoulders and a row of tiny buttons down the front. Delighted, I gave her the tiny package containing the thimble. She opened it, tried it on and smiled her joy. "Every time I wear, I think of you!"

Mama, seated in her customary place, didn't respond when I showed her the dress, so I placed my parcel before her, wrapped in brown paper. Her gaze didn't waver. I unwrapped it and lifted the lovely watercolor for her to see.

"Here, Mama. I got you something pretty to look at."

Katya ooohed and aaahed. We watched Mama's face for any sign of joy or delight. None. I sighed and went to find a nail to hang the picture on. As I drove the nail into the two by four stud to the right of the stove,

I wondered if Davy and Laura might be right. Maybe she never *would* come back.

But then I noticed a tiny, almost imperceptible reaction. When I turned back from hanging the picture, she moved her chair, ever so slightly, to gain a better angle. All Christmas day she looked at the picture instead of the stove. Progress?

The day was quiet, unlike the turmoil that boiled up inside of me. Kissing Rob McRae had set me down in the midst of uncertainty. I went about the routine tasks, but my mind was far away. Where was Rob today? What was he doing? A house full of company? Was he thinking of me? The magnitude of the contrast between our lives glared. I felt drawn to Rob with an intensity once reserved for Davy Hughes, but I couldn't let myself love him. Davy and I had been so sure of our love, and look where that led us. The realization that love could die turned my heart to lead. I kept a tight rein on my feelings, sure that I was reading more into one kiss than intended.

I put more wood on the fire and turned to Katya to distract myself.

"Would you like to visit Istvan this week? We could go on Wednesday. You could take him some of your Christmas cookies."

Her face lit up. "Yes! Kifli and nut rolls. Istvan love!" She was off in an instant, planning what to wear, what to take and what to say. I, on the other hand, was engaged in plodding thought about my father and, inevitably, Davy.

The day after Christmas I approached Mr. Shaver. "Could I have Wednesday off to go visit my father?"

"Sure. Rob and I can muddle through one day without you, can't we, Rob?"

Rob sat at his desk typing busily at some story of his. He looked up and nodded absently.

When I sat down at my desk, I felt a distance between us. Something was bothering him. He was quiet. No teasing, no banter. Just his fingers punching the keys.

Mr. Shaver gave me a questioning glance, and I raised my eyebrows in reply. For the rest of that day and the next, Rob was busy, businesslike—almost abrupt. No reference to Christmas Eve.

For me it felt like he was having regrets for leading me on—giving me false hope. He was probably afraid I'd taken his attentions to heart— wondering how he could let me down easy. I revisited my fantasy of falling in love with him and decided I'd been foolish. While the kiss meant something to me, for him it was probably nothing more than a little Christmas cheer.

Monday and Tuesday dragged on with almost no communication between us. I saw the error of my ways. How could a man like Rob McRae find me interesting? I bet he'd had a chuckle over my poor little house. He'd only been nice to me out of pity for my poverty. I should stay where I belonged, on the supper side of town. Rob belonged on the dinner side, and I shouldn't forget that.

The train ride to Pittsburgh on Wednesday was short, about an hour. We got off at the station and followed a map Rob drew for us to the Allegheny County jail. The building was impressive—all arches and spires. So much so that Katya drew her breath when she saw it. "Istvan live in castle," she said.

We entered at the opposite end of the huge, imposing tower of the courthouse. Marble floors, soaring ceilings, echoes of voices. The whole place made me, and I'm sure Katya, feel small. I approached a guard seated at a desk. "We've come from Johnstown to visit some of the prisoners."

I gave him the names, and after he scanned a list he told a police cadet to bring prisoners number 2957 and 4288 to the visitor's room.

"You have fifteen minutes."

He motioned toward a frosted glass door behind him, and we crossed the marble floor and waited for another guard to open it. Inside were two long tables, with two rows of chairs across from each other. There was a pointed, leaded-glass window up high so you couldn't look out, and the room had the echo and chill of masonry walls and high ceilings. Yet another guard stood near the back door, arms crossed, holstered pistol at the ready. We waited in the austere room for maybe ten minutes, chilled and nervous, until the door at the back opened and Istvan shuffled in, wearing dull gray, baggy clothes, wrinkled and smelly.

His appearance belied the grandeur of the building and made me wonder what the actual jail part was like. His face broke into a grin when he saw Katya, and he shuffled over to sit opposite her, his shackles clanking against the floor. Ugly iron manacles kept his wrists from touching the table top. Katya cried out and reached for his hands.

"No touching!" the guard yelled.

Katya jerked her hands back. Filled with anguish at this miscarriage of justice, I smiled anyway and nodded to Istvan as though this were a routine, happy reunion.

My father came in a few minutes later. His hair was white, and his eyes showed wrinkles, but he looked fit and almost happy. He, too, was shackled, but they didn't interfere with his movements the way Istvan's did. The difference between youth and age. Istvan resisted. Papa accepted.

"Papa."

"Pammie. How good of you to come. How is your mother?"

"Much the same, but showing signs of improvement." I told him about the watercolor and how she turned her chair to look at it. He smiled.

"I think there's hope. I think she'll get better when I come home."

"I hope so. I've been working for Mr. Shaver for almost a year now, and I love it. We're not as strapped for money as we were."

"I'm proud of you, girl. You wait and see. I'll get my job back at the Cambria works. Some Johnstown people were here visiting Hughes and Dailey, and they say we'll be welcomed back. When I get back to work, I'll apply for a loan and build us a house."

I smiled at that. "I don't know. I've grown attached to the old Oklahoma house. I'd hate to leave it. Maybe we could use it for a tool shed or a stable later on," I said with a laugh.

"You won't be around much after I get home. To hear Davy tell it, he'll be taking you off to greener pastures as soon as he gets out." Papa sighed. "A hard one, that one. Can't seem to get over his anger."

The statement sent a chill through me. My stomach turned to lead at the thought of Davy making plans without even talking to me. Did he think I'd just want to take up and leave with him as soon as Papa got home? Was he really that thick-headed? I thought we'd settled that between us a long time ago. What would it take to get him to let go?

I changed the subject and while Papa and I talked about a lot of things, the fifteen minutes drew to a close before we could get it all said. The guard escorted Istvan out the back door, leaving Katya awash in tears. She turned and hurried through the front to wait for me. When the guard returned, I asked, "May I kiss my father good-bye?"

He nodded almost imperceptibly and looked away. I leaned over and kissed Papa on the forehead. As he rose and turned to go, he asked, "That young man, that Istvan, how long is he in here for?"

"Ten years, so they say."

My father shook his head. "Take the life out of him." He rearranged his shackles for the return to his cell. "This ain't no place for a young man," he said over his shoulder as he shuffled out the door.

I sat in the barren room, gathering my thoughts—alone except for the guard—before getting up to join Katya in the outer chamber.

"You no want to see Davy?" she asked, wiping her tears.

"No." The word sounded terse and final—reflected feeling I couldn't name. Shame? Anguish? Regret? Dread?

Katya watched me, her eyes steady. "You sure?"

I looked around the cold empty room and thought of Davy alone in his cell with no one to talk to, no one to care, and was moved to do something—for the sake of what used to be. "Maybe. Maybe I will. Just because . . ."

Katya nodded, her face solemn. "You need be sure. Sure you no love any more."

I turned to the guard. "There's one other prisoner I'd like to see. David Hughes."

He consulted the list again and turned to the other guard. "Bring in number 2776."

With a backward glance at Katya, I followed the escort into the visitor's room for a second time and sat down at the same table, my hands cold, my breath shallow.

After a few minutes the door opened and Davy was ushered in, shackles jangling, his face unreadable. In a moment. he was sitting down opposite me and I was searching for the right words to close this chapter of our lives.

"You sure took your time about coming to visit."

"I have to work, Davy. To keep Mama and me."

He sniffed. "Oh, yeah. I forgot. You and that sweetie-boy newspaper reporter. That why you couldn't come to the trial? Cause Sweetie Boy had to 'cover' it? I saw him there every day, looking self-important. Someone should smash his pretty-boy face in for him. Then we'd see how important he is."

"Yes, Davy. I couldn't come to the trial because I had to work. Do we have to fight? Isn't there some way for us to be civil with each other?"

His tone softened. "Who's fightin'? I'm just letting you know I wanted to see you. I missed you." He leaned back and put an arm over the back of his chair, despite the clank and rattle of the manacles. He cocked his head to the side—like he was measuring me—the extent of my commitment.

I made no reply, thinking about how easy it would have been for us to see each other ever since the flood, except for Davy's behavior. There didn't need to be any separation at all. We could be married, raising a family by now.

"So where you wanna go when I get out? Your old man's going back to take care of your mother, so you can't hide behind that anymore. Now all we gotta do is decide where to go. I've been thinking maybe Chicago. I like a place where they've never heard of Johnstown."

It hits me like a splash in the face. For the past three years all I've thought about is getting out of Johnstown, putting it all behind me. Now I realize I don't want to go at all. I love the place. It's beautiful and ugly and backward and smart. "I don't know, Davy. Sometimes I don't think Johnstown is so bad."

"Not so bad? You want to live there in the middle of all that destruction and sorrow? All those people slogging through life, trying to forget?" He looked from side to side, sighed, and brought his manacled hands crashing back to the table. "Know that those responsible for it are still living their rich, happy lives? Not me! I'm getting' out, and you're coming with me."

I jumped at the crash, then looked him straight in the eye. "No. I'm not."

Davy stood, his shackles rattling, and stepped back from the table. He was yelling now, and the guard moved in to restrain him. "You're not? You're not? Well, we'll just see if you're not." He slammed both shackled hands down on the table in front of me. I jumped again. The guard pulled his gun and shoved it into Davy's side. "Sit down or she goes."

Davy straightened up slowly, watching my face. "So, that's how it is. How it's always going to be."

"I don't need anyone to lay down the law to me, Davy. And I won't spend the rest of my life watching you torn up by hate."

He sat down. The guard took a few steps back and holstered his gun. The tension eased. Davy rested his head on his hands, elbows on the table. The wrist shackles slipped down his arms, and the chain played a scale against the table's edge. I sat in silence for a few minutes. I was acutely aware of the slow passage of time, wanting this to be over. Fifteen minutes felt like eternity.

Davy shook his head. "I guess you'd better move on, Pam," he said softly. "I've tried to get over it. Get it out of my system. I thought you'd help me with that, but it looks like you've given up on me."

I looked at my hands, my heart pounding in my chest. I couldn't argue.

"Yes. You're right. It started the day I came to see you in the shed out back of your father's house. I knew then you were damaged. I thought time would heal you, but you're as much a victim of the flood as your mother and sisters and brother. You're a walking dead man. Dead to me. Dead to the possibilities that life still offers. I can't help you."

Tears flowed freely down my face. I rose and nodded to the guard. Davy sat silent in that huge, cold Gothic room as I turned my back and walked away.

Chapter 33

I'm beside myself waiting for Katya to come home. I go to the telephone and dial Stephen's number. Katya answers, and, while I begin the conversation with banalities, it isn't but a minute before I'm pouring out the news of Davy's visit.

"So he wants you to do him a favor? Save his rich man's reputation? That's a turnaround from the boy we used to know. Strange, isn't it, how money can turn a man's head. I hope you sent him packing!"

"I did. Told him I wasn't to be bought and neither was James."

"Good! You don't think he'll come back, do you?"

"No. My sense is that he left town right after visiting the cemetery. Probably for good."

Katya sighs. "Not for good if he has to come back here for the wedding."

I take a moment to contemplate that. Davy's son is still engaged to Ellen Duncan, and my son is still in love with her. That familiar helpless feeling that always accompanied dealing with Davy comes over me. "I wonder—if I promised never to print a story on him, could he talk his son out of marrying her?"

"Pamela! You can't go that far. Anyway, how do you think James would like his mother sticking her nose into his love life?"

A giggle escapes me. "Too late," I tell her.

"You know, I think I'd better come home. I'm worried about you. Too many possibilities for trouble."

Now I laugh out loud. "Just what I was hoping for! How soon can you get here?"

Katya arrives on the 4 o'clock bus from Geistown, carrying bags full of produce from the farm. I greet her at the top of the incline with joy and relief. She's always lent a measure of common sense to my shenanigans. Rob loved her for that.

Once in the kitchen, she ties on her apron and sorts the vegetables into piles, washes them, and puts some away. She keeps out enough for a tasty supper of kielbasa, pierogies and stewed vegetables. I realize how much I'd missed her.

We barely sit down at the table when the front door opens and James walks in. "I knew I smelled pierogies," he grins. "Can smell them a mile away. Glad to have you back, Katya. Mother's been pacing like a cop on patrol."

He pats my shoulder and gives Katya a wink while she rushes to get him a plate.

"What brings you here?" I ask.

"A healthy appetite, pierogies—and a bit of news."

Now Katya is back in her chair. "News? What news?"

"I just came from an intimate little talk with Ellen. Seems her intended's father stopped by this morning and got a little too pushy. Wanted her to quit her job at the *Clarion*. Ellen's decided she doesn't like him one bit."

"Doesn't like him? I wonder why?" I try to sound innocent in my curiosity.

"Said he was arrogant. Bossy. No respect for women."

Katya smiles. "That'd be a death knell around here," she says, with a pointed look in my direction.

James attacks his plate of pierogies with a special fervor he reserves for Katya's cooking. No worry. I know when the competition has me. I sit quiet, watching him eat, thinking of his father. Such a strong likeness. Like eating dinner with Rob again.

"So what do you think this news portends? She isn't marrying his father, you know."

"I know, but it's another crack in the wall. I'm thinking young Mr. David Hughes may be in for a fall."

"And guess who'll be there, broom in hand, to sweep up the pieces," Katya smiles.

James pushes back from the table, rubs his stomach, and thanks her for the meal. "Good to have you back, old girl," he says. "Guess I'll hang around here for a while, until after seven. Told her I'd pick her up then."

"Pick her up? You're going out?" I wince at the possibility that James could make his move too soon.

"Just to a movie. I told her she needed something to distract her from her quandary."

"Quandary?"

"Yeah, whether to marry him or me."

"That's a quandary! How did it get to this point? James, you haven't kept us up at all."

He grins. "You already know more than you need to. Leave this to me, Mother. I can tell when the time is right."

I raise an eyebrow and excuse myself from the table. I leave James to help Katya with the dishes and go upstairs. I sit down on my bed, my hands shaking. I want this too much. It isn't mine to have. I have to remember that. After a short talk with myself, I change out of my dress into a robe and go back downstairs just in time to hear James's car pull away from the curb.

"What do you suppose he's up to?" I ask Katya.

She looks at me over her glasses—one of those 'You know as well as I do what he's up to' looks.

I sit down in Rob's chair and turn the radio on. Amos ' n Andy are up to no good, along with Kingfish, the worst conniver of the lot. I listen for a while, but my thoughts keep taking me back to Davy—I'm sorry— Evan Hughes. The name change, the wealth, the pretense, the power makes me smile. I wonder what he'd say if he knew that at this very moment *my* son is working to bring disaster upon *his* son.

I leave the radio on, but my mind is years away, back there again, back where Davy and I left it off.

On the train from Pittsburgh back to Johnstown, Katya turned to me. "I not go again, Pammie. Hurt too bad. Better not see Istvan than see and have so little."

I touched her hand. "I know. Maybe letters would be better."

She nodded.

"I'll get you some paper and see to mailing them for you. Did Istvan say anything about what it was like in jail?"

"Slow. Say time pass slow. I worry he not make it. I worry he too sad."

I wanted to tell her there was hope, but I couldn't. As soon as I got back to the *Clarion* office the next day, I pestered Mr. Shaver. "Have you heard anything from the judge?"

He pointed to the calendar. "After the first of the year."

I returned to my typing, but couldn't resist asking every day, even though I always got the same answer. New Years Day was the next Sunday. I asked again on Monday and was met with nothing but a raised eyebrow. Through all of this, Rob kept his own counsel, pretending to be too busy for small talk. He didn't even ask how my visit with my father and Davy had gone. I couldn't tell if he was trying to discourage me, or if he was just respecting my privacy, giving me time to think. I longed for a return to our easy banter.

The first week of 1893 passed—quiet, busy, non-committal. The second Sunday was the eighth, and I'd set my sights on the tenth. If there wasn't any word from the judge by then, I planned to go to Ebensburg myself to plead Istvan's case, little though I knew of the law.

On the tenth we were hit with a powerful snowstorm that literally brought Johnstown to a standstill. Even the trains from Altoona were stopped while gangs of workers shoveled the tracks. The weather added to my anxiety, and I paced the office, ready to lash out at anything or anyone that tested me.

Rob watched with detached amusement. Having kept his distance since Christmas Eve, he turned away when I looked in his direction, but I saw him smile to himself when he thought I wasn't looking.

"Just what do you find so amusing, Mr. McRae?" It was the first time I'd addressed him directly since Christmas.

"You, Miss Gwynedd, acting like a caged animal. Don't you think you should relax and let the legal system work its way?"

"How is my anxiety a problem for you?"

"It's not, but it seems to be for you." He turned back to his ever-present typewriter.

Now I'd done it. Burned my last bridge. If he had any feelings for me, my shrewishness had surely put him off. I felt worse now than I did five minutes ago, and five minutes ago I was ready to scream.

I peeked into Mr. Shaver's office. "Sir, would you mind if I went home early today? I'm feeling delicate."

"Delicate is it? Well, I've just the treatment for that. What you need, young lady, is a vent for your frustration." He rose from his desk, reached behind his office door and handed me two snow shovels. "Here. You and Rob go out and work it off."

I looked at him in disbelief. Shoveling snow? He wanted me to shovel snow?

"You want to live in a man's world, you can do a man's work. Both of you. Outside. And don't come in until that sidewalk's bare."

I leaned the shovels against Rob's desk while I put on my wraps, my face set in a sullen glare. He kept typing as though he hadn't heard Mr. Shaver's directive. I picked up my shovel and stepped out into snow almost two feet deep, some of it packed by the few brave souls who'd ventured out that morning. I lowered the shovel blade to the sidewalk, scooped, and lifted. It was a dry snow, not very heavy, but the sidewalk was long and wide. In a few minutes, Rob joined me without a word, heaving two shovels full for every one of mine. Always wanting to best me. I worked along behind him, entertaining fantasies about dumping snow down his back. My thoughts worked to conjure disaster upon him. As he stood under the eaves to catch his breath, a huge wedge of snow fell down from the roof, almost burying him up to his knees. I laughed out loud.

He dropped his shovel and moved menacingly toward me. I climbed over a snow bank into the street, watching him warily. He was up over the bank in one long stride, picking me up without ceremony or consideration for my status as a lady, and depositing me bottoms up in the snow bank.

"There. Laugh, but remember there are consequences."

I lay helpless in the snow, struggling to regain my dignity. He'd already climbed down to the sidewalk and picked up his shovel. I let him resume his task before I crawled out of the bank, a fistful of snow concealed in my mitten. As he bent to pick up a shovelful, I ran by, pulled up his collar and shoved the snow down his back. He set up a howl, and I headed for the door, ducking inside just in time to avoid a reprisal.

Mr. Shaver's recipe for reducing office tension had worked its magic. We'd cleaned the whole sidewalk and were hugely tired, but laughing again. Rob put the shovels away. Lunch time.

He turned to me. "Tea Room?"

I nodded, and we went out into the street, walking along beside snow piles almost up to our shoulders. The town was so quiet without the clip of horse's hooves.

"So how was your visit to Pittsburgh?" Rob asked as we walked along mostly shoveled sidewalks on our way. The first time he'd shown any interest.

"All right. My father seems well and he's full of plans to come home and get back to work."

No response. We walked about half a block in silence. Then . . ."And Davy?"

"Same as ever. Bitter and mean. Not fit for human company."

Rob quickened his stride and smiled down at me. "That's good," he said.

"Good? Why good?"

"Just good. Frees me up to follow my plan."

I gave him a frown. "What plan?"

He ignored my question and slipped in one of his own. "Good night for a sleigh ride. We could stop by my house for hot chocolate on the way."

"Sure!" I'd answered before I realized that he was asking me to go out with him and meet his parents. I swallowed hard, hoping I hadn't let myself in for disappointment.

"I'll pick you up at seven o'clock."

As we arrived at the Tea Room, Ralph Bolton, the town telegrapher, hurried past the window, wrapped in earmuffs and a wool scarf, making his way down the slippery street. I turned and watched his progress.

"Rob, it looks like he's going to the *Clarion*. I wonder what it could be."

"Mr. Shaver'll tell us. Come on. I'm hungry."

"It might be about Istvan. I'm going back to see. You order for me." I turned and ran along the snowy sidewalk halfway down the block, keeping Mr. Bolton's back in view. He entered the *Clarion* office, and I arrived about a minute later. Mr. Shaver was just opening the telegram. Mr. Bolton passed me on his way out.

Mr. Shaver looked at me over his glasses. He held the telegram in both hands, then reached one hand out to take mine.

"We did it, Pammie! You and Mrs. Plummer and I. We saved him. The judge has declared a mistrial. Istvan is free!"

I grabbed him and danced him around the tiny office, bumping into things, knocking over a pile of books.

"Thank God! I've got to tell Katya! You go over to the Tea Room and tell Rob. You eat my lunch! I've got to go."

I tore up Main Street toward Bedford, knee deep in snow where the walks were unshoveled. I didn't care how much snow there was. Katya was sitting by the window, sewing a dress for a customer. I burst through the door, yelling.

"Katya! Istvan is free! Free! Mrs. Plummer lied at the trial, and she told the judge on the day she died. Now Istvan is free!"

Katya looked at me uncomprehendingly, her face clouded with trying to make out my meaning. "Free? You mean out of jail? Now?"

"Now, Katya. Now! Isn't it wonderful?"

She stood, carefully caught her needle in a fold of cloth and reached for me. We hugged and danced and laughed all at once. We stomped and shook the walls of the Oklahoma house, swung around the tiny room like it was a ballroom.

All the commotion disturbed Mama, and she turned in her chair to look at us. Katya and I stopped in mid-dance and looked at each other, then at Mama's direct glance.

"Mama?" I asked.

She sniffed and returned to her former posture, hands in her lap, looking at the watercolor, but it wasn't quite her former posture. She sat taller, her head cocked to the side. I walked around in front of her and stared into her calm, serene face. She didn't make eye contact with me, but I knew she was aware. I knelt at her feet and lay my head in her lap. She wasn't gone anymore.

"Oh, Mama. I've missed you."

Slowly, gently her hands caressed my shoulders.

Katya stood where I'd left her in the middle of the room, wiping her tears. Our hearts were ready to burst. We tried to calm ourselves, but the joy broke out again and again as we discussed the future.

"We get married right away. Save money. Buy farm. Be farmers again."

"Yes, Katya. You can do that. With both of you working, you'll be able to buy a farm sooner than you think."

Mama sat watching us, her fingers smoothing her apron. I took her hands in mine and talked to her. Sensibility flickered in her eyes. I searched my mind for something, anything, to keep her with me. Then I got an idea. Music. I looked about, wondering how or where I could get her some music. Then I thought of the church, and brought Mama her coat.

"Come on, Mama. We're going for a little walk."

Soon Katya, Mama and I were making our way through piles of snow down Bedford Street to Clinton and down Locust to Franklin. It was a long trek over snowy sidewalks, but the sun was already warming things up, and the snow was beginning to melt a little. When we got there, Mama seemed to recognize the Methodist Church that had stood strong against the flood. I tried the door and found it open, and the three of us walked slowly down the aisle to the piano. Mama sat down like she'd never been away and began to play. "Blessed Assurance" lifted and swelled throughout the church. Standing behind her, I marveled at the ease with which my mother's fingers caressed the keys. My body moved to the rhythm, and the words made their way through the dark memories of the flood to my lips. I was singing again.

Then I was aware of someone behind me. I didn't turn around. No need. Rob's hands encircled my waist, his breath warm on my neck as he joined in the song. As Mama played a rollicking interlude, he whispered in my ear, "You were hard to find."

I turned and smiled into his eyes. "You, too."

Spring has arrived again, and my little town is abloom with lilacs, daffodils and hyacinths. Every yard, it seems, offers some addition to the celebration. Katya is taking her time getting dressed, and I sit on the front porch, gloves on, purse in my lap. When she finally appears, she looks every inch the lovely grandmother, silver hair pinned neatly under a spring hat. I smile.

"You look fine. People will wonder which one of us is the mother of the groom."

"They'll know. No worry there. We'd better get going. Don't want to miss any of the preliminaries."

We descend the porch steps and turn left toward the Presbyterian Church, just a block away. Cars are already parked up the street, and we catch a glimpse of the bride being escorted into the church by her mother and the bridesmaids, followed by her father, carrying her veil and bouquet. As I arrive, Ellen's sister steps up to pin on my corsage.

"There's one for you, too," she tells Katya.

Katya's smile telegraphs her delight.

"There's a little room on the left at the back of the church. You can wait in there," the girl directs.

Katya and I go right in, anxious to be out of the way, but I wish I could see James beforehand. "Where do you think they've put him?" I ask.

Smiling, Katya nods in the direction of this room's twin—across the hallway. Her nod encourages me. I turn for the door and look back to see if she wants to come.

She shakes her head. "You go."

I slip out of the room and gently try the knob across the hall. It gives, and I open the heavy door to see my son, handsome as ever, glowing with pride. He rises to meet me, his eyes shining.

"Never thought you'd see this day, did you?" he asks.

"I hoped."

He takes my hands in both of his and smiles down at me. "It might not have happened if it hadn't been for you."

"And Katya. She was even more determined than I was."

He steps back as there's a knock at the door. He opens it a crack and speaks to someone in the hall. "Hang on. I'm in the middle of something here," he says.

He turns to me, takes my hands again. "Thank you, Mother, for all you did to make us a family—Dad and Kenneth and me. I've been lucky all my life—to be your son and Dad's, and to have the *Clarion* handed to me. Now I hope to fulfill your dream of becoming a grandmother." He gives me a mischievous grin.

"That would be payment enough," I tell him.

"I'll do my best."

Another knock, this one impatient, serves notice that it's time. The organ begins the wedding march, and James slips out the door and around the side aisle to the altar. I stand with Katya, ready to be ushered to our seats. She gives my hand a squeeze. We turn and look at the line of bridesmaids assembled behind us with their groomsmen, followed by the bride and her father. The usher tucks my hand into his arm, and I look up into the face of young Gerald Kirk. Didn't this all start with him?

As we walk down the aisle, my hand on Gerald's arm, Katya behind, I take them all with me: Rob and Kenneth, my mother and father, Geordie, Istvan, even Laura with her flirtatious smile. Come, let's celebrate and be thankful.

About the Author

Judith Redline Coopey was born in Altoona, PA and holds degrees from the Pennsylvania State University and Arizona State University. A passion for history drives her writing, and a love for Pennsylvania sustains it. Her previous book, *Redfield Farm* is about the Underground Railroad in and around Bedford County. *Waterproof* continues her narrative on the state that shaped her.

Redfield Farm

For Ann and Jesse Redfield, Quaker brother and sister, their hatred of slavery is as hard as Pennsylvania limestone. Ann's devotion to her older brother runs deep, so when he gets involved in the Underground Railroad, Ann asks no questions. She joins him in the struggle. Together they lie, sneak, masquerade and defy their way past would-be enforcers of the hated Fugitive Slave Law.

A NOVEL OF THE UNDERGROUND RAILROAD

REDFIELD FARM

JUDITH REDLINE COOPEY

Their dedication to the cause leads to complicated relationships with their fellow Quakers, pro-slavery neighbors, and with the fugitives themselves. When Jesse returns from a run with a deadly fever, accompanied by a fugitive, Josiah, who is also sick and close to death, Ann nurses both back to health. But precious time is lost, and Josiah, too weak for travel, stays the winter at Redfield Farm. Ann becomes his teacher, friend and confidant. When grave disappointment shakes her to her roots, Ann turns to Josiah for comfort, and comfort leads to intimacy. The result, both poignant and inspiring, is life-long devotion to each other and to their cause.

Redfield Farm is a tale of compassion, dedication and love, steeped in the details of another time but resonant with implications for today's world.

The author brings to the narrative a deep understanding of the workings of the Underground Railroad, which lends authenticity and truth to this tale of a live well-lived and a love well-founded.